THE ASSOCIATION FOR SCOTTISH LITERARY STUDIES
NUMBER FORTY

MARGARET OLIPHANT

KIRSTEEN

*

THE ASSOCIATION FOR SCOTTISH LITERARY STUDIES

The Association for Scottish Literary Studies aims to promote the study, teaching and writing of Scottish literature, and to further the study of the languages of Scotland.

To these ends, the ASLS publishes works of Scottish literature (of which this volume is an example); literary criticism and in-depth reviews of Scottish books in *Scottish Studies Review*; short articles, features and news in *ScotLit*; and scholarly studies of language in *Scottish Language*. It also publishes *New Writing Scotland*, an annual anthology of new poetry, drama and short fiction, in Scots, English and Gaelic. ASLS has also prepared a range of teaching materials covering Scottish language and literature for use in schools.

All the above publications are available as a single 'package', in return for an annual subscription. Enquiries should be sent to:

> ASLS, Department of Scottish Literature, 7 University Gardens, University of Glasgow, Glasgow G12 8QH. Telephone/fax +44 (0)141 330 5309 or visit our website at **www.asls.org.uk**

A list of Annual Volumes published by the ASLS can be found at the end of this book.

THE ASSOCIATION FOR SCOTTISH LITERARY STUDIES

MARGARET OLIPHANT

KIRSTEEN

THE STORY OF A SCOTCH FAMILY SEVENTY YEARS AGO

Edited by

ANNE M. SCRIVEN

GLASGOW

2010

Published in Great Britain, 2010
by The Association for Scottish Literary Studies
Department of Scottish Literature
University of Glasgow
7 University Gardens
Glasgow G12 8QH

ASLS is a registered charity no. SC006535

www.asls.org.uk

Hardback
ISBN: 978-0-948877-98-8

Paperback
ISBN: 978-0-948877-99-5

A catalogue record for this book
is available from the British Library.

The Association for Scottish Literary Studies acknowledges
support from Creative Scotland towards
the publication of this book.

Typeset by AFS Image Setters Ltd, Glasgow
Printed and bound by JF Print Ltd, Sparkford, Somerset

Contents

Acknowledgements

There are a number of individuals and institutions who have helped in large or small ways towards the arrival of this edition. I therefore thank: Margaret Elphinstone; Alistair Fergusson; Joseph Fodey; Josephine Haythornthwaite; Jonathan Hope; Stuart Johnson; Margery Palmer McCulloch; Mary Quaine; Alan Riach; Merryn Williams; The Carnegie Trust for Scotland; Staff of the National Library of Scotland; Staff of the British Library; Staff of the University of Strathclyde library; Staff of the University of Glasgow library; Tim Moreton of the National Portrait Gallery; Alysoun Sanders of Macmillan Archives. Special thanks must go to Dorothy Macmillan for her elegant editorial advisory skills – any remaining errors are entirely mine – and to Duncan Jones for his patient and creative production talents. My greatest thanks goes to Colum and Sam, who have tholed the presence of *Kirsteen* in our family life with the grace of gentlemen.

Note on the text

Kirsteen was initially serialised in *Macmillan's Magazine* from August 1889 to August 1890. Macmillan then published the novel in three volumes in September 1890, reprinted in December 1890. Macmillan brought out a second edition in one volume in March 1891, reprinted in October 1891, March 1895, August 1898 and January 1900. The manuscript of *Kirsteen* was destroyed in May 1924 (London, British Library, Macmillan Archive, Dep 10345, p.629). The Macmillan Editions Book for the period 1843-1911 records that electrotyped plates for the 1891 one-volume edition were made in October 1890 and eventually destroyed in 1934 (Macmillan Archive, Dep 10345, p.629).

All versions, serialisation, first and second editions, are divided into Parts I and Part II with Part I concluding at the end of Chapter IV after the departure for India of Kirsteen's sweetheart, Ronald. In the first edition the volumes divide as follows: Volume I, I-XV; Volume II, I-XV; Volume III, I-XVI. In the serialisation and 1891 edition the chapters number continuously from I-XLVI. There are some minor punctuation and spelling differences between the three-volume and the one-volume editions; there are no material differences.

The volumes do divide in appropriate places: Volume I concludes with Kirsteen's departure for London; Volume II concludes with Robbie's letter which gives Kirsteen some hope of Ronald's return, a hope that is dashed in the first chapter of Volume III, Chapter XXI, of the one-volume edition of 1891). But despite this, I believe that the renumbering of chapters for the 1890 three-volume edition was largely a publication necessity and somewhat diminishes the force of the two-part division of Kirsteen's life, especially since that two-part division is retained. For this reason and because it was the last edition published in Oliphant's lifetime, I have taken the one-volume 1891 edition as my copy text. In any case, although with *Kirsteen* Macmillan retained the practice of the three-volume format, followed by a one-volume edition, by the 1890s it was becoming increasingly unfashionable to do so.

All obvious spelling errors in the 1891 text have been

silently corrected and period spellings and punctuations have been modernized (e.g. 'dulness', p.58). Period idiom has been left unchanged (e.g. 'but imperfectly understanded of her intelligence', p.282), and Oliphant's own occasional inconsistencies with regard to character names have been preserved.

Introduction

'And thus life was over for Kirsteen; and life began.'

Kirsteen, like its heroine, had a challenging beginning. In October 1888 Margaret Oliphant wrote to William Blackwood asking him if he would be interested in serialising her new novel in *Blackwood's Edinburgh Magazine*: 'for once in a way, I think it good and worth the trouble of a more special arrangement': she asked £400 for it.[1] Blackwood's declined her offer as the firm had increasingly considered her more in the fields of biography and history.[2] Determined to have her novel in print, Oliphant immediately offered it to Macmillan and sold the publication rights for the paltry sum of £300.[3] She understood this to mean only book rights leaving serialisation rights with her but it emerged that she had in fact sold the entire copyright. When she later heard of Macmillan's plans to serialise *Kirsteen* in their magazine she sent a stinging letter to Lillie Craik of Macmillan:

> I am very much surprised by your letter just received. Of course I am exceedingly glad that "Kirsteen" should be published in the Magazine, but I had not heard a word of your intention to use it so – and our bargain was solely for its publication in book form – don't you think this is a little *brusque* on your part? I shall have great pleasure in preparing it for the Magazine and it is what I should have desired – but at the same time not a word on this subject has been said to me – this is treating me rather cavalierly, I think. Its use in the Magazine must naturally make a difference in every way – which of course I *must* revise and correct the type-setting [...] Have I done anything rude or disagreeable that your tone towards me is so dry and peremptory? I am quite unconscious of it.[4]

Pointing out to her that Macmillan was within its legal right to publish *Kirsteen* in any form, Craik nevertheless gave her a further £100 to compensate for the misunderstanding.[5] As she was always short of money it is understandable that Oliphant attempted to maximise the profits of her literary labours, but there is also the less mercenary point that Oliphant really did believe that *Kirsteen* was a significant novel which deserved better treatment.

By the time Oliphant began *Kirsteen* she had been part of the contemporary literary scene for nearly 40 years. Her first novel was published in 1849 and during her lifetime, between 1828-1897, she produced over ninety novels. Many of them are perhaps little more than pot-boilers. Left a young widow after only seven years of marriage when her husband died of tuberculosis in 1859 Oliphant had, she wrote to John Blackwood, 'nothing but [her] head and [her] hands'[6] to rely on. With two young children and in the latter stages of pregnancy, around £1,000 in debt and only a small insurance policy of £200 between her and destitution, Oliphant turned to her pen to survive. Over and above her novels, she went on to produce a staggering amount of writing – some 300 articles, 50 short stories, 25 works of non-fiction and autobiographical writing. Her reputation was to suffer from this necessary industry as critics took the line that she was 'working too fast and producing too much'.[7] Nevertheless, John Stock Clarke's defence of her work is persuasive:

> in almost all of Mrs Oliphant's novels her coolly ironic vision, her individual and intelligent approach to life, make far more impact than [her narrative] weaknesses – which scarcely affect the basic fabric of her work. Trollope wrote less than half as much as Mrs Oliphant wrote, yet he lapsed into false and conventional language and stereotyped plots and character patterns more frequently than she did.[8]

Amidst this daunting mountain of writing lay some true gems and *Kirsteen: the Story of a Scotch Family Some Seventy Years Ago* is one of them. Lifting her head up from the constant demand of deadlines and family pressures, Oliphant herself recognised this novel to be one of her best.

Contemporary opinions of *Kirsteen* for the most part bear her out. *The Athenaeum* (October 1890), pronounced it had 'an air of originality';[9] *Murray's Magazine* stated it was a story 'uncommonly well written; a literary anodyne – and something more';[10] *The Academy* viewed the story as 'carried through without hitch or flagging from beginning to end';[11] *The Scottish Review*, judged the novel to be 'much above average',[12] and in a later assessment also thought it had 'a Hardyesque passion'.[13] In other reviews the success of Oliphant's novels set in Scotland is attributed to her deep familiarity with her birth country. This confidence was remarked from the beginning of Oliphant's literary career – a letter from the founder and editor of *The Edinburgh Review*, Francis Jeffrey, forwarded to Oliphant in January 1850 by her publisher Henry Colburn, highly praises her first novel *Passages in the Life of Margaret Maitland* (1849). Jeffrey declares himself to be 'captivated' and finds one of the main characters as 'so original and yet so true to nature and to Scottish nature, [and] far beyond anything that Galt could reach'.[14] Some forty years later critics were still remarking this same talent. Alexander Allardyce commented in December 1894: 'It is only in the pages of Mrs Oliphant and Mr Stevenson that we now meet with any serious attempt at delineating Scottish character'.[15] In September 1897, J.H. Millar stated: 'In none of her stories is the effect of "atmosphere" more triumphantly attained than in those where the scene is situated in Scotland; for Mrs Oliphant knew her native country, and she knew its people.'[16] In his preface to Oliphant's *A Widow's Tale and Other Stories* (1898), J.M. Barrie described *Kirsteen* as 'the best, far the best, story of its kind that has come out of Scotland for the last score of years';[17] and W.E. Henley expostulated to Henry James: 'That you should have any pretensions to interest in literature, and should dare to say that you have not read *Kirsteen*!'[18] When he did read it however Henry James was not very impressed. He was:

> confirmed after twenty pages in my belief – I laboured through the book – that the poor thing had but a *feminine* conception of literature: such slipshod, imperfect, faltering, peeping, down-at-heel work, – buffeting along like a ragged creature in a high wind and just struggling to the goal, and falling a quivering mass of faintness and fatuity. Yes, no doubt she was a gallant woman, though no species of wisdom – but an artist, an artist![19]

It is important here to remember that James and Oliphant had very different views of the writer's duties. Reviewing *Portrait of a Lady* in *Blackwood's* Oliphant concluded that it was 'one of the most remarkable specimens of literary skill which the critic could lay his hand upon' but, nevertheless, found his heroine, Isabel Archer, 'a congeries of thoughts and questions rather than a woman'.[20] In Oliphant's view all James's attention to his art did not necessarily produce truth to human nature while James deplored Oliphant's irresponsible refusal of devotion to the art of the novelist. James's rather sour comment after Oliphant's death that 'no woman had ever, for half a century, had her personal "say" so publicly and irresponsibly'[21] has to be set alongside his half-uncomprehending admission that in spite of his reservations about its art he is 'beguiled' by *Kirsteen*, that it is 'full of life' and throws up 'a fresh, strong air'.[22]

But James's uncertainty would seem to have prevailed. As Oliphant's life drew to a close, so too did her literary reputation. Its decline can be attributed to a number of factors: her favoured format of the triple-decker novel became unfashionable; her review of Hardy's *Jude the Obscure* in January 1896 was deemed prudish and out of kilter with contemporary thought (even though it was in line with *Blackwood's* own prevailing house policy); her prolific literary output had cheapened her name; the unrelenting pressure of writing to provide for her family (and extended family) gave her little or no time for reviewing or editing her own work and the luxury of focusing on one work at a time was unknown to her; the legacy of Carlyle's famous series of lectures where he outlined the 'man of letters' as exclusive to the male species, affected the public view of any woman of letters; the posthumous publication of her self-effacing autobiography where she foregrounds the challenges of balancing the conflicting lives of family and writing and constructs herself as a minor writer, damaged her literary standing. A further factor contributing to *Kirsteen* being out of print from 1900 until the Dent edition in 1984,[23] and with no fully edited text until this present one, can be found in the negative effect of the kailyard school of writing which tainted public opinion of novels located in Scotland. The double irony here is that what contemporary critics discerned as an important aspect of the novel later may have hindered its fame, and that Oliphant herself deplored the kailyard genre, particularly its inauthentic use of the Scots language: she protested in

1895: 'Does Mr Crockett or Mr Maclaren, or any other of the many professors of this craft, think *that* is Scotch?'[24]

Thanks to a small number of scholars, Oliphant's writing had never quite disappeared from view; but it was her novels set in the fictional English Home County town of Carlingford that now became best known. Her novels set in Scotland, suffering from being written by a woman and a Scot, were quite firmly out of print.[25] It was not until the late twentieth century, when gynocriticism began to make an impact on the submerged field of Scottish women's writing, that Oliphant's writing began to appear on university reading lists. Among the wider reading public, the resuming of the Scottish parliament in 1999 put the recovery and revisioning of Scottish culture on the agenda.

And for the modern reader there is much to recommend *Kirsteen*. Oliphant's novel is a *bildungsroman*, a novel of awakening, and the awakenings are many. Some way into the novel Kirsteen speaks of her intended journey to London and comments to her sister Anne that 'it is a long journey' and 'a person can never tell if they will ever win back' (Ch.XX, p.173). As the novel progresses and Kirsteen's life and mindset take on a new and healthier state, we realise that we do not want her to 'win back', at least, not if she must relinquish all that she has valiantly gained. By the end of the novel Kirsteen has travelled a long way and not just in geographical miles.

Kirsteen opens in 1814 – the year which saw the publication of Scott's *Waverley* – and it is possibly no coincidence that Oliphant chose to situate her novel in this period. Oliphant was a great admirer of Scott's writing and was very familiar with his works. In her study *Royal Edinburgh: Her Saints, Kings, Prophets and Poets*, published by Macmillan in 1890, she devotes a chapter to Scott dubbing him 'The Shakespeare of Scotland'.[26] This book also carries the epigraph 'Mine own romantic town' – the quotation from *Marmion* underscoring Oliphant's view that Scott is central to the story of Scotland's capital. In her autobiography she records after reading Scott's journal that:

It is the nationality perhaps, the national brotherhood that makes me feel as if it were a bigger me that was speaking sometimes, as if I could enter into anything,

almost forgetting that these were not my own affairs. I
feel I know him almost as I know myself.[27]

Kirsteen is however no simple flattering imitation of
Waverley. The relationship between the novels is a complex
one.[28] Written in the late nineteenth century and set in the
cultural change of the early nineteenth century, *Kirsteen* has
a very different protagonist from Scott's earlier hero,
Edward Waverley. For a start she is female, a young
unlearned Highland girl, who is not constructed as a muse
for *Waverley's* wandering Romantic sensibility – as is the
bewitching Flora McIvor in Scott's novel – but is a flesh and
blood lass fighting at first not so much for her place in the
world, as for a simple acceptable existence. Her quest is
therefore completely different from the young Waverley's.
She is not seeking the thrill of adventure or the glamour of a
cause; she simply seeks survival and self-determination.
Whereas Edward Waverley comes to Scotland for the sake
of family honour and the thrill of military arms, Kirsteen
tells Miss Jean Brown quite simply that she has come to
London to 'work for her living – and to make my fortune if
I can' (Ch.XXII, p.188). Edward Waverley travels deep into
Scotland to find himself, Kirsteen travels away from Scotland to be free to be herself. The journey of Scott's hero is
initially in the nature of a vacation, a stravaig, a consequence of boredom, Kirsteen's journey is a necessity
although she is also in a sense seeking her fortune. Waverley's way is smoothed by an officer's commission at Dundee
and a letter of introduction to an old family friend who is
the owner of an estate in Perthshire. He travels on horseback. Kirsteen, in an imitation of Scott's Jeannie Deans,
walks from her home in Loch Fyne, Argyllshire, down to
Glasgow. Here she gets a coach to London which takes her
two and half days. Her heart is full of fear not adventure:

> Somewhere in the darkness that great city lay as the
> western world lay before its discoverer. Kirsteen
> formed an image to herself of something blazing into
> the night full of incomprehensible voices and things;
> and she had all the shrinking yet eagerness of a first
> explorer not knowing what the horrors there might be
> to encounter, but not his faith in everything good.
> (Ch.XX, p.178)

Oliphant's heroine, unlike Scott's hero on his initial encounter, sees her Highland home through unromantic eyes. Kirsteen is the daughter of a Highland laird, Douglas of Drumcarro, who is himself a complex character. Drumcarro does not display any kind of benevolent kinship with those around him. He is desperate to win back the land taken from the Douglas family, attainted for their part in the Jacobite 1745 rising (an inaccuracy on Oliphant's part as the Douglases were not strong Jacobites), but this comes over as a selfish wish which stems from an impulse of greed rather than care for other members of his clan. He has an immense pride in the Douglas name but no apparent actual care for any member of it. Oliphant's construction of Drumcarro's character is in tune with her own stance as far as Jacobitism was concerned. In a letter to John Blackwood in 1852 she declares that she is 'not much of a Jacobite'[29] and in her early novel *Katie Stewart*, published by *Blackwood's* in 1853, where her heroine is completely uninterested in the Jacobite cause, the narrator derides Charles Edward Stuart saying he has 'the look of wandering imbecile expression, like the passing shadow of an idiot's face over the face of a manful youth'[30] Her construction of Drumcarro and his bullish attitude to all is consonant with her scepticism about the Jacobite cause. As she focuses on the position and fortunes of a young Highland girl who has to run from her home or endure a forced marriage, Oliphant paints an image of the Highlands which is not one that any tourist board would wish to endorse.

The means of redemption for Edward Waverley and Kirsteen Douglas also vastly differ. Whereas Scott's hero arrives at his own sense of himself through the experience of civil war, Oliphant's heroine finds it through the quiet unlauded female industry of dressmaking. And whereas the Jacobite rising, with all its bloody battles, results in loss and failure, Kirsteen's embrace of the lowly occupation of the needle enables her to buy back her family's disinherited land. That her family refuse to acknowledge her achievement is rather amusing but also plausible as female-centred work is rarely viewed as having any relevance for the fortunes of family or country. In *Waverley*, Rose Bradwardine, whose 'very soul is in home, and in the discharge of all those quiet virtues of which home is the centre' (Vol I,

Ch.XIII), takes her direction from the strong males around her, and the bewitching Flora McIvor is deeply immersed in the Jacobite cause and under the final guidance of her brother. Neither Rose's nor Flora's own interests in bardic poetry or music or gardening serve as a means for their independence. As Arlene Young points out:

> [Oliphant] constructs the story using the most tradi-
> tional and apparently unassertive area of women's
> work – needlework – to forge a sense of female com-
> munity that simultaneously supports and subverts
> male dominance and that enables female independence
> while endorsing femininity.[31]

Oliphant's decision to have her heroine enter the world of mantua-making and to become a successful single woman, may derive from two of her own interests. Oli-phant was herself very interested in the world of sewing and fashion. In her autobiography she tells of the early influence of her mother who made all her daughter's clothes 'finer and more beautifully worked than ever child's clothes were'.[32] This influence was a lasting one: in 1876 she pub-lished *Dress*, which insists on the importance of dress for human well-being.[33] In her article 'The Looker-On' (June 1895), she elevates fashion over book collection:

> The Looker-On, he is bound to say, finds something
> interesting in this unfailing pleasure in dress, which so
> many of his comrades lose no opportunity of flinging
> in the faces of their womankind. To see an old lady
> poring over the descriptions of the fashions, with seri-
> ous brow and eager eyes, has a pathos in it. Her own
> black gown has not been changed for years. She is
> thinking no more of herself than of the Queen of
> Sheba. At the best she is pondering which will be best
> for Annie; how this and that will suit her. At the worst
> she has still the vision, if there is no Annie, of multi-
> tudes of gay figures, all shining and splendid in the
> finery which is also poetry and beauty and charm. I
> have a tender feeling for the newspapers which are full
> of Chiffon. They amuse the unamusable. They carry
> interest and even a little excitement to the dullest
> places. Not an elevating kind of interest, did you say?

Ah, well! There is nothing very elevating in a catalogue of old books, which awakens in our own bosom a kindred feeling. Nay, the old books are less elevating. You don't suppose we want to read them when we have got them? First editions are not meant (nowadays) to be read. We like to gloat upon them on our shelves, and congratulate ourselves that Dryasdust would give his head to have an example like this. It is all pride and selfishness and the love of acquisition. Whereas the old woman, wondering if that special *confection* of red and blue or pink and white would suit Annie, is on a much higher plane.[34]

In Oliphant's eyes, the fashion industry should not be belittled, but this leads us to the ironic fact that many people caught up in the early days of the industry were indeed more than belittled. For many women caught up in the early nineteenth century world of sweated trade with its inhumane working hours, poor conditions and paltry wages, the glamour of female dress was something unknown to the majority of exhausted seamstresses. It was not until the mid century that the situation of the exploited seamstress became fully known to the public.[35] As Arlene Young points out: 'To represent a character as a seamstress was to construct her as deserving of compassion; she would by definition be exploited'.[36] In Dickens's *Nicholas Nickleby* (1838) the recently impoverished and vulnerable Kate Nickleby has to take work in a dressmaking salon where she is viewed as a pretty pawn to be played with by the idle male eye. In Oliphant's *Kirsteen*, however, the issue of the exploited seamstress is not given narrative prominence, and it is only in an aside in Chapter XXX that we get a glimpse of the sinister side of the mantua-making business. Kirsteen and Miss Jean Brown have become so successful that the orders flood in, but there is an obvious consequence for the workforce behind the shop front:

This prosperous condition was in its full height in the midst of the season, the work-room so *throng* that relays of seamstresses sat up all night, there being no inspectors to bring the fashionable mantua-makers under control. (Ch.XXX, p.256)

Aware of the possible sentiments of her readers, Oliphant
opens the next chapter:

> There were no inspectors to look after the work-
> rooms of the dressmakers in these days, but perhaps
> also, at least with mistresses like Miss Jean, there was
> little need for them. If the young women in the work-
> room had sometimes to work for a part of the night it
> was only what at that time everybody was supposed
> to do in their own affairs or in their masters', when
> business was very urgent, or *throng* as was said in Scot-
> land. The head of the house sat up too, there were
> little indulgences accorded, and when the vigil was not
> too prolonged, there was a certain excitement about it
> which was not unpleasing to the work-women in the
> monotony of their calling. One of these indulgences
> was that something was now and then read aloud to
> them as they worked. (Ch.XXXI, p.257)

And, a little later in the same chapter, we are told that
'[Kirsteen] was up the whole night never flagging, while the
others managed it by relays, snatching an hour or two of
sleep, and returning to work again' (Ch.XXXI, p.258). It
may help to remember here that Oliphant herself often
worked late at night and was no stranger to hard work – as
a diary entry in 1888 attests: 'During Summer wrote for
Longman, to clear off debt with them, *Lady Car*, one
volume. During September wrote a short story, two numbers, for Blackwood (pot boiler), called *Sons and Daughters*
and began *Kirsteen.*'[37] The difference being of course that
Oliphant was always wealthy enough to have domestic help
and was also the director of her own affairs. If she sat up
at night to write it was mostly her choice. It has to be said
then that Oliphant avoids the debate about sweated labour
by ensuring that the reader is aware that the arduous conditions of the seamstresses are softened by some thoughtful
entertainment and support. She is also careful to construct
Jean Brown not as a mercenary boss, and in this way
Oliphant subverts the dominant narrative trajectory
favoured by other novelists which Beth Harris outlines as:

> a healthy young woman, who has recently been
> orphaned, or whose family has been reduced, leaves

her life in the countryside to become a seamstress in
the city. There, the woman encounters a heartless and
greedy employer and begins an irreversible decline
leading to illness and death and/or prostitution.[38]

Where Oliphant's *Kirsteen* differs from this tragic trajectory
is in her choice of heroine. The major difference between,
for example, Kate Nickleby's situation and that of Kirsteen
Douglas – apart from their working for very different
people – is that Kirsteen does not view herself as weak or a
victim and having this 'consciousness which gives courage'
(Ch.XXIII, p.199), calls Lord John to account for his shameful view that 'milliners were supposed to be very fair game'
(Ch.XXIII, p.199). Where Kate Nickleby has to be rescued
by her brother from the unwelcome advances of Sir
Mulberry Hawk and the useless Wititterleys, Kirsteen, by
contrast, who has no male protector nor expectation of
one, quells Lord John Campbell with her own dignity and
demand for respect. As Elizabeth Jay has noted: 'In novel
after novel Mrs Oliphant makes it clear that it is not a
woman's duty merely to yield unquestioning obedience to
any man, since this would effectively be abnegating a
woman's most treasured possession, her moral sense.'[39]
Oliphant's heroines are consistently constructed as
balanced and sensible woman, who unlike Dickens's often
consumptive heroines (whom Oliphant dismissed as: 'pretty
enough, amiable enough, generous enough' but falling short
of any notable individuality[40]), refuse to faint and be overcome by situations but use their heads to think through
challenges and their hands to provide the means. Dickens's
Mantalinis in *Nicholas Nickleby* are theatrically conceived –
intended to amuse and outrage the reader with their bizarre
behaviour – Jean Brown, by contrast, is not theatrical, but
a simple, honest and hardworking woman with her feet
quite firmly on the ground. She is neither caricatured nor
made an object of fun by Oliphant. And this is in tune with
Oliphant's practice of championing the intelligent single
woman – of any age – who appears repeatedly in her writing. In her essay 'Scottish National Character' (1860), we
find Oliphant praising the worth of 'this class of celibates
[who] behaved themselves with great energy and emphasis
in the world—'.[41] Oliphant's heroines are not women to be

dismissed lightly. Kirsteen Douglas, particularly as she gains prominence, is reminiscent of the impressive Catherine Vernon in Oliphant's novel *Hester* (1883) who as a young woman saves the family bank from ruin and then continues as its head for many years. In her retirement she creates 'the Vernonry' – a community composed of relations who are without the means of supporting themselves. Together, Catherine Vernon and Kirsteen Douglas would have made a formidable partnership. If Oliphant therefore refused to interrogate the fashion industry and the 'song of the shirt'[42] to its depths, what she did nevertheless do in *Kirsteen* was to elevate it both as a viable means of vital independence for her character, and thus also subvert the Victorian ideology of public and private divide.

In *Kirsteen* Oliphant also argues for female fashion to be recognised as a definite art form. Oliphant was familiar with the world of art – her husband, Frank, was a stained glass artist – and in her autobiography she records a standard practice of their quiet but bohemian life while living in London: 'What I liked best in the way of society was when we went out occasionally quite late in the evening, Frank and I, after he had left off work in his studio, and went to the house of another painter uninvited, unexpected, always welcome'.[43] And there are also numerous references to the world of art in her essays and review articles which appeared for the most part in the columns of *Maga*. Given Oliphant's own interest in dress there is a clear agenda in the description of *Kirsteen*'s Miss Macnab, who comes to make the simple ball gowns for the Douglas sisters, as 'an artist in her way' (Ch.VIII, p.77). And this scene offers clues to the future path of Kirsteen. When Miss Macnab reminisces about the young dressmakers she once had working under her who often tried their own ideas out and then came back to her methods, Kirsteen rejoins that if she were to 'take her own way': 'I would never yield, I would make it answer' (Ch.VIII, p.78). It is the simple countrywoman Miss Macnab who pinpoints the necessary qualities of a gifted dressmaker advising that: 'If ye dinna get the skirt to fall straight from the waist, ye will never mend it at the foot' and insisting that dressmaking 'wants good blood in your veins and a leddy's breeding before you'll ever make a gown that will set off a leddy' (Ch.VIII, p.79). Kirsteen unconsciously absorbs this information, which she later puts to good use, but she adds to it her own natural creativity and awareness of style. We hear a few times of Kirsteen's ability to 'handle and drape the pretty materials and to adapt them to this and that pretty wearer, as a painter likes to arrange and study the more subtle harmonies of light and shade' (Ch.XXIII, p.197), and how she would 'work with the rapidity of an inventor, throwing a piece of stuff into wonderful folds and plaitings of which no one could say what the issue was to be' (Ch.XXXI, p.262).

As a highly respected businesswoman, Kirsteen has come a long way from her beginnings and the situation which drove her to flee her family home in Argyll. Held by her father as 'a creature of no account' (Ch.XII, p.112), while her brothers are one by one sent off into the world to earn their fortunes and make a name for themselves, Kirsteen and her sisters are expected to remain at home, to work in the house and to somehow make advantageous marriages. When Kirsteen refuses to do her father's bidding and marry the kind but unattractive Glendochart who is old enough to be her father, she is threatened with physical violence.

> 'Dare to say a word but what I tell ye, and I'll dash ye – in pieces like a potter's vessel!' cried Drumcarro, taking the first similitude that occurred to him. He shook her as he spoke, her frame, though it was well-knit and vigorous, quivering in his grasp. 'Just say a word more of your damned nonsense and I'll lay ye at my feet!' (Ch.XV, p.131)

Drumcarro is represented as quite capable of laying Kirsteen at his feet: there are various references to his dark past as a slave driver. As with the issue of the exploited seamstress, Oliphant does not really engage with the wider political questions behind this sinister family history: 'Whether these supposed cruelties and horrors were all or almost all the exaggerations of a following agitation, belonging like many similar atrocities in America to the Abolitionist imagination, is a question unnecessary to discuss.' (Ch.V, p.54). Oliphant's refusal to fully discuss this issue is perhaps disappointing but, since she alludes at various points to the subject, we feel the effect of a troubled reticence rather than a decided ignorance. In Chapter XLIV, for example, Drumcarro's repressed past resurfaces to torment him:

> there surged up all manner of things. Old scenes far off and gone, incidents that had taken place in the jungle and swamp, cries and sounds of the lash, and pistol shots all long over and forgotten. One face, not white like Lord John's, but grey in its blackness, like ashes, came and wavered in the darkness before him more distinct than the others. No ghost, he had no faith in ghosts, nothing outside of him. Something within from which even if they could hang him he knew he would not get free' (p.371).

Drumcarro's colonial past functions as a submerged and silenced story in the text and is all the more powerful for Oliphant's refusal of polemic.

In the slave-driving figure of Neil Douglas of Drumcarro, Oliphant creates a character who can be read as a precursor to the brutal John Gourlay of George Douglas Brown's *The House with the Green Shutters* (1901) and R.L. Stevenson's Weir of *Weir of Hermiston* (1896) – Weir is managed by the able Kirstie much as Marg'ret Brown manages her master Drumcarro. A possible source for Oliphant's modelling of Drumcarro is contained in Lord Archibald Campbell's (1884) *Records of Argyll: Legends, Traditions, and Recollection of Argyllshire Highlanders*, which Oliphant reviewed in March 1886 in *Maga*, and includes a story, set in the seventeenth century, of 'The Fair Maid of Callard and Campbell of Inverawe', which describes 'The then proprietor of Callard' who was 'a stern disciplinarian, a morose, proud and, it is said, avaricious man, with an inordinate love of display, not often coupled with the kind of pride which he is said to have had.[44] It is this same destructive nature found in her own father that causes Kirsteen to flee her home but, although he has given her very little in material goods throughout her life, he has endowed her with a strong pride in bearing the Douglas name. Although Kirsteen packs very few material possessions to help her journey to a new existence, her belief in herself as a Douglas is tightly wound into her mental baggage. It is this pride that sustains her on her difficult journey south, it is this pride that causes her to hesitate in accepting her sister Anne's marriage, it is this pride that gives her the bearing and air of a woman of quality which in turn enhances her status as a businesswoman, and it is this pride which she eventually comes to see as irrelevant for the world outside of Argyll-shire. Kirsteen's real journey in the novel is not the hundreds of geographical miles she travels but rather involves the shedding of an old self, an old mindset: 'She was going – where? From the impossible to the possible' (Ch.XVI, p.138). Her quest, although she does not fully comprehend it, is not to find a safe haven where she can wait for her young lover to find her, but rather to find a place where she can negotiate a way of belonging to a recalcitrantly patri-archal Scotland while rejecting its valuation of women.

Kirsteen, then, adds a new dimension to the national tale as constructed by Scott. *Kirsteen* is in many ways a success story, a rags-to-riches tale, but, unlike Scott's *Waverley*, it is not resolved either by a satisfactory marriage or reunion with loved ones. Kirsteen is never fully accepted by her family and she remains single. In *Kirsteen* Oliphant explores the still little explored terrain of the relationship between women and Scotland in a new manner. Oliphant's contribu-tion to the national tale – with its formula of intrigue, romance and history – is to expose the backwardness and prejudice of Kirsteen's Argyllshire home far more radically than had been done before. It is the metropolis of London, which affords Kirsteen shelter, an income, a new career and new-found dignity. All that awaits her in her Highland home is abuse and disregard. Although Kirsteen is 'seized with a yearning now and then' for her mother, her little sister and although she may create 'an ideal picture of the beauty and perfection of nature as embodied in her own glen', Kirsteen is nevertheless aware that her home environ-ment is in reality a hostile place, a place of repression and unforgiveness. As she cries to herself: 'Go back! Oh, no; she would not if she could go back, and she could not if she would' (Ch.XXV, p.211).

From the perspective of another country, Kirsteen finds time and space to reconfigure her relationship with Scot-land and part of this renegotiation is an awakening to the texts which have previously constructed her. The respective inherited narratives of the dutiful daughter, the Douglas clan, Highland pride, the faithful lover, are narratives which she does not completely cast off but grows to recognise as working within limited spheres. And even though her family are never quite comfortable with her involvement in 'trade', she accepts their unease and continues to function effectively for their and her own good. By the end of the novel we find her in the city of Edinburgh – the city which Oliphant recognised as 'always living, always stirring'[45] and hence an appropriate final home for her vibrant heroine whose eyes, despite her advanced years, are 'still full of fire' (p.385). The narrative decision to return Kirsteen to Scotland, but not to Argyll, again demonstrates Oliphant's recognition of just how far her heroine has travelled and just how far the world has travelled with her. From the wilds of Inverarary, to London and finally to a cultured Edinburgh New Town residence in Moray Place, Kirsteen Douglas's life journey illustrates what can happen when a Scottish woman sets her sights high. In charting that journey Margaret Oliphant creates a distinctive and alternative national tale.

Anne M. Scriven
2010

Endnotes

[1] Oliphant to W. Blackwood, 8th October 1888 (Edinburgh, National Library of Scotland, MSS 4523, fols 75-6).

[2] See David Finkelstein, *The House of Blackwood: Author-Publisher Relations in the Victorian Era.* (Pennsylvania: Pennsylvania State University Press, 2002), p.33.

[3] Receipt for *Kirsteen.* London, British Library. Macmillan Archive, MSS 54919, fol 197. Previously Oliphant had been able to command figures such as £1,500 for the copyright of *The Perpetual Curate* which was published in 1864 by Blackwood's. Lillie Craik of Macmillan reasoned with Oliphant that their price of £300 was a fair one as 'we fail to get the same result from your later [novels] that we once got' (Macmillan Archive, MSS 55427, fol 212).

[4] Oliphant to G. Lillie Craik, April 17th 1889 (Macmillan Archive, MSS 54919, fol 211).

[5] G. Lillie Craik to Oliphant (Macmillan Archive, MSS 55428, fol 629).

[6] Oliphant to John Blackwood, 1868, in *The Autobiography and Letters of Mrs M.O.W. Oliphant,* ed. by Mrs Harry Coghill; with an introduction by Q.D. Leavis (Leicester: Leicester University Press, 1974), p.220. Henceforth referenced as Coghill.

[7] An example of this is the review of Oliphant's *Autobiography and*

Letters which appeared in *The Saturday Review*, 20 May 1899, where Oliphant is called a 'trades-union author' who wrote solely for money. Oliphant was also condemned by Virginia Woolf as a woman who had 'sold her brain, her very admirable brain, prostituted her culture and enslaved her intellectual liberty in order that she might earn her living and educate her children'. Virginia Woolf, *Three Guineas*. (Oxford: Oxford University Press, [1938] 1992). p.287.

[8] John Stock Clarke, *Margaret Oliphant*. Victorian Fiction Research Guides. Series XI. (St. Lucia: University of Queensland, 1986), p.1.

[9] 'Novels of the Week', *The Athenaeum*, 3286 (Oct 1890), p.509.

[10] 'Our Library List', *Murray's Magazine*. 8:47 (Nov 1890), p.717.

[11] William Wallace, 'New Novels, *The Academy*, 966 (Nov 1890), p.416.

[12] 'Contemporary Fiction', *The Scottish Review*, 17 (Jan 1891), p.258.

[13] 'Art IV – Mrs Oliphant and her rivals', *Scottish Review*, 30 (Oct 1897), p.282.

[14] Francis Jeffrey, cited in Coghill ([1899], 1974) pp.153-5.

[15] Alexander Allardyce, *Who Was Lost and Is Found* (Review), *Blackwood's Edinburgh Magazine*, 156 (Dec 1894), p.874.

[16] J.H. Millar, 'Mrs Oliphant as a Novelist', *Blackwood's Edinburgh Magazine*. 162:983 (Sept 1897), pp.305-19.

[17] J.M. Barrie, preface to Margaret Oliphant, *A Widow's Tale, and Other Stories*. (Edinburgh and London: Blackwood and Sons, [1898] 1899) p.7.

[18] Leon Edel, *Henry James: The Treacherous Years 1985-1901* (London: Rupert Hart-Davis, 1969), p.233.

[19] Edel, p.233.

[20] Oliphant, 'Recent Novels', *Blackwood's Edinburgh Magazine*, 131 (March 1882), p.374.

[21] Henry James (August 21, 1897), *Harper's Weekly*, XLI, Reprinted as 'London Notes, August 1897' in Leon Edel, ed., *Henry James: Literary Criticism*. (New York: The Library of America, 1984), p.1411.

[22] Edel, p.1413.

[23] See Oliphant, *Kirsteen: The Story of a Scotch Family Seventy Years Ago*, ed. by Merryn Williams (London: Dent, 1984).

[24] Oliphant, 'The Looker-On', *Blackwood's Edinburgh Magazine*, 67 (June 1895), pp.902-29.

[25] This remained the situation for many years until the collaborative initiative of a Glasgow-based publisher, Zeticula, under the imprint of Kennedy and Boyd, and the Centre for Scottish Cultural Studies, Department of English Studies, University of Strathclyde, brought back into print Oliphant's novels *Katie Stewart* and *The Ladies Lindores*. See: Margaret Oliphant, *Katie Stewart*, ed. by Anne McManus Scriven (Glasgow: Kennedy and Boyd, 2007) and Margaret Oliphant, *The Ladies Lindores*, ed. by Anne McManus Scriven (Glasgow: Kennedy and Boyd, 2008).

[26] Oliphant, *Royal Edinburgh: Her Saints, Kings, Prophets and Poets*. (London: Macmillan, [1890] 1893), pp.491-520.

[27] Elizabeth Jay (ed.), *The Autobiography and Letters of Margaret Oliphant*. (Ormskirk: Broadview, 2002), p.98.

[28] Pamela Perkins in her essay ' "We who have been bred upon Sir Walter": Margaret Oliphant, Sir Walter Scott, and Women's Literary History', reads Oliphant's *Kirsteen* alongside *Waverley*. Perkins's excellent essay gives much fuller discussion to the literary climates in which Scott and Oliphant respectively operated and offers the insightful comment: 'In *Kirsteen*, which pointedly opens in 1814, Oliphant thus attempts to write the novel that Scott could not, catching the texture of lived daily experience in the early nineteenth century. That, of course, is what Oliphant – and Scott – praise female novelists of the time such as Austen and Edgeworth for doing, but precisely because she is writing historical fiction, Oliphant is attempting something very different than a belated imitation of their work.' See: Pamela Perkins, *English Studies in Canada*. vol 30; issue 2 (2004), pp.90-104.

[29] Coghill, p.158.

[30] Oliphant, *Katie Stewart*. (Glasgow: Kennedy and Boyd, 2007), p.55.

[31] Arlene Young, ' "Workers" Compensation: (Needle)Work and Ideals of Femininity in Margaret Oliphant's *Kirsteen*', in Beth Harris, ed., *Famine and Fashion: Needlewomen in the Nineteenth Century*. (Aldershot: Ashgate, 2005), p.42.

[32] Jay (2002), p.56.

[33] Oliphant, *Dress*, 1876, reprinted 2005 (Boston: Adamant Media Corporation, 2005).

[34] Oliphant, 'The Looker-On', *Blackwood's Edinburgh Magazine*, 67 (June 1895), pp.902-29.

[35] See C. Walkley, *The Ghost in the Looking Glass: The Victorian Seamstress* (London: Peter Owen, 1981).

[36] Young (2005), p.41.

[37] Jay (2002), p.209.

[38] Beth Harris, ed., *Famine and Fashion: Needlework in the Nineteenth Century* (Aldershot: Ashgate, 2005), p.2.

[39] Elizabeth Jay, *Mrs Oliphant: A Fiction to Herself* (Oxford: Oxford University Press, 1995), pp.62-3.

[40] Oliphant, 'Charles Dickens', *Blackwood's Edinburgh Magazine*, 109 (April 1855), pp.451-66.

[41] Oliphant, 'Scottish National Character', *Blackwood's Edinburgh Magazine*, 87 (June 1860), pp.715-31.

[42] 'The Song of the Shirt', a poem by Thomas Hood, published in 1843, was written as a plea for the women involved in sweated labour and provided what became an iconic image of the seamstress-as-victim.

[43] Jay (2002), p.83.

[44] Lord Archibald Campbell, *Records of Argyll: Legends, Traditions, and Recollection of Argyllshire Highlanders* (Edinburgh and London: William Blackwood and Sons, 1884), pp.375-97.

[45] Oliphant, *Royal Edinburgh: Her Saints, Kings, Prophets and Poets* (London: Macmillan, 1893), p.520.

PART I

CHAPTER I

'Where is Kirsteen?'

''Deed, mem, I canna tell you; and if you would be guided by me you wouldna wail and cry for Kirsteen, night and day. You're getting into real ill habits with her to do everything for you. And the poor lassie has not a meenit to hersel'. She's on the run from morning to night. "Bring me this," and "get me that." I ken you're very weakly and life's a great trouble, but I would fain have ye take a little thought for her too.'

Mrs Douglas looked as if she might cry under Marg'ret's reproof. She was a pale pink woman seated in a large high easy-chair, so-called, something like a porter's chair. It was not particularly easy, but it was filled with pillows, and was the best that the locality and the time could supply. Her voice had a sound of tears in it as she replied –

'If you were as weak as I am, Marg'ret, and pains from head to foot, you would know better – and not grudge me the only comfort I have.'

'Me grudge ye ainything! no for the world; except just that bairn's time and a' her life that might be at its brightest; but poor thing, poor thing!' said Marg'ret, shaking her head.

The scene was the parlour at Drumcarro, in the wilds of Argyllshire, the speakers the mistress of the house *de jure*, and she who was at the head of affairs *de facto*, Marg'ret the housekeeper, cook, lady's maid, and general manager of everything. Mrs Douglas had brought Marg'ret with her as her maid, when she came to Drumcarro as a bride some thirty years before; but as she went on having child after child for nearly twenty years, without much stamina of either mind or body to support that continual strain, Marg'ret had gradually become more and more the deputy and representative, the real substitute of the feminine head of the house. Not much was demanded of that functionary so far as the management of its wider affairs went. Her husband was an arbitrary and high-tempered man, whose will was absolute in the family, who took counsel with no one, and who, after the few complaisances of a grim honeymoon, let his wife drop into the harmless position of a nonentity, which indeed was that which was best fitted for her. All her active duties one by one had fallen into the hands of Marg'ret, whose first tender impulse to save the mistress whom she loved from toils unfitted for her, had gradually developed into the self-confidence and universal assumption of an able and energetic housekeeper born to organize and administer. Marg'ret did not know what these fine words meant, but she knew 'her work', as she would have said, and by degrees had taken everything in the house and many things outside it into her hands. It was to her that the family went for everything, who was the giver of all indulgences, the only person who dared speak to 'the maister', when clothes were wanted or any new thing. She was an excellent cook, a good manager, combining all the qualities that make a house comfortable, and she was the only one in the house who was not afraid of 'the maister', of whom on the contrary he stood in a little awe. A wife cannot throw up her situation with the certainty of finding another at a moment's notice as a good housekeeper can do – even if she has spirit enough to entertain such an idea. And poor Mrs Douglas had no spirit, no health, little brains to begin with and none left now, after thirty years of domestic tyranny and a 'bairn-time' of fourteen children. What could such a poor soul do but fall into invalidism with so many excellent reasons constantly recurring for adopting the habits of that state and its pathos and helplessness – especially with Marg'ret to fall back upon, who, though she would sometimes speak her mind to her mistress, nursed and tended, watched over and guarded her with the most unfailing care? Drumcarro himself (as he liked to be called) scarcely dared to be very uncivil to his wife in Marg'ret's presence. He knew better than to quarrel with the woman who kept so much comfort with so little expense in his spare yet crowded house.

'Who is your "poor thing, poor thing"?' said a cheerful voice, with a mimicry of Marg'ret's manner and her accent (for Marg'ret said poor as if it were written with a French u, that sound so difficult to English lips). 'Would it be the colley dogue or the canary bird or maybe the mistress of the house?'

Marg'ret turned round upon the only antagonist in the house who could hold head against her, or whom she could not crush at a blow – Kirsteen, the second daughter, who came in at this moment, quite softly but with a sudden burst open of the door, a sort of compromise between the noise it would have been natural to her to make, and the quietness essential to the invalid's comfort. She was a girl of nearly twenty, a daughter of the hills, strongly built, not slim but trim, with red hair and brown eyes and a wonderful complexion, the pure whiteness like milk which so often goes with those ruddy locks, and the colour of health and fine air on her cheeks. I would have darkened and smoothed my Kirsteen's abundant hair if I could, for in those days nobody admired it. The type of beauty to which the palm was given was the pale and elegant type, with hair like night and starry eyes either blue or dark; and accordingly Kirsteen was not considered a pretty girl, though there were many who liked her looks in spite of her red hair, which was how people expressed their opinion then. It was so abundant and so vigorous and full of curl that it cost her all the trouble in the world to keep it moderately tidy, whereas 'smooth as satin' was the required perfection of ladies' locks. Her eyes were brown, not nearly dark enough for the requirements of the time, a kind of hazel indeed, sometimes so full of light that they dazzled the spectator and looked like gold – also quite out of accordance with the canons of the day. She was slightly freckled. She was, as I have said, strongly built; and in the dress of the time, a very short bodice and a very straight and scanty skirt, her proportions were scarcely elegant, but her waist was round if not very small, and her arms, in their short sleeves, shapely and well formed, and whiter than might have been expected from their constant exposure to air and sun, for Kirsteen only put on her gloves on serious occasions. The air of health and brightness and vigour about her altogether, made her appearance like that of a burst of sunshine into this very shady place.

' 'Deed,' said Marg'ret, putting her hands on each side of her own substantial waist in a way which has always been supposed to imply a certain defiance, "it was just you yoursel".'

'Me!' the girl cried with a sort of suppressed shout. She

cast a laughing glance round with an apparent attempt to discover some cause for the pity. 'What have I done wrong now?' Then her eyes came back to the troubled almost whimpering pathos of her mother's looks, and a cloud came over her bright countenance. 'What has she been saying, mother, about me?'

'She says I'm crying on you for something day and night, and that you never have a minute to yourself; and oh! Kirsteen, my dear, I fear it's true.'

Kirsteen put her arms akimbo too and confronted Marg'ret with laughing defiance. They were not unlike each other, both of them types of powerful and capable woman-hood, the elder purely and strongly practical, the other touched with fancy and poetry and perhaps some of the instincts of gentle blood, though neither in father nor mother were there many graces to inherit. 'You are just a leein' woman,' said the girl with a flash of her bright eyes. 'Why, it's my life! What would I do without my minnie? – as the song says.' And she began to sing in a fresh, sweet, but uncultivated voice—

> ' "He turned him right and round about,
>   Said, scorn not at my mither,
>   True loves I may get mony an ane,
>   But minnie ne'er anither." ' '

Before Kirsteen's song came to an end, however, her eyes suddenly filled with tears. 'What were you wanting, mother?' she said hastily as she dropped the tune, which was a very simple one, 'to make her speak?'

'Oh, I was wanting nothing – nothing in particular. I was wanting my pillows shifted a little, and the big plaiden shawl for my knees, and one of my wires that fell out of my reach, and my other clew for I'm nearly at the end of this one. Ay! that's better; there is nobody that knows how to make me comfortable but you.'

For Kirsteen in the meantime had begun to do, with swift and noiseless care, all that was wanted, finding the clew, or ball of worsted for the stocking her mother was knitting, as she swept softly past to get the big shawl, on her way to the side of the chair where she arranged the pillows with deft, accustomed skill. It did not take a minute to supply all these simple requirements. Marg'ret looked on, without moving while all was done, and caught the look, half-soothed, half-peevish, which the invalid cast round to see if there was not something else that she wanted. 'You may put down that book off the mantelpiece that Robbie left there,' Mrs Douglas said, finding nothing else to suggest, 'it will curl up at the corners and your father will be ill-pleased—'

'Weel?' said Marg'ret, 'now ye've got your slave, I'm thinking, ye've nae mair need of me, and there's the grand supper to think of, that the maister's aye sae keen about. When will ye have markit a' thae things, Miss Kirsteen? For I maun see to the laddie's packing before it's ower late.'

'There's the last half-dozen of handkerchiefs to do; but I'll not take long, and they're small things that can go into any corner. I'll do them now,' said Kirsteen with a little sigh.

'There's nae hurry;' Marg'ret paused a little, then caught the girl by the sleeve, 'just take another turn in the bonny afternoon before the sun's down,' she said in a low tone, 'there's plenty of time. Run away, my bonny lamb. I'll see the mistress wants naething.'

'And you that have the supper and the packing and all on your hands! No, no. I'll do them now. You may go to your work,' said Kirsteen with a look half-tender, half-peremptory. She carried her work to the window and sat down there with the white handkerchiefs in her hand.

'And what colour will you mark them in, Kirsteen? You have neither cotton nor silk to do it.'

Kirsteen raised her head and pulled out a long thread of her red hair. 'I am going to do it in this colour,' she said with a slight blush and smile. It was not an unusual little piece of sentiment in those days, and the mother accepted it calmly.

'My colour of hair,' she said, smoothing with a little com-plaisance her scanty dark locks under her cap, 'was more fit for that than yours, Kirsteen, but Robbie will like to have it all the same.'

Kirsteen laughed a little consciously while she proceeded with her work. She was quite willing to allow that a thread of her mother's dark hair would be better. 'I will do one with yours for Robbie,' she said, 'and the rest with mine.'

'But they're all for Robbie,' said the mother.

'Yes, yes,' Kirsteen replied with again that conscious look, the colour mantling to her cheeks, a soft moisture filling her eyes. The handkerchief was marked in fine delicate little cross stitches upon the white cambric, and though Mrs Douglas's dark hair was like a spider's web, the red of Kirsteen's shone upon the fine fabric like a thread of gold.

The handkerchiefs were not yet finished when two young men came into the room, one so like Kirsteen that there was no difficulty in identifying him as her brother, the other a swarthy youth a little older, tall and strong and well knit. Robbie was on the eve of his start in life, leaving home, and Ronald Drummond, who was the son of a gentleman in the neighbourhood, was going with him. They were both bound with commissions in the Company's service for India, where half of the long-legged youths, sons of little Highland lairds and Lowland gentlemen, with good blood and plenty of pride and no money, the Quentin Durwards of the early nineteenth century, found an appropriate career. The period was that of the brief peace which lasted only so long as Napoleon was at Elba, long enough, however, to satisfy the young men that there was to be no chance of renewed fighting nearer home and to make them content with their destination. They had been bred for this destination from their cradles, and Robbie Douglas at least was not sorry to escape from the dullness of Drumcarro to a larger life. Several of his brothers were already in India, and the younger ones looked to no other fate but that of following. As for the girls they did not count for much. He was sorry to say goodbye to Kirsteen but that did not weigh down his heart. He was in high excitement, eager about his new outfit, his uniform, all the novel possessions which were doubly enchanting to a boy who had never before possessed anything of his own. He was eighteen, and to become all at once a man, an officer, an independent individuality, was enough to turn the head of any youth.

Ronald Drummond was different. He was going from a much more genial home: he had already tasted the sweets of independence, having served in the last campaign in the Peninsula and been wounded, which was a thing that raised him still higher in the scale of life than the three years' advantage in respect of age which he had over his young comrade. He was neither so cheerful nor so much excited as

Robbie. He came and stood over Kirsteen as she drew closer and closer to the window to end her work before the light had gone.

'You are working it with your hair!' he said, suddenly, perceiving the nature of the long curling thread with which she threaded her needle.

'Yes,' she said, demurely, holding up her work to the light. 'What did you think it was?'

'I thought it was gold thread,' he said. And then he took up one of the handkerchiefs already completed from the table. 'R. D.,' he said, 'that's my name too.'

'So it is,' said Kirsteen, as if she had now discovered the fact for the first time.

'Nobody will do anything like that for me,' he added, pathetically.

'Oh, Ronald! if not the hairs of their heads but the heads themselves would do ye good ye should have them – and that ye know.'

'It is very true,' said Ronald, 'and thank you, Kirsteen, for reminding me how good they are; but,' he added, after a moment, in a low voice, 'they are not *you*.'

She gave vent to a very feeble laugh which was full of emotion. 'No, they could not be that,' she said.

'And R. D. is my name too,' said the young man. 'Kirsteen!' She looked up at him for a moment in the light that was fading slowly out of the skies. He had taken one of the handkerchiefs from the pile, and touching her sleeve with one hand to call her attention, put the little glistening letters to his lips and then placed the handkerchief carefully in the breast pocket of his coat. Standing as he did, shutting out, as she complained, all the light from Mrs Douglas, this little action was quite unseen, except by the one person who was intended to see it. Kirsteen could make no reply nor objection, for her heart was too full for speech. Her trembling hand, arrested in its work, dropped into his for a moment. He whispered something else, she scarcely knew what – and then Marg'ret marched into the room with the two candles which were all the lights ever used in Drumcarro parlour, and all was over and done.

CHAPTER II

There was 'a grand supper', as Marg'ret had announced, at
Drumcarro this evening, for which though it was almost
entirely a family party, solemn preparations were being
made. The house was full of an unusual odour of good
cheer; unusual goings and comings through the house
betrayed an excitement and sense of a great event approaching which was diffused through the family. On ordinary
occasions the family dinner took place between two and
three o'clock in the afternoon, followed by tea at seven with
much wealth of scones and jam, new-laid eggs and other
home produce – and the day ended for the elders by the
production of 'the tray' with its case of spirit-bottles and
accompanying hot water. Now and then by times, however,
this great ceremonial of a supper took place, always on the
eve of the departure of one of the boys to make their fortune in the world. These occasions were consequently not
surrounded by the brightest recollections to the grown-up
portion of the family, or to their mother. The supper
indeed to her was a feast of tears, probably as great, though
a more usual indulgence than the other characteristics of
the festival. It was rarely that Mrs Douglas ventured to
weep in presence of her lord, but on that night he said
nothing, made no comment upon her red eyes, and suffered
the whimper in her voice without any harsh, 'Hold your
tongue, woman!' such as usually subdued her. And it was
recognized in the house that it was the mother's role and
privilege on these occasions to cry. The children were not
disturbed by it as they might have been by tears which they
were less accustomed to see shed.

The dining-room was the best room in Drumcarro as in
many Scotch houses of the kind, being recognized as the
real centre of life, the special room of 'the maister' and the
scene of all the greater events in the family. There were
two windows in it, which at a time when the existence of
the window-tax curtailed the light was of itself a fine
feature, and it was well-sized and not badly furnished, with

a multitude of substantial mahogany chairs, sideboard, cellaret, and a long dining-table of very dark mahogany, shining like a black mirror, which was capable of being drawn out to almost any length, and which had attained the very highest polish of which wood was capable. Covered with a dazzling white cloth, lighted with four candles, a most unusual splendour – set in the silver candlesticks, which were the pride of the family – and surrounded by all the Douglases who still remained at home, it was an imposing sight. Flowers had not yet been thought of as decorations of a table; such frivolities were far in the depths of time. A large square dish set in a high stand of plated silver with straggling branches extending from it on every side, each of which contained a smaller dish full of confectionery, pieces of coloured 'rock' from Edinburgh, and sweeties procured from 'the merchant's' for the occasion, occupied the centre of the table. It was called the *épergne* and was considered very splendid. The central dish was piled high with ruddy apples, which gave an agreeable piece of colour, if anyone had thought of such fantastic folly. The four candlesticks, each with a pair of snuffers in its tray placed between them, completed the decorative portion of the table. The candles were not the delicate articles which advancing civilization has learned how to produce, but smoky 'moulds', which tinged the atmosphere with a perceptible emanation, especially when they stood in need of snuffing. They threw a ruddy light upon the faces closely assembled round the board, bringing out most fully those of the more youthful members of the family, and fading dismally towards the ends of the long table at which the principal personages were placed. There were but two visitors of the party, one the minister, invited in right of having more or less superintended Robbie's studies, such as they were, and seated on Mrs Douglas's right hand; the other an old Miss Douglas known as Aunt Eelen, from whom there were certain expectations, and who occupied a similar place of honour by the side of Drumcarro. The hero of the evening was at his father's left hand. The rest of the party were Mary the eldest daughter, Jeanie the youngest, Kirsteen, and two boys, aged fourteen and twelve respectively, the remaining sons of the house. The fare was excellent, and in another region might have been thought luxurious; but it was

impossible to conceal that the large dish of delicious trout
which stood smoking before Mrs Douglas, and the corres-
ponding hecatomb of grouse to which her husband helped
the company after the trout had been disposed of, came
from the loch and the moor on Drumcarro estate, and
therefore were as much home produce as the eggs and the
cream. This fact elicited a somewhat sharp criticism from
Miss Eelen at the foot of the table.

'The grouse is no doubt very good,' she said, 'and being
to the manner born as ye may say, I never tire of it; but for
a genteel supper like what you have always given to the
lads—'

'Faith,' said the laird, 'they'll find it most genteel where
they're going. The Englishmen will think it the finest table
in the world when they hear we have grouse every day; and
Robbie's no bound to condescend upon the number of
other dishes. I know what I am doing.'

'No doubt, no doubt: I was only making a remark. Now
I think a bit of cod from the sea or a made dish of fine
collops, or just a something tossed up with a bit of veal,
they're more genteel – and I know that's what you're always
thinking of, Neil – of course, for the boys' sakes—'

'There's a made dish coming, mem,' said Merran, who
was waiting.

'Oh, there's a made dish coming! I thought Marg'ret
would mind what was for the credit of the house. Robbie,
my man, ye ought to feel yourself a great personage with all
the phrase that's made for you. When Sandy went away,
who was the first, there was nothing but a haggis – but
we've learned many things since then.'

'A haggis is a very good thing, it's fit for a king's table.'

'But not what you would call refined, nor genteel. Give
me the leg and a piece of the back – there's more taste in it.
I hope you will always be grateful to your father for giving
ye such a grand set out.'

'I think,' said the minister at the other end, 'that you and
Drumcarro, mem, give yourselves more and more trouble
every son that leaves ye. This is the fifth I have seen.'

'Oh, don't say me, Mr Pyper,' said the mother. 'I know
just nothing about it – when your son's going away, and ye
think ye may never set eyes on him again, who's to think
of eating and drinking? He may do it, but not me.'

'That's very true,' said Mr Pyper. 'Still to give the lad a something pleasurable to look back upon, a last feast, so to speak, has many points in its favour. A lad's mind is full of materialism, as you may call it, and he will mind all the faces round the friendly board.'

'It's not very friendly to me,' said the mother, with a sob. 'My four bonny boys all away, and now Robbie. It just breaks my heart.'

'But what would you do with them, mem, if they were here?' said the sensible minister. 'Four big men, for they're all men by this time, about the house. No, no, my dear leddy, you must not complain. Such fine openings for them all! And every one getting on.'

'But what does that matter to me, Mr Pyper, if I am never to see one of them again?'

'Oh yes, mem, it matters – oh, ay, it matters much. The young of no species, much less the human, can bide at home. Fathers and mothers in the lower creation just throw them off, and there's an end. But you do more than that. You put them in the best way of doing for themselves, and the King himself cannot do better. Alas!' said the minister, 'no half so well, decent man – for look at all these young princes, one wilder than the other. And every one of yours doing so well.'

'Oh, yes, they're doing well enough – but such a long way away. And me so delicate. And Robbie never quite strong since he had the measles. It's borne in upon me that I will never see him again.'

'You need not say it, mother,' said Kirsteen, 'for that's what nobody can know; and it's just as likely he may be sent home with dispatches or some great grandee take a fancy to him and bring him back. And when we're sitting some day working our stockings he'll come linking in by the parlour door.'

'Oh, you're just as light as air,' said the mother; 'there's nothing serious in ye. You think going to India is just like going to the fair.'

Kirsteen darted a quick glance at her mother, but said no more. Her eyes kept filling much against her will. She was in great terror lest a big drop might brim over and run down her cheek, to be spied at once by Jeanie or the boys. For nothing would be hid from these little things: they could note at the same moment the last bit of a bird which they had all counted on, being transferred to Aunt Eelen's plate, and keep an eye upon the favourite apple each had chosen, and spy that suspicious brightness in Kirsteen's eyes. Nothing could be hid from their sharp, little, all-inspecting looks.

There was a breathless moment when the cloth was drawn, and the black gleam of the mahogany underneath changed in a moment the lights of the picture, and gave the children a delightful opportunity of surveying themselves in that shining surface. It was a moment full of solemnity. Everybody knew what was coming. The port and sherry, with their little labels, in the silver holders intended to prevent the bottles from scratching the table, were placed before Mr Douglas. Then there was also placed before him a trayful of tall glasses. He rose up: the eyes of all followed his movements: Jock and Jamie projecting their red heads forward in the smoky glow of the candles, then much in want of snuffing; Jeanie's paler locks turned the same way. Mary, who had her mother's brown smooth hair, rested her clasped hands upon the edge of the table with calm expectation. Kirsteen leant her elbows on the same shining edge, and put down her face in her hands. Miss Eelen shook her head, and kept on shaking it like a china mandarin. The laird of Drumcarro went to an old-fashioned wine-cooler, which stood under the sideboard. He took from it one bottle of champagne, which occupied it in solitary dignity. Marg'ret stood ready with a knife in her hand to cut the wire, and a napkin over her arm to wipe up anything that might be spilt. Not a word was said at table while these preliminaries were going through. Aunt Eelen, as the catastrophe lingered, went so far as to make a suppressed *Tchish Tchish!* of her tongue against her palate. The rest were full of serious excitement too important for speech. The bottle was opened finally without spilling a drop: it was perhaps not so much 'up' as it might have been. Drumcarro filled all the glasses, one for each person at table, and another one for Marg'ret. There was perhaps more foam than wine in a number of the glasses. He held up his own in his hand. 'It's Robbie's last night at Drumcarro,' he said, 'for the present. Have you all your glasses? Before the fizz is out of the wine drink to Robbie's good health and good luck to him, and to all our lads that have gone before.' He touched the foam in his glass, now fast dying away, with his lips. 'May they all come back with stars on their breasts,' he said, 'and do credit to their name – and not a laggard, nor a coward, nor one unworthy to be a Douglas among them all!'

The other male members of the party were standing up also. 'Here's to you, Robbie!' 'Here's to you, Robbie!' cried the two boys. The foam in their glasses merely moistened their throats, the minister, however, whose glass had been full, gravely swallowed its contents in little sips, with pauses between. 'A very good health to them all, and the Lord bless them,' he said with imposing authority. Mrs Douglas taking advantage of the privilege awarded to her, began to cry, and Marg'ret lifted up a strong voice, from the foot of the table where she stood with her hand upon the shoulder of the hero.

'Be a good lad, Robbie – and mind upon your minnie and a' the family – and be a credit to us a': here's to you, and to the rest o' the young gentlemen, them that's gone, and them that are to go!'

'Ye'll have to get a new bottle for the little one,' said Aunt Eelen. 'Neil, my man, for your half-dozen will be out with Jock.' She gave a harsh laugh at her own joke. 'And then there's the lasses' marriages to be thought upon,' she added setting down her glass.

Drumcarro resumed his seat, the ceremonial being over. 'Let the lasses' marriages alone,' he said impatiently. 'I've enough to think upon with my lads. Now, Rob, are you sure you're all ready? Your things packed and all your odds and ends put up? The less of them you take the better. Long before you've got the length of Calcutta ye'll be wishing you had left the half of your portmanteaux at home.'

'I've just two, father.'

'Well, ye'll be wishing ye had but one. Bring ben the hot water, Marg'ret; for wine's but a feeble drink, and cold on the stomach. My wife never moves at the right time. Will I give her a hint that you're waiting, Eelen?'

'Not on my account, Drumcarro. Your champagne's no doubt a grand drink; but a glass out of your tumbler, if you're going to make one, is more wholesome and will set all right.'

'I thought ye would say that,' said the laird. She had said it already on every such occasion – so that perhaps his divination was not wonderful. He proceeded with care to the manufacture of 'the tumbler', at which the minister looked from the other end of the table with patient interest, abiding his time.

'Snuff the candles,' said the laird, 'will nobody pay a little attention? You three little ones, you can run away with your apples, it's near your bedtime; but don't make more noise than you can help. Marg'ret, take the hot water to the minister. Champagne, as ye were saying, Eelen, is a grand drink; I think it right my sons should drink it at their father's table before they plunge into the extravagance of a mess. It teaches a lad what he's likely to meet with, and I would not have one of mine surprised with any dainty, as if he had come out of a poorhouse. But a wholesome glass like what I'm helping you to is worth twenty of it.' He was filling a wine-glass with his small silver toddy-ladle as he spoke, and the fumes of the pungent liquid rose in curls of steam pleasant to the accustomed nostrils. Robbie kept an eye upon the hot water which Mr Pyper detained, knowing that one of the privileges of his position tonight was 'to make a tumbler' for himself, with the privilege of offering it then to his sisters, as each of his brothers had done.

'Can I assist you to a glass, mem – just a drop? It will do ye good,' the minister said.

'Nothing will do me good,' said Mrs Douglas. 'I'm far past that; but I'll take a little for civility, not to refuse a friend, whether it's toddy or whether it's wine it's all sounding brass and a tinkling cymbal to me. A woman when her bairns go from her is little comforted by the like of that.'

'And yet the creature comforts have their place, a homely one but still a true one,' said the minister. 'There's a time to feast as well as a time to refrain from feasting. Miss Mary, may I have the pleasure of assisting you?'

'I'll take a little from Robbie,' said the elder daughter, wisely instructed that it was well thus to diminish the unwonted tumbler allowed to the novice. Kirsteen rose quickly to her feet as these interchanges went round.

'Mother, I think if ye'll let me I'll just give an eye to what the little ones are doing,' she said, 'and see that Robbie's

things are all ready. One of the boxes is open still and there
are these handkerchiefs.'

Kirsteen's eyes were brimming over, and as she spoke a
large drop fell upon her hand: she looked at it with alarm,
saying, 'I did not mean to be so silly,' and hastened away.

'Where is Kirsteen away to? Can she not take her share
of what is going like the rest?' said her father. 'You breed
these lasses to your own whimsies, Mistress Douglas. The
bairns are well out of the road; but them that are grown up
should bide where they are, and not disturb the family. I
have no patience with them.'

'I'm here, father,' said Mary in her mild voice.

'Oh, ay, you're there,' said the inconsistent head of the
house, 'for you're just nobody, and never had two ideas in
your head,' he continued in a lower tone. 'Now, Robbie,
my man, take your glass, there is no saying when you will
get another. It's just second nature to a Scotsman, but it's
as well for you to be out of the way of it; for though it's the
most wholesome drink, it's very seductive and you're much
better without it at your age. It's like the strange woman
that you're warned against in Scripture.'

'Drumcarro!' said Aunt Eelen. 'Oh fie! before ladies.'

'Ladies or no ladies I cannot let the occasion pass without
a word of warning,' said the father. 'Ye will have every
temptation put before ye, my lad, not drink perhaps, for
the climate will not stand it, but other things, that are
worse.'

'I'm thinking, Christina,' said the old lady, 'that now
your goodman has begun his moralities it may be as well
for us to go, for you know where that begins and you never
can tell where it may end; a man has cognizance of many
things that cannot enter into the experience of you and me.
Mind you what your father says, Robbie, but it's not
intended for your mother and me.'

CHAPTER III

Kirsteen hurried out of the room, out of the fumes of the toddy and the atmosphere of the half-festive, half-doleful occasion which made a not altogether unpleasant excitement in the monotony of the home life. She gazed in at the open door of the parlour, and saw the three younger children gathered in the firelight upon the hearthrug munching their apples, and the sweets with which they had been allowed to fill their pockets. The firelight made still more ruddy the red heads and freckled faces of the boys, and lit up Jeanie, who sat on a footstool a little higher than her brothers, in her more delicate tints. Kirsteen was much attached to her younger sister, who promised to be the beauty of the family, and thought her like an angel, especially as seen through the dew of her wet eyes. 'Dinna make a noise,' she said, 'be awfu' quiet or you'll be sent to your beds!' and then closed the door softly and stole through the dark passage towards the principal entrance. There was no light save a ruddy gleam from the kitchen in the depths of that dark passage which traversed the whole breadth of the house, and that which shone through the crevices of the dining-room door. She had to find her way groping, but she was very well used to this exercise, and knew exactly where the hall-table and the heavy wooden chairs on each side stood. The outer door stood half open according to the habit of the country where there were no burglars to fear, and little to tempt them, and a perfect capacity of self-defence inside. There was a full moon that night but it had not yet risen, though the sky was full of a misty light which preceded that event. A faint shadow of the group of trees outside was thrown upon the doorway; they were birches, slender and graceful, with their leaves half blown away by the October gales; those that remained were yellow with the first touches of the frost, and in themselves gave forth a certain light. Kirsteen stole out to a bench that stood against the wall, and sat down in a corner. She was not afraid of cold with her uncovered head and bare arms. All the moods of the elements were familiar to the Highland girl. She thought it mild, almost warm: there was no wind, the yellow birches, perceptible in their faint colour, stood up like a group of long-limbed youths dangling their long locks in the dim light: the further landscape was but faintly visible, the shoulder of the hill against the sky, and a single gleam of the burn deep down among the trees.

She sat pressing herself into the corner of the seat, and the long pent-up tears poured forth. They had been getting too much for her, like a stream shut in by artificial barriers, and now came with a flood like the same stream in spate and carrying every obstruction away. It was almost a pleasure to see (if there had been anyone to do so) the good heart with which Kirsteen wept: she made no noise, but the tears poured forth in a great shower, relieving her head and her heart. They were very heavy, but they were not bitter. They meant a great deal of emotion and stirring up of her whole being, but though her feelings were very poignant they were not without pleasure. She had never felt so elevated above herself, above every dull circumstance that surrounded her. She had been very sorry and had shed tears plentifully when the other boys went away. But this was not the same. She perhaps did not confess to herself, yet she knew very well that it was not altogether for Robbie. Robbie had his share, but there was another now. For years Kirsteen and Ronald Drummond had been good friends. When he went away before she had felt a secret pang, and had been very eager to hear the news of the battles and that he was safe: but something had changed this friendship during the last summer while he had been at home. Not a word had been said: there was no love-making; they were both too shy to enter upon any revelation of feeling, nor was there any opportunity for explanations, since they were always surrounded by companions, always in the midst of a wandering, easy-minded party which had no respect for anyone's privacy. But Kirsteen when she marked her brother's handkerchiefs with her hair had fully intended that Ronald should see it, and be struck with the similarity of the initials and ask for or take one of them at least. Her heart beat high when this happened according to her prevision; and when he stooped and whispered, 'Will ye wait for me, Kirsteen, till I come back?' the answering

whisper, 'That I will!' had come from the bottom of her
heart. She had scarcely been aware of what was said in the
hurry of the moment. But it had come back to her, every
syllable and every tone as soon as it was all over. Their
spirits had floated together in that one moment, which was
only a moment yet enough to decide the course of two
lives. They were too much bound by the laws of their
youthful existence to think of breaking any observance in
order to expand these utterances, or make assurance sure.
That Ronald should spend his last evening at home with his
mother and sister, that Kirsteen should be present at
Robbie's parting supper, was as the laws of the Medes and
the Persians to these two. No emergency could be imagined
of sufficient weight to interfere with such necessities of life.
And there was something in their simple absolutism of
youthful feeling which was better expressed in the momentary conjunction, in the sudden words so brief and preg-
nant, than in hours of lovers' talk, of which both boy and
girl would have thought shame. 'Will ye wait for me till I
come back?' What more could have been said in volumes?
and, 'That I will!' out of the fervour of a simple heart?
Kirsteen thought it all over again and again. He seemed to
stand by her side bending a little over her with a look half
smile, half tears in his eyes; and she was aware again of the
flash of the sweet discovery, the gold thread of the little
letters put to his lips, and then the question, 'Will ye wait?'
Wait! For a hundred years, for all the unfathomed depths
of life, through long absence and silence, each invisible to
the other. 'That I will!' She said it over and over again to
herself.

In those days there was no thought of the constant
communications we have now, no weekly mails, no rapid
courses overland, no telegraph for an emergency. When a
young man went away he went for good – away; every trace
of him obliterated as if he had not been. It was a four
months' voyage to India round by the Cape. Within the
course of the year his mother might hope to hear that he
had arrived. And if an Indian letter had come even at that
long interval for a girl in another family, what a host of
questions would she not have had to go through! 'A letter
for Kirsteen! Who's writing to Kirsteen? What is he writing
to her about? What is the meaning of it all? I must know

what that means!' Such would have been the inquiries that
would have surged up in a moment, making poor Kirsteen
the object of everybody's curious gaze and of every kind of
investigation. She never dreamed of any such possibility.
Robbie, when he wrote home, which he would no doubt do
in time, might mention the companion of his voyage; Agnes
Drummond might say, 'There's a letter from our Ronald.'
These were the only communications that Kirsteen could
hope for. She was very well aware of the fact, and raised no
thought of rebellion against it. When she gave that promise
she meant waiting for interminable years – waiting without
a glimpse or a word. Nor did this depress her spirits: rather
it gave a more elevating ideal form to the visionary bond.
All romance was in it, all the poetry of life. He would be as
if he were dead to her for years and years. Silence would fall
between them like the grave. And yet all the time she would
be waiting for him and he would be coming to her.

And though Kirsteen cried it was not altogether for
trouble. It was for extreme and highly wrought feeling,
sorrow and happiness combined. Through all her twenty
years of life there had been nothing to equal that moment,
the intensity of it, the expectation, the swift and sudden
realization of all vague anticipations and wishes. It was only
a minute of time, a mere speck upon the great monotonous
level of existence, and yet there would be food enough in
it for the thoughts of all future years. When the thunder-
shower of the tears was exhausted, she sat quite still in a
kind of exalted contentment, going over it and over it,
never tired. The hot room and the smoky glare of the
candles, and the fumes of the whisky and the sound of all
the voices, had been intolerable to her; but in the fresh
coldness of the night air, in that great quiet of Nature, with
the rustle of the leaves going through it like breath, and
the soft distant tinkle of the burns, what room and scope
there was for remembering; which was what Kirsteen called
thinking – remembering every tone and look, the way in
which he approached the table where her work was lying,
her wonder if he would notice, the flush of perception on
his face as he said, 'It's my name too,' and then that tender
theft, the act that left Robbie for ever without one of his
pocket-handkerchiefs – she thought with a gleam of fun
how he would count them and count them, and wonder

how he had lost it – the little visionary letters put to his
lips. Oh, that her heart had been sewn in with the hair to
give to him! But so it was, so it was! He had that pledge of
hers, but she had nothing of his, nor did she want anything
to remind her, to bind her faith to him, though it should
be years before she saw him again. The tears started into
her eyes again with that thought, which gave her a pang, yet
one which was full of sweetness: for what did it matter
how long he was away, or how dark and still the time and
space that separated them now. 'Will ye wait for me till I
come back?' that would be the gold thread that should run
through all the years.

The sound of a little movement in the dining-room from
which all this time she had heard the murmur of the voices,
the tinkle of the glasses, made her pause and start. It was
the ladies withdrawing to the parlour. She thought with a
little gasp that they would find the children scorching their
cheeks on the hearthrug, instead of being sent off to bed as
should have been done, and held her breath expecting every
moment the call of 'Kirsteen!' which was her mother's
appeal against fate. But either the general licence of the
great family event, or the sedative effect of her mouthful of
champagne and glass of toddy, or the effect of Aunt Eelen's
conversation which put her always on her defence whatever
was the subject, had subdued Mrs Douglas: there came no
call, and Kirsteen though with a slightly divided attention,
and one ear anxiously intent upon what was going on
indoors, pursued her thoughts. It gave them a more vivid
sweetness that they were so entirely her own, a secret which
she might carry safely without anyone suspecting its existence under cover of everything that was habitual and
visible. It would be her life, whatever was going on outside.
When she was dull – and life was often dull at Drumcarro
– when her mother was more exacting than usual, her father
more rough, Mary and the children more exasperating, she
would retire into herself and hear the whisper in her heart,
'Will ye wait till I come back?' – it would be like a spell
she said to herself – just like a spell; the clouds would disperse and the sun break out, and her heart would float forth
upon that golden stream.

The sound of a heavy yet soft step aroused Kirsteen at
this moment from her dreams; but she was set at ease by

the sight of a great whiteness which she at once identified
as Marg'ret's apron, coming slowly round the corner of the
house. 'I just thought I would find you here,' said Marg'ret.
'It's natural in me after that warm kitchen and a' the pots
and pans, to want a breath of air – but what are you doing
here with your bare neck, and nothing on your head? I'm
just warning you for ever, you'll get your death of cold.'

'I could not bear it any longer,' said Kirsteen, 'the talking
and all the faces and the smell of the toddy.'

'Hoot,' said Marg'ret, 'what ails ye at the smell of the
toddy? In moderation it's no an ill thing – and as for the
faces you wouldna' have folk without faces, you daft bairn;
that's just a silly speech from the like of you.'

'There's no law against being silly,' Kirsteen said.

'Oh, but that's true. If there was, the jails would be ower
full: though no from you, my bonny dear. But I ken weel
what it is,' said Marg'ret, putting her arm round the girl's
shoulder. 'Your bit heart's a' stirred up and ye dinna ken
how ye feel. Tak' comfort, my dear bairn, they'll come
back.'

Kirsteen shed a few more ready tears upon Marg'ret's
shoulder, then she gave that vigorous arm a push, and burst
from its hold with a laugh. 'There's one of Robbie's handkerchiefs lost or stolen,' she said. 'Where do ye think he'll
ever find it? and R. D. worked upon it with a thread of my
hair.'

'Bless me!' said Marg'ret with alarm, 'who would meddle
with the laddie's linen? but you're meaning something mair
than meets the eye,' she added, with a pat upon the girl's
shoulder; I'll maybe faddom it by and by. Gang away ben,
the ladies will be wondering where ye are, and it's eerie out
here in the white moonlight.'

'Not eerie at all: ye mean soft and sweet,' said Kirsteen,
'the kind of light for thinking in; and the moon is this
minute up. She's come for you and not for me.'

'I cannot faddom you the nicht any more than I can
faddom what ye say,' said Marg'ret. 'There's mair in it than
Robbie and his handkerchief. But I maun go in and fasten
up the straps and put his keys in his pocket or he'll forget
them. Laddies are a great handful, they're aye forgetting.
But they're like the man's wife, they're ill to have, but
worse to want. Gang in, gang in out of the night air,' said

Marg'ret with a faint sob, softly pushing Kirsteen before
her. The smell of the peat fires which was pleasant, and of
the smoke of the candles which was not, and of the penetrating fumes of the toddy again filled Kirsteen's nostrils as
she came in. She had no right to be fastidious, for she had
been brought up in the habit and knowledge of all these
odours. When she entered, another scent, that of the tea
with which the ladies were concluding the evening, added
its more subtle perfume. In those days people were not
afraid of strong tea mixed with a great deal of green to
modify the strong black Congou, and it had been 'masking'
for half an hour before the fire: they were not afraid of
being 'put off their sleep'.

'And do ye mean to say, Christina, that there's nobody
coming about the house that would do for your girls?'

'Oh, for mercy's sake, Eelen, say not a word about that:
we've had trouble enough on that subject,' said Mrs
Douglas in her injured voice.

'Are you meaning Anne? Well, I mind Drumcarro's
vow, but there is no doubt that was a misalliance. I'm meaning men in their own position of life.'

'Where are they to see men in their own position, or
any men?' said the mother, shaking her head. 'Bless me,
Kirsteen, is that you? I don't like people to go gliding about
the house like that, so that ye never can hear them. When
your aunt and me were maybe talking – what was not meant
for the like of you.'

'Hoot, there was no hairm in it,' said Aunt Eelen, 'if all
the lasses in the town had been here.'

'But it's an ill custom,' said Mrs Douglas. 'However, as
you're here ye may just get me my stocking, Kirsteen, and
take up a stitch or two that I let fall. Na, na, no strangers
ever come here. And now that my Robbie's going, there will
be fewer than ever. I wish your father would not keep that
laddie out of his bed, and him starting so early. And, eh,
me, to think that I'm his mother, and most likely will never
see him in this world again!'

CHAPTER IV

Robbie went away next morning very early, before the October day was fairly afloat in the skies. They had no carriage at Drumcarro except 'the gig', and it was perched up in this high conveyance, looking very red with tears and blue with cold, that the household, all standing round the door, saw the last of the boy mounted beside his father, with a large portmanteau standing uncomfortably between them. His other baggage had been sent off in the cart in the middle of the night, Jock as a great favour accompanying the carter, to the great envy and wrath of Jamie, who thought it hard that he should miss such a 'ploy', and could see no reason why his brother should be preferred because he was two years older. Jamie stood at the horse's head looking as like a groom as he could make himself, while his father made believe to hold in the steady honest mare who knew the way as well as he did, and was as little troubled by any superfluous fun or friskiness. Mrs Douglas had remained in bed dissolved in tears, and her boy had taken his leave of her in those congenial circumstances. 'Be a good lad, Robbie, and sometimes think upon your poor mother, that will never live to see you again.' 'Oh, mother, but I'll be back long before that,' he cried vaguely, doing his best to behave like a man, but breaking out in a great burst of a sob, as she fell back weeping upon her pillows. The girls at the door were in different developments of sorrow, Mary using her handkerchief with demonstration, Kirsteen with her eyes lucid and large with unshed tears through which everything took an enlarged, uncertain outline, and little Jeanie by turns crying and laughing as her attention was distracted from Robbie going away to Jamie standing with his little legs wide apart at the mare's respectable head. Robbie was not at all sorry to go away: his heart was throbbing with excitement and anticipation of all the novelties before him; but he was only eighteen, and it was also full for the moment of softer emotions. Marg'ret stood behind the girls, taller than any of them, with her apron to her eyes.

She was the last person on whom his look rested as his
father called out, 'Stand away from her head,' as if honest
Mally had been a hunter, and with a friendly touch of the
whip stirred the mare into motion. Robbie looked back at
the grey house, the yellow birches waving in the wind, the
hillside beyond, and the group round the door, and waved
his hand and could not speak. But he was not sorry to go
away. It was the aim of all his breeding, the end looked forward to for many years. 'It's me the next,' said Jock, who
was waiting at Inveralton, from which place by fishing-
smack and coach Robbie was to pursue his way to Glasgow
and the world. Travellers had but few facilities in those
days: the rough fishing boat across the often angry loch; the
coach that in October did not run 'every lawful day', but
only at intervals; the absence of all comfortable accommodation would grievously affect the young men nowadays
who set out in a sleeping carriage from the depths of the
Highlands to take their berths in a P. and O. Robbie
thought of none of these luxuries which were not yet
invented. His parting from his father and brother was not
emotional: all that had been got over when the group about
the doors had waved their last goodbye. He was more
anxious about the portmanteaux, upon which he looked
with honest pride, and which contained among many other
things the defective half-dozen of handkerchiefs. Ronald
Drummond met him at the side of the loch with his boxes,
which contained a more ample outfit than Robbie's and
the sword-case which had been in the Peninsula, a distinction which drew all eyes. 'It's me the next,' Jock shouted as
a parting salutation, as the brown sail was hoisted and the
boat, redolent of herrings, carried the two adventurers
away.

'Weel,' said Marg'ret, 'the laddie's gane, and good go
with him. It's ane less to think of and fend for. And we
must just all go back to our work. Whoever comes or whoever goes, I have aye my dinner to think of, and the clean
clothes to be put into the drawers, and the stockings to
darn a' the same.'

'If you'll put an iron to the fire, Marg'ret, I'll come and
do the collars,' said Mary, 'he was always so particular,
poor Robbie. There will be no fyke now with trying to
please him.'

'I cannot settle to work,' said Kirsteen, 'and I will not. I'm not just a machine for darning stockings. I wish I was Robbie going out into the world.'

'Oh, Kirsteen, come and see the rabbits he gave me,' said Jeanie. 'He would not trust one of them to the boys, but gave them to me. Come and take them some lettuce leaves. It will keep us in mind of Robbie.' There was perhaps some danger that the recollection of the brother departed would not last very long. So many had gone before him and there were still others to go.

But Kirsteen avoided Jeanie and the rabbits and suddenly remembered something she had to get at the 'merchant's', which was a full mile off – worsted for her mother's knitting and needles for herself, who was always, to the reprobation of the elder members of the family, losing her needles. She was glad to represent to herself that this errand was a necessity, for a house without needles how can that be? and poor mother would be more dependent than ever on everything being right for her work, on this melancholy day. It was still quite early, about nine o'clock, and it was with a compunction that Kirsteen gave herself the indulgence of this walk. A morning away from work seemed to her almost an outrage upon life, only to be excused by the circumstances and the necessity of the errand. She walked along the familiar road not noting where she went, her thoughts far away, following the travellers, her mind full of an agitation which was scarcely sorrowful, a sort of exaltation over all that was common and ordinary. The air and the motion were good for her, they were in harmony with that condition of suppressed excitement in which from the depths of her being everything seemed bubbling up. Kirsteen's soul was like one of the clear pools of the river by which she walked, into which some clear, silvery, living thing had leaped and lived. Henceforward it was no more silent, no longer without motion. The air displaced came up in shining globules to the surface, dimpling over the water, a stir was in it from time to time, a flash, a shimmering of all the ripples. Her mind, her heart were like the pool – no longer mirroring the sky above and the pathway ferns and grasses on the edge, but something that had an independent life. She roamed along without being able to tell had anyone asked her where she was. The road was a beautiful road by the

side of a mountain stream, which was only called the burn,
but which was big enough for trout or even now and then
salmon – which ran now along the side of the hill, now
diving deep down into a ravine, now half hid with big over-
reaching banks, now flinging forth upon a bit of open
country, flowing deep among the rocks, chattering over the
shallows, sometimes bass, sometimes treble, an unaccoun-
table, unreasonable, changeable stream. Red rowan-tree
berries hung over it reflecting their colour in the water. The
heather on the hill came in deep russet tones of glory
defeated, and the withered bracken with tints of gold, all
gaining a double brilliancy from the liquid medium that
returned their image. To all these things Kirsteen was so
well accustomed that perhaps she did not at any time stop
to note them as a stranger might have done. But today she
did not know what was about her; she was walking in more
beautiful landscapes, in the lands of imagination by the
river of love, in the country of the heart. The *pays du tendre*
which was ridiculous when all the fine ladies and gentlemen
postured about in their high-heeled shoes is not absurd
when a fresh and simple maiden crosses its boundary. She
went down the glen to the merchant's and chose her wool,
and bought her needles, and said a few words to the women
at their doors, and shed a few more tears when they were
sorry for her about her brother's going away, without ever
leaving that visionary country, and came back from the
village more deeply lost in it than ever, and hearing the
whisper of last night in every motion of the branches and
every song of the burns. 'Will ye wait for me, Kirsteen?'
though it was only this morning that he went away, and
years and years must pass before he came back – 'Ay, that I
will! That I will.'

She had nearly reached home again, coming back from
the merchant's – for even her reverie and the charm of it
could not keep Kirsteen's step slow, or subdue its airy
skimming tread – when she came up to the carter with his
cart who had carried Robbie's luggage to Inveralton. She
stopped to speak to him, and walked along by his side
timing her steps to those of his heavy slow tread and the
movement of the laborious patient horse. 'Did you see him,
Duncan?' she said.

'Oh, ay, I saw him – and they got away fine in James

Macgregor's boat; and a quick wind that would carry them over the loch in two or three minutes.'

'And how was he looking, Duncan?'

''Deed, Miss Kirsteen, very weel: he's gaun to see the world – ye canna expect a young boy like that to maen and graen. I have something here for you.'

'Something for me!' She thought perhaps it was something that had been put into the gig by mistake, and was not excited, for what should there be for her? She watched with a little amusement Duncan's conflict with the different coats which had preserved his person from the night cold. He went on talking while he struggled.

'The other laddie, Jock, I left to come home with the maister in the gig. He thought it was fine – but I wouldna wonder if he was regretting Duncan and the cart – afore now. Here it is at last, and a' fecht to get it. It is a book from Maister Ronald that you gave him a loan of – or something o' that kind if I could but mind what gentles say—'

'Gave him – a loan of—?' cried Kirsteen, breathless. She had to turn away her head not to exhibit to Duncan the overwhelming blush which she felt to cover her from head to foot. 'Oh, yes – 'she added after a moment, taking the little parcel from his hand, 'I – mind.'

Let us hope that to both of them the little fiction was forgiven. A loan of – she had nothing to lend nor had he ever borrowed from her. It was a small paper parcel, as if it contained a little book. Kirsteen never could tell how she succeeded in walking beside the carter for a few steps further, and asking him sedately about his wife and the bairns. Her heart was beating in her ears as if it would burst through. It was like a bird straining at its bonds, eager to fly away.

Then she found herself at home where she had flown like the wind, having informed Duncan that she was 'in a great hurry' – but in the passage on the way to her own room, she met Mary, who was coming from the kitchen with a number of shining white collars in her arms which she had been ironing. 'Where have you been?' said Mary. 'My mother has been yammering for you. Is this an hour of the day to go stravaighing for pleasure about the roads?'

Mary pronounced the last word 'rods', though she prided herself on being very correct in her speech.

'Me – I have been to the merchant's for my mother's

fingering for her stockings,' Kirsteen said breathlessly.

'It was wheeling she wanted,' said Mary with exasperating calm; 'that's just like you, running for one thing when it's another that's wanted. Is that it in that small parcel like a book?'

'No, that's not it,' said Kirsteen, clasping the little parcel closer and closer.

'It's some poetry-book you've had out with you to read,' said her sister as if the acme of wrong-doing had been reached. 'I would not have thought it of you, Kirsteen, to be reading poetry about the rods, the very morning that Robbie's gone away. And when my mother is so ill she cannot lift her head.'

'I've been reading no poetry,' cried Kirsteen with the most poignant sense of injury. 'Let me pass, Mary. I'm going up the stair.'

But it was Marg'ret now who interposed, coming out at the sound of the altercation. She said, 'Miss Kirsteen, I'm making some beef-tea for the mistress. Come in like a dear and warm your hands, and ye can carry it up. It will save me another trail up and down these stairs.'

Kirsteen stood for a moment obstructed on both sides with a sense of contrariety which was almost intolerable. Tears of vexation rose to her eyes. 'Can I not have a moment to myself?' she cried.

'To read your poetry!' Mary called after her in her mild little exasperating voice.

'Whist, whist, my lamb, say nothing,' said Marg'ret. 'Your mother canna bide to have a talking. Never you mind what she says, think upon the mistress that's lying up there, wanting to hear everything and canna – wanting to be in the middle of everything and no equal to it. It was no that I grudge going up the stairs, but just to keep a' things quiet. And what's that you've gotten in your hand?'

'It's just a small parcel,' said Kirsteen, covering it with her fingers. 'It's just a – something I was buying—'

'Not sweeties,' said Marg'ret solemnly, 'the bairns had more than plenty last night—'

'Never you mind what it is,' said Kirsteen with a burst of impatience, thrusting it into her pocket. 'Give me the beef-tea and I'll take it upstairs.'

Mrs Douglas lay concealed behind her curtains, her face

almost in a fluid state with constant weeping. 'Oh, set it
down upon the table,' she said. 'Do they think there's comfort in tea when a woman has parted with her bairn? And
where have ye been, Kirsteen? just when I was in want of ye
most: just when my head was sorest, and my heart like to
break – Robbie gone, and Mary so taken up with herself,
and you – out of the way—'

'I'm very sorry, mother,' said poor Kirsteen. 'I ran down
to the merchant's to get you your yarn for your knitting. I
thought you would like to have it ready.'

Mrs Douglas rocked her head back and forward on her
pillow. 'Do I look like a person that's thinking of yarn or of
stockings, with my head aching and my heart breaking?
And none of you can match a colour. Are you sure it's the
same? Most likely I will just have to send Marg'ret to
change it. What's that bulging out your pocket? You will
tear every pocket you have with parcels in it as if you were
a lad and not a lass.'

'It's only a very small thing,' said Kirsteen.

'If that's the yarn ye should never let them twist it up so
tight. It takes the softness all out of it. Where are ye going
the moment you've come back? Am I to have nobody near
me, and me both ill in body, and sore, sore distrest in mind?
Oh, Kirsteen, I thought ye had a truer heart.'

'Mother, my heart's true,' cried the girl, 'and there's
nothing in the world I would not do to please you. But let
me go and put away my things, let me go for a moment, just
for a moment. I'll be back again before you've missed me.'

'You're not always so tidy to put away your things,' said
the invalid, 'sit down there by my bedside, and tell me
how my bonny lad looked at the last? Did he keep up his
heart? And was your father kind to him? And did you see
that he had his keys right, and the list of all his packages?
Eh me, to think I have to lie here and could not see my
laddie away.'

'But, mother, you have never done it,' said Kirsteen, 'to
any of the boys – and Robbie never expected—'

'You need not mind me,' said Mrs Douglas, 'of the waik
creature I've always been. Aye in my bed or laid up, never
good for anything. If you'll lift me up a little, Kirsteen, I
might maybe try to swallow the beef-tea; for eh! I have
much, much need of support on such a doleful day. Now

another pillow behind my back, and put the tray here; I
cannot bear the sight of food, but I must not let my
strength run down. Where are you going now, you restless
thing? Just stay still where you are; for I cannot do without
you, Kirsteen. Kirsteen, do you hear me? The doctor says
I'm never to be left by myself.'

It was not till a long time after that Kirsteen was free.
Her eager expectation had fallen into an aching sense of suspense, a dull pang that affected both mind and body.
Instead of the rapid flight to her room full of anticipation in
which she had been arrested in entering the house, she went
soberly, prepared for any disenchantment. The room was
shared with her younger sister Jeanie, and it seemed quite
probable that even a moment's solitude might be denied
her. When she found it empty, however, and had closed
the door upon herself and her secret, it was with trembling
hands that she opened the little parcel. It might be the handkerchief sent back to her, it might be some other plain intimation that he had changed his mind. But when the
covering was undone, Kirsteen's heart leaped up again to
that sudden passion of joy and content which she had first
known yesterday. The parcel contained the little Testament
which Ronald had carried to church many a Sunday, a small
book bound in blue morocco, a little bent and worn with
use. On the flyleaf were his initials R. D., the letters of the
handkerchief, and underneath C. D. freshly written. He had
made rather clumsily, poor fellow, with a pencil, a sort of
runic knot of twisted lines to link the two names together.
That was all. Nowadays the young lover would at least have
added a letter; seventy years ago he had not thought of it.
Kirsteen's heart gave a bound in her breast, and out of
weariness and contradiction and all the depressing influ-
ences of the morning, swam suddenly into another world: a
delicious atmosphere of perfect visionary bliss. Never were
public betrothals more certain, seldom so sweet. With a
timid movement, blushing at herself, she touched with her
lips the letters on the title-page.

PART II

CHAPTER V

Mr Douglas of Drumcarro was the son of one of the Scotch lairds who had followed Prince Charlie, and had been attainted after the disastrous conclusion of the Forty-Five. Born in those distracted times, and learning as their very first lessons in life the expedients of a hunted man to escape his pursuers, and the anguish of the mother as to the success of these expedients, the two half-comprehending children, twin boys, had grown up in great poverty and seclusion in a corner of a half-ruined house which belonged to their mother's father, and within cognizance of their own real home, one of the great houses of the district which had passed into alien hands. When they set out to make their fortune, at a very early age, their mother also having in the meantime died, two half-educated but high-spirited and strongly feeling boys, they had parted with a kind of vow that all their exertions should be addressed to the task of regaining their old possessions and home, and that neither should set foot again upon that beloved alienated land until able in some measure to redeem this pledge. They went away in different directions, not unconfident of triumphantly fulfilling the mutual promise; for fame and fortune do not seem very difficult at sixteen, though so hard to acquire at a less hopeful age. Willie, the younger, went to England where some relations helped him on and started him in a mildly successful career. He was the gentlest, the least determined of the two, and fortune overtook him in a manner very soothing after his troubled boyhood in the shape of a mild competency and comfort, wife and children, and a life altogether alien to the romance of the disinherited with which he had begun.

But Neil Douglas, the elder, went further afield. He went to the West Indies, where at that period there were fortunes for the making, attended, however, by many accessories of which people in the next generation spoke darkly, and which still, perhaps, among unsophisticated people survive in tradition, throwing a certain stain upon the planter's for-

tunes. Whether these supposed cruelties and horrors were
all or almost all the exaggerations of a following agitation,
belonging like many similar atrocities in America to the
Abolitionist imagination, is a question unnecessary to discuss. Up to the time at which this story begins, whenever
Mr Douglas of Drumcarro quarrelled with a neighbour over
a boundary line or a shot upon the hillside, he was called
'an auld slave-driver' by his opponent, with that sense of
having power to exasperate and injure which gives double
piquancy to a quarrel. And of him as of many another such
it was told that he could not sleep of nights; that he would
wake even out of an after-dinner doze with cries of remorse,
and that dreams of flogged women and runaways in the
marshes pursued him whenever he closed his eyes. The one
thing that discredited these popular rumours among all
who knew Drumcarro was that he was neither tender-
hearted nor imaginative, and highly unlikely to be troubled
by the recollection of severities which he would have had
no objection to repeat had he had the power. The truth was
that he had by no means found fortune so easily as he had
hoped, and had worked in every way with a dogged and
fierce determination in spite of many failures, never giving
up his aim, until at last he had found himself with a little
money, not by any means what he had looked for and
wanted, but enough to buy a corner of his old inheritance,
the little Highland estate and bare little house of Drumcarro. Hither he came on his return from Jamaica, a fierce,
high-tempered, arbitrary man, by no means unworthy of
the title of 'auld slave-driver', so unanimously bestowed
upon him by his neighbours, who, however, could not
ignore the claims of his old Douglas blood however much
they might dislike the man.

He had married a pretty little insipid girl, the daughter
of one of his brother's friends in 'the south country', who
brought with her a piano and a few quickly fading airs and
graces to the Highland wilds, to sink as soon as possible
into the feeble and fanciful invalid, entirely subject to her
husband's firmer will and looking upon him with terror,
whom the reader has already seen. Poor Mrs Douglas had
not vigour enough to make the least stand against her fate.
But for Marg'ret she would have fallen at once into the
domestic drudge which was all Drumcarro understood or

wanted in a wife. With Marg'ret to preserve her from that lower depth, she sank only into invalidism – into a timid complaining, a good deal of real suffering, and a conviction that she was the most sorely tried of women. But she bore her despotic husband seven boys without a blemish, robust and long-limbed lads equal to every encounter with fate. And this made him a proud man among his kind, strongly confident of vanquishing every adverse circumstance, in their persons at least, if not, as Providence seemed to have forbidden, in his own. He set his whole heart upon these boys – struggling and sparing to get a certain amount of needful education for them, not very much it must be allowed; and by every means in his power, by old relation-ships half-forgotten, by connections of his West Indian per-iod, even by such share as he could take in politics, contrived to get appointments for them, one after another, either in the King's or the Company's service for India. The last was much the best of any; it was a fine service, with per-petual opportunities of fighting and of distinction, not so showy as the distinctions to be gained in the Peninsula, but with far better opportunities of getting on. The four eldest were there already, and Robbie had started to follow them. For Jock, who took to his books more kindly than the others, there was a prospect of a writership. It was more easy in those days to set young men out in the world than it is now. Your friends thought of them, your political leaders were accessible; even a passing visitor would remark the boys in your nursery and lend a friendly hand. Nobody lends a friendly hand nowadays, and seven sons is not a quiverful in which a poor man has much reason to rejoice.

On the other hand the girls at Drumcarro were left with-out any care at all. They were unlucky accidents, tares among the wheat, handmaids who might be useful about the house, but who had no future, no capabilities of ad-vancing the family, creatures altogether of no account. Men in a higher position than the laird of Drumcarro might have seen a means of strengthening their house by alliances, through the means of four comely daughters, but the poor little Highland lairdlings, who were their only possible suitors, were not worth his trouble, and even of them the supply was few. They too went out into the world, they did not remain to marry and vegetate at home. Mr Douglas felt

that every farthing spent upon the useless female portion
of his household was so much taken from the boys, and the
consequence was that the girls grew up without even the
meagre education then considered necessary for women,
and shut out by poverty, by pride, by the impossibility of
making the appearance required to do credit to the family,
even from the homely gaieties of the countryside. They
grew up in the wilds like the heather and the bracken, by
the grace of nature, and acquired somehow the arts of reading and writing, and many housewifely accomplishments,
but without books, without society, without any break in
the monotony of life or prospect in their future. Their
brothers had gone off one by one, depriving them in succession of the natural friends and companions of their youth.
And in this way there had happened a domestic incident
never now named in Drumcarro; the most awful of cata-
strophes in the experience of the younger members of the
family. The eldest of the girls, named Anne, was the hand-
somest of the three elder sisters. She was of the same type
of beauty which promised a still more perfect development
in the little Jeanie, the youngest of the daughters; with fair
hair just touched with a golden light, blue eyes soft and
tender, and a complexion somewhat pale but apt to blush at
any touch of sentiment or feeling into the warmest variable
radiance. She sang like a bird without any training, she
knew all the songs and stories of the district, and read every
poetry-book she could find (they were not many – The
Gentle Shepherd, an old copy of Barbour's Bruce, some
vagrant volumes of indifferent verse); she was full of sentiment and dreamy youthful romance without anything to
feed upon. But just at the time when her favourite brother
Nigel went away, and Anne was downcast and melancholy,
a young doctor came temporarily to the district, and came
in the usual course to see Mrs Douglas, for whose case he
recommended certain remedies impossible to be carried
out, as doctors sometimes do. He advised change of air,
cheerful company, and that she should be kept from everything likely to agitate or disturb her. 'That's sae easy –
that's sae likely,' said Marg'ret under her breath. But Anne
listened anxiously while the young doctor insisted upon
his remedies. He came again and again, with an interest in
the patient which no one had ever shown before. 'If you

could take her away into the sunshine – to a brighter place, where she would see new faces and new scenes.' 'Oh, but how could I do that,' cried Anne, 'when I have no place to take her to, and my father would not let me if I had?' 'Oh, Miss Anne, let me speak to your father,' the young man pleaded. 'You shall have a pleasant house to bring your mother to, and love and service at her command if you will but listen to me.' Anne listened, nothing loth, and the young doctor, with a confidence born of ignorance, afterwards asked for an interview with Drumcarro. What happened was never known; the doctor departed in great haste, pale with wrath, Mr Douglas's voice sounding loud as the burn when in spate after him as he strode from the door; and Anne's cheeks were white and her eyes red for a week after. But at the end of that week Anne disappeared and was no more seen. Marg'ret, who had risen very early in the middle of the wintry dark, to see to some great washing or other household work, found, as was whispered through the house, a candle flickering down in the socket upon the hall-table, and the house door open. To blow out the last flickering flame, lest it should die in the socket and so foreshadow the extinction of the race, was Marg'ret's first alarmed precaution; and then she shut the open door, but whether she saw or heard anything more nobody ever knew. A faint picture of this scene, the rising and falling of the dying light, the cold wind blowing in from the door, the wild darkness of the winter morning, with its belated stars in a frosty sky looking in, remained in the imagination of the family surrounding the name of Anne, which from that day was never pronounced in the house. Where she went or what became of her was supposed by the young ones to be absolutely unknown. But it is to be hoped that even Drumcarro, savage as he was, ascertained the fate of his daughter even while he cursed her. It came to be understood afterwards that she had married her doctor and was happy; but that not for a long time, nor to the sisters thus taught by the tremendous force of example what a dreadful thing it was to look at any upstart doctor or minister or insignificant person without a pedigree or pretensions like their own.

This was the only shape in which love had come near the door of Drumcarro, and if there was a certain attraction

even in the tragic mystery of the tale, there was not much
encouragement for the others to follow Anne's example,
thus banished summarily and for ever from all relations
with her family. Also from that time no doctor except the
old man who had brought the children into the world was
ever allowed to enter those sacred doors, nor any minister
younger or more seductive than Mr Pyper. As for other eligible persons there were none in the countryside, so that
Mary and Kirsteen were safe from temptation. And thus
they went on from day to day and from year to year, in a
complete isolation which poverty made imperative more
even than circumstances, the only event that ever happened
being the departure of a brother, or an unusually severe
'attack' of their mother's continued ever-enduring illness.
They were not sufficiently educated nor sufficiently
endowed to put them on a par with the few high-born ladies
of the district, with whom alone they would have been
allowed to associate; and there was native pride enough in
themselves to prevent them from forming friendships with
the farmers' daughters, also very widely scattered and few
in number, who, though the young ladies of Drumcarro
were so little superior to themselves in any outward attri-
bute, would have thought their acquaintance an honour.
Nothing accordingly could exceed the dullness, the monotony of their lives, with no future, no occupation except
their work as almost servants in their father's house, no
hope even of those vicissitudes of youth which sometimes
in a moment change a young maiden's life. All was bald and
grey about them, everything but the scenery, in which, if
there is nothing else, young minds find but an imperfect
compensation. Mary indeed had a compensation of another
kind in the comfortable apathy of a perfectly dull and stolid
character, which had little need of the higher acquirements
of life. But Kirsteen with her quick temper and high spirit
and lively imagination was little adapted for a part so blank.
She was one of those who make a story for themselves.

CHAPTER VI

Marg'ret was perhaps the only individual in the world who dared to remonstrate with Mr Douglas as to the neglect in which his daughters were losing their youth and all its pleasures and hopes. Aunt Eelen it is true made comments from time to time. She said: 'Puir things, what will become of them when Neil's deed? They've neither siller nor learning; and no chance of a man for one of them than I can see.' 'And yet they're bonny lassies,' said the sympathetic neighbour to whom on her return home after Robbie's departure she made this confidence. 'Oh, they're well enough, but with a silly mother and a father that's just a madman, what can any person do for them?' Miss Eelen Douglas was not quite assured in her own mind that it was not her duty to do something for her young relations, and she took a great deal of pains to prove to herself that it was impossible.

'What if you had them over at the New Year? There's aye something going on, and the ball at the Castle.'

'The ball at the Castle!' cried Miss Eelen with a scream. 'And what would they put on to go to the ball at the Castle? Potato-bags and dishclouts? Na, na, I'm of his mind so far as that goes. If they cannot appear like Drumcarro's daughters, they are best at home.'

'Bless me,' said the kind neighbour, 'a bit white frock is no ruinous. If it was only for a summer Sabbath to go to the kirk in, they must have white frocks.'

'Ruinous or no ruinous it's more than he'll give them,' said Miss Eelen, shutting up her thin lips as if they had been a purse. She was very decided that the white frocks could not come from her. And indeed her means were very small, not much more than was absolutely necessary to maintain her little house and the one maid who kept her old mahogany and her old silver up to the polish which was necessary. Naturally all her neighbours and her cousin Neil, who hoped to inherit from her, exaggerated Miss Eelen's income. But though she was poor, she had a compunction. She felt that the white frocks ought to be obtained somehow, if even by the further pinching of her own already pinched living, and that the great chance of the ball at the Castle ought to be afforded to Drumcarro's neglected girls. And she had to reason with herself periodically as to the impossibility of this, demonstrating how it was that she could not do it, that it was not her part to do it, that if the father and the mother saw no necessity, how was she, a cousin once removed, to take it upon her? For though they called her aunt she was in reality Neil Douglas of Drumcarro's cousin and no more. Notwithstanding all these arguments a compunction was always present in Miss Eelen's worn out yet not extinguished heart.

'Besides,' she began again more briskly, 'what would be the use? Ye'll no suppose that Lord John or Lord Thomas would offer for Drumcarro's lasses. They're as good blood, maybe better; for it's cauld watery stuff that rins in those young lads' veins. But Neil Douglas is a poor man; if he had all or the half that rightly belongs to him, it would be anither matter. We'll say nothing about that. I'm a Douglas myself, and it just fires me up when I think of it. But right or wrong, as I'm saying, Drumcarro's a poor man, and it's no in the Castle his lasses will find mates. And he's a proud man. I think upon Anne, puir thing, and I cannot say another word. Na, na, it's just a case where nobody can interfere.'

'But Miss Anne's very happy, and plenty of everything, as I hear.'

'Happy, and her father's doors closed upon her, and her name wiped out as if she were dead – far more than if she were dead! And bearing a name that no man ever heard of, her, a Douglas!' Miss Eelen's grey cheek took on a flush of colour at the thought. She shook her head, agitating the little grey ringlets on her forehead. 'Na, na,' she said, 'I'm vexed to think upon the poor things – but I cannot interfere.'

'Maybe their father, if you were to speak to him—'

'Me speak to him! I would as soon speak to Duncan Nicol's bull. My dear, ye ken a great deal,' said Miss Eelen with irony, 'but ye do not ken the Douglases. And that's all that can be said.'

This, however, was not all that a more devoted friend, the only one they had who feared neither Drumcarro nor

anything else in the world, in their interest, found to say.
Marg'ret was not afraid of Drumcarro. Even she avoided
any unnecessary encounter with 'the auld slave-driver', but
when it was needful to resist or even to assail him, she did
not hesitate. And this time it was not resistance but attack.
She marched into the laird's room with her head held high,
trumpets playing and banners flying, her broad white cap-
strings finely starched and streaming behind her with the
impulse of her going, an unusual colour in her cheeks, her
apron folded over one hand, the other free to aid the eloquence of her speech. Several months had passed in great
quiet, the little stir of Robbie's departure having died away
along with the faint excitement of the preparations for his
departure, the making of his linen, the packing of his portmanteaux. All had relapsed again into perfect dullness and
the routine of every day. Jamie, the next boy, was only
fourteen; a long time must elapse before he was able to
follow his brother into the world, and until his time should
come there was no likelihood of any other event stirring
the echoes at Drumcarro. As for Marg'ret, the routine was
quite enough for her. To think what new variety of scone
she could make for their tea, how she could adapt the
remains of the grouse to make a little change, or improve
the flavour of the trout, or compound a beef-tea or a pud-
ding which would tempt her mistress to a spoonful more,
was diversion enough for Marg'ret among the heavier
burdens of her work. But the bairns – and above all
Kirsteen, who was her special darling. Kirsteen had carried
her head very high after Robbie went away. She had been
full of musings and of dreams, she had smiled to herself
and sung to herself fragments of a hundred little ditties,
even amid the harassments of her sick mother's incessant
demands, and all the dullness of her life. But after a month
or two that visionary delight had a little failed, the chill of
abandonment, of loneliness, of a life shut out from every
relaxation, had ceased to be neutralized by the secret
inspiration which kept the smile on her lips and the song in
her heart. Kirsteen had not forgotten the secret which was
between her and Ronald, or ceased to be sustained by it;
but she was young, and the parting, the absence, the silence
had begun to tell upon her. He was gone; they were all gone,
she said to herself. With everything in the world to sustain

the young sufferer, that chill of absence is always a sad
one. And her cheerfulness, if not her courage, had flagged.
Her heart and her head had drooped in spite of herself. She
had been found moping in corners, 'thinking', as she had
said, and she had been seen with her eyes wet, hastily drying the irrepressible tears. 'Kirsteen greetin'!' One of the
boys had seen it, and mocked her with a jibe, of which
afterwards he was much ashamed; and little Jeanie had seen
it, and had hurried off awestricken to tell Marg'ret,
'Kirsteen was in the parlour just with nobody, and greetin'
like to break her heart.'

'Hoot awa' with ye, it'll be that auld pain in her head,'
said Marg'ret sending the little girl away. But this report
brought affairs to a crisis. 'The bairn shall not just be left to
think and think,' she said to herself, adding however prudently, 'no if I can help it.' Marg'ret had managed one way
or other to do most things she had set her heart upon, but
upon this she could not calculate. Drumcarro was not a
man to be turned easily from his evil ways. He was a 'dour
man'. The qualities which had enabled him in the face of
all discouragement to persevere through failure and disappointment until he had at last gained so much if no more
and become Drumcarro, were all strong agents against the
probability of getting him to yield now. He had his own
theories of his duty, and it was not likely that the represen-
tations of his housekeeper would change them. Still
Marg'ret felt that she must say her say.

He was seated by himself in the little room which was
specially his own, in the heaviness of the afternoon. Dinner
was over, and the air was still conscious of the whisky and
water which had accompanied it. A peat fire burned with an
intense red glow and his chair and shabby writing-table
were drawn close to it. No wonder then that Drumcarro
dozed when he retired to that warm and still seclusion.
Marg'ret took care not to go too soon, to wait until the
afternoon nap was over; but the laird's eyes were still heavy
when she came in. He roused himself quickly with sharp
impatience; though the doze was habitual he was full of
resentment at any suspicion of it. He was reading in his
room; this was the version of the matter which he expected
to be recognized in the family: a man nowadays would say
he had letters to write, but letters were not so universal an

occupation then. A frank or an opportunity, a private hand, or sure messenger with whom to trust the missive were things of an occasional occurrence which justified correspondence; but it was not a necessity of every day. Mr Douglas made no pretence of letters. He was reading; a much crumpled newspaper which had already passed through several hands was spread out on the table before him. It was a Glasgow paper, posted by the first reader the day after publication to a gentleman on Loch Long, then forwarded by him to Inveralton, thence to Drumcarro. Mr Pyper at the Manse got it at fourth hand. It would be difficult to trace its wanderings after that. The laird had it spread upon his table, and was bending over it, winking one eye to get it open when Marg'ret pushed open the door. She did not knock, but she made a great deal of noise with the handle as she opened it, which came to much the same thing.

'Well,' he said, turning upon her snappishly, 'what may ye be wanting now?'

'I was wanting – just to say something to ye, Drumcarro, if it's convenient to ye,' Marg'ret said.

'What do ye want? That's your way of asking, as I know well. What ails ye now, and what long story have ye to tell? The sooner it's begun, the sooner it will be ended,' he said.

'There is truth in that,' replied Marg'ret sedately; 'and I canna say I am confident ye will be pleased with what I'm going to say. For to meddle between a father and his bairns is no a pleasant office, and to one that is but a servant in the house.'

'And who may this be,' said Mr Douglas grimly, 'that is coming to interfere between a father and his bairns – meaning me and my family, as I'm at liberty to judge?'

Marg'ret looked her master in the face, and made him a slight but serious curtsey. ''Deed, sir, it's just me,' she said.

'You!' said the laird with all the force of angry indignation which he could throw into his voice. He roused himself to the fray, pushing up his spectacles upon his forehead. 'You're a bonny one,' he said, 'to burst into a gentleman's private room on whatever errand let alone meddling in what's none of your concerns.'

'If ye think sae, sir,' said Marg'ret, 'that's just anither point we dinna agree about; for if there's a mair proper person to speak to ye about your bairns than the person that has brought them up, and carried them in her arms, and made their parritch and mended their clo'es all their life, I'm no acquaint with her. Eh me, what am I saying? There is anither that has a better right – and that's their mother. But she's your wife, puir lamb, and ye ken weel that ye've sae dauntened her, and sae bowed her down, that if ye were to take a' their lives she would never get out a word.'

'Did she send ye here to tell me so?' cried Drumcarro.

'But me,' said Marg'ret unheeding the question, 'I'm not to be dauntened neither by words nor looks. I'm nae man's wife, the Lord be thankit.'

'Ye may well say that,' said the laird, seizing an ever-ready weapon, 'for it's well known ye never could get a man to look the way ye were on.'

Marg'ret paused for a moment and contemplated him, half moved by the jibe, but with a slight wave of her hand put the temptation away. 'I'm no to be put off by ony remarks ye can make, sir,' she said; 'maybe ye think ye ken my affairs better than I do, for well I wot I ken yours better than you. You're no an ill father to your lads. I would never say sae, for it wouldna' be true; ye do your best for them and grudge naething. But the lasses are just as precious a gift from their Maker as their brothers, and what's ever done for them? They're just as neglecktit as the colley dogues: na, far mair, for the colleys have a fine training to make them fit for their work – whereas our young ladies, the Lord bless them—'

'Well,' said the father sharply, 'and what have you to do with the young ladies? Go away with you to your kitchen, and heat your girdle and make your scones. That's your vocation. The young ladies I tell ye are no concern of yours.'

'Whose concern should they be when neither father nor mother take ony heed?' said Marg'ret. 'Maister Douglas, how do you think your bonny lads would have come through if they had been left like that and nobody caring? There's Miss Kirsteen is just as clever and just as good as any one o' them; but what is the poor thing's life worth if she's never to see a thing, nor meet a person out of Drum-carro House? Ye ken yoursel' there's little company in Drumcarro House – you sitting here and the mistress maybe in her bed, and neither kin nor friend to say a plea-sant word. Lord bless us a'! I'm twice her age and mair: but I would loup ower the linn the first dark day, if I was like that lassie without the sight of a face or the sound of a voice of my ain kind.'

'You're just an auld fool,' said Drumcarro, 'the lassie is as well off as any lassie needs to be. Kirsteen – oh ay, I mind now, ye have always made a pet of Kirsteen. It's maybe that that has given her her bold tongue and set that spark in her eye.'

'Na,' said Marg'ret, 'it was just her Maker did that, to make her ane of the first in the land if them she belongs to dinna shut her up in a lonesome glen in a dull hoose. But naebody shall say I'm speaking for Kirsteen alone; there's your bonny little Jeanie that will just be a beauty. Where she got it I cannot tell, ony mair than I can tell where Kirsteen got her grand spirit and yon light in her ee. No from her poor mother, that was a bonny bit thing in her day, but never like that. Jeanie will be just the flower o' the haill country-side, if ye can ca' it a country-side that's a' howkit out into glens and tangled with thae lochs and hills. If she were in a mair open country there's no a place from Ayr to Dumfries but would hear of her for her beauty in twa or three years' time. Ye may say beauty's but skin deep, and I'm saying nothing to the contrary; but it's awfu' plea-sant to the sight of men; and I'll just tell you this, Drum-carro – though it's maybe no a thing that's fit for me to say – there's no a great man in a' the land that bairn mightna' marry if she had justice done her. And maybe that will move ye, if naething else will.'

A gleam had come into Drumcarro's eyes as she spoke, but he answered only by a loud and harsh laugh, leaning back in his chair and opening wide a great cavern of a mouth. 'The deil's in the woman for marrying and giving in marriage!' he said. 'A bit lassie in a peenny? It's a pity the Duke marriet, Marg'ret, but it cannot be mended. If she's to get a prince he'll come this way when she's old enough. We'll just wait till that time comes.'

'The time has come for the rest, if no for her,' said

Marg'ret, unexpectedly encouraged by this tone. 'And eh? if ye would but think, they're young things, and youth comes but ance in a lifetime, and ye can never win it back when it's past. The laddies, bless them, are all away to get their share; the lassies will never get as much, but just a bit triflin' matter – a white gown to go to a pairty, or a sight of Glasgow, or—'

'The woman's daft!' said the laird. 'Glasgow! what will they do there? a white gown! a fiddlestick – what do they want that they haven't got – plenty of good meat, and a good roof over their heads, and nothing to do for't but sew their seams and knit their stockings and keep a pleasant tongue in their heads. If ye stir up nonsense among them, I'll just turn ye bag and baggage out of my house.'

'I would advise ye to do that, sir,' said Marg'ret calmly. 'I'll no need a second telling. And ye'll be sorry but ance for what ye have done, and that'll be a' your life.'

'Ye saucy jade!' said the laird: but though he glared at her with fiery eyes, he added no more on this subject. 'The lassies!' he said, 'a pingling set aye wanting something! To spend your money on feeding them and clothing them, that's not enough it would appear! Ye must think of their finery, their parties and their pleasures. Tell Kirsteen she must get a man to do that for her. She'll have no nonsense from me.'

'And where is she to get a man? And when she has gotten a man – the only kind that will come her gait—'

Mr Douglas rose up from his chair, and shook his clenched fist. Rage made him dumb. He stammered out an oath or two, incapable of giving vent to the torrent of wrath that came to his lips. But Marg'ret did not wait till his utterances became clear.

CHAPTER VII

This was one of the days when Mrs Douglas thought she felt a little better, and certainly knew it was very dull in her bedroom, where it was not possible to keep even Kirsteen stationary all day, so she had ventured to come downstairs after the heavy midday dinner which filled the house with odours. A little broth, served with what was considered great delicacy in Drumcarro, in a china dish on a white napkin, had sufficed for her small appetite; and when everything was still in the house, in partial somnolence after the meal, she had been brought to the parlour with all her shawls and cushions, and established by the fire. The news of the great ball at the Castle which had moved Marg'ret to the desperate step she had just taken had its effect in the parlour too. Kirsteen, who had said at first proudly, 'What am I heeding?' had notwithstanding everything begun to wake up a little to the more usual sensations of a girl of twenty when any great event of this description is about to take place. It would be bonny to see – it would be fine just for once to be in grand company like the old Douglases her forbears, and to see how the lords and ladies behaved themselves, if they were really so different from common folk. And then Kirsteen began to think of the music and the sound of the dancers' feet upon the floor, in spite of herself – and the imaginary strains went to her head. She was caught in the measure of her dreams, swaying a little involuntarily to keep time, and interjecting a real step, a dozen nimble twinklings of her feet in their strong country shoes as she went across the room to fetch a new clew for her mother's knitting.

'What's that you're doing, Kirsteen, to shake the whole place?' said Mrs Douglas.

'Oh, it's just nothing, mother.'

'She's practising her steps,' said Mary, 'for the grand ball.'

'Dear me, dear me,' Mrs Douglas said. 'How well I know by myself! Many's the time I've danced about the house so that nothing would keep me still – but ye see what it all comes to. It's just vanity and maybe worse than vanity – and fades away like the morning dew.'

'But, mother,' said Kirsteen, 'it was not your dancing nor the pleasure you've had that made you ill; so we cannot say that's what it comes to.'

'Pleasure!' said her mother. 'It's very little pleasure I have had in my life since I marriet your father and came to this quiet place. Na, na, it's no pleasure – I was very light-hearted in my nature though you would not think it. But that's a thing that cannot last.'

'But you had it, mother,' said Mary, 'even if it was short. There was that ball you went to when you were sixteen, and the spangled muslin you had on, and the officer that tore it with his spurs.'

Mrs Douglas's eyes lit up with a faint reflection of bygone fire. 'Eh, that spangled muslin,' she said, 'I'll never forget it, and what they all said to me when I came home. It was not like the grand gowns that are the fashion now. It was one of the last of the old mode before those awfu' doings at the French Revolution that changed everything. My mother wore a hoop under her gown standing out round her like a cartwheel. I was not old enough for that; but there was enough muslin in my petticoat to have made three of these bit skimpit things.'

'I just wish,' said Mary with a sigh, 'that we had it now.'

'It would be clean out of the fashion if ye had it; and what would ye do with a spangled muslin here? Ye must have parties to go to, before ye have any need for fine claes.'

Mary breathed again that profound sigh. 'There's the ball at the Castle,' she said.

'Lord keep us!' cried her mother. 'Your faither would take our heads off our shoulders if ye breathed a word of that.'

'But they say the whole country's going,' said Kirsteen; 'it's like as if we were just nobody to be always held back.'

'Your father thinks of nothing but the boys,' said Mrs Douglas, with a feeble wail; 'it's aye for them he's planning. Ye'll bring nothing in, he says, and he'll have you take little out.'

There was a pause after this – indignation was strong in

Kirsteen's heart, but there was also a natural piety which
arrested her speech. The injustice, the humiliation and hard
bondage of the iron rule under which she had been brought
up, but which she had only now begun to look upon as anything more than the rule of nature, was what was upper-
most in her thoughts. Mary's mind was not speculative. She
did not consider humiliation or injustice. The practical
affected her more, which no doubt was in every way a more
potent argument. 'I just wonder,' she said, 'that he has not
more sense – for if we were away altogether we would take
nothing out – and that cannot be if nobody knows that we
are here.'

'Your father's a strange man,' said Mrs Douglas. 'You're
old enough to see that for yourselves. When there are men
coming about a house, there's more expense. Many's the
dinner he got off my father's table before he married me –
and to have your lads about the house would never please
him. Many is the thought I take about it when ye think I
have nothing in my head but my own trouble. He would
never put up with your lads about the house.'

'Mother!' cried Kirsteen, with indignation, 'we are not
servant lasses with men coming courting. Who would dare
to speak like that of us?'

Mary laughed a little over her work. She was darning
the stockings of the household, with a large basket before
her, and her hand and arm buried in a large leg of grey-blue
worsted. She did not blush as Kirsteen did, but with a little
simper accepted her mother's suggestion. 'If we are ever to
get away from here, there will have to be lads about the
house,' she said, with practical wisdom; 'if we're not to do
it Anne's way.'

'Lord bless us, what are you saying? If your father heard
you, he would turn us all to the door,' said Mrs Douglas, in
dismay. 'I've promised him on my bended knees I will
never name the name of that – poor thing, poor thing,' the
mother cried suddenly, with a change of voice, falling into
trembling and tears.

'I've heard she was real well off,' said Mary, 'and a good
man, and two servant maids keepit for her. And it's just an
old fashion thinking so much of your family. The old
Douglases might be fine folk, but what did they ever do for
us?'

'Mary! hold your peace,' cried Kirsteen, flaming with scorn and wrath. 'Would ye deny your good blood, and a grand race that were as good as kings in their day? And what have we to stand upon if it's not them? We would be no more than common folk.'

The conviction of Kirsteen's indignant tones; the disdainful certainty of being, on the natural elevation of that grand race, something very different from common folk, overawed the less convinced and less visionary pair. Mrs Douglas continued to weep, silently rocking herself to and fro, while Mary made what explanations she could to her fiery assailant.

'I was meaning nothing,' she said, 'but just that they're all dead and gone, and their grandeur with them. And the fashion's aye changing, and folk that have plenty are more thought upon than them that have nothing, whatever may be their name.'

'Do you think,' said Kirsteen, 'if we had my mother's old gown to cut down for you and me, or even new gowns fresh from the shop – do you think we would be asked to the Castle or any other place if it were not for the old Douglases that ye jeer at. It's not a spangled muslin, but an old name that will carry us there.'

'There's something in that,' said Mary, cowed a little. 'But,' she added with a sigh, 'as we're not going it's no thanks to them nor any person. When the ladies and gentlemen are going to the ball we'll be sitting with our seams with one candle between us. And we may just spend our lives so, for anything I can see – and the old Douglases will never fash their heads.'

'Lord bless us! there's your father!' cried Mrs Douglas with a start, hastily drying her eyes. Her ear was keener for that alarming sound than the girls', who were caught almost in the midst of their talk. The laird came in, pushing open the door with a violent swing which was like a gale of wind, and the suspicious silence that succeeded his entrance, his wife having recourse to her knitting in sudden desperation, and the daughters bending over their various tasks with devotion, betrayed in a moment what they desired to hide from his jealous eye.

'What were ye colleaguing and planning, laying your heads together – that you're all so still when I come in?'

'We were planning nothing, Neil, just nothing,' said Mrs Douglas, eagerly. 'I was telling the bairns a bit of an auld story – just to pass the time.'

'They'll pass the time better doing their work,' said their father. He came first to the fireside round which they were sitting, and stared into the glowing peat with eyes almost as red: then he strode towards the only window, and stood there shutting out the light with his back towards them. There was not too much light at any time from that narrow and primitive opening, and his solid person filled it up almost entirely. Kirsteen laid down her work upon her lap. It was of a finer kind than Mary's, being no less than the hemming of the frills of Drumcarro's shirts, about which he was very particular. He had certain aristocratic habits, if not much luxury, and the fineness of his linen was one of these. Kirsteen's hemming was almost invisible, so small were the stitches and the thread so delicate. She was accomplished with her needle according to the formula of that day.

'Drumcarro,' said his wife timidly after a few minutes of this eclipse, 'I am not wanting to disturb ye – but Kirsteen cannot see to do her work – it's little matter for Mary and me.'

'What ails Kirsteen that she cannot do her work?' he said roughly, turning round but keeping his position. 'Kirsteen here and Kirsteen there, I'm sick of the name of her. She's making some cursed nonsense I'll be bound for her ain back.'

'It's for your breast, father,' said Kirsteen; 'but I'll stop if you like, and put it by.'

He eyed her for a moment with sullen opposition, then stepped away from the window without a word. He had an uneasy sensation that when Kirsteen was his opponent the case did not always go his way. 'A great deal ye care, any of ye, for me and my wishes,' he said. 'Who was it sent that deevil of a woman to my own business-room, where, if any place, a man may expect to be left in peace? No to disturb me! Ye would disturb me if I was on my deathbed for any confounded nonsense of your ain.'

'I am sure, Drumcarro,' his wife replied, beginning to cry.

'Sure – you're sure of nothing but what she tells ye. If it

were not for one thing more than another I would turn
her out of my house.'

'Dinna do that – oh, dinna do that, if it's Marg'ret you're
meaning,' cried Mrs Douglas, clasping her hands. 'She's just
a stand-by for everything about the place, and the best cook
that ever was – and thinks of your interest, Drumcarro,
though maybe ye will not believe it, far above her own.
And if you take away Marg'ret I'll just lie down and die –
for there will be no comfort more.'

'You're very keen to die – in words; but I never see any
signs in you of keeping to it,' he said; then drawing forward
a chair to the fire, pushing against Kirsteen, who drew back
hurriedly, he threw himself down in it, in the midst of the
women who moved their seats hastily on either side to give
him room. 'What's this,' he said, 'about some nonsense
down at the Castle that is turning all your silly heads? and
what does it mean?'

Mrs Douglas was too frightened to speak, and as for
Kirsteen she was very little disposed to take advantage of
the milder frame of mind in which her father seemed to be
to wheedle or persuade him into a consent.

It was Mary who profited by the unusual opportunity.
'It's just the ball, father that the Duke gives when he comes
home.'

'The Duke,' said he. 'The Duke is as auld a man as I am,
and balls or any other foolishness, honest man, I reckon
they're but little in his way.'

'He does not do it for himself, father – there's the young
lords and ladies that like a little diversion. And all the folk
besides from far and near – that are good enough,' Mary
said adroitly. 'There are some that say he's too particular
and keeps many out.'

'Nobody can be too particular, if he's a duke or if he's a
commoner,' said Mr Douglas. 'A good pedigree is just your
only safeguard – and not always that,' he added after a
moment, looking at her steadily. 'You'll be one that likes a
little diversion too?'

'And that I am, father,' said Mary, suddenly grown into
the boldest of the party, exhilarated and stimulated, she could
scarcely tell how, by a sentiment of success that seemed to
have got into the air. Mrs Douglas here interposed, anxious
apparently lest her daughter should go too far.

'No beyond measure, Drumcarro – just in reason, as once I liked it well myself.'

'You,' said Drumcarro hastily, 'ye were never an example. Let them speak for themselves. I've heard all the story from beginning to end. They're weary of their life here, and they think if they went to this folly, they might maybe each get a man to deliver them.'

'Father!' cried Kirsteen springing to her feet, with blazing eyes. To her who knew better, who had not only the pride of her young womanhood to make that suggestion terrible, but the secret in her heart which made it blasphemy – there was something intolerable in the words and laugh and jibe, which roused her mother to a wondering and tremulous confidence, and made Mary's heart bound with anticipated delight. But no notice was taken of Kirsteen's outcry. The laird's harsh laugh drew forth a tremulous accompaniment, which was half nervous astonishment and half a desire to please him, from his more subservient womankind.

'Well, Drumcarro,' said his wife timidly, 'it would just be the course of nature; and I'm sure if it was men that would make them happy, it's no me that would ever say them nay.'

'You!' said her husband again. 'Ye would not say nay to a goose if ye saw him waddlin' ben. It's not to your judgment I'm meaning to trust. What's Kirsteen after there, with her red head and her e'en on fire? Sit down on your chair and keep silent if ye have nothing pleasant to say. I'm not a man for weirdless nonsense and promiscuous dancing and good money thrown away on idle feasts and useless claes. But if there's a serious meaning at the bottom of it, that's just another matter. Eelen, I suppose that's in all the folly of the place and well known to the Duke and his family, as she has a good right to be from her name, will understand all about it, and how to put them forth and set them out to the best advantage. It must be well done, if it's done at all.'

'There's a great many things that they will want, Drumcarro; none of mine are fit to wear, and the fashions all changed since my time. They will want—'

'Oh, mother, not half what you think; I've my cairngorms that Aunt Mary left me. And Kirsteen, she has a very

white skin that needs nothing. It's just a piece of muslin
for our gowns—'

'Eh me,' said Mrs Douglas, 'when I mind all my bonny
dyes, and my pearlins and ribbons, and high-heeled shoes,
and my fan as long as your arm; and washes for my skin
and cushions for my hair!' She sat up in her chair forgetting
her weakness, a colour rising in her pale cheeks, her spirit
rising to the unaccustomed delightful anticipation which
was half regret and recollection, so that for once in her life
she forgot her husband and escaped from his power. 'Ah!'
she exclaimed again with a little outcry of pain, 'if I had but
thought upon the time I might have lasses of my ain and
keepit them for my bairns—'

'Ye may make yourself easy on that point,' said Drumcarro, pushing back the chair he had taken, 'for ye never
had a thing but was rubbish, nothing fit for a daughter of
mine.'

'It's not the case, it's not the case,' said the poor lady
touched in the tenderest point. 'I had my mother's garnets,
as bonny a set as ever was seen, and I had a brooch with a
real diamant inside it, and a pearl pin – and – oh, I'm no
meaning to say a word to blame your father, but what do
men ken of such things? And it's not the case! It's not the
case! Ye're not to believe him,' she said with a feverish flush
upon her cheeks.

'Bits of red glass and bits of white, and a small paste head
on the end of a brass preen,' said Drumcarro with a mocking laugh.

'Father, let her be,' cried Kirsteen. 'I'll not have her
crossed, my bonny minnie, not for all the balls that ever
were.'

'You'll not have her crossed! You're a bonny one to lift
your face to your father. If you say another word ye shall
not go.'

'I care not if I should never go – I will not have my
mother vexed, not for the Duke nor the Castle nor a'
Scotland,' cried Kirsteen with fire gleaming in her hazel
eyes.

'Oh, ye fool, ye fool! and him for once in a good key,'
cried Mary, in her sister's ear.

CHAPTER VIII

Mrs Douglas was the first to echo this prudent advice when after she had wept away the sting of that atrocious accusation and minutely described her 'bonny dyes' (her pretty things) to her children who indeed had heard all about them often, and knew the pearl pin and the garnets by heart, and had been comforted with a cup of tea, she came to herself. And by that time Kirsteen's indignation too had cooled, and thoughts of the heaven of the Castle, with fine ladies and grand gentlemen pacing forth as in the ballads, and music playing and the sound of the dancers' feet, began to buzz in her young head and fill it with longings. If *he* had been at home he would have been there. It would never now be what it might have been had it happened before. But even with that great blank of absence Kirsteen was but twenty, and her heart did not refuse to throb a little at this unthought of, unhoped for prospect. Just to see it, and how great persons behaved, and what like the world was, when you were in it, that world which represents itself in so many different ways to the youthful imagination. Kirsteen felt that at the Castle she would see it in all its glory, nothing better in the King's own court – for was it not under the shadow of the Duke, and what could fancy desire more? She would need no further enlightenment or experience of the aspect of society, and what it was and how it looked, than she could get there. This was the Highland girl's devout belief; *Vedi Napoli e poi morire*; earth could not have anything to show more fair.

Marg'ret would have been more than a woman had she not been all-glorious over this event. 'I just daured him to do it,' she said, 'to let the occasion pass by and nane of his daughters seen, and a' their chances lost.' 'Did ye speak of chances for me?' cried Kirsteen in youthful fury. 'Me that would not look at one of them, if it was the prince out of the story book. Me that—!' She turned away to dash a hot tear from her dazzling wet eyes – 'me that am waiting for him!' Kirsteen said in her heart. Her faithful champion looked at her with anxious eyes. 'If she would but say that's what she's meaning,' was Marg'ret's commentary. 'Eh, I wonder if that's what she's meaning? but when neither the ane nor the ither says a word how is a person to ken?' It slightly overclouded her triumph to think that perhaps for her favourite the chances were all forestalled, and even that trouble might come out of it if somebody should throw the handkerchief at Kirsteen whom her father approved. The cold chill of such an alarm not seldom comes across the designer of future events when all has been carefully arranged to quicken the action of Providence. But Marg'ret put that discouraging alarm hastily out of her mind. Right or wrong it was always a good thing that her nurslings should see the world. When the roll of white muslin arrived that was to make the famous gowns, and when Miss Macnab (who was not without claims in some faraway manner to be connected with a family in as near as the tenth remove from the laird of Macnab's own sovereign race) came over with her little valise, and her *nécessaire* full of pins and needles, and was put into the best room, and became for the time the centre of interest in the household – Marg'ret could scarcely contain herself for pleasure. 'A' the hoose' with the exception of the boys, who at this stage of their development counted for little, snatched every available moment to look in upon Miss Macnab – who sat in state, with a large table covered with cuttings, and two handmaids at least always docile beside her, running up gores or laying hems. It might be thought indeed that the fashion of that time required no great amount of labour in the construction of two white dresses for a pair of girls. But Miss Macnab was of a different opinion. She did not know indeed the amount of draping and arranging, the skill of the artist in the fine hanging of folded stuffs, or even the multitudinous flouncings of an intermediate age into which the art of dress was to progress. The fashions of 1814 look like simplicity itself; the long, straight, narrow skirt, the short waist, the infantile sleeves, would seem to demand little material and less trouble for their simple arrangement. But no doubt this was more in appearance than in reality, and the mind of the artist is always the same whatever his materials may be. Miss Macnab kept the young ladies under hand for hours fitting every line – not folds, for folds there

were none – so that the skirt might cling sufficiently without
affording too distinct a revelation of the limbs beneath, an
art perhaps as difficult as any of the more modern con-
trivances. Mary stood like a statue under the dressmaker's
hands. She was never weary; so long as there was a pleat or
seam that needed correction, a pinch too little here, a fullness too much there, she was always ready. The white gown
was moulded upon her with something like a sculptor's
art. Miss Macnab with her mouth full of pins, and her
fingers seamed with work, pinned and pulled, and stretched
out and drew in with endless perseverance. She was an
artist in her way. It was terrible to her as a mistake on the
field of battle to a general, to send forth into the world a
gown that did not fit, a pucker or a twist in any garment she
made. There are no Miss Macnabs nowadays, domestic professors of the most primitive yet everlasting of arts. The
trouble she took over her composition would tire out a
whole generation of needlewomen, and few girls even for a
first ball would stand like Mary to be manipulated. And
there is no such muslin now as the fine and fairy web, like
the most delicate lawn, which was the material of those
wonderful gowns, and little workmanship so delicate as that
which put together the long seams, and made invisible hems
round the scanty but elaborate robe. Kirsteen, who was
not so patient as her sister, looked on with a mixture of
contempt and admiration. It did not, to her young mind
and thoughts occupied with a hundred varying interests,
seem possible at first to give up all that time to the perfection even of a ball-dress. But presently the old seamstress
with her devotion to her art began to impress the open-
minded girl. It was not a very rich living which Miss
Macnab derived from all this labour and care. To see her
kneeling upon her rheumatic knees, directing the easy fall
of the soft muslin line to the foot which ought to peep from
underneath without deranging the exactness of the delicate
hem, was a wonder to behold. A rivulet of pins ran down
the seam, and Miss Macnab's face was grave and careful as
if the destinies of a kingdom were upon that muslin line.

'What trouble you are taking!' cried Kirsteen. 'And it's
not as if it were silk or velvet, but just a muslin gown.'

Miss Macnab looked up from where she knelt by Mary's
knee. She had to take the pins out of her mouth before

she could speak, which was inconvenient, for no pin-
cushion is ever so handy. 'Missie,' she said, 'my dear, ye
just show your ignorance: for there's nothing so hard to
take a good set as a fine muslin; and the maist difficult is aye
the maist particular, as ye would soon learn if ye gave
yoursel' to ainy airt.'

Kirsteen, who knew very little of any art, but thought it
meant painting pictures, here gave vent, to her own shame
afterwards, to a little laugh, and said hastily, 'I would just
set it straight and sew it up again if it was me.'

'I have no objection that ye should try,' said Miss
Macnab, rising from her knees, 'it's aye the best lesson.
When I was in a lairger way of business, with young ones
working under me, I aye let them try their ain way; and
maistly I found they were well content after to turn to mine
– that is if they were worth the learning,' she added composedly; 'there are many that are just a waste of time and
pains.'

'And these are the ones that take their own way? But if I
were to take mine I would never yield, I would make it
answer,' said Kirsteen. She added with a blush, 'I just
cannot think enough of all your trouble and the pains ye
take.'

Miss Macnab gave the blushing girl a friendly look. She
had again her mouth full, so that speech was impossible,
but she nodded kindly and with dignity in return for this
little burst of approval which she knew to be her due; and
it was with all the confidence of conscious merit and a
benign condescension that she expounded her methods
afterwards. 'If ye dinna get the skirt to fall straight from the
waist, ye will never mend it at the foot,' she said. 'I can
see you're ane that can comprehend a principle, my bonny
missie. Take a' the trouble ye can at the beginning, and the
end will come right of itsel'. A careless start means a double
vexation in the finish. And that ye'll find to apply,' said this
mild philosopher, 'to life itsel' as well as to the dressmaking, which is just like a' the airts I ever heard tell of, a
kind of epitome of life.'

Kirsteen could not but break out into a laugh again,
notwithstanding her compunction, at the dressmaker's high
yet mild pretension; but she listened with great interest
while Mary stood and gave all her thoughts to the serious

subject of the skirt and how it would hang. 'I just pay no attention to what she's saying, but I would like my gown to hang as well as any there, and you must take trouble for that,' was Mary's report afterwards when the gown was found to be perfect. And what with these differing motives and experiences the workroom was the opening of new interests in Drumcarro as important as even the ball at the Castle. The excitement and the continued interest made the greatest improvement in Mrs Douglas's health, who came and sat in Miss Macnab's room and gave a hundred directions which the dressmaker received blandly but paid no attention to. Marg'ret herself was stirred by the presence of the artist. She not only excelled herself in the scones she made for Miss Macnab's tea, but she would come in the afternoon when she was not 'throng' and stand with her hands upon each side of her ample waist and admire the work and add no insignificant part to the conversation, discoursing of her own sister, Miss Jean Brown, that was in a very large way of business in London, having gone there as a lady's maid twenty years before. The well born Miss Macnab allowed with a condescending wave of her hand that many began in that way. 'But my opinion is that it wants good blood in your veins and a leddy's breeding before you'll ever make a gown that will set off a leddy,' she said to the little circle, but only, not to hurt her feelings, after Marg'ret was gone.

While these proceedings were occupying all his family, Drumcarro himself proceeded with the practical energy which hitherto had only been exercised on behalf of his sons to arrange for his daughters' presentation to the world. More exciting to the country than a first drawing-room of the most splendid season was the ball at the Castle which was by far the finest thing that many of the Argyllshire ladies of those days ever saw. Even among those who like the family of Drumcarro owned no clan allegiance to the Duke, the only way of approaching the *beau monde*, the great world which included London and the court as well as the Highlands, was by his means. The Duke in his own country was scarcely second to the far off and unknown King whose throne was shrouded in such clouds of dismay and trouble, and the Duchess was in all but name a far more splendid reality than the old and peevish majesty, without beauty or prestige, who sat in sullen misery at Windsor. To go to London, or even to Edinburgh, to the Lord High Commissioner's receptions at Holyrood, was a daring enter-prise that nobody dreamed of; but to go to the Castle was the seal of good blood and breeding. When he had got this notion into his head Drumcarro was as determined upon it as the fondest father could have been. The girls were of no consequence, but his daughters had their rights with the best, and he would not have the family let down even in their insignificant persons; not to speak of the powerful sug-gestion of relieving himself from further responsibility by putting them each in the way of finding 'a man'.

He made his appearance accordingly one afternoon in the little house inhabited by Miss Eelen, to the great sur-prise of that lady. It was a very small, grey house, standing at a corner of the village street, with a small garden round it, presenting a curious blank and one-eyed aspect, from the fact that every window that could be spared, and they were not abundant to start with, had been blocked up on account of the window-tax. Miss Eelen's parlour was dark in consequence, though it had originally been very bright, with a corner window towards the loch and the quay with all its fishing boats. This, however, was completely built up, and the prospect thus confined to the street and the merchant's opposite – a little huckster's shop in which everything was sold from needles to ploughshares. Miss Eelen was fond of this window, it was so cheerful; and it was true that nobody could escape her who went to Robert Duncan's – the children who had more pennies to spend than was good for them, or the servant girls who went sur-reptitiously with bottles underneath their aprons. Miss Eelen kept a very sharp eye upon all the movements of the town, but even she acknowledged the drowsiness that comes after dinner, and sat in her big chair near the fire with her back turned to the window, 'her stocking' in her lap, and her eyes, as she would have described it, 'gathering straes', when Mr Douglas paid her that visit. Her cat sat on a footstool on the other side, majestically curling her tail around her person, and winking at the fire like her mistress. The peats were burning with their fervent flameless glow, and comfort was diffused over the scene. When Drumcarro came in Miss Eelen started and instinctively put up her

hands to her cap, which in these circumstances had a way
of getting awry.

'Bless me, Drumcarro! is this you?'

'It's just me,' he said.

'I hope they're all well?'

'Very well, I'm obliged to you. I just came in to say a
word about – the Castle—'

'What about the Castle?' with astonished eyes.

'I was meaning this nonsense that's coming on – the ball,'
said Mr Douglas, with an effort. A certain shamefacedness
appeared on his hard countenance – something like a blush,
if that were a thing possible to conceive.

'The ball? Bless us all! have ye taken leave of your senses,
Neil?'

'Why should I take leave of my senses? I'm informed that
the haill country – everybody that's worth calling gentry
will be going. You're hand and glove with all the clanjamfry.
Is that true?'

'Who ye may mean by "clanjamfry" I cannot say. If ye
mean that his Grace and her Grace are just bye ordinary
pleasant, and the young lords and ladies aye running out
and in – no for what I have to give them, as is easy to be
seen—'

'I'm not surprised,' said Drumcarro; 'one of the old
Douglas family before the attainder was as good as any one
of their new-fangled dukes.'

'He's no' a new-fangled duke, as you know well; and as
for the Douglas family, it is neither here nor there. Ye were
saying ye had received information?' Miss Eelen divined
her kinsman's errand, though it surprised her, but she
would not help him out.

'Just that,' said Drumcarro; 'I hear there's none left out
that are of a good stock. Now I'm not a man for entertainment, or any of your nonsense of music and dancing, nor
ever was. I have had too much to do in my life. But I'm told
it will be a slight to the name if there's none goes from
Drumcarro. Ye know what my wife is – a complaining
creature with no spirit to say what's to be done, or what's
not—'

'Spirit!' cried Miss Eelen. 'Na, she never had the spirit
to stand up to the like of you; but, my word, you would
soon have broken it if she had.'

'I'm not here,' said Mr Douglas, 'to get any enlightenment on her character or mine. I've always thought ye a
sensible woman, Eelen, even though we do not always
agree. They tell me it'll be like a scorn put upon Drumcarro
if the lasses are not at this ploy. Confound them a' and their
meddling, and the fools that make feasts, and the idiots that
yammer and talk! I've come to you to see what you think.
There shall come no scorn on Drumcarro while I'm to the
fore.'

'Well, Neil, if you ask me,' said Miss Eelen, 'I would have
taken the first word, and given ye my opinion if I had
thought it would be of any use; but it's just heaven's truth;
and farewell to the credit of Drumcarro when it's kent there
are two young women, marriageable and at an age to come
forward, and not there. It is just the truth. It will be said –
for that matter it is said already – that ye're so poor or so
mean that ye grudge the poor things a decent gown, and
keep them out of every chance. I would not have said a
word if you had not asked me, but that's just what folk
say.'

Drumcarro got up hastily from his chair and paced about
the room, and he swore an oath or two below his breath
that relieved his feelings. There was a great deal more in
Miss Eelen's eyes. The 'auld slave-driver' knew that his
name did not stand high among his peers, and his imagination was keen enough to supply the details of the gossip of
which his cousin gave so pleasant a summary. 'Ye may tell
them then,' he said, 'with many thanks to you for your
candid opinion, that Drumcarro's lasses, when he pleases,
can just show with the best, and that I'll thole no slight to
my name, any more than I would were I chief of this whole
country as my forbears were. And that's what ye can tell
your gossips, Eelen, the next time ye ask them to a dish of
tea – no' to say you're a Douglas yourself and should have
more regard for your own flesh and blood.'

'Bless me!' cried Miss Eelen, 'the man's just like a tempest, up in a moment. Na, Drumcarro, I always gave ye
credit if but your pride was touched. And it's just what I
would have wished, for I was keen for a sight of the ploy
mysel' but too old to go for my own pleasure. You will just
send them and their finery over to me in the gig, and I'll
see to all the rest. Bless me, to think of the feeling that

comes out when ye least expect it. I was aye convinced that if once your pride was touched. And who knows what may come of it? There's plenty of grand visitors at the Castle – a sight of them's as good as a king's court.'

'I hope a man will come of it, to one or the other of them,' Drumcarro said.

CHAPTER IX

Mr Douglas himself went to the ball at the Castle. He was of opinion that when a thing is to be done, it is never so well done as when you do it in your own person, and like most other people of similar sentiments, he trusted nobody. Miss Eelen as one of the race, was no doubt on the whole in the interests of the family, but Drumcarro felt that even she was not to be trusted with so delicate a matter as the securing of 'a man' for Mary or Kirsteen. It was better that he should be on the spot himself to strike when the iron was hot, and let no opportunity slip. It is true that his costume was far from being in the latest fashion; but to this he was supremely indifferent, scarcely taking it into the most cursory consideration. If he went in sackcloth he would no less be a Douglas, the representative of the old line upon whose pedigree there was neither shadow nor break. He was very confident that he could not appear anywhere without an instant recognition of his claims. Those of the Duke himself were in no way superior: that potentate was richer, he had the luck to have always been on the winning side, and had secured titles and honours when the Douglases had attainder and confiscation – but Douglas was Douglas when the Duke's first forbear was but a paidling lairdie with not a dozen men to his name. Such at least was the conviction of Drumcarro; and he marched to the Castle in his one pair of black silk stockings – with his narrow country notions strangely crossed by the traditions of the slave-driving period, with all his intense narrow personal ambitions and grudges, and not an idea beyond the aggrandizement of his family – in the full consciousness of equality (if not superiority) to the best there, the statesman Duke, the great landowners and personages who had come from far and near. Such a conviction sometimes gives great nobleness and dignity to the simple mind, but Drumcarro's pride was not of this elevating kind. It made him shoulder his way to the front with rising rage against all the insignificant crowd that got before him, jostle as he might; it did not give him the consolatory assurance that where he was, there must be the most dignified place. It must be allowed, however, in defence of his attitude that to feel yourself thrust aside into a crowd of nobodies when you know your place to be with the best, is trying. Some people succeed in bearing it with a smile, but the smile is seldom warm or of a genial character. And Drumcarro, at the bottom of the room, struggling to get forward, seeing the fine company at the other end, and invariably, persistently, he scarcely knew how, put back among the crowd, was not capable of that superlative amiability. The surprise of it partially subdued him for a time, and Miss Eelen's exertions, who got him by the arm, and endeavoured to make him hear reason.

'Drumcarro! bless the man – can ye not be content where ye are? Yon's just the visitors, chiefly from England and foreign parts – earls and dukes, and such like.'

'Confound the earls and the dukes! what's their titles and their visitors to me? The Douglases have held their own and more for as many hundred years—'

'Whisht, whisht, for mercy's sake! Lord, ye'll have all the folk staring as if we were some ferly. Everybody knows who the Douglases were; but man, mind the way of the world that ye are just as much affected by as any person. Riches and titles take the crown of the causeway. We have to put up with it whether we like it or no. You're fond of money and moneyed folk yourself—'

'Haud your fuilish tongue, ye know nothing about it,' said Drumcarro. But then he felt that he had gone too far. 'I'm so used to my wife I forget who I'm speaking to. You'll excuse me, Eelen?'

'The Lord be praised I'm not your wife,' said Miss Eelen devoutly. She added, perceiving a vacant chair a little higher up near the edge of the privileged line, 'I see my harbour, Drumcarro, and there I'll go, but no further;' and with an able dive through the throng and long experience of the best methods, managed adroitly to settle herself there. She caught by the elbow as she made her dart a gentleman who stood by, a man with grey hair still dressed in a black silk bag in the old-fashioned way which was no longer the mode. 'Glendochart,' she said, 'one word. I'm wanting your help; you were always on the Douglas' side.'

'Miss Eelen?' he cried with a little surprise, turning round. He was a man between fifty and sixty, with a fresh colour, and gentle, friendly air, much better dressed and set up than Drumcarro, but yet with something of the look of a man more accustomed to the hillside and the moor than to the world.

'For gudesake look to my cousin, Neil, of Drumcarro; he's just like a mad bull raging to be in the front of everything. Auld Earl Douglas, our great forbear, was naething to him for pride. He will just shame us all before the Duke and Duchess and their grand visitors, if someone will not interfere.'

The gentleman thus appealed to turned round quickly with a glance at the two girls, who with difficulty, and a little breathless and blushing with excitement, had emerged out of the crowd behind Miss Eelen, less skilled in making their way than she. 'These young ladies,' he said, 'are with you? they'll be—'

'Just Drumcarro's daughters, and the first time they've ever been seen out of their own house. But yonder's their father making everybody stand about. For ainy sake, Glendochart.'

'I'll do your bidding, Miss Eelen.'

The girls both thought, as his look dwelt upon them, that he was a most kind and pleasant old gentleman, and sighed with a thought that life would be far easier and everything more practicable if their father was but such another. But alas, that was past praying for. They had a little more space now that they had gained this comparative haven at the side of Miss Eelen's chair to take breath and look about them, and shake themselves free of the crowd.

The muslin gowns had been very successful; the skirts fell in a straight line from the waistband high under their arms to their feet, one with a little edge of fine white embroidery, the other with a frill scarcely to be called a flounce round the foot. The bodices were no longer than a baby's, cut in a modest round with a little tucker or lace against the warm whiteness of the bosom: the sleeves were formed of little puffs of muslin also like a baby's. Mary wore her necklace of cairngorms with much pride. Kirsteen had nothing upon her milk-white throat to ornament or conceal it. Nothing could have been whiter than her throat, with the soft warmth of life just tingeing its purity; her red hair which goes so well with that warm whiteness, was done up in what was called a classic knot at the back of her head, but there were some little curls which would not be gainsaid about her forehead and behind her ear. Her arms were covered with long silk gloves drawn up to meet the short sleeves. She was in a great tremor of excited imagination and expected pleasure. She was not thinking of partners indeed, nor of performing at all in her own person. She had come to see the world – to see the fine ladies and gentlemen, to hear some of their beautiful talk perhaps, and watch the exquisite way in which they would behave themselves. This was the chief preoccupation of her mind. She looked round her as if it had been 'the play'. Kirsteen knew nothing at all of the play, and had been brought up to believe that it was a most depraved and depraving entertainment, but still there had never been any doubt expressed of its enthralling character. The ball she had decided from the first day it had been mentioned, would be as good as going to the play.

Miss Eelen very soon found an old lady sitting near with whom she could talk, but Mary and Kirsteen stood together looking out upon the faces and the moving figures and speaking to no one. They scarcely cared to talk to each other, which they could do, they both reflected, very well at home. They stood pressing close to each other, and watched all the coming and going. In the position which they had gained they could see all the sets, the great people at the head of the room, the humbler ones below. Kirsteen had an advantage over her sister. She had met Lady Chatty several times at Miss Eelen's and had admired her, half for herself, half for her position, which had a romantic side very delightful to her simple imagination. 'That's Lady Chatty,' she whispered to Mary, proud of her superior knowledge. 'I don't think much of her,' said Mary, whispering back again. This gave Kirsteen a shock in the perfect pleasure with which she watched the graceful movements and animated looks of the future beauty. She had felt a disinterested delight in following the other girl through her dance, admiring how happy she looked and how bright; but Mary's criticism had a chilling effect.

A long time passed thus, and Kirsteen began to feel tired

in spite of herself; the pleasure of watching a room full of
animated dancers very soon palls at twenty. Her expectation of pleasure gradually died away. It was very bonny, but
not the delight she had thought. Mary stood with a smile
which had never varied since they entered the room, determined to look pleased whatever happened – but Kirsteen
was not able to keep up to that level. If *he* had but been
here! then indeed all things would have been different. It
gave her a singular consolation to think of this, to feel that
it was in some sort a pledge of her belonging to him that
she was only a spectator in the place where he was not; but
she was too sensible not to be aware that her consolation
was a fantastic one, and that she would in fact have been
pleased to dance and enjoy herself. She and her sister were
pushed a little higher up by the pressure of the crowd
which formed a fringe round the room, and which consisted of a great many young men too timid to break into
the central space where the fine people were performing,
and of tired and impatient girls who could not dance till
they were asked. Somehow it began to look all very foolish
to Kirsteen, not beautiful as she had hoped.

And then by ill luck she overheard the chatter of a little
party belonging to the house. It was the kind of chatter
which no doubt existed and was freely used at the balls
given by the Pharaohs (if they gave balls), or by Pericles, or
at least by Charlemagne. 'Where do all these funny people
come from?' 'Out of the ark, I should think,' the young
lords and ladies said. 'Antediluvian certainly – look, here is
a pair of very strange beasts.' The pair in question seemed
to Kirsteen a very pretty couple. The young man a little
flushed and blushing at his own daring, the girl, yes! there
could be no doubt, Agnes Drummond, Ronald's sister, of
as good family as any in the room. But the young ladies and
gentlemen from London laughed 'consumedly'. 'Her gown
must have been made in the year one.' 'And no doubt that's
the coat his grandfather was married in.' But all their impertinences were brought to a climax by Lord John, one of
the family, who ought to have known better. 'Don't you
know,' he said, 'it's my mother's menagerie? We have the
natives once a year and make 'em dance. Wait a little till
they warm to it, and then you shall see what you shall see.'
Kirsteen turned and flashed a passionate glance at the young

speaker, which made him step backwards and blush all over his foolish young face; for to be sure he had only been beguiled into saying what the poor young man thought was clever, and did not mean it. Kirsteen's bosom swelled with pride and scorn and injured feeling. And she had thought everybody would be kind! and she had thought it would all be so bonny! And to think of a menagerie and the natives making a show for these strangers to see!

'Miss Kirsteen, there is a new set making up, and your sister would be glad of you for a *vees-à-vis* if ye will not refuse an old man for a partner.' Kirsteen looked round and met the pleasant eyes, still bright enough, of Glendochart, whom Miss Eelen had bidden to look after the indignant Drumcarro. Kirsteen looked every inch Drumcarro's daughter as she turned round, an angry flush on her face, and her eyes shining with angry tears.

'I will not dance. I am obliged to you, sir,' she said.

'Not dance,' said Mary, in an indignant whisper, 'when we're both asked! And what would ye have? We cannot all have young men.'

'I will not dance – to make sport for the fine folk,' said Kirsteen in the same tone.

'You are just like my father,' said Mary, 'spoiling other folks' pleasure. Will ye come or will ye not? and the gentleman waiting – and me that cannot if you will not.'

'Come, my dear,' said old Glendochart. He patted her hand as he drew it through his arm. 'I have known your father and all your friends this fifty years, and ye must not refuse an old man.'

Neither of the girls were very much at their ease in the quadrille, but they watched the first dancers with anxious attention, and followed their example with the correctness of a lesson just received. Kirsteen, though she began very reluctantly, was soothed in spite of herself by the music and the measure, and the satisfaction of having a share in what was going on. She forgot for a moment the gibes she had listened to with such indignation. A quadrille is a very humdrum performance nowadays to those who know nothing so delightful as the wild monotony of the round dance. But in Kirsteen's time the quadrille was still comparatively new, and very 'genteel'. It was an almost solemn satisfaction to have got successfully through it, and her old partner was very kind and took her out to the tea-room afterwards with the greatest attention, pointing out to her the long vista of the corridor and some of the pictures on the walls, and everything that was worth seeing. They were met as they came back by a very fine gentleman with a riband and a star, who stopped to speak to her companion, and at whom Kirsteen looked with awe. 'And who may this bonny lass be?' the great man said. 'A daughter of yours, Glendochart?'

'No daughter of mine,' said the old gentleman in a testy tone. 'I thought your Grace was aware I was the one of your clan that had not married. The young lady is Miss Kirsteen Douglas, a daughter of Drumcarro.'

'I beg your – her pardon and yours; I ought to have known better,' said the Duke. 'But you must remember, Glendochart, when you are in such fair company, that it is never too late to mend.'

'He should indeed have known better,' said Glendochart, when they had passed on. 'These great folk, Miss Kirsteen, they cannot even take the trouble to mind – which kings do, they say, who have more to think of. And yet one would think my story is not a thing to forget. Did you ever hear how it was that John Campbell of Glendochart was a lone auld bachelor? It's not a tale for a ballroom, but there's something in your pretty eyes that makes me fain to tell.'

'Oh, it is little I care for the ballroom,' cried Kirsteen, remembering her grievance, which she told with something of the fire and indignation of her original feeling. He laughed softly, and shook his head.

'Never you fash your head about such folly. When my Lord John goes to St James's the men of fashion and their ladies will say much the same of him, and you will be well avenged.'

'It's very childish to think of it at all,' said Kirsteen, with a blush. 'And now will you tell me?' She looked up into his face with a sweet and serious attention which bewitched the old gentleman, who was not old at all.

'I was away with my regiment on the continent of Europe and in the Colonies and other places for many years, when I was a young man,' Glendochart said.

'Yes?' said Kirsteen, with profoundest interest – for was not that the only prospect before *him* too?

'But all the time I was confident there was one waiting for me at home.'

'Oh, yes, yes,' said Kirsteen, as if it had been her own tale.

'The news from the army was slow in those days, and there was many a mistake. Word was sent home that I was killed when I was but badly wounded. I had neither father nor mother to inquire closely, and everybody believed it, and she too. I believe her friends were glad on the whole, for I was a poor match for her. Her heart was nearly broke, but she was very young and she got over it, and, whether with her own will or without it I cannot tell, but when I came home at last it was her wedding-day.'

'Oh!' Kirsteen cried almost with a shriek, 'was that the end of her waiting? Me, I would have waited and waited on—'

'Wait now and ye will hear. The marriage was just over when I came to her father's house thinking no evil. And we met; and when she saw me, and that I was a living man, and remembered the ring that was on her finger and that she was another man's wife she went into her own maiden chamber that she had never left and shut to the door. And there she just died, and never spoke another word.'

'Oh, Glendochart!' cried Kirsteen with an anguish of sympathy, thinking of Ronald, and of the poor dead bride, and of the sorrow which seemed to her throbbing heart impossible, as if anything so cruel could not have been. She clasped his arm with both her hands, looking up at him with all her heart in her face.

'My bonny dear!' he said with surprised emotion, touching her clasped hands with his. And then he began to talk of other things: for they were in the ballroom, where, though everyone was absorbed in his or her own pleasure, or else bitterly resenting the absence of the pleasure they expected, yet there were a hundred eyes on the watch for any incident. Kirsteen, in the warmth of her roused feelings, thought nothing of that. She was thinking of the other who was away with his regiment, for who could tell how many years – and for whom one was waiting at home – one that would never put another in his place, no, not for a moment, not whatever news might come!

CHAPTER X

'It was just a very bonny ball,' said Mary. 'No, I was not disappointed at all. I danced with young Mr Campbell of the Haigh, and once with old Glendochart, who is a very well-mannered man, though he is not so young as once he was.'

'He was by far, and by far, the nicest there,' cried Kirsteen with enthusiasm.

'For them that like an auld joe,' said Mary demurely. Kirsteen had no thought of 'joes' old or young, but she thought with pleasure that she had gained a friend.

'The Duke took me for his daughter – and oh! if there was such a person she would be a happy lass. Aunt Eelen, did you ever hear—'

Kirsteen cast a glance round and checked further question, for her father consuming a delicate Loch Fyne herring, with his attention concentrated on his plate, and Mary seated primly smiling over her scone, were not at all in sympathy with the tale she had been told last night. Miss Eelen, with the tray before her on which stood the teapot and teacups, peering into each to count the lumps of sugar she had placed there, did not appear much more congenial, though there were moments when the old lady showed a romantic side. No trace of the turban and feathers of last night was on her venerable head. She wore a muslin mutch, fine but not much different from those of the old wives in the cottages, with a broad black ribbon round it tied in a large bow on the top of her head; and her shoulders were enveloped in a warm tartan shawl pinned at the neck with a silver brooch. The fringes of the shawl had a way of getting entangled in the tray, and swept the teaspoons to the ground when she made an incautious movement; but nothing would induce Miss Eelen to resign the tea-making into younger hands.

'Did I ever hear?' she said. 'I would like to know, Kirsteen Douglas, what it is I havena heard in my long pilgrimage of nigh upon seventy years. But there's a time for everything. If ye ask me at another moment I'll tell ye the whole story. Is it you, Drumcarro, that takes no sugar in your tea? No doubt you've had plenty in your time in yon dreadful West Indies where you were so long.'

'What's dreadful about them?' said Drumcarro. 'It's ignorance that makes ye say so. Ye would think ye were in paradise if ye were there.'

'Oh, never with all those meeserable slaves!'

'You're just a set of idiots with your prejudices,' said the laird, who had finished his herrings and pushed away his plate. 'Slaves, quo' she! There's few of them would change places, I can tell ye, with your crofters and such like that ye call free men.'

'Ye were looking for something, father,' said Mary.

'I'm looking for that mutton bone,' said her father. 'Fish is a fine thing; but there's nothing like a bit of butcher's meat to begin the day upon.'

'It's my ain curing,' said Miss Eelen. 'Ye can scarcely call it butcher's meat, and it's just a leg of one of your own sheep, Drumcarro. Cry upon the lassie, Kirsteen, and she'll bring it ben in a moment. We're so used to womenfolk in this house, we just forget a man's appetite. I can recommend the eggs, for they're all our own laying. Two-three hens just makes all the difference in a house; ye never perceive their feeding, and there's aye a fresh egg for an occasion. And so you were pleased with your ball? I'm glad of it, for it's often not the case when lassies are young and have no acquaintance with the world. They expect ower much. They think they're to get all the attention like the heroines in thae foolish story-books. But that's a delusion that soon passes away. And then you're thankful for what you get, which is a far more wholesome frame of mind.'

Kirsteen assented to this with a grave face, and a little sigh for the beautiful visions of ideal pleasure which she had lost.

But Mary bridled, and declared that all her expectations had been fulfilled. 'I got a great deal of attention,' she said, 'and perhaps I had not such grand fancies as other folk.'

'I have bidden Glendochart to come and see us at Drumcarro. Ye'll have to see to the spare cha'amer, and that he gets a good dinner,' said Mr Douglas. 'Him and me we have many things in common. He's one of the best of his name, with a good record behind him – not to match with our auld Douglas line, but nothing to snuff at, and not far off the head of the house himsel'.'

'You would be at the school together, Drumcarro,' Miss Eelen said.

'No such a thing – he's twenty years younger than me,' said Mr Douglas angrily. 'And I was at no schule, here or there, as ye might well mind.'

'Twenty years! If there's ten between ye that's the most of it. There's no ten between ye. When I was a young lass in my teens John Campbell was a bit toddling bairn, and ye were little mair, Drumcarro. Na, na, ye need not tell me. If there's five, that's the most. Ye might have been at the schule together and nothing out of the common. But he's had none of the cares of a family, though maybe he has had as bad to bear; and a man that is not marriet has aye a younger look. I ken not why, for with women it's just the contrair.'

'Mr Campbell is a very personable man,' said Mary. 'I'm no judge of ages, but I would say he was just in middle life.'

'It's but little consequence what you say,' said her father roughly. 'If Kirsteen was to express an opinion—'

Kirsteen's mind had a little wandered during this discussion. Glendochart's age appeared to this young woman a subject quite unimportant. He was of the age of all the fathers and old friends. Had she been a modern girl she would have said he was a darling, but no such liberties were taken in her day.

'And that I will,' she said, 'for we made friends though I've only seen him one night. He is just a man after my own heart,' said Kirsteen with warmth, with a sigh at the thought of his sad story, and a rising colour which was due to the fact that her imagination had linked the idea of young Ronald with that of this old and delightful gentleman who had been what her young lover was – but born to a less happy fate.

'Well,' said Drumcarro, 'now ye've spoken, Kirsteen, ye've made no secret of your feelings; and, so far as I can judge, he has just as fine an opinion of you. And if you give your attention to making him comfortable and let him see the mettle you're of, there is no saying what may happen. And it's not me that will put obstacles in the way.'

'Drumcarro,' cried Miss Eelen, 'ye get credit for sense among your own kind, but if ever there was a donnered auld fool in affairs of a certain description! Cannot ye hold your tongue, man, and let things take their course? They will do that without either you or me.'

Mr Douglas had disposed of a great deal of the mutton ham. He had made a very good breakfast, and he felt himself free to retire from the table with a final volley. 'If you think,' he said, 'that I am going to give up my mind to manage, as you womenfolks call it, and bring a thing about, and draw on the man and fleech the lassie, ye are just sair mistaken, Eelen. When I say a word in my house I'm accustomed to see it done, and no nonsense about it. If a man comes seeking that I approve of, it's my pleasure that he shall find what he's askin' for. I'll have no picking and choosing. Men are no so plenty, and lasses are just a drug in the market. You have never got a man yourself.'

'The Lord be praised!' said Miss Eelen. 'I would have broken his heart, or he would have broken mine. But I've kent them that would have married me, Neil Douglas, if it was for me or for my tocher I leave you to judge. I'm thankful to think I was never deceived for a moment,' said the old lady with a nod which sent the black bow upon her head into a little convulsion of tremulous movement. 'I name nae names,' she said.

Drumcarro walked to the window discomfited, and turned his back upon the party, looking out upon the village street. To tell the truth he had forgotten that trifling incident in his life. To taunt a woman who has refused you with never having got a man is a little embarrassing, and his daughters exchanged astonished looks which he divined, though it took place behind his back. Their opinion did not interest him much, it is true, but the thought that they had discovered a humiliation in his past life filled him with rage, insignificant as they were. He stood there for a moment swallowing his fury; then, 'There's the gig,' he said, thankful for the diversion. 'Ye'll better get on your things and get back to your work, and mind your mother and the concerns of the house instead of senseless pleasure. But it's just what I said, when ye begin that kind

of thing there's no end to it. When the head's once filled
with nonsense it's a business to get it out.'

'Well, father,' said Mary, 'the ball's done, and there is
no other coming if we were ever so anxious. So you need
not be feared. It's a little uncivil to Auntie Eelen to rise up
the moment we've swallowed our breakfast.'

'Oh, dinna take me into consideration,' said Miss Eelen.
'Ye must do your father's bidding, and I'll never lay it to
your charge. But you'll take a piece of yon fine seed cake to
your mother, poor thing, and some of the bonny little bis-
cuits that were round the trifle at the supper. I just put
them in my pocket for her. It lets an invalid person see the
way that things are done – and a wheen oranges in a basket.
She has very little to divert her though, poor thing, she
has got a man.'

Drumcarro did not appear to take any notice of this
Parthian arrow, though he fumed inwardly. And presently
the girls' preparations were made. The muslin dresses did
not take up so much room as ball-dresses do nowadays, and
had been carefully packed early in the morning in a box
which was to go home by the cart in the afternoon. And
they tied on their brown bonnets and fastened their cloth
pelisses with an activity becoming young persons who were
of so little account. To mount beside their father in the
gig, squeezed together in a seat only made for two persons,
and in which he himself took an undiminished share, with
a basket upon their knees, and several parcels at their feet,
was not an unalloyed pleasure, especially as he gave vent to
various threats of a vague description, and instantly
stopped either daughter who ventured to say a word. But
they had few pleasures in their life, and the drive home,
even in these circumstances, was not without its compen-
sations. The girls knew that every cottar woman who came
out to the door to see them pass was aware that they had
been at the ball at the Castle, and looked after them with
additional respect. And even the shouting children who ran
after the gig and dared a cut of Drumcarro's whip in their
effort to hang on behind amused them, and gave them a
feeling of pleased superiority. Coming home from the ball –
it was perhaps the best part of it, after all. When they were
drawing near the house their father made a speech to them
which Kirsteen at least listened to without alarm but with

much wonder. 'Now,' he said suddenly, as if adding a last word to something said before, 'I will have no nonsense whatever you may think. If a man comes to my door that I approve, I'll have no denial thrown into his teeth. You're all ready enough when it's to your own fancy, but, by —— this time I'll make ye respect mine.'

'What is it, father?' said Kirsteen with astonished eyes.

Mary gave her sister a smart poke with her elbow. 'We'll wait till we're asked before we give any denial,' she said.

'Ye shall give none whether or no,' said Drumcarro, unreasonably it must be allowed; 'but it's no you I'm thinking of,' he added with contempt.

Kirsteen felt herself deficient in Mary's power of apprehension. It was not often that this was the case, but her sister had certainly the better of her now. There were, however, many things said by Drumcarro to which his family did not attach a great interest, and she took it for granted that this was one of the dark sayings and vague declarations in which, when he was out of humour, he was wont to indulge. Her heart was not overwhelmed with any apprehension when she jumped lightly down from the gig glad to escape from these objurgations and feeling the satisfaction of having news to tell, and a revelation to make to the eager household which turned out to the door to meet her: Marg'ret in the front with cap-ribbons streaming behind her and her white apron folded over her arm, and little Jeanie with her hair tumbled and in disorder, her mouth and her ears open for every detail, with one or two other heads in the background – they had never seen the Castle, these ignorant people, never been to a ball. The mortifications of the evening all melted away in the delight of having so much to tell. Certainly the coming home was the best; it brought back something of the roseate colour of the setting out. And what a world of new experiences and sensations had opened up before Kirsteen since yesterday. 'Was it bonny?' said little Jeanie. 'Did you see all the grand folk? Was it as fine as ye thought?' And then Mrs Douglas's voice was heard from the parlour, 'Come ben, come ben, this moment, bairns. I will not have ye say a word till ye're here.' She was sitting up with a delicate colour in her cheeks, her eyes bright with anticipation. 'Now just begin at

the beginning and tell me everything,' she said. Certainly
the best of it was the coming home.

Mary gave her little narrative with great composure and
precision, though it surprised her sister. 'Everybody was
just very attentive,' she said. 'It was clear to be seen that the
word had been passed who we are. It was young Mr Campbell of the Haigh that took me out at the first, but I just
could not count them. They were most ceevil. And once I
saw young Lord John looking very hard at me, as if he
would like to ask me, but there was no person to introduce
him. And so that passed by.'

'Oh, Mary, I wish ye had danced with a lord and a
Duke's son,' cried little Jeanie, clapping her hands.

'Well, he was no great dancer,' said Mary. 'I liked the
young laird of the Haigh far better, and even old Glendochart – but he was Kirsteen's one.'

'He was the nicest of all,' cried Kirsteen. 'But, Jeanie, ye
should have seen all the bonny ladies with their diamonds
like sparks of light. You would have thought the Duchess
had stars on her head – all glinting as they do in a frosty sky
– and a circle about her neck that looked just like the King's
Ellwand,[1] but far more of them. It's not like stones or
things out of the earth, as folks say. It's like wearing little
pieces of light.'

'Oh, I wish I had seen them,' said Jeanie.

'Whisht, whisht. I've seen diamonds many a time, but I
never thought them like pieces of light. They're more like
bits of glass, which I have seen just as bonny. And who was
it you danced with most, Kirsteen? You have not given us
a list like Mary.'

'I danced with Glendochart,' said Kirsteen, looking down
a little. 'I stood a long time just looking about me. When
you are dancing you cannot see the rest of the ball, and it
was very bonny. Glendochart took me into the tea-room
and showed me all the pictures and things.'

'But Lord John never looked in that fixed way at you?'

'No,' said Kirsteen very shortly, perceiving that it was
inexpedient to repeat the little episode of Lord John.

---

[1] The belt of Orion.

'Then ye were not so much taken notice of as Mary?' cried Jeanie with disappointment.

'But she spoke to the Duke – or at least he spoke to Glendochart when Kirsteen was on his arm – and there was Lady Chatty that made great friends with her,' said Mary with benevolence, not to leave her sister quite in the background. But there was a momentary pause of disappointment, for they all felt that Lady Chatty was not so suggestive – had not in her name so many possibilities as Lord John.

'I hear of nothing but Glendochart,' said Mrs Douglas; 'if he is the man I mind upon, he will be the same age as your father; and what was he doing dancing and hanging about the like of you, a man at his time of life?'

Mary gave a little laugh, and repeated, 'He was Kirsteen's one.'

'What is the meaning of that, Kirsteen?'

'The meaning of it is that Glendochart, though he is old, is a real gentleman,' said Kirsteen; 'and he saw that we were strangers and neglected, and nobody looking the way we were on—'

At this there was an outcry that drowned the rest of the sentence. Strangers, the daughters of Drumcarro! – neglected when Mary had just said how attentive everybody had been! 'You are just in one of your ill keys, Kirsteen,' said her mother.

'No,' said Mary, 'but she's looking for him tomorrow: for my father has asked him, and she is feared you will not like him when ye see him. But my opinion is, though he is old, that he is still a very personable man.'

CHAPTER XI

A few days afterwards Glendochart appeared at Drumcarro riding a fine horse, and dressed with great care, in a costume very different from the rough and ill-made country clothes to which the family were accustomed. Jock and Jeanie who had come home from school rushed emulously to take the horse to the stable, and the household was stirred to its depths with the unaccustomed sensation of a visitor, a personage of importance bringing something of the air of the great world with him. He was conducted to the laird's room by Marg'ret herself, much interested in the stranger – and there remained for a short time to the great curiosity of the family, all of whom were engaged in conjectures as to what was being said within those walls, all but Kirsteen, who, being as it appeared most closely concerned, had as yet awakened to no alarm on the subject, and assured her mother quietly that there was nothing to be fluttered about, 'for he is just very pleasant, and makes you feel at home, and like a friend,' she said. Mrs Douglas had come down to the parlour earlier than usual in expectation of this visit. She had put on her best cap; and there was a little fresh colour of excitement in her cheeks. 'But what will he be saying to your father?' she said. 'Sitting so long together, and them so little acquainted with each other.' 'Oh, but they were at the school together, and at the ball they were great friends,' replied Kirsteen. She was the only one about whom there was no excitement. She sat quite cheerfully over her work 'paying no attention', as Mary said.

'Why should I pay attention? I will just be very glad to see him,' replied Kirsteen. 'He is just the kind of person I like best.'

'Whisht, Kirsteen, whatever you may feel ye must not go just so far as that.'

'But it's true, mother, and why should I not go so far? He's a very nice man. If he had daughters they would be well off. He is so kind, and he sees through you, and sees what you are thinking of.'

'You must not let him see what you are thinking of, Kirsteen!'

'Why not?' she said, glancing up with candid looks. But after a moment, a vivid colour came over Kirsteen's milk-white forehead. Then a smile went over it like a sudden ray of sunshine. 'I would not be feared,' she cried, 'for he would understand.' She was thinking of his own story which he had told her, and of the one who was like him, away in a far distant country. How well he would understand it! and herself who was waiting, more faithful than the poor lady who had not waited long enough. Oh, but that should never be said of Kirsteen!

Presently the two gentlemen were seen to be walking round the place, Drumcarro showing to his visitor all that there was to show in the way of garden and stables and farm offices, which was not much. But still this was the right thing for one country gentleman to do to another. The ladies watched them from the window not without an acute sense of the shortcomings of the place, and that there was no horse in the stable that could stand a moment's comparison with Mr Campbell of Glendochart's beautiful beast. Drumcarro was a house in the wilds, standing on a grassy bank without so much as a flower plot near, or any 'grounds' or 'policy', or even garden to separate and enclose it, and a sense of its shabbiness and poverty came into the minds of all, instinctively, involuntarily. 'If that's what he's thinking of he will never mind,' Mrs Douglas said under her breath. 'Whisht, mother,' said Mary. Kirsteen did not even ask Mary what her mother meant. Mrs Douglas indeed said a great many things that meant little or nothing, but this did not quite explain the fatal unconsciousness of the girl upon whose preoccupied ear all these warnings seemed to fall in vain.

The dinner had been prepared with more than usual care, and Marg'ret herself carried in several of the dishes in order to make a further inspection of the visitor. She had not been precisely taken into anybody's confidence, and yet she knew very well that he had come more or less in the capacity of a suitor, and that Drumcarro's extreme politeness and the anxiety he displayed to please and propitiate the stranger were not for nothing. Marg'ret said to herself that if it had been anybody but the laird, she would have

thought it was a question of borrowing money, but she
knew that Drumcarro would rather die than borrow, with a
horror and hatred not only of debt but of the interest he
must have had to pay. So it could not be that; nor was the
other gentleman who was so well preserved, so trim, 'so
weel put on', at all like a moneylender. It became clear to
her, as she appeared in the dining-room at intervals, what
the real meaning was. Glendochart had been placed next to
Kirsteen at table, and when he was not disturbed by the
constant appeals of Drumcarro, he talked to her with an
evident satisfaction which half flattered, half disgusted the
anxious spectator. He was a real gentleman, and it was a
compliment to Miss Kirsteen that a man who had no doubt
seen the world and kings' courts and many fine places
should distinguish her so – while on the other hand the
thought was dreadful that, in all her bloom of youth,
Kirsteen should be destined to a man old enough to be her
father. As old as her father! and she so blooming and so
young. But Marg'ret was perhaps the only one in the party
who thought so. The others were all excited by various
interests of their own, which might be affected by this union
between January and May. Mrs Douglas, with that fresh
tint of excitement on her cheeks, was wholly occupied by
the thought of having a married daughter near her, within
her reach, with all the eventualities of a new household to
occupy and give new interest to life; and Mary with a sense
that her sister's house to visit, in which there would be
plenty of company and plenty of money, and opportunity
of setting herself forth to the best advantage, would be like
a new existence. The young ones did not know what it was
that was expected to happen, but they too were stirred by
the novelty and the grand horse in the stable, and Glendochart's fine riding-coat and silver-mounted whip. Kirsteen herself was the only one who was unexcited and
natural. There was little wonder that Glendochart liked her
to talk to him. She was eager to run out with him after
dinner, calling to little Jeanie to come too to show him the
den, as it was called, where the burn tumbled over succes-
sive steps of rock into a deep ravine, throwing up clouds of
spray. She took care of the old gentleman with a frank and
simple sense that it was not he but she who was the best
able to guide and guard the other and used precautions to

secure him a firm footing among the slippery rocks without a single embarrassing thought of that change of the relationship between old and young which is made by the fictitious equality of a possible marriage. Far, very far were Kirsteen's thoughts from anything of the kind. She felt very tenderly towards him because of the tragedy he had told her of, and because he had gone away like Ronald, and had trusted in someone less sure to wait than herself. The very sight of Glendochart was an argument to Kirsteen, making her more sure that she never could waver, nor ever would forget.

When they came back from this expedition to the dish of tea which was served before the visitor set out again, Mrs Douglas exerted herself to fill out the cups, a thing she had not been known to do for years. 'Indeed,' she said, 'I have heard of nothing but Mr Campbell since they came back from the ball: it has been Glendochart this and Glendochart that all the time, and it would ill become me not to show my gratitude. For I'm but a weak woman, not able myself to go out with my daughters; and they are never so well seen to, Mr Campbell, when they are without a mother's eye.'

Drumcarro uttered a loud 'Humph!' of protest when this bold principle was enunciated; but he dared not contradict his wife, or laugh her to scorn in the presence of a visitor so particular and precise.

'You might trust these young ladies, madam,' said Glendochart gallantly, 'in any company without fear; for their modest looks would check any boldness, whatever their beauty might call forth.'

This was still the day of compliments, and Glendochart was an old beau and had the habits of his race.

'Oh, you are very kind,' said Mrs Douglas, her faint colour rising, her whole being inspired. 'If gentlemen were all like you, there would be little reason for any uneasiness; but that is more than we can expect, and to trust your bairns to another's guidance is always a very heavy thought.'

'Madam, you will soon have to trust them to the guidance of husbands, there can be little doubt.'

'But that's very different: for then a parent is free of responsibility,' said the mother, rising to the occasion; 'that is just the course of nature. And if they are so happy as to chance upon good, serious, God-fearing men.'

'Let us hope,' said Glendochart, not without a glance at Kirsteen, 'that your bonny young misses will be content with that sober denomination; but they will no doubt add for themselves, young and handsome and gay.'

'No, no,' Mrs Douglas said, led away by enthusiasm, 'you will hear no such wishes out of the mouths of lassies of mine.'

'Let them answer for themselves,' said Drumcarro, 'they're old enough: or maybe they will wait till they're asked, which would be the wisest way. Glendochart, I am very sorry to name it, and if ye would take a bed with us, I would be most pleased. But if you're determined to go today, I must warn ye the days are short and it's late enough to get daylight on the ford.'

'If ye would take a bed—' Mrs Douglas repeated.

The visitor protested that he was much obliged but that he must go. 'But I will take your permission to come again,' he said, 'and my only fear is that you will see too much of me, for there are strong temptations here.'

'Ye cannot come too often nor stay too long; and the more we see of you, the more we will be pleased,' said the mistress of the house. And the girls went out to see him mount his horse, which the boys had gone to fetch from the stable. Never was a visitor more honoured. A third person no doubt might have thought the welcome excessive and the sudden interest in so recent an acquaintance remarkable. But no one, or at least very few are likely to consider themselves and the civilities shown to them in the same light as an impartial spectator would do. It seems always natural that friends new or old should lavish civilities upon ourselves. Glendochart rode away with a glow of pleasure. He was not at all afraid of the ford, dark or light. He was as safe in his saddle as he ever had been, and had no fear of taking cold or getting damp. He feared neither rheumatism nor bronchitis. He said to himself, as he trotted steadily on, that fifty-five was the prime of life. He was a little over that golden age, but not much, nothing to count; and if really that bonny Kirsteen with her Highland bloom, and her fine spirits, and her sense— It was a long time since that tragedy of which he had told her. Perhaps, as his Grace had said, it was never too late.

'Ye havering woman,' said Drumcarro to his wife, 'you

are just like your silly kind. I would not wonder if going so fast ye had not just frightened the man away.'

'I said nothing but what ye said I was to say,' said Mrs Douglas, still strong in her excitement; 'and it was never me that began it, and if him and you are so keen, it's not for me to put obstacles in the way.'

Drumcarro stood for a moment astonished that his feeble wife should venture to indulge in a personal effort even when it was in his own aid; then he gave a shrug of his shoulders. 'A man knows when to speak and when to refrain from speaking,' he said; 'but you womenfolk, like gabbling geese, ye can never keep still if once you have anything to cackle about.'

CHAPTER XII

All this time, strange to say, Kirsteen took no fright about old Glendochart whom she had calmly set down, as is not unusual at her age, upon the footing of a man of eighty or so, an old, old gentleman to whom she could be as kind as her friendly young soul dictated, giving him her hand to lead him down the rough road to the linn, and feeling with her foot if the stones were steady before she let him trust his weight to them. It had been quite natural to come out to the door to see him mount and ride away, to stroke and pat the shining well-groomed horse, who looked as great an aristocrat as his master beside the sober and respectable matron Mally, who drew the gig and sometimes the cart, and had carried barebacked all the children at once as carefully as if she had been their mother. Kirsteen was even pleased with the sense that she herself was Glendochart's favourite, that he had talked more to her than to anyone, perhaps even had come to see her rather than the rest, with the pleasant partiality of an old friend. To be preferred is delightful to everybody, and especially to a girl who has had little petting in her life. It was an exhilarating consciousness, and she took the little jibes that flew about in the family and the laugh of Mary and the shout of the boys with perfect good humour. Yes, very likely Glendochart liked her best. He was a true gentleman, and he had seen her standing neglected and had come to her help. But for him the ball, if indeed always an experience and a fine sight, would have left only a sting in Kirsteen's mind instead of the impression bitter-sweet which it had produced. If she were glad now that she had gone, and pleased with the sight and the fact of having been there, it was to Glendochart chiefly that the credit was due. She had taken him into her heart warmly in the position of an old friend, an old kind and true gentleman whom she would always run to meet and brighten to see. In this easy state of mind, pleased with him and even better pleased with herself because of his liking for her, she received calmly all the family jests, quite satisfied that they were true.

Glendochart became a frequent visitor. He would ride over, or sometimes drive over, in a high gig much better appointed than the old gig at Drumcarro, saying that he had come 'to his dinner' or to eat one of Marg'ret's scones, or to see how they all were this cold weather. And he would permit Jock to drive the gig for a mile or two to the boy's delight, though it took all the strength of his young wrists to hold in the horse. Once even upon a great occasion Glendochart managed to persuade Drumcarro, who was ready to attend to all his suggestions, to bring the girls to a great hurling-match, at which – for he was a master of the game – he himself appeared to great advantage and not at all like the old, old gentleman of Kirsteen's thoughts. And when the New Year came he brought them all 'fairings', beautiful boxes of sweets such as had never been seen in the Highlands, and gloves wonderful to behold, which he begged Mrs Douglas's permission to offer to her daughters. These visits and his pleasant ways, and the little excitement of his arrival from time to time, and the hurling-match which afforded a subject of conversation for a long time, and the little presents, all quickened existence at Drumcarro, and made life more pleasant for all concerned. Kirsteen had taken him by this time for many a walk to the edge of the linn, springing down before him, by the side of the waterfall, to point out which of the stepping-stones were safe to trust to.

'Put your foot here, and it is quite steady, but take care of that moss, Glendochart, for it's very soft, and I've nearly sunk into it,' she would call to him stopping in mid-descent, her young voice raised clear above the roar of the water, and her hand held out to help. If there was one thing that fretted the elderly suitor it was this, and sometimes he would make a spring to show his agility, not always with successful results. 'You see you should do as I bid you,' said Kirsteen gravely, helping him to get up on one such occasion, 'and let me try first whether it will bear you or not.'

'I will always do as you bid me,' said the old gentleman, trying to look younger and younger, and as if he did not mind the fall at all; 'but it is my part to take care of you, and not you of me.'

'Oh no, not when the moss is so wet and the stones so shoogly,' Kirsteen said.

All this was very pretty fooling; but Drumcarro was not the man to be kept hanging upon the chances of a propitious moment when it might please the wooer to make the leap. The additional cheerfulness of the household did not extend to him. He became very tired of Glendochart's 'daidling', and of the overdelicacy of his attentions. His eyes grew fiery and his grizzled eyebrows menacing. He would come into the parlour where the visitor was making himself very agreeable, keeping up the pleasantest conversation, paying compliments to Mrs Douglas (whose health had greatly improved at this period), and with a devotion which was half fatherly, though he had no such intention, distinguishing Kirsteen who was always pleased to think that he liked her best. Drumcarro would come in with his hands thrust into the depths of his pockets and his shoulders up to his ears. 'Are ye not tired yet of the weemen, Glendochart? Weel, I would not sit there phrasin' and smilin', not for a king's ransom.' 'Perhaps, my friend, I'm getting more than any king's ransom, for what could buy such kind looks?' the old beau would reply. And then Drumcarro, with an oath muttered under his breath, would fling out again, not concealing his impatience, 'I cannot put up with such daidling!' Whether Glendochart understood, or whether his host took the matter into his own hands, never was known by the female portion of the household. But one morning shortly after the New Year, Glendochart having paid a long visit on the day before, Kirsteen received a most unexpected summons to attend her father in his own room.

'My father wants to speak to me! You are just sending me a gowk's errand,' she said to Jock who brought the message.

'It's no a gowk's errand. It's just as true as death,' said Jock. 'He sent me hissel'.'

'And what can he want to say to me in his own room?' cried Kirsteen.

'He did not tell me what he wanted to say; but I can guess what it is,' said Jock.

'And so can I,' said Jeanie.

'What is it, ye little mischief?' cried Kirsteen. 'I have done nothing. I have a conscience void of offence, which is more than you can say.'

Upon this they both gave vent to a burst of laughter loud and long.

'It's about your auld joe, Kirsteen. It's about Glendochart,' they cried in concert.

'About Glendochart? – he is just my great friend, but there is no harm in that,' she cried.

'Oh, Kirsteen, just take him, and I'll come and live with ye,' said Jeanie.

'And I'll come,' added Jock encouragingly, 'whenever we have the play.'

'Take him!' said Kirsteen. She bade them with great dignity to hold their tongues and went to her father's room with consternation in her breast.

Mr Douglas was sitting over his newspaper with the air of being very much absorbed in it. It was no less than a London paper, a copy of *The Times* which Glendochart had brought, which had been sent to him from London with the news of the escape of Boney, news that made Drumcarro wild to think that Jock was but fourteen and could not be sent off at once with such chances of promotion as a new war would bring. He had given the lad a kick with a 'Useless monkey! Can ye not grow a little faster'; as Jock had clattered up to bed in his country shoes the previous night. But he was not reading, though he pretended still to be buried in the paper when Kirsteen came in. He took no notice of her till she had been standing for a minute before him repeating, 'Did you want me, father?' when he looked up, as if surprised.

'Oh, you're there. I calculated ye would take an hour to come.'

'Jock said you wanted to speak to me, father.'

'And so I did – but you might have had to put your gown on, or to brush your hair or something – for anything I knew.'

'I never do that at this time of the day.'

'Am I to mind your times of day? Kirsteen, I have something to say to you.'

'So Jock told me, father.'

'Never mind what Jock told ye. It is perhaps the most serious moment of all your life; or I might say it's the beginning of your life, for with the care that has been taken of ye, keepit from the cold and shadit from the heat, and your

meat provided and everything you could require – the like
of you doesn't know what life is as long as ye bide in your
father's house.'

Kirsteen's heart gave a throb of opposition, but she did
not say or scarcely think that this position of blessedness
had never been hers. She was not prepared to blaspheme
her father's house.

'Well! now that's all changed, and ye'll have to think of
acting for yourself. And ye are a very lucky lass, chosen
before your sister, who is the eldest, and according to the
law of Laban— But I think he was too particular. What the
deevil maittered which of them was to go first so long as
he got them both safe off his hands.'

'I have no light,' said Kirsteen with suppressed impatience, 'as to what you're meaning, father!'

'Oh, ye have no light! Then I'll give ye one, and a fine
one, and one that should make ye thankful to me all your
days. I've settled it all with Glendochart. I thought he was
but a daidlin' body, but that was in appearance, not in
reality. He's just very willing to come to the point.'

Kirsteen said nothing, but she clasped her hands before
her with a gesture which was Marg'ret's, and which had
long been known to the young people as a sign of im-
movable determination. She did not adopt it consciously,
but with the true instinct of hereditary action, an impulse
so much misrepresented in later days.

'Very willing,' said Drumcarro, 'to come to the point;
and all the settlements just very satisfactory. Ye will be a
lucky woman. Ye're to have Glendochart estates for your
life, with remainder, as is natural, to any family there may
be; and it's a very fine downsitting, a great deal better house
than this, and a heap of arable land. And ye're to have—'

'For what am I to have all this, father?' said Kirsteen in
a low voice with a tremble in it, but not of weakness.

'For what are ye to have it?' He gave a rude laugh. 'For
yourself I suppose I must say, though I would think any
woman dear at the price he's willing to pay for ye.'

'And what does Glendochart want with me?' said
Kirsteen with an effort to steady her voice.

'Ye fool! But you're not the fool ye pretend to be. I
cannot wonder that you're surprised. He wants to mairry
ye,' her father said.

Kirsteen stood with her hands clasped, her fine figure swayed in spite of her with a wave of agitation, her features moving. 'Glendochart!' she said. 'Father, if he has friends ye should warn them to keep him better and take care of him, and not let him be a trouble to young women about the country that never did any harm to him.'

'Young women,' said Drumcarro, 'there is not one I ever heard of except yourself, ye thankless jaud!'

'One is plenty to try to make a fool of,' said Kirsteen.

'I would like to see him make a fool of one belonging to me. Na, it's the other way. But that's enough of this non-sense,' he added abruptly; 'it's all settled. Ye can go and tell your mother. He's away for a week on business, and when he comes back ye'll settle the day. And let it be as soon as possible, that we may be done wi't. It's been as much as I could do to put up with it all this time. Now let any man say I've done much for my sons and little for my daughters!' said Drumcarro, stretching his arms above his head with the gesture of fatigue. 'I've got them their commissions and outfit and all for less trouble than it has cost me to get one of you a man!' He yawned ostentatiously and rubbed his eyes, then opening them again to see Kirsteen still standing in the same attitude before him he gave vent to a roar of dismissal. 'G'away with ye. Go and tell your mother. I've said all I have to say.'

'But I have something more to say,' said Kirsteen. 'I'll not marry Glendochart. It's just been a mistake, and I'm sorry, but—'

'You'll not mairry Glendochart! Ye shall marry whatever man I choose for ye.'

'No, father!' said Kirsteen clasping her hands more closely.

'No!' he said, pushing back his chair. He was honestly astonished, taken completely by surprise. 'No! Lord, but ye shall though when I say it. And what ails ye at Glendochart? And him running after ye like a fool the whole winter, and nothing but pleasant looks for him till now?'

'I'm very sorry,' repeated Kirsteen. 'I'm very sorry – I never, never thought of that. He's an old man, and it seemed all kindness, to one as much as another. Oh, I'm sorry, father. Tell him I would not have vexed him for the world.'

'I'll tell him no such thing. I'll tell him ye're very proud
and pleased, as sets ye better; and I'll take you to Glasgow
to buy your wedding gown.' He said this with an attempt at
seduction, perhaps a little startled by the first idea that to
subdue Kirsteen by violence would not be so easy as he
thought.

'Father, you're meaning it for great kindness; but oh, if
ye would just understand! I cannot marry Glendochart. I
could not if there was no other man.'

'It is just Glendochart ye shall marry, and no other. It's
all settled. You have nothing more to do with it but what
I've promised and fixed for ye.'

'No, father—'

'But I say yes,' he said, bringing down his clenched fist
on the table with a noise that made the windows ring.

'It cannot be settled without me,' said Kirsteen, growing
first red and then pale, but standing firm.

'You're not of the least importance,' he said, foam flying
from his lips. 'What are ye? A creature of no account. A
lass that has to obey her father till she gets a man, and then
to obey him. Say what ye like, or do what ye like, it will
never alter a thing I've fixed upon; and of that ye may be as
sure as that you stand there. G'away to your mother, and
tell her it's to be soon, in a month or so, to get done with it
– for I've made up my mind.'

Kirsteen stood silent for a moment, not daunted but
bewildered, feeling with a force which no girl in her situation would now recognize the helplessness of her position,
not a creature to take her part, seeing no outlet. She burst
forth suddenly when a new idea occurred to her. 'I will
speak to him myself! He is a good man, he will never hold
me to it. I will tell him—'

'If ye say a word to him,' cried Drumcarro rising from
his chair and shaking his clenched hand in her face, 'one
word! I'll just kill ye where ye stand! I'll drive ye from my
doors. Neither bit nor sup more shall ye have in this house.
Ye may go and tramp from door to door with a meal-pack
on your shoulder.'

'I would rather do that,' cried Kirsteen, 'far rather than
make a false promise and deceive a good man. Oh, father,
I'll do anything ye bid me. I'll be your servant, I'll ask for
nothing; but dinna, dinna do this! for I will not marry Glen-

dochart, not if you were to kill me, not if you were to turn me from the door.'

'Hold your peace, ye lang-tongued—; ye shall do what I bid you, that and nothing else.'

'No, father, no, father!' cried Kirsteen trembling; 'I will not – for nothing in the world.'

'Go out of my sight,' he cried, 'and hold your tongue. Away this moment! Ye shall do just what I say.'

'Father—'

'None of your fathers to me. Get out of my sight, and make yourself ready to do what I tell ye. It shall be in a fortnight. That's all you shall make by your rebellion. Not another word, or I'll turn you out of my house.'

Kirsteen retired as he made a step towards her with his hands raised to her shoulders, to put her out. His fiery eyes, the foam that flew from his lips, the fury of his aspect frightened her. She turned and fled from the room without any further attempt to speak.

CHAPTER XIII

Kirsteen rushed out of the house with the instinct of passion, to shake off all restraint, to get into the free air, where an oppressed bosom might get breath. She flew like a hunted deer, flashing past the window where Mary, sitting at her seam, saw her hurried escape and divined more or less what was the meaning of it.

'Who's that?' said Mrs Douglas, conscious of the flying shadow.

'It's Kirsteen, and my father will have told her, and she's just beside herself.'

'Beside herself!' said the mother tranquilly over her knitting. 'She may well be that; for who would have thought of such a prospect for the like of her, at her age.' Mary was not so sure that the agitation was that of joy, but she said nothing. And Kirsteen was out of sight in a moment, darting by.

She went towards the linn, without knowing why. The stream was strong with the winter floods, and the roar of it as it poured down the rocky cleft was enough to make all voices inaudible, and to deaden more or less even the sound of one's thoughts buzzing in one's head with the passion and the sweep of them, themselves like a hurrying stream. Kirsteen fled as to a covert to the 'den', down which this passionate rivulet, swollen into a torrent, stormed and poured, flinging its spray over the wet and spongy turf into which her feet sank. She cared nothing for this in the absorption of her excitement, and flung herself down upon that damp slope, feeling the spray on her forehead and the roar of the water in her ears as a sort of relief from herself. Her feelings had been like to burst her heart and her brain together as she flew along, like some struggling things shut up in a space too narrow for them. She could not get her breath nor contain the hurry and confusion of her own being. But in that damp retreat where nobody would be likely to pursue her, where she could scarcely even hear the thumping of her own heart nor any voice calling her, nor be subject to interruption of any kind, Kirsteen after a moment began to come to herself. The shock, the fright, the horror quieted a little; her mind became accustomed, as it does so rapidly, to the new alarm, to the frightful danger which had suddenly revealed itself. It was a danger which Kirsteen had not expected or foreseen. She had very well understood when she pledged herself to wait for Ronald what that meant. It was in all the traditions of romance with which she was acquainted – not waiting relieved by constant communication, and with a certain distinct boundary, but silent, unbroken, perhaps for life, certainly for years. In the beginning at least such a visionary burden may be taken up with enthusiasm, and Kirsteen had been proud of it and of the deep secret of which there was nothing to tell, which was in spirit alone, with no bond to be displayed in the sight of men. But it had never occurred to her that she might be bidden to forswear herself as she said, that she might have to struggle against all about her for the right to keep her vow. This danger had never appeared before her as a possibility. She had not thought of any wooer, nor had any such presented himself to her consciousness. Without warning, without thought of precaution or self-defence, the danger had come.

To marry Glendochart: Glendochart – there burst through Kirsteen's distressful thoughts a sudden picture of the old gentleman descending the side of the linn guided by her hand, the safe places selected for him; and then his little plunge, his slip, her cry, 'Oh, Glendochart, you have hurt yourself!' and there burst from her in the midst of her trouble an irrepressible laugh, which rang into the roar of the linn and went down with it into the depths echoing among all the rocks. Kirsteen had been ashamed to laugh when that accident happened for fear of hurting his feelings, but all the ludicrousness of the incident burst upon her now. He had got so red, poor old gentleman! he had seized upon a thorn bush to pull him up, rather than take her hand. He had said that it was nothing, nothing, though her keen young senses, compunctious of their own perceptions, had seen how he limped up the bank again. She had not dared to offer her support any more than to laugh, seeing it hurt his feelings. And it was because he wanted to marry her, her – Kirsteen, troth-plighted to her own lad – and him as old as her father. Oh, for shame, for shame!

That laugh did Kirsteen good. It liberated her soul; she escaped as from the hand of fate and became able to think. And then a wild anger swept over her mind against her father, who wanted nothing but to get her, as he said, off his hands, and against Glendochart for daring to think that she would take him, an old, old man. All the sense of his kindness disappeared in this illumination as to his motives: indeed the more Kirsteen esteemed him before, the more she despised and hated him how. She thought of auld Robin Gray, but that was too good for him. The old, ill man, to tell her a story of faithfulness and make her cry and mix him up in her mind with Ronald and her own love, and then to betray her, and want to marry her – doubly faithless, to her that died for him, and to Kirsteen that had wept for him! It was for constancy and pity and true love that the girl had been so sorry, so touched in her heart, so wishful to please him and make him smile. And now to turn upon her, to try to tear her from her own lad, to make her mansworn! There was nothing that was too bad for him, the old, ill man! Kirsteen saw herself stand before him indignant, her eyes flashing with injured honour and a sense of wrong.

But then suddenly all this sustaining force of anger went from her as Glendochart's kind and gentle face so full of feeling came before her imagination. Oh, he knew better than that! If she could but speak to him, and tell him! perhaps show him that little blue Testament, whisper to him that there was One – away with his regiment, fighting for the King, like Glendochart himself, like the story he had told her! Tears filled Kirsteen's eyes. Her father might be dour and hard, but Glendochart would understand. It was just his own story; he would never let her break her heart and die on her wedding-day like his own lass. Oh, no! oh, no! he would never do that. He would never let it happen twice, and all for him. With a quick gleam of her imagination, Kirsteen saw herself in her white wedding-gown, lying at his feet, the second bride that had burst her heart! Oh, no! oh, no! Glendochart would never do that: the tears streamed from Kirsteen's eyes at the thought, but her quivering mouth smiled with generous confidence. No, no! She had only to speak to Glendochart and all would be well.

But then came her father's threat, his blazing fiery eyes, his hand clenched and shaken in her face, the fury of his outcry: 'I'll just kill ye where ye stand – I'll put you to the door.' Kirsteen remembered Anne, and her soul sank. Anne had a husband to take care of her, she had a house, wherever it was; but Kirsteen would have nothing. And what would become of her if she were put to the door? Where would she go to find a shelter? Another grotesque vision – but not so grotesque to her imagination – of the poor beggar-woman with a meal-pack on her shoulder which her father had evoked, flitted before her mind. No, she would not be like that. She would take care of bairns, or keep a house, or even make muslin gowns like Miss Macnab. There were plenty of things she could do! – it would be long, long before she need come to the meal-pack. But then there burst over Kirsteen's mind another revelation: the shame of it! She, a Douglas – one of the old Douglases, that had been the lords of the whole land, not only of poor Drumcarro – a gentlewoman of as good blood as the Duchess or any grand lady, and one that could not be hidden or made to appear as if she were a common person! And the scandal of it, to open up the house and all its concerns to ill talk – to make it open to all the world to say that Drumcarro was an ill father, and the house a cruel house, or that the Douglas lassies were not what ladies should be, but light-headed and ill-conducted, rebels against their own kith and kin. This was the most terrible thought of all. The others seemed to open up a way of escape, but this closed the door; it is an ill bird that flies its own nest. How could Kirsteen do that? shame her family so that even Sandy and Nigel and Charlie and Donald in India, even little Robbie, should hear of it and think shame – so that *he* should hear that Kirsteen had let herself be talked about? so that Drumcarro should be lightly spoken of and all its secrets laid bare? This new suggestion brought back all the passion and the confusion that the influence of the air and the freedom out of doors, and the quiet time to think had calmed down. To endure is always possible if you set your heart to do it, whatever happens; but to shame and to expose your own house!

'Where have ye been, Kirsteen?' said Mrs Douglas. 'I never saw a person like you for running out when you're

most wanted. You should not take your walks in the fore-
noon when we're all at work.'

'Did you want me, mother? I was not fit to sit down to
my work. I had a – buzzing in my head.'

' 'Deed I think ye have always a buzzing in your head.
Sometimes I speak to ye three times before ye answer me.'

'She's uplifted with her prospects,' said Mary, 'and no
wonder. I think ye should excuse her this day.'

Mary intended to be very kind to Kirsteen. She had made
up her mind to be a very frequent visitor at her sister's
house.

'Well, well,' said Mrs Douglas, 'that may be true enough;
but I think she might have come and told me the news herself, instead of letting me find it out through your father –
not that I had not judgment enough to see what was coming
this many a day.'

Kirsteen was still trembling with the results of her self-
argument at the linn – which indeed had come to no result
at all save the tremor in her frame and the agitation in her
heart. She had knelt down by her mother's side to wind the
wool for which it appeared Mrs Douglas had been waiting,
and she was not prepared with any reply.

'She doesn't seem to have much to say to us now,
mother,' said Mary.

'Kirsteen, you should not be so proud. You will be a finer
lady than ever your mother was, with a carriage and horses
of your own, and no doubt everything that heart can desire;
for an auld man is far more silly than a young one.'

Kirsteen gave the wool a jerk which tangled it wildly.
'Mother, I just wonder what you are all havering about,'
she said.

'Kirsteen, I'm well used to rude speaking,' cried the
mother, ready to cry at a moment's notice; 'but not from
my own bairns.'

'Oh, mother, I beg your pardon. It was not you that was
havering. Dinna speak to me, for I cannot bear it. My heart
is just like to break.'

'With pleasure?' said Mary in her soft tones.

Kirsteen darted a glance of fire at her calm sister, but
turned nervously to her occupation again and answered
nothing. She had enough to do with her yarn which, in sympathy with her confused thoughts, had twisted itself in

every possible way and refused to be disentangled. Her mother remarked the tremor of her hands.

'Ye have got the hank into a terrible tangle, and what are ye trembling at, Kirsteen – is it the cold?'

'I'm not trembling, mother,' said Kirsteen.

'Do ye think I am blind or doited and cannot see? Na, I'm a weak woman, sore held down with many infirmities; but I'm thankful to say my eyes are as good as ever they were. Ye're all trembling, Kirsteen; is it the cold?'

'She has gotten her gown all wet, mother. She has been down by the linn, it's no wonder she's trembling. She ought to go and change her things.'

'Are your feet wet, Kirsteen?'

'Oh,' said Kirsteen springing to her feet, 'if ye would just let me alone; I'm neither wet nor cold, but my heart's like to break. I don't know what I am doing for misery and trouble. If ye would only have peety upon me and let me alone!'

'Dear Kirsteen, how can ye speak like that? Where will ye get any person you can open your heart to like your mother? Just tell me what's wrong and that will ease your mind. What can Mary and me mean but what is for your good? Eh, I never thought but what you would be pleased, and a blithe woman this bonny day.'

'She'll maybe open her mind best between you two, if I were away,' said Mary rising. She was really full of good feeling towards her sister, with no doubt an anticipation of good to come to herself, but yet a certain amount of solid sympathy genuine enough of its kind.

'Now, Kirsteen, my bonny woman, just tell me what's the maitter,' said Mrs Douglas when Mary was gone.

'It seems you know what has happened, mother, and how can you ask me? Am I likely to be a blithe woman as ye say when it's just been told me?'

'That a good man and a good house are waiting for ye, Kirsteen? And one that's very fond of ye, and asks no better than to give ye all ye can desire?'

'That I'm to be turned out of the house,' cried Kirsteen; 'that I'm no more to see your face; that I'm to go from door to door with a meal-pack like a beggar-woman!'

'Whisht, whisht, and don't speak nonsense: that will be some of your father's joking. Whiles he says things that are hard to bear. What should bring all this upon ye, Kirsteen? You will be the Leddy of Glendochart and an honoured woman, holding your head as high as ainy in the whole country, and silk gowns as many as ye desire, and coaches and horses; and what ye'll like best of all, my bonny bairn, the power to be of real service and just a good angel to them that ye like best.'

'Oh, mother, mother,' cried Kirsteen, burying her face in her mother's lap, 'that is the worst of it all! Oh, if ye have any peety don't say that to me!'

'But I must, for it's all true. Oh, Kirsteen, I hope I'm not a complaining woman; but just you think what it would be to me to have my daughter's house from time to time to take shelter in. Many and many a time have I been advised change of air, but never got it, for who dared name it to your father? I have been thinking this whole morning it would make me just a new woman. To get away for a while from this hole – for it's just a hole in the winter though it may be bonny at other times – and to see my bairn sitting like a queen, happy and respectit.'

'Not happy, mother!'

'That's just your fancy, my dear. You think he's old, but he's not really old, and as kind a face as ever I saw, and full of consideration, and not one that ever would say ye had too many of your own folk about ye, or that ye ought to forget your father's house. Oh, Kirsteen, it's very little a lassie knows: ye think of a bonny lad, a bright eye or a taking look, or a fine figure at the dancing, or the like of that. But who will tell ye if he may not be just a deevil in the house? Who will tell ye that he may not just ding ye into a corner and shame ye before your bairns, or drive ye doited with his temper, or make your bed and your board a hell on earth? Oh,' cried poor Mrs Douglas in accents of deep conviction, 'it's little, little a lassie kens! She thinks she will please her fancy, or she listens to a flattering tongue, or looks to a bonny outside. And all the time it's just meesery she's wedding, and not a bonny lad. But, Kirsteen,' she said, giving a furtive little kiss to the rings of hair on Kirsteen's milk-white forehead, 'Kirsteen, my bonny woman, when ye take a man that everybody knows, that is just kent for a good man and a kind man, and one that loves the very ground you tread on, oh, my dear! what does

it maitter that he's not just that young? Is it anything against
him that he knows the world and has had trouble of his
own, and understands what it is to get a bonny lass and a
good bairn like you? And oh, Kirsteen, think what ye can
do for us all if you take him, for your sisters and for the
callants, he's just made the house a different thing already;
and though that's scarcely worth the thinking of, for I'm
very near my grave and will want nothing long – Kirsteen,
for me, too!—'

'Oh, mother, mother!' cried the girl with her face still
hidden in her mother's lap, 'ye just break my heart.'

'Na, na,' said Mrs Douglas in soft quick tones like one
who consoles a child, 'we'll have no breaking of hearts. Ye
will not be a month marriet before ye'll think there's no
such a man in the world. And there's nothing he will deny
ye, and from being of little account ye'll be one of the first
ladies in the countryside. Whisht, whisht, my darling! Ye'll
make him a happy man, and is not he worthy of it?
Kirsteen! Rise up and dry your eyes. I hear your father
coming. And dinna anger him, oh! dinna anger him, for he
never minds what ill words he says!'

CHAPTER XIV

Mrs Douglas retired to her room after dinner in a very tearful mood. She had made a great effort and she had not been successful, and all her hopes which had been gradually built up into a palace of delight came tumbling down about her ears. The only comfort she could feel now was in the source of her chief troubles. 'Ye may say what you like to me,' she cried as Kirsteen helped her to take off her cap and arrange herself comfortably upon her bed, 'but your father will never put up with it. It would have been more natural in ye, Kirsteen, if ye had yielded to your mother, for well I wot ye'll have to yield to him, whether ye like it or no.'

'Oh, mother, I think ye might understand,' Kirsteen said.

'Understand! it's easy enough to understand. Ye've got a silly notion in your head that ye cannot mairry an old man. Better than you have done it before ye, and it would be a blessing to all your family, and maybe help me to live to see some of my boys come back. But na, ye will never think of that, of nothing but your own pleasure. And you'll see what your father will say to you,' said Mrs Douglas, with a vindictive satisfaction, while Kirsteen drew the coverlet over her and arranged the pillow for her head.

'Are ye comfortable, mother?'

'Oh, ay, as much as I can be, so little considered as I am. Ye need not wait. Put my stick within my reach, I'll chap upon the floor if I want ye, or ye can send Mary if it's too much trouble,' the angry mother said. She had been very tender up to this point, very anxious to show how entirely it was for everybody's advantage that this step should be taken. But to spend your strength thus upon an unconvinced and unyielding child is hard to bear, and Mrs Douglas's disappointment had turned to wrath. 'Oh, mother,' Kirsteen said with anguish, but the remonstrance met with no reply except a fretful 'Go away!' She went downstairs very slowly and reluctantly to the parlour where Mary sat at the household mending, in all the placid superiority of one who is at peace with the world. She had

rejected no one's advice. She had not crossed her father or
her mother, or disappointed her family. When Kirsteen
sat down and took her work, Mary looked at her, and gave
utterance to a faint 'tshish, tshish' of mild animadversion,
but for some time nothing was said. When the silence was
broken it was by a question from Mary, 'Ye'll not be
expecting Glendochart today?'

'Me expecting him? I never expected him! He just came
of his own will,' Kirsteen cried, moved in her anger and
wretchedness to a few hasty tears.

'Well, well, I'm saying nothing; but I suppose he's not
expected, if that's the right way.'

'I know nothing about it,' said Kirsteen: which indeed
was not quite true.

'It was just to tell Marg'ret she need take no extra trouble
about the scones. It's been a great expense a visitor like
that, especially when it comes to nothing: often to his
dinner, and still oftener to his tea. And always new scones
to be made, and jam on the table, and the boys partaking
freely: for how could I tell Jock and Jamie before a stranger,
"It's no for you." And all to come to nothing!' said Mary,
holding up her hands.

'What could it have come to?' cried Kirsteen. 'I think I
will be just driven out of my senses between my mother
and you.'

'Poor mother,' said Mary. 'She had just set her heart
upon it. It would have been a grand change to her to go and
visit ye. It would have done her health good, but there are
some that never think on such things. I just wish it had
been me that had got the chance.'

'And so do I, with all my heart,' cried Kirsteen, with a
hot and angry blush. She felt, however, that there was
something like a dishonesty, an irritating attempt to despoil
her of something belonging to her in Mary's wish.

'I would have put myself in the background,' said Mary.
'I would not have thought whether I liked it or not. I would
just have taken the man however old he had been. I would
have said, it will be fine for my mother and a good thing for
Kirsteen and all the bairns; and I would just have taken
him and never said a word.'

'That would have been pleasant for him – that you
should take him for the sake of the family.'

'He would have been none the wiser,' said Mary composedly. 'There would have been no necessity to tell him. And he would never have found it out. They say men are very vain; they just think ye are in love with them whether ye are or not. And I would have managed Glendochart fine. But it was not me that had the chance.'

Kirsteen cast a gleam of mingled indignation and contempt at her sister, who went on diligently with her mending while she gave vent to these sentiments. Mary was fitting on a patch upon one of the boys' undergarments, carefully laying it by the thread. Her mending was famed in the family; nobody made repairs so neatly. She spoke very softly, never lifting her eyes from the work, which indeed required all her attention. And there is a special power, especially for irritation, in the words of wisdom that are thus addressed to one without any lifting of the eyes.

'But that's just the way of the world,' Mary said with a sigh. 'The one that would do it, that would not think of herself, but just do it, is never the one that has it in her power. I've seen the same thing many a time. The wilful one that will please herself, it is her that folk seek—'

Kirsteen's heart swelled high with mortification and pain. If there was anything that she had desired in her visionary moods it had been to sacrifice herself, to do some great thing for her mother, to be the saving of little Jeanie. She had made many a plan how to do this, how to perform prodigies for them, to deliver them from dangers. In her dreams she had saved both from fire and flood, from the burning house which fancy sacrificed lightly to give her the chance of a piece of heroism, or from the roaring stream when it ran to its highest, cutting off Drumcarro, which was a thing that had happened once. And now the smooth and smiling Mary, who would have thought of nobody in such a strait but herself, could reproach Kirsteen! And it was a true reproach. Here was the way, with no need to set the house on fire, or flood the country: here was a deliverance to be accomplished, that was within her power, that she could do so easily with no trouble to anyone save to him who was far away, who perhaps would never hear of it, who might have changed his mind and forgotten Kirsteen long before he heard of it. All the best part of her seemed to rise against Kirsteen, demanding of her this sacrifice. Oh, it was so easy to do it in your head, to make a sacrifice of everything when nothing was wanted! – but when the time came—

And as if this was not enough, little Jeanie came running after Kirsteen when the poor girl escaped and wandered out again towards the linn in hope of a little soothing from Nature – Jeanie stole her hand into Kirsteen's and rubbed her golden locks against her sister's sleeve. 'When ye go to Glendochart take me with you,' said Jeanie. 'Oh, I would like to live in a grand house. I would like a powney to ride, and to play upon the harpsichord as my mother did when she was young. They say ye'll be very rich, Kirsteen, when you go with Glendochart.'

'But I will never go with Glendochart!' Kirsteen cried.

'Oh, will ye no? And why will ye no, Kirsteen? Will ye send him away? Oh, you could never be so cruel as to do that! Will he come here no more? – and everything be just as it used to be? Oh, Kirsteen!' cried Jeanie, 'I wish you would marry Glendochart! I would if it was me. He is the kindest man in the whole world. He speaks to me as if he was— No, fathers are not kind like that. I like him, Kirsteen, I am awfu' fond of him; and so is Jock and Jamie – Oh, I wish ye would change your mind!'

'But, Jeanie, ye would not wish me to be meeserable,' cried poor Kirsteen.

'No,' said Jeanie – but she added with youthful philosophy, 'you wouldna be meeserable when me and the rest were so happy. And it is us that will be meeserable if you send him away that has been so good to us all. And how would ye like that?'

Jeanie's small voice became almost stern as she asked the question, 'How would ye like that? – to make all the rest meeserable – when the alternative was nothing more than being meeserable yourself?' Kirsteen had nothing to say against that logic. She told Jeanie to run to a certain drawer where she would find some oranges and share them with the boys. They were Glendochart's oranges like everything pleasant in the house. And he was the kindest man in the world. And he would be miserable too as well as her mother and Jeanie and the laddies. Oh, poor Kirsteen, with all her best feelings turning traitors to her! would it not be

far easier to consent and make them all happy, and just be
miserable herself?

But she was not to be left free even now. Before she had
got to the side of the linn, to be deafened with the roar and
drenched with the spray, which were the only things she
could think of in which any solace was, Marg'ret coming
round the back of the house interrupted her on her way.
'Where are ye going, down by the linn to get your death of
cold and maybe an accident into the bargain? You have
nothing upon your head, and no gloves on your arms, and
the grass is drookit. No, my bonny lamb, ye must not go
there.'

'Let me be, Marg'ret. What do I care! If I get my death
it will be all the better; but I'll no get my death.'

'Lord, save us, to hear her speak! Ye'll no get your death
– it's just a figure of speech; but ye may get the cauld or a
sair throat, or something that will settle on your chest, and
that's as bad. What for would ye go and tempt Providence?
Come into my bonny kitchen that is all redd up and like a
new pin, and get a good warm.'

'Neither warm nor cold is of any consequence to me,'
said Kirsteen, 'if folk would just leave me alone.'

'What's the maitter with my bonny doo? Many a time
you've come to Marg'ret with your trouble and we've
found a way out of it.'

'I see no way out of it,' said Kirsteen. She had reached
that point of young despair when comfort or consolation is
an additional aggravation of the evil. She preferred to be
told that everything was over, and that there was no hope.

'Ye may tell me a' the same,' said Marg'ret, putting her
arm round her nursling, and drawing her close. 'It's about
auld Glendochart, that's plain for all the world to see.'

'You call him auld Glendochart,' cried Kirsteen.

'Weel, and what would I call him? He's auld compared
to the like of you. He's no blate to come here with his grey
pow and choose the best of the flock. But dinna break your
heart for that, Kirsteen. Ye must say to him that ye canna
have him. He will take a telling. A man of that age he kens
most things in this world. He will just mount his horse
again, and ride away.'

'It's easy speaking,' cried Kirsteen, 'but it's me that dare
not say a word. For my father is just red-weed, and will

have it, Marg'ret. And my mother, she wants it too. And all of them they are upon me because I cannot consent: for oh, I cannot consent! – whatever folk may think or say, it's just this, that I cannot do it. I would sooner die.'

'There is nobody that will force you,' said Marg'ret. 'Dinna lose heart, my bonny bairn. The laird himself is very fierce sometimes, but his bark is worse than his bite. Na, na, ye must just keep up your heart. Glendochart will soon see, he will let nobody force ye. Things like that never come to pass noo. They're just a relic of the auld times. Maybe the auld Douglases that we hear so much about, that had the rights of fire and sword, and dark towers and dungeons to shut ye up in, might have done it. But where would he shut ye up here? There's no a lock to any room door in this house!' Marg'ret's laugh had a cheerful sound in the air, it broke the spell. 'Your father may want to frighten you, and bring ye to his will – but he will do nae mair; and as for the mistress, she will reproach ye for a day and then it'll be a' done.'

Kirsteen was obliged to confess that there was something in this. Her mother had been in despair for twenty-four hours, and 'just her ordinary' the day after on many previous occasions. It might all 'blow over' as Marg'ret said, especially if Glendochart should see with his own eyes how little disposed was the bride whom the family were so anxious to put into his arms. No doubt his feelings would be hurt, which was a thing Kirsteen did not like to think of. But somebody must suffer it was clear, and if so, perhaps it was better that it should be Glendochart who was an old man, and no doubt used to it, and who was also a rich man, and could go away and divert himself as Marg'ret suggested.

Marg'ret was of opinion that though it might hurt his feelings it was not likely at his age that it would break his heart. For hearts are more fragile at twenty than at sixty – at least in that way.

CHAPTER XV

Marg'ret had said with truth that the troubles of her young favourite had often been smoothed away after a consultation with herself. The best of us have our weak points, and the excellent Marg'ret was perhaps a little vain of the faculty of 'seeing a way out of it', which she believed herself to possess. She had seen a way out of it in many family tribulations which had a way of appearing less desperate when she took them in hand. And her last grand success in respect to the ball at the Castle had no doubt added to her confidence in herself. But after having turned it over in her mind for the best part of the night Marg'ret found that even her courage did not sustain her when she thought of confronting Drumcarro and requiring of him that he should give up the marriage on which he had evidently set his heart. Marg'ret was conscious that she was herself partly to blame: had she not set before him in the famous argument about the ball the fact that in no other way was there any likelihood of finding 'a man' for either of his daughters? Alas, the man had been but too easy to find, and how was she to confront him now and bid him let go his prize? Marg'ret's heart sank, though it was not given to sinking. She lay awake half the night turning it over and over in her mind, first representing to herself under every light the possible argument with Drumcarro and what he would say, and what she would say. She heard herself remonstrating, 'Sir, ye canna force your ain bairn, to make her meeserable,' and the response, 'What the deevil have you to do with it, if I make her meeserable or no?' She had been *dans son droit* when she had interfered about the muslin gowns and the ball, and the necessity of letting the young ladies be seen in the world – but who was she to meddle with a marriage when everybody was pleased but just the poor lassie herself? A poor lassie will change her mind as Marg'ret knew, and will sometimes be very thankful to those who opposed her foolish youth, and made her do what turned out to be so good for her. There was nothing so little to be calculated upon, as the sentiments of a girl whose position would be unspeakably improved by marriage, and whose silly bits of feeling might change at any moment. It is true that Kirsteen was not silly but full of sense far beyond her years. But even she might change her mind, and who could doubt that Drumcarro's daughter would be far better off as Glendochart's wife?

All this 'dautoned' Marg'ret as she would herself have said. She began even to glide away from her conviction that the master must be wrong. This is a fine working sentiment, and helps to surmount many difficulties, but when a reasonable soul is smitten by hesitation and feels that it is possible for even a habitual wrongdoer to be for once in the right, it takes the strength out of all effort. Finding herself less and less likely to be able with any comfort to object, Marg'ret began instinctively to turn to the other side of the question; and she found there was a great deal to be said on that other side. Glendochart was old – but after all he was not so dreadfully old, not in the stage of extreme age, as Kirsteen supposed. He was a 'personable man'. He would give his young wife everything that heart of woman (in Argyllshire) could desire. She would have a carriage to drive about in and a saddle-horse to ride. She would get a spinet, or a harpsichord, or the new-fangled thing that was called a piany to play upon if she pleased; and as many books as she could set her face to; and maybe a sight of London and the King's court, 'decent man! if he were but weel again,' said Marg'ret to herself, for the name of the Prince Regent was not in good odour. All this would be Kirsteen's if she could but just get over that feeling about the old man. And after all, Marg'ret went on, reasoning herself into a more and more perfect adoption of the only practicable side, he was not such an old man. Two or three years younger than Drumcarro – and Drumcarro had life enough in him, just a very born devil as fierce as ever he was. They would be bold that would call the laird an old man, and Glendochart was three at least, maybe five years younger. Not an old man at all – just a little over his prime; and a well-made personable man, doing everything that the youngest did, riding every day and out stalking on the hills in the season, and hurling, as Kirsteen herself had allowed, with the best. When everything was done and said what should hinder her to take Glendochart? He was a far finer gentleman than anybody that Kirsteen was likely to meet with. He was a good man, everybody said. He was what you might call a near kinsman of the Duke's, not more than four or five times removed. She would be in the best of company at Glendochart, invited out to dinner, and to all the diversions that were going. What could a lassie want more? Marg'ret woke in the morning in a great hurry, having overslept herself after a wakeful night, with the same conviction in her mind which was so strongly impressed upon all the others. It was just for everybody's advantage that Kirsteen should marry Glendochart, and for her own most of all.

Kirsteen herself had been much calmed and invigorated by her consultation with Marg'ret. That authority had made so little of the obstacles and the dangers, as if it would be the easiest thing in the world to shake off Glendochart, and convince Drumcarro that nothing could be done. For the moment Kirsteen's heart rose. She was accustomed to put great trust in Marg'ret, to see her cheerful assurances more or less justified. Many a storm had blown over which had filled the girl with terror, but which Marg'ret had undertaken should come to nothing. And if that was what Marg'ret thought now, all might be well. That day Kirsteen bore herself with great courage, getting back her colour, and singing about the house as was her wont, though it was only by a great effort that she dismissed the foreboding from her heart. And this brave front she kept up heroically during the greater part of the week of Glendochart's absence, finding her best help in silence and a determined avoidance of the subject – but the courage oozed out at her fingertips as the days stole away. They seemed to go like conspirators one by one bringing her near the dreadful moment which she could not avoid. It had been on Thursday that her father had spoken to her, and now the week had gone all but a day. Kirsteen had just realized this with a sick fluttering at her heart, as she stood at the door watching the ruddy colours of the sunset die out of the heavens. Something of the feeling of the condemned who watches his last sun setting had come into her mind in spite of herself: what might have happened to her before tomorrow? Would her father's curse be on her, or the still heavier malison of a creature mansworn, false to her dearest vow?

While she was thus musing, all her fictitious courage forsaking her, she felt herself suddenly and roughly caught by the arm from behind. 'Well,' said her father, 'are ye thinking what'll ye say to your joe? He's to be here tomorrow to his dinner, and he'll expect to find it all settled. Have ye fixed with your mother about the day?'

'Father,' cried Kirsteen in a wild sudden panic, 'you know what I said to ye. There's no day to be settled. I will tell him I cannot do it. I cannot do it. There's no question about a day.'

He swung her round with that iron grasp upon her arm so that she faced him. His fierce eyes blazed upon her with a red light from under his heavy eyelids. 'Dare to say a word but what I tell ye, and I'll dash ye – in pieces like a potter's vessel!' cried Drumcarro, taking the first similitude that occurred to him. He shook her as he spoke, her frame, though it was well-knit and vigorous, quivering in his grasp. 'Just say a word more of your damned nonsense and I'll lay ye at my feet!'

Kirsteen's heart fluttered to her throat with a sickening terror; but she looked him in the face with what steadiness she could command, and a dumb resolution. The threat gave her back a sense of something unconquerable in her, although every limb shook.

'Ye'll see Glendochart when he comes – in my presence – ye'll have the day fixed and all put in order. Or if ye want to appear like a woman and not a petted bairn before your man that is to be, you'll settle it yourself. I give you full liberty if you'll behave yourself. But hearken,' he said, giving her another shake, 'I'll have no confounded nonsense. If ye go against me in a strange man's presence and expose the family, I will just strike ye down at my feet, let what will come of it. Do you hear what I say?'

'He will not let you strike me,' she cried in terror, yet defiance.

'Ye'll be at my feet before he has the chance,' cried Drumcarro. 'And whose will be the wyte if your father, the last of the Douglases, should be dragged to a jail for you? If ye expose my family to scorn and shame, I'll do it more. Do you hear me? Now go and settle it with your mother,' he said, suddenly letting her go. Kirsteen, thrown backward by the unexpected liberation, fell back with a dizzying shock against the lintel of the door. She lay against it for a moment sick and giddy, the light fading from her eyes; and for a minute or two Kirsteen thought she was going to die. It is a conviction that comes easily at such a crisis. It seemed to the girl so much the best way out of it, just to be done with it all.

'The only art her guilt to cover,
To hide her shame from every eye,
To bring repentance to her lover,
And wring his bosom –'

Poor Kirsteen had no guilt, nor had she any clear apprehension what this meant, or what guilt it was – it might have been only the guilt of disobedience, the shame of exposing the family for anything she knew; but the words flashed through her mind in her half-faint, lying speechless against the door. It would bring repentance to them all and wring their bosoms – it would save the shame of a disturbance and the dreadful sight of a struggle between father and daughter. The only art – just to die.

He had said, 'Go to your mother.' This came vaguely back to her mind as she came to herself. Her mother – no, her mother would say just the same, they would all say the same. She had no one to go to. Then Kirsteen's gradually quickening senses heard something which sounded like an approaching footstep. She roused herself in a moment, and still sick and faint, with a singing in her ears, turned and fled – not to her mother, to Marg'ret in the kitchen, who was her only hope.

The kitchen was, as Marg'ret had said, 'like a new pin' at that hour, all clear and bright, the fire made up, the hearth swept, the traces of dinner all cleared away. It was the moment when Marg'ret could sit down to needlework or spell out some old, old newspaper which even the minister had done with; her assistant Merran was out in the byre looking after the kye, and Marg'ret was alone. When Kirsteen rushed in unsteadily and threw herself down in the big wooden chair by the fireside, Marg'ret was threading a needle which was a work of patience. But this sudden invasion distracted her completely and made her lay down both thread and needle with a sigh.

'My bonny woman! what is the matter now?'

'Marg'ret, I nearly fainted standing against the door.'

'Fainted! bless the bairn! na, na, no so bad as that! Your head's cool and so is your hand. What was it, Kirsteen?'

'Or nearly died would be more like it, and that would maybe have been the best.' And then with moist eyes fixed upon her anxious companion and a tremulous smile about her mouth, Kirsteen repeated her verse—

> ' "The only art her guilt to cover,
> To hide her shame from every eye,
> To bring repentance to her lover,
> And wring his bosom – is to die." '

'Kirsteen! what is that you are saying?' cried Marg'ret, a sudden flush showing even upon her ruddy colour. 'Guilt and shame! What have those dreadfu' things to do with you?'

'I am disobeying both father and mother,' said the girl solemnly, 'isna that guilt? And oh, it's shaming all belonging to me to stand against them; but I canna help it, I canna help it. Oh, Marg'ret, hide me from him, find me a place to go to! What will I do! What will I do!'

'My dear, my dear,' said Marg'ret, 'you make my heart sair. What can I say to you? I have ever taken your pairt as you ken weel – but oh, my bonny woman, I canna but think you're a little unreasonable. What ails you at Glendochart? He's a good man and an honourable man, and it would please everybody. To think so much of his age when there's no other objection is not like you that had always such sense. And ye would be far happier, Kirsteen, in a house of your own. Because there's white on his head is that a cause to turn your heart from a good man?'

Kirsteen said nothing for a moment: she looked with wistful eyes and a faint smile in Marg'ret's face, shaking her head; then suddenly rising up went away out of the kitchen, hurrying as much as her limbs, still feeble with the late shock and struggle, would let her. Marg'ret stood aghast while her hurried irregular step was audible going upstairs.

'Now I have just angered her,' said Marg'ret to herself, 'and cast back her bit heart upon herself, and made her feel she has no true friend. Will I go after her – or will I wait till she comes back?'

This question was settled for her as she stood listening

and uncertain, by the sound of Kirsteen's return. Marg'ret
listened eagerly while she came downstairs again step by
step. She came into the kitchen with the same vague deprecating smile upon her face. She had a little Testament in
its blue boards in her hand. She said nothing, but opening
it held out to her faithful adviser the flyleaf upon which
there stood the initials together of R. D. and C. D., connected with the feeble pencilling of the runic knot. Kirsteen
said not a word, but held it out open, pointing to this
simple symbol with her other hand. 'R. D.,' said Marg'ret,
'wha' is that? C. D., that will just stand for yourself. It's not
one of Robbie's books – it's – it's – Oh!' she cried with
sudden enlightenment, 'now I understand!'

Kirsteen put the little page solemnly to her trembling lips,
a tear almost dropped upon it, but she shut the book
quickly that no stain should come upon it, even of a tear.
She did not say a word during this little tender revelation of
her heart, but turned her eyes and her faint propitiatory
smile to Marg'ret as if there was no more to be said.

'And this has been in your heart all the time!' cried
Marg'ret, drying her eyes with her apron. 'I thought of that,
twa-three times. There was something in his look yon day
he gaed away, but I never said a word, for who can tell?
And this was in your heart a' the time?'

'He said, "Will ye wait till I come back?" and I said,
"That I will!"' 'said Kirsteen, but very softly, the sweetness
of the recollection coming back to soothe her in the midst
of all the pain.

'And that's how they've tied their lives, thae young
things!' said Marg'ret also with a kind of solemnity. 'A
word spoken that is done in a moment, and after that – a'
thae long and weary years – and maybe for all they ken
never to see ilk ither again.'

'And if it should be so,' said Kirsteen, 'it would just be
for death instead of life, and all the same.'

'Oh, weel I ken that,' said Marg'ret shaking her head.
She made a pause, and then she added hurriedly, 'What's
to be done with you, lassie? If Glendochart's coming the
morn to mairry ye there's no time to be lost.'

'Marg'ret, I will just go away.'

'Where will ye go to? It's easy speaking: a creature like
you cannot travel the countryside like a servant lass going

to a new place. And ye've nae friends that will take such a charge. Miss Eelen would be frightened out of her wits. I know nobody that will help you but Glendochart himself – and you couldna go to him.'

'What is that letter on the table, Marg'ret, and who is it from?'

'The letter? What's in the letter? Can ye think of that at sic a moment? It's a letter from my sister Jean.'

'Marg'ret, that's just where I am going! I see it all in a flash like lightning. I am going to London to your sister Jean.'

'The bairn is clean out of her senses!' cried Marg'ret almost with a scream.

And then they stood and looked at each other for a long rapid minute, interchanging volumes in the silent meeting of their eyes. Kirsteen had sprung in a moment from the agitated creature who had come to Marg'ret to be hidden, to be sheltered, not knowing what could be done with her, to the quick-witted, high-spirited girl she was by nature, alive with purpose and strong intuition, fearing nothing. And Marg'ret read all this new world of meaning in the girl's eyes more surely than words could have told her. She saw the sudden flash of the resolution, the clearing away of all clouds, the rise of the natural courage, the Kirsteen of old whom nothing could 'dauton' coming back. 'Oh, my lamb!' she breathed under her breath.

'There's not a moment to be lost,' said Kirsteen, 'for I must go in the morning before anybody is up. And ye must not tell a living creature but keep my secret, Marg'ret. For go I must, there is no other thing to do. And maybe I will never come back. My father will never forgive me. I will be like Anne cut off from the family. But go I must, for no more can I bide here. Give me the letter from your sister to let her see it's me when I get there. And give me your blessing, Marg'ret – it's all the blessing I will get. And let me go!'

'Not tonight, Kirsteen!'

'No, not tonight; but early – early in the morning before daylight. Dinna say a word – not a word. It's all clear before me. I'll be at nobody's charges, I'll fend for myself; and your sister Jean will show me the way.'

There was another silence during which Kirsteen, quite

regardless of the rights of propriety which existed no more between Marg'ret and herself than between mother and daughter, took possession of Miss Jean Brown's letter, while Marg'ret stood reflecting, entirely alarmed by the revelation made to her, and by the sudden rebirth of the vehement young creature who had been for a time so sub-dued and broken down by her first contest with the world. To keep Kirsteen back was, in the circumstances and with the strong convictions of the Scotch serving woman as to the force of a troth-plight and the binding character of a vow, impossible. But to let her go thus unfriended, unaided, alone into an unknown world, far more unknown to Marg'ret than the ends of the earth would be to her repre-sentative now, was something more than could be borne. She suddenly exclaimed in a sharp tone with a cruel hope: 'And where are ye to get the siller? It's mad and mad enough anyway, but madder still without a penny in your pocket. How are ye to get to London without money? It's just impossible.'

'I can walk, others have done it before me. I'm well and strong and a grand walker,' said Kirsteen, but not till after a pause of consternation, this consideration not having crossed her mind before.

'Walk! it's just hundreds of miles, and takes a week in the coach,' cried Marg'ret. 'Ye cannot walk, no to say ye would want money even then, for I'm no supposing that you mean to beg your bread from door to door. Without money ye canna go a step. I'll not permit it. Have ye any-thing of your ain?'

'I have the gold guinea my grandmother left me in her will; but I have no more. How should I have any more?'

Marg'ret stood for a moment undecided, while Kirsteen waited a little eager, a little expectant like a child. It did not occur to her to deprecate help from Marg'ret as a more high-minded heroine might have done. Marg'ret was a little Providence at Drumcarro. She had store of everything that the children wanted, and had been their resource all their lives. And Kirsteen had not realized the difference between money and other indispensable things. She waited like a child, following Marg'ret with her eyes until some expedi-ent should be thought of. She breathed a sigh of suspense yet expectation when Marg'ret hurried away to her bedroom at the back of the house, seating herself again in the big chair to wait, not impatiently, for the solution of the problem. Marg'ret came back after a few minutes with a work-box in her hand. All kinds of things had come out of that box in the experience of the children at Drumcarro, things good and evil, little packets of powders for childish maladies, sweeties to be taken after the nauseous mouthful, needles and thimbles and scissors when these needful implements had all been lost, as happened periodically, even a ribbon or a pair of gloves in times of direst need. She began to turn over the well-remembered contents – old buttons, hooks and eyes from old gowns long departed, Marg'ret's two brooches that formed all her jewellery, wrapped up in separate pieces of paper. 'My sister Jean,' said Marg'ret with her head bent over the box, 'has often bidden me to come and see her in London town. You ken why I couldna go. I couldna thole to leave you that are leavin' me without a tear. And she sent me what would do for my chairges. It was never touched by me. It took me a great deal of trouble to get Scotch notes for it, and here it is at the bottom of my box with many an auld relic on the top of it – just a' I'll have of ye when ye've got your will,' said Marg'ret, a tear dropping among the miscellaneous articles in the box. She took from the bottom a little parcel in an old letter, folded square and written closely to the very edge of the seal. 'Hae! take it! and ye maun just do with it what pleasures yoursel',' Marg'ret cried.

CHAPTER XVI

The 12th of January was a still grey winter day, not very cold and exceedingly calm, the winds all hushed, the clouds hanging low, with a possibility – of rain a possibility which is never remote in a Highland landscape. As the slow daylight began to bring the hills into sight, not with any joyous sunrising but with a faint diffusion of grey upon the dark, a gradual growing visible of the greater points, then very slowly of the details of the landscape, there came also into sight, first ghostlike, a moving, noiseless shadow, then something which consolidated into the slim figure of a woman, a solitary traveller moving steadily along the dewy mountain road. It came in sight like the hills, not like an interruption to the landscape but a portion of it, becoming visible along with it, having been in the dark as well as in the light. Before the day was fully awake it was there, a gliding shadow going straight up the hills and over the moors, at the same measured pace, not so much quick as steady, with a wonderful still intensity of progress. The road was more than dewy, it was glistening wet with the heavy damps of the night, every crevice among the rocks green and sodden, every stone glistening. The traveller did not keep exactly to the road, was not afraid of the wet hillside turf, nor even of a grey dyke to climb if it shortened the way. She passed lightly over bits of moss among the rustling, faded heather, and spots of suspicious greenness which meant bog, choosing her footing on the black roots of the wild myrtle, and the knolls of blackberries, like one to the manner born. She gave a soul to the wild and green landscape, so lonely, so washed with morning dews. She was going – where? From the impossible to the possible – from the solitudes of the hills into the world.

Kirsteen had been walking for hours before she thus came into sight, and the dark and the silence had filled her with many a flutter of terror. It took something from what might have been in other circumstances the overwhelming excitement of thus leaving home to encounter that other bewildering and awful sensation of going out into the night, with everyone asleep and all wrapped in the profound blackness of winter, through which it was hard enough even for the most familiar to find a way. This horror and alarm had so occupied her mind, and the sensation of being the one creature moving and conscious in that world of dark-ness that she had scarcely realized the severance she was making, the tearing asunder of her life. Even Marg'ret, repressing her emotion lest a sob should catch some wake-ful ear in the sleeping house, had faded from Kirsteen's mind when she took the first step into the dark. She knew there were no wild beasts who could devour her, no rob-bers who would seize her, as she had fancied when a child: she had a trembling sense that God would protect her from ghosts and spiritual evils; but her young soul trembled with fears both physical and spiritual, just as much as when she had wandered out in the dark at six years old. Reason con-vinces but does not always support the inexperienced spirit. When the ever wakeful dogs at the little clachan heard the faint footfall upon the edge of the path and barked, Kirsteen was half consoled and half maddened with terror. If someone should wake and wonder, and suspect a mid-night thief, and burst open a door and find her; but on the other hand it was a little comfort to feel that even a dog was waking in that black expanse of night.

She had already come a long way, before the daylight, when she and the landscape that enclosed her came dimly, faintly into sight in the first grey of the morning. Her eyes had got accustomed to the darkness, her heart a little calmed and sustained by the fact that nothing had happened to her yet, no hidden malefactor in the dark, nor sheeted whiteness from the churchyard interrupting her on her way. Her heart had beat while she passed, loud enough to have wakened the whole clachan, but nothing had stirred, save the dogs – and safe as in the warmest daylight she had got by the graves. Nothing could be so bad as that again. Partly by familiar knowledge and partly by the conscious-ness of certain gradations in the darkness as she became used to it, she had got forward on her way until she had reached the head of the loch where the water was a guide to her. Kirsteen had resolved that she would not venture to approach the town or cross the loch in the boat, the usual

way, but taking a large sweep round the end of the loch,
strike at once into the wilds which lay between her and the
comparatively higher civilization of the regions within reach
of Glasgow. If she could but reach that great city, which
was only second in her dim conceptions to London itself,
she would feel that she was safe, but not before. She came
round the head of the loch in the beginnings of the dawn
and had pushed her way far into the gloomy mystery of
Hell's Glen, with its bare hills rising to the dim sky on
either side, before the height of noon. It is gloomy there
even when the height of noon means the dazzling of a Highland summer day. But when the best of the daylight is a dull
grey, the long lines of the glen unbroken by anything but a
shepherd's hut here and there at long intervals, and the
road that could be seen winding through like a strip of
ribbon all the way gave the fugitive a mingled sense of
serenity and of that tingling, audible solitude and remote-
ness from all living aid or society which thrills every nerve.
When she was halfway through the glen, however, the thrill
was subdued by that experience of no harm as yet which is
the most perfect of support, and Kirsteen began to be conscious that she had eaten nothing and scarcely rested since
she set out. She had swallowed a mouthful as she walked –
she had thrown herself down for a moment on the hillside
– but now it seemed possible to venture upon a little real
rest.

Kirsteen was dressed in a dark woollen gown of home-
spun stuff, made like all the dresses of the time, with a
straight, long, narrow skirt, and a short bodice cut low
round her shoulders. Over this she had a warm spencer,
another bodice with long sleeves, rising to her throat, where
it was finished with a frill. She had strong country shoes
and woollen stockings just visible under her skirt. Her
bonnet was a little of the coal-scuttle shape but not very
large; and flung back over it, but so that she could put it
down over her face at a moment's notice, was a large black
veil, such an imitation of Spanish lace as was practicable at
the time, better in workmanship, worse in material than
anything we have now. The large pattern with its gigantic
flowers in thick work hid the face better than any lighter
fabric, and it hung over the bonnet when thrown back like
a cloud. She had a bundle on one arm, done up carefully in

a handkerchief containing two changes of linen, and another gown, carefully folded by Marg'ret into the smallest possible space; and on the other a camlet cloak, dark blue, with a fur collar and metal clasps, which was Marg'ret's own. This was sore lading for a long walk, but it was indispensable in face of the January winds, and the cold on the coach, of which Marg'ret knew dreadful things. To Kirsteen it seemed that if she could but reach that coach, and pursue her journey by the aid of other legs than her own, and with company, all her troubles would be over. She sat upon the hillside anxiously watching the path lest any suspicious figure should appear upon it, and took out from her wallet the last scones of Marg'ret's she was likely to eat for a long time. Should she ever eat Marg'ret's scones again? Salt tears came to Kirsteen's eyes and moistened her comely face. It was done now – the dreadful step taken, never to be altered, the parting made. Her life and her home lay far behind her, away beyond the hills that shut her in on every side. She said to herself with trembling lips that the worst was over; by this time everyone in Drumcarro would know that she was gone. They would have looked for her in every corner, up on the hill and down by the linn where the water poured into the vexed and foaming gulf. Would it come into anybody's head that she had thrown herself in and made an end of everything?

> The only art her guilt to cover.

Would they send and tell Glendochart, poor old gentleman – would they warn him not to come to a distressed house? Or would he be allowed to come and her father say to him: 'She is not worthy of a thought. She is no bairn of mine from this day'? 'And my mother will go to her bed,' said Kirsteen to herself with a tear or two, yet with the faint gleam of a smile. She could see them all in their different ways – her father raging, her mother weeping, and Mary telling everybody that she was not surprised. And Marg'ret – Marg'ret would put on a steady countenance so that nobody could tell what she knew and what she didn't know. It almost amused Kirsteen though it made her breath come quick, and brought the tears to her eyes, to sit thus in the deep solitude with the silence of the hills all thrilling round, and look down as it were upon that other scene, a

strangely interested spectator, seeing everything, and her
own absence which was the strangest of all.

But perhaps she sat too long and thought too much, or
the damp of the sod had cramped her young limbs, or the
tremendous walk of the morning told more after an interval
of rest, for when she roused herself at last and got up again,
Kirsteen felt a universal ache through her frame, and
stumbled as she came down from her perch to the road
below. How was she to get through Glencroe to Arrochar –
another long and weary course? The solitude of the glen
came upon her again with a thrill of horror. If she could
not walk any better than this it would be dark, dark night
again before she came to the end of her journey – would
she ever come to the end of her journey? Would she drop
down upon the hill and lie there till someone found her? A
wave of discouragement and misery came over her. There
was a house within sight, one of those hovels in which still
the Highland shepherd or crofter is content to live. Kirsteen
knew such interiors well – the clay floor, the black,
smoke-darkened walls, the throng of children round the
fire: there was no room to take in a stranger, no way of
getting help for her to push on with her journey. All the
pictures of imagination fled from her, scant and troubled
though they had been. Everything in the world seemed wept
out except the sensation of this wild solitude, the aching
of her tired limbs, the impossibility of getting on, her own
dreadful loneliness and helplessness in this wild, silent,
unresponsive world.

Kirsteen could scarcely tell how she dragged herself to
the entrance of the glen. A little solitary mountain farm or
gillie's house stood at some distance from the road,
approached by a muddy cart-track. The road was bad
enough, not much more than a track, for there were as yet
no tourists (nay, no magician to send them thither) in those
days. A rough cart came lumbering down this path as she
crept her way along, and soon made up to her. Kirsteen had
made up her mind to ask for a 'cast' or 'lift' to help her
along, but her courage failed her when the moment came,
and she allowed the rude vehicle to lumber past with a heart
that ached as much as her limbs to see this chance of ease
slip by. She endeavoured as much as she could to keep
within a certain distance of the cart 'for company', to cheat

the overwhelming loneliness which had come over her. And perhaps the carter, who was an elderly rustic with grizzled hair, perceived her meaning, perhaps he saw the longing look in her eyes. After he had gone on a little way he turned and came slowly back. 'Maybe you're ower genteel for the like of that,' he said, 'but I would sooner ye thought me impident than leave you your lane on this rough long road. Would you like a lift in the cart? There's clean straw in it, and you're looking weariet.'

Poor Kirsteen had nearly wept for pleasure. She seated herself upon the clean straw with a sense of comfort which no carriage could have surpassed. It was a mode of conveyance not unknown to her. The gig had seldom been vouchsafed to the use of the girls in Drumcarro. They had much more often been packed into the cart. She thanked the friendly carter with all her heart. 'For I am weariet,' she said, 'and the road's wet and heavy both for man and beast.'

'Ye'll have come a far way,' he said, evidently feeling that desire for information or amusement which unexpected company is wont to raise in the rustic heart.

Kirsteen answered that she had come from a little place not far from Loch Fyne, then trembled lest she had betrayed herself.

'It's very Hieland up there,' said the carter; 'that's the country of the Lord their God the Duke, as Robbie Burns calls him. We have him here too, but no so overpowering. Ye'll be a Campbell when you're at hame.'

'No, I am not a Campbell,' said Kirsteen. It occurred to her for the first time that she must give some account of herself. 'I'm going,' she said, 'to take up – a situation.'

'I just thought that. 'Twill be some pingling trade like showing or hearing weans their letters, keeping ye in the house and on a seat the haill day long.'

'Something of that kind,' Kirsteen said.

'And you're a country lass and used to the air of the hills. Take you care – oh, take care! I had one mysel' – as fine a lass as ye would see, with roses on her cheeks, and eyes just glancing bright like your ain; and as weel and as hearty as could be. But before a twelvemonth was o'er, her mother and me we had to bring her hame.'

'Oh,' cried Kirsteen, 'I am very sorry – but she's maybe better.'

'Ay, she's better,' said the carter. 'Weel – wi' her Faither which is in heaven.'

'Oh, I'm sorry, sorry!' cried Kirsteen with tears in her eyes.

'Thank ye for that: ye have a look of her: I couldna pass ye by: but eh, for Gudesake if ye have faither and mother to break their hearts for you, take care.'

'You must have liked her well, well!' said the girl. Fatigue and languor in herself added to the keen sense of sympathy and pity. 'I wish it had been me instead of her,' she said hastily.

'Eh,' said the man, 'that's a sair thing to say! Ye must be an orphan with none to set their hearts on you – but you're young, poor thing, and there's nae telling what good may come to ye. Ye must not let down your heart.'

The cart rumbled on with many a jolt, the carter jogged by the side and talked, the sound and motion were both drowsy, and Kirsteen was extremely tired. By and by these sounds and sensations melted into a haze of almost beatitude, the drowsiness that comes over tired limbs and spirit when comparative ease succeeds to toil. After a while she lost consciousness altogether and slept nestled in the straw, like a tired child. She was awakened by the stoppage of the cart, and opening her eyes to the grey yet soft heavens above and the wonder of waking in the open air, found herself at the end of a road which led up to a farmstead at the mouth of Glencroe where the valley opens out upon the shore of that long inlet of the sea which is called Loch Long.

'I'm wae to disturb ye, but I must take the cairt back to the town, and my ain house is two miles down the loch. But there's a real dacent woman at the inn at Arrochar.'

'It's there I was going,' said Kirsteen, hurriedly sliding from her place. She had been covered with her camlet cloak as she lay, and the straw had kept her warm. 'I'm much obliged to you,' she said – 'will ye take a – will ye let me give you—'

'No a farden, no a farden,' cried the man. 'I would convoy ye to Mrs Macfarlane's door, but I have to supper my horse. Will ye gie me a shake of your hand? You're a bonny lass and I hope ye'll be a guid ane – but mind there's awfu' temptations in thae towns.'

Kirsteen walked away very stiff but refreshed, half angry, half amused by this last caution. She said to herself with a blush that he could not have known who she was – a lady! or he would not have given her that warning which was not applicable to the like of her. They said poor lassies in service, out among strangers, stood in need of it, poor things. It was not a warning that had any meaning to a gentlewoman; but how was the man to know?

She went on still in a strange confusion of weariness and the haze of awakening to where the little town of Arrochar lay low by the banks of the loch. It was dark there sooner than in other places, and already a light or two began to twinkle in the windows. Two or three men were lingering outside the inn when Kirsteen reached the place, and daunted – her she who was never daunted. She went quickly past, as quickly as her fatigue would admit, as if she knew where she was going. She thought to herself that if anyone remarked it would be thought she was going home to her friends, going to some warm and cheerful kent place – and she a waif and outcast on the world! When she had passed, she loitered and looked back, finding a dim corner where nobody could see her, behind the little hedge of a cottage garden. Presently a woman in a widow's cap came briskly out to the door of the little inn, addressing a lively word or two to the loitering men which made them move and disperse; and now was Kirsteen's time. She hurried back and timidly approached the woman at the inn door as if she had been a princess. 'Ye'll maybe be Mistress Macfarlane?' said Kirsteen.

'I'm just that; and what may ye be wanting? Oh, I see you're a traveller,' said the brisk landlady; 'you'll be wanting lodging for the night.'

'If you have a room ye can give me – with a bed – I've had a long walk – from near Loch Fyne,' said Kirsteen, feeling that explanation was necessary, and looking wistfully in the face of the woman on whom her very life seemed to depend. For what if she should refuse her, a young girl all alone, and turn her away from the door?

Mrs Macfarlane was too good a physiognomist for that – but she looked at Kirsteen curiously in the waning light. 'That's a far way to come on your feet,' she said, 'and you're a young lass to be wandering the country by yourself.'

'I'm going – to take up a situation,' said Kirsteen. 'If ye should have a room—'

'Oh, it's no for want of a room. Come in, there's plenty of room. So ye're going to take up a situation? Your minnie must have been sair at heart to let you gang afoot such a weary way.'

'There was no other – convenience,' said Kirsteen, sick and faint. She had to make an effort not to cry. She had not thought of this ordeal, and her limbs would scarcely sustain her.

'Come in,' said the woman. 'Would you rather go to your bed, or sit down by the fire with me? Lord bless us, the poor thing's just fainting, Eelen. Take her into the parlour, and put her in the big chair by the fire.'

'I'm not fainting – I'm only so tired I cannot speak,' said Kirsteen, with a faint smile.

'Go ben, go ben,' said Mrs Macfarlane, 'and I'll make the tea, and ye shall have a cup warm and strong. There's naething will do you so much good.'

And to lie back in the big chair by the warm fire seemed like paradise to Kirsteen. This was her fortunate lot on her first night from home.

CHAPTER XVII

She had, however, much questioning to go through. There was but little custom to occupy the woman of the inn, and the mingled instincts of kindness and gossip and that curiosity which is so strong among those who have little to learn save what they can persuade their neighbours to tell them, had much dominion over Mrs Macfarlane. Kindness perhaps was the strongest quality of all. Her tea was hot and strong and what she considered well 'masket' before the fire; and when the Highland maid, who could speak little English, but hung about in silent admiration of the unexpected visitor, who was a new incident in the glen, had 'boilt' some eggs, and placed a plate of crisp cakes – the oatcakes which were the habitual bread of Scotland at that period – and another of brown barley scones, upon the table, the mistress herself sat down to encourage her guest to eat.

'There's some fine salt herrings if ye would like that better, or I could soon fry ye a bit of ham. We've baith pork hams and mutton hams in the house. But a fresh boilt egg is just as good as anything, and mair nat'ral to a woman. Ye'll be gaun to Glasco where everybody goes.'

'Yes,' said Kirsteen, with a doubt in her heart whether it was honest not to add that she was going further on.

'I wonder what they can see in't – a muckle dirty place, with long lums pouring out smoke. I wouldna gie Arrochar for twenty o't.'

'I suppose,' said Kirsteen, 'it's because there is aye plenty doing there.'

'I suppose sae. And ye're going to take up a situation? It's no a place I would choose for a young lass, but nae doubt your mother kens what she's doing. Is it a lady's maid place, or to be with bairns, or— I'm sure I beg your pardon! You'll be a governess, I might have seen.'

Kirsteen had grown very red at the thought of being taken for a lady's maid, but she said to herself quickly that her pride was misplaced, and that it was the best service

anyone could do her to think her so. 'Oh, no,' she said,
'I'm not clever enough to be a governess. I'm going – to a
mantua-maker's.'

'Weel, weel – that's a very genteel trade, and many a puir
leddy thankful to get into it,' said Mrs Macfarlane. 'I'm
doubting you're one yoursel', or else ye have lived with
better kind of folk, for ye've real genty ways, and a bonny
manner. Take heed to yourself in Glasco, and take up with
none of thae young sprigs in offices that think themselves
gentlemen. Will ye no take another cup? Weel, and I
wouldna wonder ye would be better in your bed than any
other place. And how are ye going on in the morning?
There's a coach from Eelensburgh, but it's a long walk to
get there. If ye like Donald will get out the gig and drive
you. It would be a matter of twelve or maybe fifteen shil-
lings if he couldna get a job back – which is maist unlikely
at this time of the year.'

With many thanks for the offer Kirsteen tremblingly
explained that she could not afford it. 'For I will want all
my money when I get to Glasgow,' she said.

'Weel,' said Mrs Macfarlane, 'ye ken your ain affairs best.
But there's sturdy beggars on the road, and maybe ye'll
wish ye had ta'en my offer before you win there.'

Kirsteen thought she never would sleep for the aching of
her limbs when she first laid herself down in the hard bed
which was all the little Highland inn, or even the best
houses in Scotland afforded in that period. Her mind was
silenced by this strange physical inconvenience, so that she
was quiescent in spirit and conscious of little except her
pangs of fatigue. Youth, however, was stronger than all her
pangs, and the influence of the fresh mountain air, though
charged with damp, in which she had pursued her journey –
and she slept with the perfect abandon and absolute repose
of her twenty years, never waking from the time she laid
her head upon the pillow until she was awakened by Eelen,
the Highland maid, whom she opened her eyes to find
standing over her with the same admiring looks as on the
previous evening.

'Your hair will be like the red gold and your skin like
the white milk,' said Eelen; 'and it's chappit acht, and it's
time to be wakening.'

Kirsteen did not spring from her bed with her usual alertness, for she was stiff with her first day's travels. But she rose as quickly as was possible, and got downstairs to share the porridge of a weakly member of the family who was indulged in late hours, and had a little cream to tempt her to consume the robust food.

'I would have given ye some tea but for Jamie,' said Mrs Macfarlane, 'maybe he'll take his parritch when he sees you supping yours with sic a good heart.' Though she was thus used as an example Kirsteen took leave of the kind inn-keeper with a sense of desolation as if she were once more leaving home. ' 'Deed, I just wish ye could bide, and gie the bairns their lessons and please a' body with your pleasant face,' the landlady said. Kirsteen went on her way with a 'piece' in her pocket and many good wishes. It was a bright morning, and the sun, as soon as he had succeeded in rising over the shoulders of the great hills, shone upon Loch Long as upon a burnished mirror, and lit up the path which Kirsteen had to travel with a chequered radiance through the bare branches of the trees, which formed the most intri-cate network of shadow upon the brown path. The deep herbage and multitudinous roadside plants all wet and glis-tening, the twinkle of a hundred burns that crossed the road at every step, the sound of the oars upon the rowlocks of a fisher-boat upon the loch, the shadows that flew over the hills in swift, instantaneous succession added their charms to the spell of the morning, the freshest and most rapturous of all the aspects of nature. Before long Kirsteen forgot everything, both trouble of body and trouble of mind. The fascination of the morning brightness entered into her heart. In a sunny corner she found a bit of yellow blossom, of the wild St John's wort, that 'herb of grace' which secures to the traveller who is so happy as to find it unawares a prosperous day's journey, and in another the rare, delicate star of the Grass of Parnassus. These with a sprig of the 'gale', the sweet wild myrtle which covers those hills, made a little bouquet which she fastened in the belt of her spencer with simple pleasure. She hesitated a moment to wear the badge of the Campbells, and then with a fantastic half-amused sentiment reminded herself that if she had become the lady of Glendochart as she might have done (though ignorant folk took her for a governess or even a lady's waiting woman) she would have had a right to wear

it. Poor Glendochart! It would hurt his feelings to find that
she had flown away from her home to escape him. Kirsteen
was grieved beyond measure to hurt Glendochart's feelings.
She put the gale in her belt with a compunctious thought
of her old, kind wooer. But at that moment her young
spirit, notwithstanding all its burdens, was transported by
the morning and the true delight of the traveller, leaving all
that he has known behind him for love of the beautiful
and the new. It seemed to Kirsteen that she had never seen
the world so lovely nor the sun so warm and sweet before.

She had walked several miles in the delight of these novel
sensations and was far down Loch Long side, without a
house or sign of habitation nigh, when there suddenly rose
from among the bushes of brown withered heather on the
slope that skirted the road a man whose appearance did not
please Kirsteen. He had his coat-sleeve pinned to his breast
as if he had lost an arm, and a forest of wild beard and hair
enclosing his face. In these days when the wars of the Peninsula were barely over, and Waterloo approaching, nothing
was so likely to excite charitable feelings as the aspect of an
old soldier – and the villainous classes of the community
who existed then, as now, were not slow to take advantage
of it. This man came up to Kirsteen with a professional
whine. He gave her a list of battles at which he had been
wounded which her knowledge was not enough to see were
impossible, though her mind rejected them as too much.
But he was an old soldier (she believed) and that was
enough to move the easily flowing fountains of charity. No
principle on the subject had indeed been invented in those
days, and few people refused a handful of meal at the house
door, or a penny on the road to the beggar of any degree,
far less the soldier who had left the wars with an empty
sleeve or a shattered leg. Kirsteen stopped and took her
little purse from her pocket and gave him sixpence with a
look of sympathy. She thought of the boys all away to the
endless Indian wars, and of another besides who might be
fighting or losing his arm like this poor man. 'And I'm very
sorry for ye, and I hope ye will win safe home,' said
Kirsteen passing on. But different feelings came into her
mind when she found that she was being followed, and that
the man's prayer for 'anither saxpence' was being repeated
in a rougher and more imperative tone. Kirsteen had a great

deal of courage as a girl so often has, whose natural swift impulses have had no check of practical danger. She was not at first afraid. She faced round upon him with a rising colour and bade him be content: 'I have given ye all I can give ye,' she said, 'for I've a long, long journey before me and little siller.'

'Ye have money in your purse, my bonny lady, and no half so much to do with it as me.'

'If I've money in my purse it's my own money for my own lawful uses,' said Kirsteen.

'Come, come,' cried the man, 'I'll use nae violence unless ye force me. Gie me the siller.'

'I will not give ye a penny,' cried Kirsteen. And then there ensued a breathless moment. All the possibilities swept through her mind. If she took to flight he would probably overtake her, and in the meantime might seize her from behind when she could not see what he was doing. She had no staff or stick in her hand but was weighted with her bundle and her cloak. She thought of flinging the latter over his head and thus blinding and embarrassing him to gain a little time, but he was wary and on his guard. She gave a glance towards the boat on the loch, but it was in mid-water, and the bank was high and precipitous. Nowhere else was there a living creature in sight.

'Man,' said Kirsteen, 'I cannot fight with ye, but I'm not just a weak creature either, and what I have is all I have, and I've a long journey before me – I'll give ye your six-pence if you'll go.'

'I'll warrant ye will,' said the sturdy beggar, 'but I'm no so great a fuil as I look. Gie me the purse, and I'll let ye go.'

'I'll not give ye the purse. If ye'll say a sum and it's within my power I'll give ye that.'

'Bring out the bit pursie,' said the man, 'and we'll see, maybe with a kiss into the bargain,' and he drew nearer, with a leer in the eyes that gleamed from among his tangled hair.

'I will fling it into the loch sooner than ye should get it,' cried Kirsteen, whose blood was up – 'and hold off from me or I'll push you down the brae,' she cried, putting down her bundle, and with a long breath of nervous agitation pre-paring for the assault.

'You're a bold quean though ye look so mim – gie me a pound then and I'll let ye go.'

Kirsteen felt that to produce the purse at all was to lose it, and once more calculated all the issues. The man limped a little. She thought that if she plunged down the bank to the loch, steep as it was, her light weight and the habit she had of scrambling down to the linn might help her – and the sound of the falling stones and rustling branches might catch the ear of the fisher on the water, or she might make a spring up upon the hill behind and trust to the tangling roots of the heather to impede her pursuer. In either case she must give up the bundle and her cloak. Oh, if she had but taken Donald and the gig as Mrs Macfarlane had advised!

'I canna wait a' day till ye've made up your mind. If I have to use violence it's your ain wyte. I'm maist willing to be friendly,' he said with another leer pressing upon her. She could feel his breath upon her face. A wild panic seized Kirsteen. She made one spring up the hill before he could seize her. And in a moment her bounding heart all at once became tranquil and she stood still, her terror gone.

For within a few paces of her was a sportsman with his gun, a young man in dark undress tartan scarcely distinguishable from the green and brown of the hillside, walking slowly downwards among the heather bushes. Kirsteen raised her voice a little. She called to her assailant, 'Ye can go your way, for here's a gentleman!' with a ring of delight in her voice.

The man clambering after her (he did 'hirple' with the right foot, Kirsteen observed with pleasure) suddenly slipped down with an oath, for he too had seen the new-comer, and presently she heard his footsteps on the road hurrying away.

'What is the matter, my bonny lass?' said the sportsman; 'are ye having a quarrel with your joe? Where's the impudent fellow? I'll soon bring him to reason if you'll trust yourself to me.'

Kirsteen dropped over the bank without reply with a still more hot flush upon her cheeks. She had escaped one danger only to fall into another more alarming. What the country folk had said to her had piqued her pride; but to be treated by a gentleman as if she were a country lass with her joe was more than Kirsteen could bear.

He had sprung down by her side, however, before she could do more than pick up the bundle and cloak which the tramp had not touched.

'He's a scamp to try to take advantage of you when you're in a lone place like this. Tell me, my bonny lass, where ye are going? I'll see you safe over the hill if you're going my way.'

'It is not needful, sir, I thank ye,' said Kirsteen. 'I'm much obliged to you for appearing as you did. It was a sturdy beggar would have had my purse; he ran at the sight of a gentleman; but I hope there are none but ill-doers need to do that,' she added with heightened colour drawing back from his extended hand.

The young man laughed and made a step forward, then stopped and stared. 'You are not a country lass,' he said. 'I've seen you before – where have I seen you before?'

Kirsteen felt herself glow from head to foot with over-powering shame. She remembered if he did not. She had not remarked his looks in the relief which the first sight of him had brought, but now she perceived who it was. It was the very Lord John whose remarks upon the antediluvians had roused her proud resentment at the ball. He did not mistake the flash of recognition, and a recognition which was angry, in her eyes.

'Where have we met?' he said. 'You know me, and not I fear very favourably. Whatever I've done I hope you'll let me make my peace now.'

'There is no peace to make,' said Kirsteen. 'I'm greatly obliged to you, sir; I can say no more, but I'll be more obliged to you still if you will go your own gait and let me go mine, for I am much pressed for time.'

'What! and leave you at the mercy of the sturdy beggar?' he cried lightly. 'This is my gait as well as yours, I'm on my way across Whistlefield down to Roseneath – a long walk. I never thought to have such pleasant company. Come, give me your bundle to carry, and tell me, for I see you know, where we met.'

'I can carry my own bundle, sir, and I'll give it to nobody,' said Kirsteen.

'What a churl you make me look – a bonny lass by my side overweighted, and I with nothing but my gun. Give me the cloak then,' he said, catching it lightly from her arm.

'If you will not tell me where we met tell me where you're going, and I'll see you home.'

'My home is not where I am going,' said Kirsteen. 'Give me back my cloak, my Lord John. It's not for you to carry for me.'

'I thought you knew me,' he cried. 'Now that's an unfair advantage, let me think, was it in the schoolroom at Dalmally? To be sure! You are the governess. Or was it—?'

He saw that he had made an unlucky hit. Kirsteen's countenance glowed with proud wrath. The governess, and she a Douglas! She snatched the cloak from him and stood at bay. 'My father,' she cried, 'is of as good blood as yours, and though you can scorn at the Scots gentry in your own house you shall not do it on the hillside. I have yon hill to cross,' said the girl with a proud gesture, holding herself as erect as a tower, 'going on my own business, and meddling with nobody. So go before, sir, or go after, but if you're a gentleman, as ye have the name, let me pass by myself.'

The young man coloured high. He took off his hat and stood aside to let her pass. After all there are arguments which are applicable to a gentleman that cannot be applied to sturdy beggars. But Kirsteen went on her way still more disturbed than by the first meeting. He had not recognized her, but if they should ever meet again he would recognize her. And what would he think when he knew it was Drumcarro's daughter that had met him on the hillside with her bundle on her arm, and been lightly addressed as a bonny lass. The governess at Dalmally! Hot tears came into Kirsteen's eyes as she made her way across the stretch of moorland which lies between Loch Long and the little Gairloch, that soft and verdant paradise. She walked very quickly neither turning to the right hand nor the left, conscious of the figure following her at a distance. Oh, the governess! She will be a far better person than me, and know a great deal more, thought Kirsteen with keen compunction, me to think so much of myself that am nobody! I wish I was a governess or half so good. I'm a poor vagrant lass, insulted on the roadside, frighted with beggars, scared by gentlemen. Oh, if I had but taken the honest woman's offer of Donald and the gig!

CHAPTER XVIII

Kirsteen passed that night at Helensburgh, or Eelensburgh as everybody called it, and next day arrived at Glasgow a little after noon. She had the address there of a friend of Marg'ret where she would once again find herself in the serenity of a private house. She seemed to herself to have been living for a long time in public places – in houses where men could come in to drink or any stranger find a shelter, and almost to have known no other life but that of wandering solitude, continual movement, and the consciousness of having no home or refuge to which she belonged. Kirsteen had never made a day's journey in her life before that dreadful morning when she set out in the dark, leaving all that was known and comprehensible behind her. She had never been in an inn, which was to her something of a bad place given over to revellings and dissipation, and profane noise and laughter, the 'crackling of thorns under the pot'. These ideas modify greatly even with a single night's experience of a quiet shelter and a kind hostess – but she looked forward to the decent woman's house to which Marg'ret's recommendation would admit her, with the longing of a wanderer long launched upon the dreary publicity of a traveller's life, and feeling all the instincts of keen exclusivism, which belonged in those days to poorer Scotch gentry, jarred and offended at every turn. To find the house of Marg'ret's friend was not easy in the great grimy city which was Kirsteen's first experience of a town. The crowded streets and noises confused her altogether at first. Such visions of ugliness and dirt, the squalid look of the high houses, the strange groups, some so rich and well-to-do, some so miserable and wretched, that crowded the pavements, had never entered into her imagination before. They made her sick at heart; and London, people said, was bigger (if that were possible) and no doubt more dreadful still! Oh that it could all turn out a dream from which she might wake to find herself once more by the side of the linn, with the roar of the water, and no sickening clamour of ill tongues in her ear! But already the linn, and the far-off life by its side were away from her as if they had passed centuries ago.

She found the house at last with the help of a ragged laddie upon whose tangled mass of nondescript garments Kirsteen looked with amazement, but who was willing apparently to go to the end of the world for the sixpence which had been saved from the tramp. It was in a large and grimy 'land' not far from Glasgow Green, a great block of buildings inhabited by countless families, each of which had some different trace of possession at its special window – clothes hanging to dry, or beds to air, or untidy women and girls lolling out. The common stair, which admitted to all these different apartments, was in a condition which horrified and disgusted the country girl. Her courage almost failed her when she stepped within the black portals, and contemplated the filthy steps upon which children were playing, notwithstanding all its horrors, and down the well of which came sounds of loud talking, calls of women from floor to floor and scraps of conversation maintained at the highest pitch of vigorous lungs. 'It's up at the very top,' said the urchin who was her guide. Kirsteen's expectations sank lower and lower as she ascended. There were two doors upon each stairhead, and often more than one family enclosed within these subdivisions, all full of curiosity as to the stranger who invaded their grimy world with a clean face and tidy dress. 'She'll be some charity leddy seeking pennies for the puir folk.' 'We hae mair need to get pennies than to give them.' 'She'll be gaun to see Allison Wabster, the lass that's in a decline.' 'She'll be a visitor for Justin Macgregor, the proud Hieland besom, that's ower grand for the like of us.' These were the pleasant words that accompanied her steps from floor to floor. Kirsteen set it all down to the score of the dreadful town in which every evil thing flourished, and with a sad heart and great discouragement pushed her way to the highest storey, which was cleaner than below though all the evil smells rose and poisoned the air which had no outlet. The right-hand door was opened to her hurriedly before she could knock, and an old woman with a large mutch upon her head and a tartan shawl on her shoulders came out to meet her. 'Ye'll be the leddy from Loch Fyne,' she said with a homely curtsey. 'Come ben, my bonny leddy, come ben.'

After the purgatory of the stair Kirsteen found herself
in a paradise of cleanliness and order, in a little lantern of
light and brightness. There were three small rooms – a
kitchen, a parlour so called, with a concealed bed which
made it fit for the combined purposes of a sleeping and
living room, and the bedroom proper into which she was
immediately conducted, and which was furnished with a
tent-bed, hung with large-patterned chintz, each flower
about the size of a warming-pan, and with a clean knitted
white quilt which was the pride of Jean Macgregor's heart.
There was a concealed bed in this room too, every con-
trivance being adopted for the increase of accommodation.
Perhaps concealed beds are still to be found in the much-
divided 'lands' in which poor tenants congregate in the
poorer parts of Glasgow. They were formed by a sort of
closet completely filled by the spars and fittings of a bed,
and closed in by a dismal door, thus securing the exclusion
of all air from the hidden sleeping-place.

The decent woman, who was Marg'ret's old friend, took
Kirsteen's bundle from her hands, and opening it, spread
out the contents on the bed.

'I'll just hang them out before the fire to give them air,
and take out the creases. And, mem, I hope you'll make
yoursel' at home and consider a' here as your ain.'

'Did ye know I was coming?' said Kirsteen, surprised.

'Only this morning. I got a scart of the pen from Marg'ret
Brown, that is my cousin and a great friend, though I have
not seen her this twenty years. She said it was one o' the
family, a young leddy that had to travel to London, and no
man nor a maid could be spared to gang with her; and I
was to see ye into the coach, and take good care of ye; and
that I will, my bonny leddy, baith for her sake, and because
ye've a kind face of your ain that makes a body fain.'

In the relief of this unexpected reception, and after the
misery of the approach to it which had sunk Kirsteen's
courage, she sat down and cried a little for pleasure. 'I am
glad ye think I've a kind face, for oh, I have felt just like a
reprobate, hating everything I saw,' she cried. 'It's all so
different – so different – from home.'

Home had been impossible a few days ago; it looked like
heaven – though a heaven parted from her by an entire
lifetime – now.

'Weel,' said the old woman, 'we canna expect that Glasco, a miserable, black, dirty town as ever was, can be like the Hielands with its bonny hills and its bright sun. But, my honey, if ye let me say sae, there's good and bad in baith places, and Glasco's no so ill as it looks. Will ye lie down and take a bit rest, now you're here – or will I make ye a cup of tea? The broth will not be ready for an hour. If I had kent sooner I would have got ye a chuckie or something mair delicate; but there wasna time.'

Kirsteen protested that she neither wanted rest nor tea, and would like the broth, which was the natural everyday food, better than anything. She came into the parlour and sat down looking out from the height of her present elevation upon the green below, covered with white patches in the form of various washings which the people near had the privilege of bleaching on the grass. The abundant, sweet air so near the crowded and noisy streets, the freedom of that sudden escape from the dark lands and houses, the unlooked-for quiet and cheerful prospect stirred up her spirit. The lasses going about with bare feet, threading their way among the lines of clothes, sprinkling them with sparkling showers of water which dazzled in the sun, awakened the girl's envy as she sat with her hands crossed in her lap. A flock of mill-girls were crossing the green to their work at one of the cotton-factories. They were clothed in petticoats and short gowns, or bedgowns as they are called in England, bound round their waists with a trim white apron. Some of them had tartan shawls upon their shoulders. A number of them were barefooted, but one and all had shining and carefully dressed hair done up in elaborate plaits and braids. Kirsteen's eyes followed them with a sort of envy. They were going to their work, they were carrying on the common tenor of their life, while she sat there arrested in everything. 'I wish,' she said, with a sigh, 'I had something to do.'

'The best thing you can do is just to rest. Ye often do not find the fatigue of a journey,' said Mrs Macgregor, 'till it's over. Ye'll be more and more tired as the day goes on, and ye'll sleep fine at night.'

With these and similar platitudes the old woman soothed her guest; and Kirsteen soothed her soul as well as she could to quiet, though now when the first pause occurred

she felt more and more the eagerness to proceed, the impossibility of stopping short. To cut herself adrift from all
the traditions of her life in order to rest in this little
parlour, even for a day, and look out upon the bleaching of
the clothes, and the mill-girls going to work, had the wildest
inappropriateness in it. She seized upon the half-knitted
stocking, without which in those days no good housewife
was complete, and occupied her hands with that. But
towards evening another subject was introduced, which
delivered Kirsteen at once from the mild ennui of this
compulsory pause.

'Ye'll maybe no ken,' said the old woman, 'that there is
one in Glasco that you would like weel to see?'

'One in Glasgow?' Kirsteen looked up with a question in
her eyes. 'No doubt there is many a one in Glasgow that I
would be proud to see; but I cannot think of company nor
of what I like when I'm only in this big place for a day.'

'It's no that, my bonny leddy. It's one that if you're near
sib to the Douglases, and Meg does not say how near ye
are, would be real thankfu' just of one glint of your e'e.'

'I am near, very near,' said Kirsteen, with a hot colour
rising over her. She dropped the knitting in her lap, and
fixed her eyes upon her companion's face. She had already
a premonition who it was of whom she was to hear.

'Puir thing,' said Mrs Macgregor, 'she hasna seen one of
her own kith and kin this mony a day. She comes to me
whiles for news. And she'll sit and smile and say, "Have ye
any news from Marg'ret, Mrs Macgregor?" never letting
on that her heart's just sick for word of her ain kin.'

'You are perhaps meaning – Anne,' said Kirsteen,
scarcely above her breath.

'I'm meaning Mrs Dr Dewar,' said the old woman. 'I
think that's her name – the one that marriet and was cast
off by her family because he was just a doctor and no a
grand gentleman. Oh, missie, that's a hard, hard thing to
do! I can understand a great displeasure, and that a difference might be made for a time. But to cut off a daughter –
as if she were a fremd person, never to see her or name her
name, oh, that's hard, hard! It may be right for the Lord
to do it, that kens the heart (though I have nae faith in that),
but no for sinful, erring man.'

'Mrs Macgregor,' said Kirsteen, 'you will remember that

it's my – my near relations you are making remarks
upon.'

'And that's true,' said the old lady. 'I would say nothing
to make ye think less of your nearest and dearest – and that
maybe have an authority over ye that Scripture bids ye aye
respect. I shouldna have said it; but the other – the poor
young leddy – is she no your near relation too?'

Kirsteen had known vaguely that her sister was supposed
to be in Glasgow, which was something like an aggravation
of her offence: for to live among what Miss Eelen called the
fremd in a large town was the sort of unprincipled prefer-
ence of evil to good which was to be expected from a girl
who had married beneath her; but to find herself confronted with Anne was a contingency which had never
occurred to her. At home she had thought of her sister with
a certain awe mingled with pity. There was something in
the banishment, the severance, the complete effacing of her
name and image from all the family records, which was very
impressive to the imagination, and brought an ache of compassion into the thought of her, which nobody ventured
to express. Kirsteen had been very young, too young to
offer any judgment independent of her elders, upon Anne's
case when she had gone away. But she had cried over her
sister's fate often, and wondered in her heart whether they
would ever meet, or any amnesty ever be pronounced that
would restore poor Anne, at least nominally, to her place in
the family. But it had not entered into her mind to suppose
that she herself should ever be called upon to decide that
question, to say practically, so far as her authority went,
whether Anne was to be received or not. She kept gazing at
her hostess with a kind of dismay, unable to make any
reply. Anne – who had married a man who was not a gentleman, who had run away, leaving the candle dying in the
socket. A strong feeling against that family traitor rose up
in Kirsteen's breast. She had compromised them all – she
had connected the name of the old Douglases, the name of
the boys in India, with a name that was no name, that of a
common person – a doctor, one that traded upon his education and his skill. There was a short but sharp struggle in
her heart. She had run away herself, but it was for a very
different reason. All her prejudices, which were strong, and
the traditions of her life were against Anne. It was with an

effort that she recovered the feeling of sympathy which
had been her natural sentiment. 'She is my near relation,
too. But she disobeyed them that she ought to have
obeyed.'

'Oh, missie, there are ower many of us who do that.'

Kirsteen raised her head more proudly than ever. She
gave the old woman a keen look of scrutiny. Did she know
what she was saying? Anyhow, what did it matter? 'But if
we do it, we do it for different reasons – not to be happy, as
they call it, in a shameful way.'

'Oh, shameful – na, na! It's a lawful and honest marriage,
and he's a leal and a true man.'

'It was shameful to her family,' cried Kirsteen doubly
determined. 'It was forgetting all that was most cherished. I
may be sorry for her—' she scarcely was so in the vigour
of her opposition – 'but I cannot approve her.' Kirsteen
held her head very high and her mouth closed as if it had
been made of iron. She looked no gentle sister, but an
unyielding judge.

'Weel, weel,' said the old woman with a sigh, 'it's nae
business of mine. I would fain have let her have a glimpse,
puir thing, of someone belonging to her; but if it's no to be
done it's nane of my affairs, and I needna fash my thoom.
We'll say no more about it. There's going to be a bonny
sunset if we could but see it. Maybe you would like to take
a walk and see a little of the town.'

Kirsteen consented, and then drew back, for who could
tell that she might not meet someone who would recognize
her. Few as were the people she knew, she had met one on
the wild hillsides above Loch Long, and there was no telling
who might be in Glasgow, a town which was a kind of
centre to the world. She sat at the window, and looked out
upon the women getting in their clothes from the grass
where they had been bleaching, and on all the groups about
the green – children playing, bigger lads contending with
their footballs. The sky became all aglow with the glory of
the winter sunset, then faded into grey, and light began to
gleam in the high windows. Day passed, and night, the
early, falling, long-continuing night, descended from the
skies. Kirsteen sat in the languor of fatigue and in a curious
strangeness remote and apart from everything about as in
a dream. It was like a dream altogether – the strange little

house so near to the skies, the opening of the broad green
space underneath and the groups upon it – place and people
alike unknown to her, never seen before, altogether un-
related to her former life – yet she herself introduced here
as an honoured guest, safe and sheltered, and surrounded
by watchful care. But for Marg'ret she must have fought
her way as she could, or sunk into a dreadful obedience.
Obedience! that was what she had been blaming her sister
for failing in, she who had so failed herself. She sat and
turned it over and over in her mind while the light faded
out from the sky. The twilight brought softening with it.
She began to believe that perhaps there were circumstances
extenuating. Anne had been very young, younger than
Kirsteen was now, and lonely, for her sisters were still
younger than she, without society. And no doubt the man
would be kind to her. She said nothing while the afternoon
passed, and the tea was put on the table. But afterwards
when Mrs Macgregor was washing the china cups, she
asked suddenly, 'Would it be possible if a person desired it,
to go to that place where the lady you were speaking of,
Mrs Dr—? If you think she would like to see me I might
go.'

CHAPTER XIX

If it was strange to sit at that window looking out over the world unknown, and feel herself an inmate of the little house so different from everything she had ever seen, the guest and companion of the old woman whose very name she had never heard till a few days before, it was still more strange to be in the thronged and noisy streets full of people, more people than Kirsteen had supposed to be in the world, under the glaring of the lights that seemed to her to mock the very day itself, though they were few enough in comparison with the blaze of illumination to which we are now accustomed – going through the strange town in the strange night to see Anne. That was the climax of all the strangeness. Anne, whose name was never named at home, whom everybody remembered all the more intensely because it was forbidden to refer to her. Anne, who had gone away from her father's house in the night leaving the candle flaring out in the socket and the chill wind blowing in through the open door. That scene had always been associated in Kirsteen's mind with her sister's name, and something of the flicker of the dying candle was in the blowing about of the lights along the long range of the Trongate, above that babel of noises and ever shifting phantasmagoria of a great city. She could not make any reply to the old woman who walked beside her, full of stories and talk, pointing out to her a church or a building here and there. Kirsteen went through a little pantomime of attention, looking where she was told to look, but seeing nothing, only a confused panorama of crowded dark outlines and wind-blown lights, and nothing that she could understand.

At length they struck into a long line of monotonous street where there were no shops and no wayfarers, but some lamps which flickered wildly, more and more like the dying candle. Mrs Macgregor told her the name of the street, and explained its length and beauty, and how it had been built, and that it was a very genteel street, where some of the bailies and a number of the ministers lived. 'The houses are dear,' she said, 'and no doubt it was a fight for Dr Dewar to keep up a house in such a genteel place. But they external things are of great consequence to a doctor,' she added. Kirsteen was dazed and overawed by the line of the grim houses looming between her and the dark sky, and by the flaring of the wild lights, and the long stretch of darkness which the scanty unavailing lamps did not suffice to make visible. And her heart began to beat violently when her guide stopped at a door which opened invisibly from above at their summons and clanged behind them, and revealed a dark stair with another windy lamp faintly lighting it, a stair in much better order than the dreadful one where Mrs Macgregor was herself living, but looking like a gloomy cleft among the dark walls. Now that she had come so far, Kirsteen would fain have turned back or delayed the visit to which she seemed to be driven reluctantly by some impulse that was not her own. Was it not an aggravation of her own rebellion that she should thus come secretly to the former rebel, she who had been discarded by the family and shut out from its records? She shrank from the sight of the house in which poor Anne had found refuge, and of the husband who was a common person, not one of their own kind. Drumcarro at his fiercest could not have recoiled more from a common person than his runaway daughter, whose object it was to establish herself with a mantua-maker in London. But Kirsteen felt her own position unspeakably higher than that of her sister.

She followed her companion tremulously into the little dark vestibule. 'Oh, ay, the mistress is in: where would she be but in, and hearing the bairns say their bits of lessons?' said an active little maid who admitted them, pointing to the glow of ruddy firelight which proceeded from an inner door. And before she was aware Kirsteen found herself in the midst of a curious and touching scene. She had not heard anything about children, so that the sight so unexpected of two little things seated on the hearthrug, as she remembered herself to have sat in her early days under Anne's instructions, gave her a little shock of surprise and quick-springing kindness. They were two little roundabout creatures of three and four, with little round rosy faces faintly reddened by the flickering light, which shone in the

soft glow, their hair half flaxen, half golden. Their chubby
hands were crossed in their laps. Their mother knelt in
front of them, herself so girlish still, her soft yellow hair
matured into brown, her face and figure fuller than of old,
teaching them with one hand raised. 'Gentle Jesus, meek
and mild,' she was saying: 'Dentle Desus, meet and mild,'
said the little pupils: 'listen to a little child.' There was no
lamp or candle in the room: nothing but the firelight. The
two dark figures in their outdoor dresses stood behind in
the shadow, while all the light concentrated in this family
group. The mother was so absorbed in her teaching that she
continued without noticing their entrance.

'You are not saying it right, Dunny; and Kirsty, my pet,
you must try and say it like me – Gentle Jesus.'

'Dentle Desus,' said the little ones with assured and smiling incorrectness incapable of amendment. Kirsteen saw
them through a mist of tears. The name of the baby on the
hearth had completed the moving effect of old recollections
and of the familiarity of the voice and action of the young
mother. The voice had a plaintive tone in it, as so many
voices of Scotchwomen have. She stood behind in the background, the rays of the fire taking a hundred prismatic tints
as she looked at them through the tears upon her eyelashes.
Her heart was entirely melted, forgetful of everything but
that this was Anne, the gentle elder sister who had taught
her childhood too.

'I have brought a young leddy to see you, Mrs Dewar,'
said the old woman. Anne sprang up to her feet at the
sound of the voice.

'I did not hear anybody come in,' she said. 'I was hearing
them their hymn to say to their papa tomorrow. Is it you,
Mrs Macgregor? You're kind to come out this cold night.
Dunny, tell Janet she must put ye to your bed, for I'm busy
with friends.'

'Na,' said the old lady, 'we'll not interrupt. I'm going
ben to say a word to Janet mysel'. And she'll no interrupt
you putting your bairns to their bed.'

She drew Kirsteen forward into the influence of the firelight, and herself left the room, leaving the sisters together.
Anne stood for a little gazing curiously at the silent figure.
She was puzzled and at a loss; the black silk spencer, the
beaver bonnet, were common enough articles of dress, and

the big veil that hung like a cloud over Kirsteen's bonnet kept the face in the shade. 'Do I know ye?' she said, going timidly forward. Then with a cry, 'Is it Kirsteen?'

The little children sat still on the hearthrug with their little fat hands crossed in their laps; they were not concerned by the convulsions that might go on over their heads. They laughed at the glancing firelight and at each other in one of those still moments of babyhood which come now and then in the midst of the most riotous periods; they had wandered off to the edge of the country from whence they came. When the two sisters fell down on their knees by the side of the little ones, the mother showing her treasures, the young aunt making acquaintance with them, the rosy little faces continued to smile serenely upon the tears and suppressed passion. 'This is Kirsty that I called after you, Kirsteen.' 'But oh, ye mean for my mother, Anne?' 'Kirsty, me!' said the little three-year-old, beating her breast to identify the small person named. 'She's Kistina; I'm Duncan,' said the little boy, who was a whole year older, but did not generally take the lead in society. 'They are like two little birdies in a nest,' said Kirsteen; 'oh! the bonny little heads like gold – and us never to know.'

'Will I send them to Janet, or will ye help me to put them to their bed?' said the proud mother. For a moment she remembered nothing but the delight of exhibiting their little round limbs, their delightful gambols, for so soon as the children rose from that momentary abstraction they became riotous again and filled the room with their 'flichterin' noise and glee'. 'I never light the candles till David comes in,' Anne said apologetically. 'What do I want with more light? For the bairns are just all I can think of; they will not let me sew my seam, they are just a woman's work at that restless age.' She went on with little complaints which were boasts as Kirsteen looked on and wondered at the skilled and careful manipulation of her sister's well-accustomed hands. The bedroom to which the group was transferred was like the parlour lighted only by the fire, and the washing and undressing proceeded while Anne went on with the conversation, telling how Dunny was 'a rude boy', and Kirsty a 'very stirring little thing', and 'just a handful'. 'I have enough to do with them, and with making and mending for them, if I had not another thing on my

hands,' said Anne; 'they are just a woman's work.' Kirsteen
sat and looked on in the ruddy flickering light with strange
thoughts. Generally the coming on of motherhood is
gradual, and sisters and friends grow into a sort of amateur
share in it. But to come suddenly from the image of Anne
who had left the house door open and the candle dying in
the socket, to Anne the cheerful mother kissing the rosy
limbs and round faces, her pretty hair pulled by the baby
hands, her proud little plaints of the boy that was 'rude'
and the girl that was 'very stirring', was the most curious
revelation to Kirsteen. It brought a little blush and uneasiness along with affection and pleasure, her shy maidenhood
shrinking even while warm sympathy filled her heart.

When the children were in bed, the sisters returned to
the parlour, where Kirsteen was installed in the warmest
corner by the fire. 'Would you like the candles lighted? I
aye leave it till David comes home: he says I sit like a
hoodie crow in the dark,' said Anne. There was a soft tone
in her voice which told that David was a theme as sweet to
her as the children; but Kirsteen could not bring herself to
ask any questions about the doctor, who was a common
person, and one who had no right ever to have intruded
himself into the Douglases' august race. Anne continued for
a time to give further details of the children, how they were
'a little disposed to take the cold', and about the troubles
there had been with their teeth, all happily surmounted,
thanks to David's constant care. 'If ye ever have little
bairns, Kirsteen, ye will know what a comfort it is to have a
doctor in the house.'

'I don't know about the bairns, but I am sure I never will
have the doctor,' said Kirsteen in haste and unwarily, not
thinking what she said.

'And what for no?' said Anne, holding herself very erect.
'Ye speak like an ignorant person, like one of them that
has a prejudice against doctors. There's no greater mistake.'

'I was meaning no such thing,' cried Kirsteen eagerly.

'Well, ye spoke like it,' said Anne. 'And where would
we all be without doctors? It's them that watches over failing folk, and gives back fathers and mothers to their
families, and snatches our bonny darlings out of the jaws of
death. Eh! if ye knew as much about doctors as I know
about them,' she cried with a panting breath.

'I am sorry if I said anything that was not ceevil,' said Kirsteen; 'it was without meaning. Doctors have never done anything for my mother,' she added with an impulse of self-justification.

'And whose blame is that? I know what David ordered her – and who ever tried to get it for her? He would have taken her to his own house, and nursed her as if she had been his own mother,' cried Anne with heat.

Kirsteen with difficulty suppressed the indignation that rose to her lips. 'Him presume to consider my mother as if she were his own!' Kirsteen cried within herself. 'He was a bonny one!' And there fell a little silence between the two sisters seated on opposite sides of the fire.

After a while Anne spoke again, hesitating, bending across the lively blaze. 'Were ye, maybe, coming,' she said with an effort, 'to tell me – to bring me – a message?'

Kirsteen saw by the dancing light her sister's eyes full of tears. She had thought she was occupied only by the babies and the changed life, but when she saw the beseeching look in Anne's eyes, the quivering of her mouth, the eager hope that this visit meant an overture of reunion, Kirsteen's heart was sore.

'Alack,' she said, 'I have no message. I am just like you, Anne. I have left my home and all in it. I'm a wanderer on the face of the earth.'

'Kirsteen!' Anne sprang to her sister and clasped her in her arms. 'Oh, my bonny woman! Oh, my Kirsty!' She pressed Kirsteen's head to her breast in a rapture of sympathetic feeling. 'Oh, I'm sorry and I'm glad. I canna tell ye all my feelings. Have ye brought him with you? Where is he, and who is he, Kirsteen?'

Kirsteen disengaged herself almost roughly and with great though suppressed offence from her sister's arms. 'If ye think there is any he in the maitter, ye are greatly mistaken,' she said. 'If ye think I would take such a step for such a motive.'

Anne drew back wounded too. 'Ye need not speak so stern – I did it myself, and I would not be the one to blame you. And if there's a better reason I don't know what it is. What reason can a young lass have to leave her hame, except that there's one she likes better, and that she's bid to follow, forsaking her father and mother, in the very Scripture itself.'

Mrs Dr Dewar returned to her seat – throwing back her head with an indignant sense of the highest warrant for her own conduct. But when she resumed her seat, Anne began to say softly: 'I thought you had come to me with maybe a word of kindness. I thought that maybe my mother – was yearning for a sight of me as me for her – and to see my bairns. Oh, it would do her heart good to see the bairns. It would add on years to her life. What are ye all thinking of that ye cannot see that she's dwining and pining for a pleasant house and a cheerful life; David said it before – and he was most willing to be at all the charges – but they would not listen to him, and no doubt it's a great deal worse now.'

'If you are meaning my mother, she is no worse,' said Kirsteen. 'She is just about the same. Robbie has gone away to India like the rest; and she just bore it as well as could be expected. I have not heard,' said the girl, feeling the corners of her mouth quiver and a choking in her throat, 'how she's borne this.'

Both of them had the feeling that their own departure must have affected the invalid more strongly than any other.

'But she has not heard about your children, Anne. She would have said something.'

Anne's lips were quivering too. She was much wounded by this assertion. She shook her head. 'My mother's no one,' she said, 'that tells everything – especially what's nearest to her heart. Ye may be sure she knows – but she wouldna maybe be ready to speak of it to young lasses like you.'

Kirsteen thought this argument feeble, but she said nothing in reply.

'And so Robbie's away,' said Anne. 'He was just a bit laddie that I put to his bed like my own. Eh, but time goes fast, when ye hear of them growing up that ye can mind when they were born. I tell David our own will just be men and women before we think.' This thought brought a smile to her face and much softening of the disappointment. 'Oh, but I would like my mother to see them!' she said.

Kirsteen reflected a little bitterly that this was all Anne thought of, that her curiosity about her sister had dropped at once, and that the children and the wish that her mother should see them – which was nothing but pride – was all that occupied Anne's thoughts. And there ensued another pause; they sat on either side of the fire with divided hearts, Anne altogether absorbed in her own thoughts of the past and present, of her old girlish life which had been full of small oppressions, and of her present happiness, and the prosperous and elevated position of a woman with a good man and bairns of her own, which was her proud and delightful consciousness, and which only wanted to be seen and recognized by her mother to make it perfect. Kirsteen on her side felt this superiority as an offence. She knew that her mother had 'got over' Anne's departure, and was not at all taken up by imaginations concerning her and her pos-sible children – though she could not but recognize the possibility that her own flight might have a much more serious effect, and she sat by her sister's hearth with a jealous, proud sensation of being very lonely, and cut away from everything. She said to herself that it was foolish, nay, wrong to have come, and that it was not for her to have thus encouraged the bringing down of her father's house. There was no such thing she proudly felt in her own case.

Suddenly Anne rose up, and lifting two candlesticks from the mantelpiece placed them on the table. 'I hear David's step,' she said with a beaming face.

'Then I will just be going,' said Kirsteen.

'Why should ye go? Will ye no wait and see my husband? Maybe you think Dr Dewar is not good enough to have the honour of meeting with the like of you. I can tell you my husband is as well respected as any in Glasgow, and his name is a kent name where the Douglases' was never heard.'

'That can scarcely be in Scotland,' cried Kirsteen proudly, 'not even in Glasgow. Fare ye well, Anne. I'm glad to have seen ye.' She paused for a moment with a shake in her voice and added hurriedly, 'And the bairns.'

'Oh, Kirsteen!' cried Anne rushing to her side, 'oh, Kirsteen, bide! Oh, bide and see him! Ye will never be sorry to have made friends with my man.'

'Who is that, Anne,' said a voice behind them, 'that ye are imploring in such a pitiful tone to bide? Is it some unfriend of mine?'

'No unfriend, Dr Dewar,' said Kirsteen, turning round upon him, 'but a stranger that has little to do here.'

'It is one of your sisters, Anne!'

'It's Kirsteen,' cried Anne with wet eyes. 'Oh, David, make her stay.'

CHAPTER XX

Dr Dewar was a man of whose appearance his wife had reason to be proud. None of the long-descended Douglases were equal to him either in physical power or in good looks. He was tall and strong, he had fine hands, a physician's hands full of delicacy yet force, good feet, all the signs that are supposed to represent race – though he was of no family whatever, the son of a shopkeeper, not fit to appear in the same room in which ladies and gentlemen were. Kirsteen had stopped short at sight of him and there can be no doubt that she had been much surprised. In former times she had indeed seen him as her mother's doctor, but she had scarcely noticed the visitor, who was of no interest to a girl of her age. And his rough country dress had not been imposing like the black suit which now gave dignity and the air of a gentleman which Kirsteen had expected to find entirely wanting in her sister's husband. His somewhat pale face, large featured, rose with a sort of distinction from the ample many-folded white neckcloth, appropriate title! which enveloped his throat. He looked at the visitor with good-humoured scrutiny, shading his eyes from the scanty light of the candles. 'My wife is so economical about her lights,' he said, 'that I can never see who is here, though I would fain make myself agreeable to Anne's friends. Certainly, my dear, I will do what is in me to make your sister bide. I would fain hope it is a sign of amity to see ye here tonight, Miss Kirsteen.'

'No,' said Kirsteen, 'it is not a sign of amity. It was only that I was in Glasgow, and thought I would like to see her – at least,' she added, 'I will not take to myself a credit I don't deserve. It was Mrs Macgregor put it into my head.'

'Well, well,' said Dr Dewar, 'so long as you are here we will not quarrel about how it was. It will have been a great pleasure to Anne to see you. Are the bairns gone to their beds, my dear?'

'They're scarcely sleeping yet,' said Anne, smiling at her husband with tender triumph. 'Go ben,' she said putting one of the candlesticks into his hand, 'and see them; for I know that's what has brought ye in so soon – not for me but the weans.'

'For both,' he said, pressing her hand like a lover as he took the candle from it. Anne was full of silent exultation for she had remarked Kirsteen's little start of surprise and noticed that she said nothing more of going away. 'Well?' she said eagerly, when he had disappeared.

'Well,' said Kirsteen, 'I never heard that Dr Dewar was not a very personable man, and well-spoken. It will maybe be best for me to be getting home, before it's very late.'

'Will ye no stay, Kirsteen, and break bread in my house? You might do that and say nothing about it. It would be no harm to hide an innocent thing that was just an act of kindness, when you get home. If I am never to get more from my own family,' cried Anne, 'but to be banished and disowned as if I were an ill woman, surely a sister that is young and should have some kind thought in her heart, might do that. Ye need say nothing of it when you get home.'

'I will maybe never get home more,' said Kirsteen, overcome at last by the feeling of kindred and the need of sympathy.

'Oh, lassie,' cried Anne, 'what have ye done? What have ye done? – And where are ye going? – If ye have left your home ye shall bide here. It's my right to take care of you, if ye have nobody else to take care of ye, no Jean Macgregor, though she's very respectable, but me your elder sister. And that will be the first thing David will say.'

'I am much obliged to you,' said Kirsteen, 'but you must not trouble your head about me. I'm going to London – to friends I have there.'

'To London!' cried Anne. There was more wonder in her tone than would be expressed now if America had been the girl's destination. 'And you have friends there!'

Kirsteen made a lofty sign of assent. She would not risk herself by entering into any explanations. 'It's a long journey,' she said, 'and a person never can tell if they will ever win back. If you are really meaning what you say, and that I will not be in your way nor the doctor's, I will thankfully bide and take a cup of tea with ye – for it's not like being among strangers when I can take your hand – and give a kiss to your little bairns before I go.'

Anne came quickly across the room and took her sister in her arms, and cried a little upon her shoulder. 'I'm real happy,' she said sobbing; 'ye see the bairns, what darlin's they are – and there never was a better man than my man; but eh! I just yearn sometimes for a sight of home, and my poor mother. If she is weakly, poor body, and cannot stand against the troubles of this world, still she's just my mother, and I would rather have a touch of her hand than all the siller in Glasgow – and eh, what she would give to see the bairns!'

Kirsteen, who was herself very tremulous, here sang in a broken voice, for she too had begun to realize that she might never again see her mother, a snatch of her favourite song:

'True loves ye may get many an ane
But minnie ne'er anither.'

'No, I'll not say that,' said Anne. 'I'll not be so untrue to my true love – but oh, my poor minnie! how is she, Kirsteen? Tell me everything, and about Marg'ret and the laddies and all.'

When Dr Dewar entered he found the two sisters seated close together, clinging to each other, laughing and crying in a breath over the domestic story which Kirsteen was telling. The sole candle twinkled on the table kindly like a friendly spectator, the fire blazed and crackled cheerfully, the room in the doctor's eyes looked like the home of comfort and happy life. He was pleased that one of Anne's family should see how well off she was. It was the best way he felt sure to bring them to acknowledge her, which was a thing he professed to be wholly indifferent to. But in his heart he was very proud of having married a Douglas, and he would have received any notice from Drumcarro with a joy perhaps more natural to the breeding of his original station than dignified. He felt the superiority of his wife's race in a manner which never occurred to Anne herself, and was more proud of his children on account of the 'good Douglas blood' in their veins. 'Not that I hold with such nonsense,' he would say with a laugh of pretended disdain, 'but there are many that do.' It was not a very serious weakness, but it was a weakness. His face beamed as he came in: though Kirsteen had said that her presence was not a sign of amity he could not but feel that it was, and a great one. For certainly the laird's opposition must be greatly modified before he would permit his daughter to come here.

'Well,' he said, making them both start, 'I see I was not wanted to persuade her to bide. I am very glad to see you in my house, Miss Kirsteen. Ye will be able to tell them at home that Anne is not the victim of an ogre in human form, as they must think, but well enough content with her bargain, eh, wifie?' He had come up to them, and touched his wife's cheek caressingly with his hands. 'Come, come,' he said, 'Anne, ye must not greet, but smile at news from home.'

'If I am greetin' it's for pleasure,' said Anne, 'to hear about my mother and all of them and to see my bonny Kirsteen.'

'She has grown up a fine girl,' said the doctor looking at her with a professional glance and approving the youthful vigour and spirit which were perhaps more conspicuous in Kirsteen than delicacy of form and grace. Her indignation under this inspection may be supposed. She got up hastily freeing herself from Anne's hold.

'I must not be late,' she said, 'there's Mrs Macgregor waiting.'

'Tell the lass to bring the tea, Anne – if your sister is with friends—'

'I'm telling her that her place is here,' cried Anne, 'it is no friends, it is just old Jean Macgregor who is very respectable, but not the person for Kirsteen. And we have a spare room,' she added with pride. 'The doctor will hear of none of your concealed beds or dark closets to sleep in. He insists on having a spare room for a friend. And where is there such a friend as your own sister? We will send Jean to bring your things, Kirsteen.'

Kirsteen put a stern negation upon this proposal. 'Besides,' she said, 'it would be no advantage, for I am going on to London without delay.'

'To London?' cried the doctor. 'That's a long journey for ye by yourself. Are you really going alone?'

'I'm told,' said Kirsteen composedly, 'that the guards are very attentive, and that nobody meddles with one that respects herself. I have no fear.'

'Well, perhaps there is no fear – not what ye can call fear;
for, as you say, a woman is her own best protector, and
few men are such fools as to go too far when there's no
response. But, my dear young lady, it's a long journey and a
weary journey; I wonder that Drumcarro trusted you to go
alone; he might have spared a maid, if not a man to go with
ye.' The doctor's weakness led him to enhance the importance of Drumcarro as if it were a simple matter to send a
maid or a man.

'Oh, but Kirsteen says,' Anne began, remembering the
strange avowal, which she did not at all understand, that her
sister had made. Kirsteen took the words out of her mouth.

'It's not as if I were coming back today or tomorrow,'
she said quickly, 'and to send any person with me would
have been – not possible – I will just keep myself to myself
and nobody will harm me.'

'I am sure of that,' said the doctor cheerfully. 'I would
not like to be the man that spoke a word displeasing to ye
with those eyes of yours. Oh, I'm not complaining; for no
doubt ye have heard much harm of me and little good – but
ye have given me a look or two, Miss Kirsteen. Does not
this speak for me?' he added, raising Anne's face which
glowed with pleasure and affection under his touch – 'and
yon?' pointing to the open door of the room in which the
babies slept.

Kirsteen was much confused by this appeal. 'It was far
from my mind to say anything unceevil,' she said, 'and in
your own house.'

'Oh, never mind my own house, it's your house when
you're in it. And I would like ye to say whatever comes into
your head, for at the end, do what you will, my bonny lass,
you and me are bound to be friends. Now come, wifie,
and give us our tea.'

The dining-room in Dr Dewar's house was more dignified
than the parlour. It was used as his consulting room in
the morning, and Kirsteen was impressed by the large
mahogany furniture, the huge sideboard, heavy table, and
other substantial articles, things which told of comfort and
continuance, not to be lightly lifted about or transferred
from one place to another. And nothing could be more
kind than the doctor who disarmed her at every turn, and
took away every excuse for unfriendliness. After the dread-

ful experiences of her journey, and the forlorn sense she had of being cut off from everything she cared for, this cordial reception ended by altogether overcoming Kirsteen's prejudices, and the talk became as cheerful over the tea as if the young adventurer had indeed been a visitor, received with delight in her sister's house. She went away at last with the old woman greatly against Anne's will who tried every entreaty and remonstrance in vain. 'Surely ye like me better than Jean Macgregor,' she said. 'Oh, Kirsteen, it's far from kind – and the spare room at your disposition, and the kindest welcome – I will let you give the bairns their bath in the morning. Ye shall have them as long as you please,' she said with the wildest generosity. It was Dr Dewar himself who interrupted these entreaties.

'My dear,' he said, 'Kirsteen has a great deal of sense, she knows very well what she's doing. If there is a difficulty arisen at home as I'm led to conclude, it will just make matters worse if she's known to be living here.'

'I was not thinking of that,' cried Kirsteen, feeling the ungenerosity of her motives.

'It may be well that ye should. I would not have you anger your father, neither would Anne for any pleasure of hers. She is in a different position,' said the doctor. 'She's a married woman, and her father cannot in the nature of things be her chief object. But Kirsteen, my dear, is but a girl in her father's house, and whatever her heart may say she must not defy him by letting it be known that she's living here. But tomorrow is the Sabbath-day. The coach does not go, even if she were so far left to herself as to wish it; and it could not be ill taken that you should go to the kirk together and spend the day together. And then if ye must go, I will engage a place in the coach for ye and see ye off on Monday morning.'

'Oh, I must go, and I almost grudge the Sabbath-day,' said Kirsteen. 'I am so restless till I'm there. But I must not give you all that trouble.'

'It's no trouble. I'll go with ye as far as the coach-office. I wish I was not so busy,' said Dr Dewar with a delightful sense of his own consequence and popularity, and of the good impression it would make. 'I would convoy ye to London myself. But a doctor is never at his own disposition,' he added, with a shake of his head.

The Sunday which followed was strange yet delightful to
Kirsteen. It was like the last day of a sailor on shore before
setting forth upon the unknown, but rather of a sailor like
Columbus trusting himself absolutely to the sea and the
winds, not knowing what awaited him, than the well-guided
mariners of modern days with charts for every coast and
lighthouses at every turn. Kirsteen looked

> On land and sea and shore,
> As she might never see them more.

All was strange to her even here, but how much stranger,
dark, undeciphered, unknown was that world upon the
edge of which she stood, and where there was absolutely
nothing to guide her as to what she should encounter!
Kirsteen was not quite sure whether she could understand
the language which was spoken in London; the ways of the
people she was sure she would not understand. Somewhere
in the darkness that great city lay as the western world lay
before its discoverer. Kirsteen formed an image to herself
of something blazing into the night full of incomprehensible
voices and things; and she had all the shrinking yet eagerness of a first explorer not knowing what horrors there
might be to encounter, but not his faith in everything good.
The Sunday came like a strange dream into the midst of this
eagerness yet alarm. She was almost impatient of the interruption, yet was happy in it with the strangest troubled
happiness; though it was so real it was bewildering too, it
was a glimpse of paradise on the edge of the dark, yet unreal
in its pleasure as that vast unknown was unreal. She played
with the children, and she heard them say their prayers,
the two little voices chiming together, the two cherub faces
lifted up, while father and mother sat adoring. It was like
something she had seen in a dream – where she was herself
present, and yet not present, noting what everyone did.
For up to this time everything had been familiar in her life
– there had been no strangeness, no new views of the relationship of events with which she was too well acquainted
to have any room for flights of fancy.

And then this moment of pause, this curious, amusing,
beautiful day passed over, and she found herself in the dark
of the wintry morning in the street all full of commotion
where the coach was preparing to start. She found her

brother-in-law (things had changed so that she had actually begun to think of him as her brother-in-law) in waiting for her to put her in her place. Kirsteen's chief sensation in all that crowded, flaring, incomprehensible scene, with the smoky lamps blazing, and the horses pawing and champing, and everyone shouting to everyone else about, was shame of her bundle and fear lest the well-dressed, carefully brushed doctor should perceive with what a small provision it was that she was going forth into the unknown. No hope of blinding his eyes with the statement that she was going to friends in London if he saw what her baggage consisted of. He put her, to her surprise, into a comfortable corner in the interior of the coach, covering her up with a shawl which he said Anne had sent. 'But I was going on the outside,' said Kirsteen. 'Ye canna do that,' he said hastily. 'You would get your death of cold, besides there was no place.' 'Then there is more money to pay,' she said feeling for her purse, but with a secret pang, for she was aware how very little money was there. 'Nothing at all,' he said waving it away, 'they are just the same price, or very little difference. Goodbye, Kirsteen, and a good journey to you. A doctor's never at his own disposition.' 'But the money, I know it's more money.' 'I have not another moment,' cried the doctor darting away. Was it possible that she was in debt to Dr Dewar? She had almost sprung after him when Mrs Macgregor appeared carrying the bundle and put it on Kirsteen's knee. 'Here is your bundle, Miss Kirsteen; and here's a little snack for you in a basket.' Thank heaven he had not seen the bundle, but had he paid money for her? Was she in debt to Anne's husband, that common person? There was no time, however, to protest or send after him. With a clatter upon the stones, as if a house were falling, and a sound on the trumpet like the day of judgment, the coach quivered, moved and finally got under way.

CHAPTER XXI

It was dark again on the second afternoon when Kirsteen, all dizzy, feverish, and bewildered, attained once more, so to speak, to solid ground, after so much that had flown past her, endless, monotonous whirling in inconceivable flats and levels through night and through day. She put her foot upon the pavement timidly, and gave a frightened glance about her, knowing herself to be in London – that fabulous place of which she had never been sure whether it were not altogether a fairy tale. The journey had been like a dream, but of a different kind. She had seemed to herself to be sitting still as in an island in the seas and seeing the wastes of earth sweep past her, field pursuing field. There were hills too, but little ones, not much worthy the attention, and they too went coursing after each other, with all the sheep upon them and the trees and villages at their feet. There were pauses in the dream in which a great deal of commotion went on, and horses champed, and men shouted, and the coach swayed to and fro; but she formed to herself no definite idea of anything that was going on. People came to the coach door and spoke of dinner and supper, but Kirsteen was too shy to eat, though now and then she stepped down, feeling that she was stiffening into stone. And then the long night came, through which went the same roll and jar and jolt of the coach, and now and then a feverish interval of noise and distraction breaking the doze into which she had fallen. She was too much agitated, too unassured, too conscious of the break with all her former life and habits which she was making, to enjoy the journey or the sight of so many new places or the novelty in everything. And yet there was a certain wild pleasure in the rush through the night, even in the languor of weariness that crept over her and betrayed her into sleep, and the strange awakening to feel that it was no dream but that still, even while she slept, the fields and hedges were flying past and the journey going on. The second day, however, was one long bewilderment and confusion to Kirsteen, who was altogether unaccustomed to the kind of fatigue involved in travelling; and when she was set down finally in the midst of all the lights and commotion, the passengers tumbling down from above and from behind, the little crowd of people awaiting their friends, the ostlers, the coachmen, the porters with the luggage, her bewilderment reached its climax. She was pushed about by men running to and fro, getting out boxes and bags and every kind of package, and by the loiterers who had gathered to see the coach come in, and by the people who had not found their friends, some of whom came and peered into her face, as if she might perhaps be the person for whom they looked. Kirsteen at length managed to get out of the crowd, and stood in a corner waiting till the din should be over, observing with all the keenness that was left in her till she found someone whose face she could trust. She found at last a man who was 'a decent-like man', whom she thought she could venture to address, and, going up to him, asked if he could direct her to Miss Jean Brown's the mantua-maker? 'I have got the address in my pocket,' she said, 'but perhaps ye will know.' 'No, miss,' said the decent-like man, 'there's a many Browns. I think I knows half a hundred.' 'She is a person from Ayrshire,' said Kirsteen. 'They don't put up where they comes from, not commonly,' said her friend, with a grin; 'but if you 'as a letter, miss, I advise you to look at it.' Kirsteen had doubts about betraying the whereabouts of her pocket in this strange place, but another glance assured her that he was an unusually decent-like man; and, besides, what could she do? She took out cautiously the letter with Miss Jean Brown's address. 'Chapel Street, Mayfair, will that be near hand?' she said.

'Bless you, that's the West End, that is – it's miles and miles away.'

Kirsteen's heart sank so that she could have cried – miles and miles! – after her long jolting in the coach. The tears came to her eyes. But after a moment she recovered herself, feeling the utter futility of yielding to any weakness now. 'Could you direct me the way to go?' she said, 'for I'm a stranger in London.' To see her standing there, with her bundle in her hand and her cloak on her arm, making this very unnecessary explanation was a pathetic sight. The decent-like man was touched – perhaps he had daughters of his own.

'I might find the way,' he said, 'for I'm a Londoner born, but a stranger like you, fresh from the country, as anybody can see, and ready to believe whatever is told you – no, no! The thing you've got to do, miss, is to take a coach—'

'A coach!' said Kirsteen in horror. 'Is London such a big place, then, that it wants a coach to go from one part to another?'

'It's a hackney coach, if you have ever heard of such a thing,' said the man. 'I'll call one for you if you please. It is the best thing to do. You could never find your way by night even though you might in the day.'

Kirsteen hesitated for a moment. 'It will cost a great deal,' she said, looking wistfully from the yard into the crowded street, with its flaring lamps and the hoarse cries that came from it. She shrank back to the side of her new friend as she gazed, feeling more than ever like a shipwrecked mariner, not knowing among what kind of savages she might fall. 'Oh, will ye tell me what to do?' she said, with a quite unjustifiable faith in the decent-like man.

However, it is sometimes good to trust, and the result of Kirsteen's confidence was that she soon found herself in a hackney coach, driving, a very forlorn wayfarer indeed, through what seemed to be an endless succession of streets. She had asked her friend humbly whether he would take it amiss if she offered him a shilling for his kindness, and he had taken a load off her mind by accepting the coin with much readiness, but in return had filled her with confusion by asking where was her luggage? 'Oh, it will be quite right when I get there,' Kirsteen had said, deeply blushing, and feeling that both the coachman and her acquaintance of the yard must think very poorly of her. And then that long drive began. Every corner that was turned, and there were she thought a hundred, Kirsteen felt that now at last she must have reached her journey's end; and on each such occasion her heart gave a wild throb, for how could she tell how Miss Jean would receive her, or if there would be rest for her at last? And then there would come a respite, another long ramble between lines of dark houses with muffled lights in the windows, and then another corner and another leap of her pulses. She thought hours must have

elapsed before at last, with a jar that shook her from head
to foot, the lumbering vehicle came to a stop. Kirsteen
stepped out almost speechless with excitement, and gave
something, she could scarcely tell what, to the coachman;
and then even this conductor of a moment, whose face she
could scarcely see in the dark, clambered up on his box
and trotted away, leaving her alone. She thought, with a
pang, that he might have waited just a moment to see
whether they would let her in. It would only have been kind
– and what could she do in that dreadful case if they did
not? And what was she to Miss Jean Brown that they should
let her in? Her loneliness and helplessness, and the very
little thread of possibility that there was between her and
despair, came over Kirsteen like a sudden blight as she
stood outside the unknown door in the dark street. She
began to tremble and shiver, though she tried with all her
might to subdue herself. But she was very tired – she had
eaten scarcely anything for two days. And this great gloomy
town which had swallowed her little existence seemed so
dark and terrible. There was no light to show either
knocker or bell, and she stood groping, almost ready to give
up the attempt and sit down upon the steps and be found
dead there, as she had heard poor girls often were in
London. She had come to this pitch of desperation when
her hand suddenly touched something that proved to be a
bell. Immediately her heart stood still, with a new and
keener excitement. She waited clinging to the railing,
holding her breath.

It seemed a long time before there was any response.
Finally a door opened, not the door at which Kirsteen
stood, but one below, and a faint light shone out upon a
little area into which stepped a figure half visible. 'Who is
there? And what may you be wanting?' said a voice.

'I was wanting to speak to Miss Jean Brown,' Kirsteen
said.

'Miss Brown never sees anybody at this hour. Ye can
come tomorrow if ye want to see her.'

'Oh,' cried Kirsteen, her voice shrill with trouble, 'but I
cannot wait till tomorrow! It's very urgent. It's one from
her sister in Scotland. Oh, if ye have any peety ask her –
just ask her! for I cannot wait.'

Another figure now came out below, and there was a

short consultation. 'Are ye the new lass from the Hielands?'
said another voice.

Even at this forlorn moment the heart of Kirsteen
Douglas rose up against this indignity. 'I am from the Hielands,' she said: then anxiety and wretchedness got the
better of her pride. 'Yes, yes,' she cried, 'I am anything ye
please; but let me in, oh, let me in, if ye would not have me
die!'

'Who is that at the front door? Can ye not open the front
door? Is there not a woman in the house that has her hearing but me that am the mistress of it?' cried a new voice
within; a vigorous footstep came thumping along the passage, the door was suddenly thrown open, and Kirsteen
found herself in front of a flaring candle which dazzled her
eyes, held up by a woman in a rustling silk dress half
covered by a large white muslin apron. Perhaps the white
apron made the most of the resemblance, but the worn-out
girl was not in a condition to discriminate. She stumbled
into the house without asking another question, and crying
'Oh, Miss Jean!' half fell at the feet of Marg'ret's sister,
feeling as if all her cares were over and her haven reached.

'Yes, I am just Miss Jean,' said the mistress of the house,
holding her candle so as to throw its full light on Kirsteen's
face. 'But who are you? I dinna ken ye. You're from the
auld country, that's easy to be seen; but I canna take in
every Scots lass that comes with Miss Jean in her mouth.
Who are ye, lassie? But ye're no a common lass. The Lord
keep us, ye'll never be my sister Marg'ret's young leddy
from Drumcarro?'

Miss Jean put down her candle hastily on a table, and
took Kirsteen's hands. 'You're cauld and you're in a
tremble, and ye dinna say a word. Come in, come in to the
fire, and tell me, bairn, if it's you.'

Then there followed a few moments or minutes in which
Kirsteen did not know what happened. But the clouds
cleared away and she found herself in a room full of warm
firelight, seated in a great chair, and herself saying (as if it
was another person), 'I thought I had got home and that it
was Marg'ret.'

'But you called me Miss Jean.'

'Ah,' said Kirsteen, now fully aware what she was saying
and no longer feeling like another person. 'I knew it was

Miss Jean, but it was my Marg'ret too. It was maybe this,' she said touching the white apron, 'but it was mostly your kind, kind eyne.'

'I'm feared you're a flatterer,' said Miss Jean; 'my eyne might be once worth taking notice of, but not now. But you're just worn out, and famishing and cauld and tired. Eh, to think a Miss Douglas of Drumcarro should come to my house like this, and nobody to meet you, or receive you, or pay you any attention! It was just an inspiration that I went to the door myself. But your room will be ready in a moment, and ye shall have some supper and a cup of tea.' She paused a moment and cast a glance round. 'Did you bring your – luggage with ye?' she said.

Kirsteen laughed, but blushed a little. 'I have nothing but my bundle; I came away in such a hurry – and on my feet.'

Miss Jean blushed far more than Kirsteen did. She 'thought shame for the servants'. 'We must say ye left it at the office and it's coming tomorrow,' she said anxiously. And then care and warmth and a sense of well-being and comfort and rest so enveloped Kirsteen that she remembered little more. There was a coming and going of various faces into the light, a bustle of preparation, Miss Jean's keys taken out and brought back, consultations about the spare room, and the well-aired sheets, through all of which she sat happy and passive, seeing and hearing everything once more as if she were another person. The dark seas seemed to have been traversed, the unknown depths fathomed, and paradise attained. Perhaps the blazing fire, the fragrant tea, the little hasty meal, were not very paradisaical elements; but even these creature comforts acquire a sentiment after a long, tedious journey, especially when the tired traveller retains all the quick sensations of youth, and is delivered from the horrible exaggerated terrors of inexperience as well as the mere fatigue of body and soul.

CHAPTER XXII

The journey over and the end attained! This was the thought that came to Kirsteen's mind as she opened her eyes upon the morning – not so tired, she reflected, as she had been at the inn at Arrochar, at Mrs Macfarlane's, after her first day's walk. Was that a year ago? she asked herself. The adventures by the way, the long lines of loch and hill, the villages and the silent kirks which had seemed to make her safer whenever she saw them, the great flaring dark image of Glasgow, relieved by the sight of Anne and her babies, and the green with the bleaching, the whirl of the long unbroken journey, rattling, jolting, rolling, hour after hour through day and night – the strange passage in the dark through unknown London, and finally this little room in which she opened her eyes, lying still and closing them again to enjoy the sensation of rest, then opening them to see the yellow fog of the morning like a veil against the two small windows already shrouded by curtains, to which Kirsteen was unaccustomed and which seemed to shut out all air and light – if that could be called light that pressed upon the panes with a yellow solidity just touched by a wintry sun. Were all her journeyings over, and had she reached the new world in which she was to live?

Her bundle had been carefully opened, her linen laid out in a drawer half open to show her where to find it, her second gown hung carefully up, shaken out of its creases by a skilful hand. Miss Jean herself had done this, still 'thinking shame for the servants' of the newcomer's scant possessions. It was already known all through the house that a distinguished visitor, Miss Douglas of Drumcarro, had arrived, a visitor of whose name Miss Jean was very proud, though a little mystified by her arrival, and wondering much to know what such a phenomenon as the arrival of a girl of good family unattended in London and at her house might mean. She was proud to give the needed hospitality, but why it should be to her, and not to any of her 'grand connections', that Kirsteen had come, mystified the dressmaker. And Marg'ret in her letter had given no explanation; 'Miss Kirsteen will tell you everything herself,' was all she had said. The seamstresses down below, and the servants still lower down who had mistaken the young lady for a new lass, were all in much excitement discussing the strange event. It was probably some story with love in it, the young women thought, and were all eager for a glimpse of the newcomer or for any contribution to her history.

She was nearly dressed when Miss Jean came with a gentle tap at the door. 'I was thinking you would perhaps like your breakfast in bed, my dear young lady. You have had a dreadful journey. From Glasgow in two days, and cramped up in the coach the whole time. But bless me, you are already dressed,' she added, scanning the gown in which Kirsteen had just clothed herself, from head to foot, or rather from hem to throat. Miss Jean looked it all over, and gave it a twitch here and there, and smoothed the shoulders with her hand. 'It's not ill made for the country,' she said, 'and fits you well enough, but these little puffed sleeves are out of fashion for morning dress. You must let me put you in the mode, Miss Douglas, before ye are seen in the world.'

Miss Jean herself wore a stuff gown, crossed over upon the bosom, and open at the neck which was covered with a neckerchief of voluminous white net underneath the gown. She wore a brown front with little curls, and a close cap tied under her chin for morning wear, with a large and long muslin apron trimmed round with muslin work and lace. She had a large and ruddy countenance, with eyes like Marg'ret's, kind and soft. Kirsteen was surprised to find, however, how little in the morning was the resemblance which she had thought so great in the night. Marg'ret, though the virtual mistress of the house at home, never changed the dress and aspect of a servant woman for anything more becoming the housekeeper. But Miss Jean was more imposing than many of the country ladies, with a large gold watch like a small warming-pan hooked to her side, and her handkerchief fastened by a brooch of real pearls. To have this personage addressing her so respectfully, looking forward to her entry into the grand world, overwhelmed the girl who already felt she owed her so much.

'Oh,' she said, 'Miss Jean – I have not come to London

to be seen in the world. I'm just a poor runaway from
home. I promised Marg'ret I would tell you everything.
Nothing can change the Douglas blood. We have that, but
we have little more; and all my father thinks of is to push
on the boys and restore the old family. The lassies are just
left to shift for themselves.'

'That is often the case, my dear young lady. Ye must just
marry, and do as well for yourselves in that way.'

'We are three of us at home, and we can do nothing,
and what does it matter being a Douglas if ye have no siller?
I've come away, not to see the world, but to make my
fortune, Miss Jean.'

Miss Jean threw up her hands in dismay. 'Bless the bairn,
to make her fortune!' she cried.

'That's just what I intend,' cried Kirsteen. 'I'll not marry
a man to deceive him when I care for nothing but his
money. I'll marry no man, except – and I've just come to
London to work for my living – and make my fortune if I
can.'

'Whisht, whisht, whisht!' cried Miss Jean, 'that's all very
well in a lad – and there's just quantities of them goes into
the city without a penny and comes out like nabobs in their
carriages – but not women, my dear, let alone young lassies
like you.'

'I will not be a young lass for ever, Miss Jean.'

'No,' said the dressmaker shaking her head, 'ye may be
sure of that, my dear lamb. That's just the one thing that
never happens. But ye'll be married, and happy, and bairns
at your knee, before your youth's past, for that,' she said,
with a sigh, 'I'm thinking, my dear, is the best way. I was
never one that had much to do with the men. There's some
does it, and some not. Look at Marg'ret and me, ne'er had
such a thought; but now we're getting old both the one
and the other, and who will we have to lay our heads in the
grave? – not one belonging to us. We're just as the auld
Queen said, dry trees.'

'Not Marg'ret,' cried Kirsteen, 'not while one of us is to
the fore! I am not wishing to lay her head in the grave, but
for love and faithfulness she will never lack as long as there
is a Douglas to the fore.'

'It's a real pleasure to me,' said Miss Jean, putting her
handkerchief to her eyes, 'to hear ye speak. And well I

know Marg'ret would want before you wanted, any one of
the family. So it's on both sides, and a grand thing to see a
faithful servant so respected. Now, Miss Douglas—'
   'My name is Kirsteen.'
   'Well, Miss Kirsteen. You'll just take a good rest, and
look about you, and see the follies of London before ye
think anything more about making your fortune. Eh, to
hear those bairns speak! Ye would think it was the easiest
thing in the world to make a fortune. Ye would think ye
had but to put forth your hand and take it. That's just my
nephew John's opinion, that has got a small place in an
office in Fleet Street, and is thinking what grand things he'll
have in the show the year he's Lord Mayor. He was not
satisfied at all with the last one,' said Miss Jean, with a
hearty laugh. ' "Auntie," says he, "it shall be very different
when it comes to my turn." And the laddie has fifteen shil-
lings a week, and to fend for himself! But, my dear,' she
said, smoothing Kirsteen's shoulder once more, and giving
a twitch to the one line in her gown which did not hang as
Miss Jean approved, 'by the time we have put ye into the
last fashion, and ye've been at a grand party or two, ye'll
have changed your tune.'
   'Who will bid me to grand parties?' said Kirsteen; but
Miss Jean had disappeared and did not hear. It gave
Kirsteen a little pang to think there was nobody who could
interfere, no 'grand connections' such as the mantua-maker
supposed, to call her to the world, a pang not so much for
herself as for the mortification involved in Miss Jean's discovery of the fact. As for grand parties Kirsteen had found
out that they were a delusion. The ball at the Castle had
filled her with dreams of pleasure, but yet nothing but harm
had come of it. She had been neglected while there, and
received none of the homage which every girl is taught to
expect, and she had found only Glendochart, whose suit
had cost her her home and everything that had been dear.
A tear stole to Kirsteen's eye as she made this reflection,
but it never fell, so quickly did her heart rise to the excitement of the novelty around her. She said to herself that
even if there was no Glendochart she would not now go
back. She would stay and work and make her fortune, and
make Jeanie an heiress, and get every dainty that London
could provide to send to her mother. She would buy a

carriage for her mother, and easy couches and down pillows and everything that heart could desire; and then when *he* came back – the tear rose again, but only to make brighter the triumphant smile in Kirsteen's eyes. Let the others go to grand parties if they could (Mary would like it) but as for her, she would make her fortune, and be a help to everyone that bore her name. She knelt down by her bedside to say her prayers, her heart so throbbing with purpose and anticipation that she could scarcely go through these devout little forms which had been the liturgy of her childhood. 'Oh, that I may make my fortune and help them all,' was the real petition of her heart. To suggest anything so worldly to her Maker would have been blasphemy according to the creed which Kirsteen had been taught, but this was the breath of intense aspiration that carried up the little innocent petitions. She rose from her knees in a thrill of purpose and feeling. 'They shall not be shamed as they think, they shall be thankful there was Kirsteen among the lassies, as well as seven sons to make Drumcarro great again. Oh, maybe not Drumcarro but the old Douglas country!' Kirsteen said to herself. And so went downstairs glowing to see what the new sphere was in which she was to conquer the world. And then when *he* came back!

Kirsteen was quite unacquainted with the kind of house, tall and straight and thin, in which, as in the fashionable quarter, Miss Jean had established herself. The thread of narrow street filled with a foggy smoky air through which the red morning sun struggled – the blank line of houses opposite, and the dreary wall of the church or chapel which gave it its name, seemed to her petty and dingy and small beyond description, all the more that Miss Jean evidently expected her visitor to be impressed with the fashionable character of the locality. 'The rooms were a great deal bigger where we were, near Russell Square,' she said, 'and more convenient for the work; but fashion is just everything, and this is where all my leddies live. You could not be expected to go back to Bloomsbury having once got foot in Mayfair.' Naturally Kirsteen was quite incapable of contradicting this axiom, which everybody in the workroom considered incontrovertible. The workroom was a long room built out at the back of the house, with many windows, and walls which had no decoration except a few plates of the fashions pinned to them, as being particularly lovely. A long table ran down the middle at which were seated a number of young women, every one of whom to Kirsteen's inexperienced perceptions was infinitely more fashionable, more imposing than her highest conception of herself had ever come to; and they spoke fine English, with an accent which was to be sure not so easily understood as her own, but had an air of refinement which impressed Kirsteen much. Were they all gentlewomen, come like herself to make their fortunes? She made a timid question on this subject to Miss Jean which was answered almost indignantly, 'Gentlewomen! Not one of them – havering, glaikit lassies!' was the reply.

'They speak such fine English,' said Kirsteen.

Miss Jean kept her word and took her to see all the 'ferlies', London Bridge, and the Exchange, and the Guild-hall, with Gog and Magog guarding the liberties of the city, and to take a walk in the park which was just like the country, and where a glass of new milk warm from the cow was given her as a treat. And she was taken to see the coaches come in with the news from the Continent about Boney's escape and the progress that adventurer was making, and the orders to the troops that were to crush him. Kirsteen thanked God that neither her brother nor *him* were in the King's army, but away in India where, indeed, there was fighting going on continually though nobody knew much about it. And she likewise saw Westminster and St Paul's, both of which overawed her but did not connect themselves with any idea of worship; her little kirk at home, and the respectable meeting-house at Glasgow to which she had gone with Anne, being all she knew of in that way. She maintained her composure wonderfully through all these sightseeings, showing no transport either of admiration or wonder, something to the disappointment of Miss Jean. This was not owing to want of interest, however, but partly to a Scotch shyness of expressing herself, and the strong national objection to demonstration or rhapsodies of any kind – and partly to the high tension in which her mind was – a sort of exaltation which went beyond any tangible object, and even made most things a little disappointing, not so splendid as imagination had suggested. The one thing that did overcome Kirsteen's composure was the extent of

the streets, tedious, insignificant, and unlovely but endless,
going on and on to the end of all things, and of the crowd,
which she did not admire in itself, which was often dirty,
noisy, and made her shrink, but which also was endless,
abounding everywhere. You left it in Fleet Street only to
find it again in Piccadilly, Kirsteen thought, gaping at the
coaches before the White Horse Cellar just as it had gaped
at her own coach where she arrived, which was, she was
told, far away in the city. Where did the people come from?
Where did they disappear to? Did they live anywhere or
sleep in bed, or were they always about the streets day and
night? This was one of the things that made her more indifferent to the sights; for her eyes were always wandering
away after the people about whom she did not like to ask
questions. She saw the Prince Regent riding out accompanied by his gentlemen, 'the grandest gentlemen in the
land,' Miss Jean explained, telling Kirsteen a name here and
there which were completely unknown to the Highland girl
– who did not admire her future sovereign. In this way a
week passed, Kirsteen vainly attempting to be suffered to
do something more than sit in the parlour and read a book
(it was the *Ladies' Museum*, a magazine of the time in many
volumes, and containing beautiful prints of the fashions,
which was the chief literature at Miss Brown's), or walk out
whenever business permitted Miss Jean an hour of freedom
– which was generally in the morning – to see the sights.
One day her patience could bear it no longer: she burst
forth—

'Miss Jean, Miss Jean! I would rather see no more ferlies.
I take you out and spend your time and give a great deal
of trouble when all I want is to learn my work, and put to
my hand.'

'To make your fortune?' said Miss Jean.

'Perhaps at the end – but to learn first,' said Kirsteen
pausing with a deep passing colour, the colour of pride –
'my trade.'

'Your trade! What would your father say, good gentleman, if he heard you say such words? – Or your mother,
poor lady, that has so little health?'

'I've left both father and mother,' cried Kirsteen, 'but
not to come upon others – and ye cannot tear me from my
purpose whatever may be said. There's reasons why I will

never go back to Drumcarro, till – I will tell you some day, I cannot now. But I'm here to work and not to be a cumberer of the ground. I want to learn to be a mantua-maker to support myself and help – other folk. Miss Jean, if you will not have me I'll have to ask some other person. I cannot be idle any more.'

'Miss Kirsteen, there will be grand connections seeking you out and angry at me that let you have your will – and I will lose customers and make unfriends.'

'I have no grand connections,' said Kirsteen. 'You see for yourself nobody has troubled their heads about me. I'm just as lone as the sparrow on the housetop. I've left my own folk and Marg'ret, and I have nobody but you in the world. Why should ye stop me? When my heart's set upon it nobody can stop me,' Kirsteen cried, with a flash of her eyes like the flash in her father's when his blood was up.

'Lord keep us! I can weel believe that to look at you,' said Miss Jean.

CHAPTER XXIII

It followed as a matter of course that Kirsteen very soon accomplished her purpose. She took her place in the work-room to the great surprise and partial confusion of the workwomen who did not at first know how to teach the lady who had come among them, her qualities and position much magnified by Miss Jean. Some of them were disposed to be impertinent, some scornful, some to toady the young newcomer, who, whatever she might be in herself, was undoubtedly Miss Brown's favourite, and able to procure favours and exemptions for those who were her friends. The standing feud between Scotch and English, and the anger and jealousy with which the richer nation regarded the invasions of the poorer, had not yet fallen into the mild dislike which is all that can be said to subsist nowadays in the way of hostile feeling between the two countries. Fierce jests about the Scotch who came to make their fortune off their richer neighbours, about their clannishness and their canniness, and their poverty and their pride, and still lower and coarser jibes about other supposed peculiarities were then still as current as the popular crows of triumph over the French and other similar antipathies; and Kirsteen's advent was attended by many comments of the kind from the sharp young Londoners to whom her accent and her slower speech, and her red hair and her ladyhood were all objects of derision.

But it was soon found that it was not easy to overcome Miss Kirsteen, which was the name she chose to be called by. 'I think no shame of my work, but I will not put my father's name in it, for he is old-fashioned and he would think shame,' Kirsteen had said – and Miss Jean approved greatly. 'It would never do to let these lassies say that there was a Miss Douglas in the workroom with them.' Kirsteen had a shrewd suspicion that the Miss Robinsons and Miss Smiths of the workroom would derive little idea of dignity or superiority from the name of Douglas; but even she was not quite so emancipated as to believe them quite ignorant

of its importance. When she discovered from the revelations of a toady that they called her Miss Carrots, or Miss
Scotchy behind her back, Kirsteen was angry, but dignified,
and took no notice, to the great disappointment of her
informant. 'I did not choose the colour of my hair,' she said
with much stateliness, little foreseeing a time to come when
red hair should be the admiration of the world. But the
young women soon heard that their shafts passed over
Kirsteen's head and fell innocuous, which is the most safe
and speedy extinguisher of malice. To make covert allusions
which the object of them never finds out, and utter jibes
that are not even heard by the intended butt of the company is poor sport.

Kirsteen had the safeguard of having a great many things
to think of. Her thoughts strayed to her mother who would
miss her, for whom perhaps she ought to have suffered
everything rather than abandon. But what good would I
have been to her if they had married me to Glendochart?
she said to herself. And then she would ask herself what
Glendochart would do, kind man whom she was wae to dis-
appoint or harm, and how Marg'ret would meet the inquiries addressed to her, how much she would be forced to
reveal, how much she could hide. And then her thoughts
would fly to Anne, and the two babies on the hearthrug,
and the doctor, who, no doubt, was well-looking and well-
spoken and kind, and who had taken thought for Kirsteen's
comfort in a way she had little title to, considering how
many prejudices, not yet by any means dispersed, she entertained against him. After these subjects were exhausted,
and sometimes before they were begun, her mind, or rather
her heart, would fly to wild, unknown landscapes; dimly
imagined wastes of arid heat, in the midst of which a white
encampment, and one there of whom she could follow only
the personal image, not knowing what he might be doing
nor what was the course of that far-off Indian life. He might
be in the midst of a battle while Kirsteen, with her head
bent over her work and her needle flying, was thinking of
him; or travelling in strange ways, on camels over the
desert, or mysterious big elephants. The letters of her
brothers had been brief records of their own health and
appointments and removals and little more. She knew no
details of the life of the East. Her imagination could only

trace him vaguely through sunshine and splendours unknown. But with all these varied thoughts to fill her mind it may be imagined that Kirsteen was very little affected by the references to Carrots or to the Scotchies who took the bread out of the mouths of English folks. When she did hear them she took them at first with great good humour. 'There are plenty of English folk in Scotland,' she said. 'I've heard that the lady's maids and the bairns'-maids are all from here – to teach the children to knap English, which is a little different, as perhaps ye know, from the way we speak.' And as for the Carrots she disposed of that very simply. 'At home it is Ginger the bairns cry after me,' she said. After a while, when she caught the sound of those recurring words among her many thoughts, she would raise her eyes and send a flash among them which daunted the whisperers. But generally Kirsteen neither noticed nor heard the impertinences of her fellow workwomen, which was the most effectual check of all.

It may not be thought a very high quality in a heroine, but Kirsteen soon developed a true genius for her craft. She had never forgotten Miss Macnab's little lecture upon the accuracy of outline necessary for the proper composition of a gown – and thus had acquired the first principles almost without knowing it. She followed up this, which is the heart of the matter, by many studies and compositions in which her lively mind found a great deal of pleasure. She was not, perhaps, very intellectual, but she was independent and original, little trained in other people's ideas and full of fancies of her own, which, to my thinking, is the most delightful of characteristics. I remember that Mr Charles Reade has endowed one of the most charming women whom he has introduced to the knowledge of the world with the same gift. Mrs Lucy Dodd only, I think, made and invented mantles; but Kirsteen tried her active young powers upon everything, being impatient of sameness and monotony, and bent upon securing a difference, an individual touch in every different variety of costume. She was delighted with the beautiful materials, which were thrown about in the workroom, the ordinary mantua-maker having little feeling for them except in a view of their cost at so much a yard. But Kirsteen, quite unused to beautiful manufactured things, admired them all, and found a pleasure in heaping together and contrasting with each other the soft silken stuffs, many of them with a sheen of two blended colours called 'shot' in those days. Manufactures had not come to such perfection then as now, but there were no adulterated silks or cheap imitations; the very muslins, sprigged and spotted with many fanciful variations, were as costly as brocade nowadays – the kind of brocade which the later nineteenth century indulges in. To be sure, on the other hand, the plain straight gown required very much less material than is necessary now.

I do not myself think that dress was pretty in those days – but every fashion is beautiful to its time. And how the ladies of the early century managed to make themselves comfortable in white muslin gowns in December, even with a cloth pelisse over them, is more than I can divine, though I find in Miss Jean Brown's copy of the *Ladies' Museum* that this was the case. However that may be – and I do not suppose that Kirsteen was before her time, or more enlightened than the rest of the world – it is certain that she applied herself to the invention of pretty confections and modifications of the fashions with much of the genuine enjoyment which attends an artist in all crafts, and liked to handle and drape the pretty materials and to adapt them to this and that pretty wearer, as a painter likes to arrange and study the more subtle harmonies of light and shade. Miss Jean, who had herself been very successful in her day, but was no longer quite so quick to catch the value of a tint, or so much disposed to stand over a subject and attain perfection in the outline of a skirt, was wise enough to perceive the gifts of her young assistant, and soon began to require her presence in the showroom, to consult with her over special toilettes and how to secure special effects. She did this at first, however, with some reluctance, always haunted by the fear that Kirsteen might thus be exposed to remark, and even that she herself might suffer for her audacity in employing a gentlewoman in so exalted a rank of life. 'What if some of your grand connections or acquaintances should see ye?' she said. 'I have no grand connections,' said Kirsteen, vexed to have this want brought back and back upon her consciousness. 'For ye see I have all the nobility coming about the place,' said Miss Jean proudly; 'and now that the season has begun it is different from the winter.' 'I know nothing about the nobility,' cried Kirsteen again. She was angered at last by the assumption, all the more that her want of acquaintance with what was so clearly understood to be her own class, now became so evident to her as to be a grievance – a grievance that she had never been conscious of before.

It happened one day, however, that there came into the showroom, while Kirsteen was there, a very distinguished party indeed, which Miss Jean advanced to the door to meet, curtseying to the ground, and which consisted of a large and imposing mother, a beautiful, tall girl, at sight of whom Kirsteen precipitately retired into a corner, and a young gentleman whom in her surprise she did not notice. It appeared, however, that this was not at all the case with him. He glanced round with a yawn as a young man in compulsory attendance on his mother and sister may be excused for doing, then, observing a young figure in the corner, began to take instant measures to discover whether there might not be something here to amuse himself with while the ladies were occupied with their dressmaker. Now it is not easy for a young person in a mantua-maker's showroom persistently to keep her back turned upon a party of customers, and Kirsteen, to give herself a countenance, began to arrange carefully the draping of a piece of silk over a stand, so as to appear to be very much occupied and absorbed in her occupation. That it should really happen to her after all to find a grand acquaintance among Miss Jean's nobility! The discovery was painful, yet gave her a certain gratification, for at least to be able to say to Miss Jean that she must run away when the Duchess came in was something, and vindicated her gentility. On the other hand she said to herself with a little bitterness that most likely they would look her in the face, even Lady Chatty, and never know that they had seen her before.

The young man all this time kept roaming about, looking as it appeared at the mantles and the bonnets, but aiming at the stand where Kirsteen, bending over her silk, was pinching and twisting it so as to show its full perfection. He said 'Oh!' with a start, when he got into a position in which he could obtain a glimpse of the half-hidden face. She looked up in the surprise of the moment; and there stood the critic of the ball, the sportsman of Loch Long side, he who had been of so much service to her yet had affronted her more than the tramp, Lord John himself – with a delighted smile and mischievous air of satisfaction. 'Ho, ho! my pretty maiden – so this was where you were going?' he said to her in a low tone – 'I am delighted to see you again.'

The colour rushed to Kirsteen's face. She looked up at him defiantly for a moment; then feeling that discretion was the better part of valour, edged away from where he was standing, bending over her draperies again and drawing the stand softly after her. But Lord John was not to be so easily daunted.

'You can't dismiss me again in that grand style,' he said. 'Loch Long is one thing and a milliner's in London quite another. Do you think I will believe that you have come here for nothing but to fit gowns on women not half so pretty as yourself?'

Angry words rushed to Kirsteen's lips in a flood – angry, scornful, defiant words, full of contempt and indignation. She was deeply indignant at this attempt to take advantage of what he thought her weakness; but she knew that she was not weak, which is a consciousness that gives courage. Had she been one of the other girls in the workroom to be flattered or frightened or compromised no doubt she would have done some imprudence, implored his silence, or committed herself in some other way. But Kirsteen was out of the range of such dangers. She turned from the stand she had been draping to another piece of work without any visible sign of the disturbance in her mind, and made no reply.

Lord John was not to be shaken off so easily. The time had no very high standard either of morals or manners, and to seize the opportunity of speaking to a pretty girl wherever he found her, was rather expected from, than disapproved in a young man. These were the days in which it was still a civility on the part of a gallant to kiss a pretty maidservant as he gave her half a crown. And milliners were supposed very fair game. He followed her as she opened with much show of zeal a box of French flowers. 'Come,' he said, 'I must choose some of these; I must buy something of you. You'll find me an excellent customer. Choose the prettiest for me, and I'll give you whatever you ask for

them. If I had but known when we met last that you were
coming here!'

'Miss Kirsteen,' said Miss Jean, who had somehow an
eye about her to observe what was going on behind. 'Will
ye please to bring me that new box of French flowers?'

It was a relief yet a new alarm. Kirsteen lifted the light
box, and came slowly towards the group. Now it would be
seen that they had no more recollection of her than if she
had been a stock or a stone. The Duchess did not turn
round, but Lady Chatty, conscious of the presence of
another girl, and also perhaps vaguely aware that her
brother had already found an interest in the opposite
corner, looked straight at Miss Jean's new assistant. She
gave a start, and clasped her hands; then crying out, 'It is
Kirsteen!' darted upon her, throwing the box with all the
beautiful new French flowers to the ground.

'Oh, dear me, how clumsy I am! Oh, I hope the flowers
will take no harm! But it is Kirsteen. Mamma, do you see?
Kirsteen Douglas from our own country. Oh, I'm so glad to
see you,' cried Lady Chatty, seizing her by both the hands
out of which her lively onslaught had thrown the box.
'You're like a breath of Highland air, you're like the heather
on the hills.'

And indeed it was a good metaphor as Kirsteen stood
confused, with her russet locks a little ruffled as their
manner was, and her hazel eyes glowing and her bright face
confused between pleasure and vexation and shame.

'It is true that it is me, Lady Chatty,' she said, 'but you
should not have made me let fall the flowers.'

'I will help you to pick them up,' said the young lady;
and Lord John, taking a long step forward as if his attention
had been suddenly roused, said, 'Can I be of use? I'll help
too.'

Meantime her Grace, who had turned round at Lady
Chatty's cry, stood for a moment surprised, regarding the
group all kneeling on the floor, picking up the flowers, and
then turned back to have a colloquy with Miss Jean, in
which the words 'Drumcarro's daughter', and 'Glendochart', and 'a wilful girl', and 'a good marriage', and Miss
Jean's deprecating explanation, 'I told her so. I told her so,
your Grace, but she would not listen to me,' came to
Kirsteen's ears in her anxiety, while she eluded the touch of

Lord John's hand, and tried to respond to all Lady Chatty's eager questions. 'Oh, Kirsteen, you should hear what Miss Eelen says of you,' said Lady Chatty, 'and poor old Glen-dochart, who is such a nice old man. Why were you so unkind? But I would not marry an old gentleman myself, not if he were a royal duke,' cried the girl, raising her voice a little not without intention. 'And how clever it was of you to think of coming here! Nobody would ever have found you here if mamma had not taken it into her head to come to Miss Jean's today. But oh, Kirsteen, it is a pity, for they will send you home again. I am glad to have seen you, but I am sorry, for mamma is coming to talk seriously to you. I can see it in her face. And papa will hear of it, and he will think it his duty to take an interest. And between them they will make you go home again. And when once they get you back, they will marry you to old Glen-dochart, whether you like or not!'

CHAPTER XXIV

And indeed the Duchess did come forward with the gravest looks, after the flowers had all been gathered up and restored to the box and her talk was over with Miss Jean.

'Miss Douglas,' she said, 'I am much surprised to find you here.'

'Your Grace,' said Kirsteen, 'I am very well here.'

'That is just your silly notion. A young person of your age is not fitted to dispose of her own life. Your worthy parents had looked out a most suitable match for you, and I cannot but say it was very wrong and a shame to all belonging to you that you should run away.'

'I would rather say nothing about it, madam,' said Kirsteen. 'Whether that was the cause or not, the heart knoweth its own bitterness; and every one of us, however small we may be, understands their own affairs best.'

'No, young lady,' said the Duchess, 'that's not so. You are not at an age when you are fit to judge. It is just nothing but childish folly,' she added, raising her voice also in-tentionally, and casting a glance towards her daughter, 'to object to a good man and a gentleman of a good family, and who is hale and hearty and full of sense – because he is not just as young as some long-legged fool that you may think better worth your pains.'

'Like me, for instance,' said Lord John in an audible aside.

Her Grace's eyes softened as her look rested for a moment upon her scapegrace. Then she turned back to Kirsteen with her severest look. 'It is a very bad example to other foolish young creatures that you have set in running away. But I hope you will think better of it, and be per-suaded, and go back to your family,' she said.

'I do not think I can do that,' said Kirsteen, 'for there's nothing changed that I know, and the reason that brought me away is still there.'

'Miss Douglas,' said the Duchess, 'his Grace himself has heard all about this from one and another, and I make little doubt that when he hears where you are and that we have seen you, and what an unsuitable place you are in for a gentleman's daughter, he will take it into his own hands, and just insist that you must go back.'

Kirsteen had been standing in a respectful attitude listening to the great lady, answering for herself, it is true, with much steadiness, but also with deference and humility. She raised her head now, however, and looked the Duchess in the face. 'I am meaning no disrespect,' she said, 'but, madam, I am not his Grace's clanswoman, that he should insist. The Douglases I have always heard tell were sovran in their own place, and gave no reverence to one of another name.'

'Young lady,' cried the Duchess astonished, 'you are a very bold person to speak of his Grace in that tone.'

'I am meaning no disrespect,' Kirsteen said. But she stood so firm, and met her Grace's eye with so little shrinking, that even the Duchess herself was embarrassed. It is unwise to profess an intention of interfering and setting everything straight before you have ascertained that your impulse will be obeyed. The great lady coloured a little and felt herself worsted. It was only natural that she should lose her temper; she turned upon Miss Jean, who stood by very tremulous, half sympathizing with Kirsteen, half overawed by her visitor.

'Then, Miss Brown,' she said, 'it should be your duty to interfere. It ill becomes you, a person so well supported by the Scots gentry, to back up a young girl of family in rebellion against her own kith and kin.'

Miss Jean was much taken by surprise, yet she was not unequal to the occasion. 'I have told Miss Kirsteen,' she said, 'on several occasions that this was what would happen; that her grand friends would step in, and that we would all be called to account. I hope your Grace will excuse me, but I cannot say more. I have no authority. If your Grace cannot move her, how will she heed the like of me?'

'She is a very self-willed young person,' said the Duchess; 'but I will see that her friends are communicated with, and no doubt her father will send someone to fetch her away. We will just leave the other question till another time. Charlotte, come away.'

'But I must have my gown, mamma,' cried Lady Chatty;
'indeed I'm not going without my gown. What should I do
with all the balls coming on, and nothing to wear? You can
go away if you please and send the carriage back for me,
or John will take me home. But if all the world were falling
to pieces, I must have my gown. You must know, Miss
Jean, it is for the birthday, and I must have something of
your very best. Kirsteen, what is the prettiest thing she has?
for you must know. I want some of that silver gauze that
is like a mist, and I have it in my head exactly how I want it
made. Oh, mamma, don't stand and look so glum, but just
go away, please, and send the carriage back for me.'

The Duchess hesitated for a moment, but in the end took
her daughter's advice, as was her custom. 'You will not
forget, Miss Jean, what I have said. And as for you, young
lady, I hope you will reflect upon your position and take
the proper steps to put things right,' she said severely.
'John, you will give me your arm downstairs. And see that
you are ready, Charlotte, in a quarter of an hour, when the
carriage comes back.'

With these words the Duchess went away. She could
not stand against her beautiful daughter and the necessity
of the new gown, but she would not sanction in her own
person the example of rebellion and self-assertion. 'You will
come back for Chatty,' she said to her son, relaxing a little
when she got outside that home of insubordination. 'She is
far too free with common people; and that young woman
is a very bold-looking person and not society for your
sister.'

'She is a very pretty person,' said Lord John; 'I could
not think where I had seen her before.'

'Pretty! with that red hair!' cried his mother, shaking her
head as she got into her carriage and drove away.

'Now, Kirsteen,' cried Lady Chatty, 'quick, quick, now
that mamma's gone her bark is a great deal worse than her
bite – tell me all about it. They wanted to make you marry
old Glendochart? Oh, parents are like that everywhere –
they want me, too. And couldn't you just face them and get
over them as I do? Couldn't you just? – Miss Jean, she is
crying – but I meant no harm.'

'Lady Chatty,' said Kirsteen, 'will you try and get her
Grace not to write? If I were ever so willing my father would

never more let me come back. Oh, if I might just be left
alone! – for I cannot tell you everything. My family is not
like other families. If I was dying for it they would never
more take me home again. Oh, if I might just be let alone!'

'I told you, Miss Kirsteen, what would be the end of it,'
said Miss Jean, 'and that you would bring me into trouble
too.'

'Oh, never mind these old people, they are all the same,'
cried Lady Chatty. 'But,' she added, 'I almost wonder after
all, Kirsteen, you did not marry old Glendochart; he would
have freed you from all the rest, and he would have done
whatever you pleased. And nobody could have put a question or said a word. So long,' said this experienced young
lady, looking in Kirsteen's face, 'as there was not someone
else. Oh, but I see!' she cried, clapping her hands, 'there is
someone else.'

'Will your leddyship look at this? – it is the gauze ye were
inquiring after,' said Miss Jean. 'I will just put it about
you over your shoulder, and you will see the effect. And
Miss Kirsteen, who has wonderful taste, will give us her
advice. Look now in the cheval glass. What does your ladyship think of that?'

'It's divine,' cried Lady Chatty, clapping her hands; and
interesting though the other subject was, the new gown and
its possibilities, and a delightful discussion as to certain
novel effects, carried the day. Miss Jean threw herself
ecstatically into Lady Chatty's devices by way of changing
the subject, and finally in a whirlwind of questions and suggestions, petitions for Kirsteen's confidence and recommen-
dations of silver trimmings, the visitor was got away at
last. Miss Jean, when she was gone, threw the silvery stuff
with some impatience upon the floor.

'I have humoured all her whims just to get you clear of
her,' she said. 'Oh, Miss Kirsteen, did I not tell ye what
would happen when you were discovered by your grand
friends?'

Curiously enough, however, even to Kirsteen's own
mind there was a certain solace in the thought that these
very great people, who knew so little about her, thought
her of sufficient importance to interfere personally in her
affairs. Her trouble and confusion before the Duchess's
reproof was wonderfully modified by the soothing sense

of this distinction. It had been humbling to feel that she had no grand connections, nobody that could interfere. There was consolation in the fulfilment of Miss Jean's prophecy.

And it may be imagined what excitement ran through the house from the garret to the basement some days after when the Scotch maid came into the workroom breathless, with the thrilling news that my Lord Duke was in the parlour waiting to see Miss Douglas. His Grace himself! 'Lord bless us!' cried Miss Jean, 'ye must go down quick, for a great person's time is precious, and I will come myself just when I think the interview's over, for no doubt he will want to give his directions to me.' All the needles in the workroom stopped with the excitement of this visit, and the boldest held her breath. A duke, no less, to see Miss Carrots, the Scotchy with the red hair! 'But that's how they do, they all hangs together,' was the comment afterwards, couched in less perfect language perhaps than the supposed pure English which Kirsteen admired. Kirsteen herself rose, very pale yet very determined, from her seat at the long table, and brushed from her dress the fragments of thread and scraps of silk. She said nothing, but walked away to this alarming interview with her heart thumping in her breast, though externally all seemed calm. Kirsteen had a strong inclination to run away once again and be no more seen, when she reached the parlour door; and it was chiefly pride that supported her through the ordeal. She went in with much internal trembling but a pale resolution which no duke nor other potentate could break down.

He was standing playing with his eyeglass against the window, blocking out most of the light – a large man enveloped in the huge folds of his neckcloth, and in layer upon layer of waistcoats, enormous at the shoulders but dwindling towards the legs in tight pantaloons. Truth to tell, his Grace was more nervous, so far as appearances went, than the little girl whom he had been sent to bring to a sense of her duty. He said 'How d'ye do?' very ceremoniously, and offered her a chair. 'You're one of our county neighbours, Miss Douglas, I hear. My land marches with Drumcarro, perhaps you will know. It is on the edge of the old Douglas country, which as luck will have it, now chiefly belongs to me, though it is no doing of mine.'

'But my father represents the old Douglases, your Grace, though we have so little of the land.'

'It is a long time since,' said the Duke, 'but it is perhaps true; and you have a right to stand up for your own side. The more reason for the Duchess's great concern at finding you here.'

'I am very well here, my lord Duke,' said Kirsteen rigidly; she had to keep so much control upon herself not to tremble that she had become as stiff as a wooden image, and was well aware of the fact, which did not add to her comfort.

'You are not my clanswoman, Miss Douglas,' said his Grace, using her own expression, 'and you know as well as I do I have no power over you. But I think I am perhaps implicated in what has happened from the foolish mistake I made in taking you for the daughter of Glendochart on the occasion when we had the pleasure of seeing you at the Castle. You may have thought from that that he was considered an old man, but he is nothing of the sort. He is younger than I am,' said the Duke, waving his hand with an air of conscious youth; 'he is a man in the prime of life. As for assuming you to be his daughter, it was only a foolish jest, my dear young lady. For I knew he had no daughter nor child of any kind, being an unmarried man. I hope this explanation will smooth matters,' the Duke said, with a demonstrative wave of his hand.

'Oh, it never was that,' cried Kirsteen, 'it never was that! And I have never said a word about Glendochart, nor given that as my reason. I had other reasons,' she said.

'My dear young lady, however you explain it, it was very foolish,' said his Grace, 'for all you needed to have done was to have said a word to Glendochart himself. He would never have had pressure put upon you. He is as true a gentleman as you will find between this and him. He would never have taken a bride by force. A word to him would have been enough.'

'I know that well,' said Kirsteen, 'oh, I know that well.' She added, 'But if it please your Grace, I never said it was because of Glendochart. I had – other reasons.'

'Oh, you had other reasons?' said the Duke, perplexed. 'But I hope now that we have talked it over you will see what is suitable, and just go quietly home.'

Kirsteen made no reply.

'I feel convinced,' said the Duke, 'that though you may be a little headstrong, you are not just a rebel, liking your freedom, as the Duchess was disposed to think; and now that I have set it all before you, you will just take your foot in hand, as we say in Scotland, and go cannily home.'

'I cannot do that, your Grace,' said Kirsteen.

'And why cannot you do that? You may depend upon it, it is the only right way. "Children, obey your parents," is the word of Scripture. You must really go home. Your forbears and mine have known each other when the Douglases were more on a level perhaps with my family than they are now, so you see I have a certain right to speak. My dear young lady, you will just come home.'

'I cannot do that, my lord Duke.'

'Hush, hush, ye will allow I must know better from my position and all that. Pack up your things, and I will see that you have a post-chaise ready and a servant to take care of you. You see we take a great interest in you, both the Duchess and myself.'

'I am much obliged to your Grace – and to the Duchess—'

'Yes, yes; but that's nothing. I will tell somebody to order the post-chaise for you, and you'll find, with a little judgment, that all will go well.'

He patted her arm softly, stroking her down as if she had been a cat or a child. 'Just go cannily home,' he said, 'that's always the best place for a girl – just go cannily home.'

At this moment Miss Jean, unable to contain herself longer, tapped at the door, and Kirsteen made her escape, leaving these high powers to concert the method of her going – a futile proceeding so long as the will of the proposed traveller remained unchanged.

CHAPTER XXV

In view of this important reservation, the arrangements made and sanctioned by Duke and Duchess, and feebly but faithfully supported by Miss Jean – who had become fully sensible of the value to herself of Kirsteen's services, yet could not but back up the higher authorities – did not come to very much. Passive resistance is a great power, and even when a child says 'I will not', it is policy on the part of his superiors to be quite sure of their power either to convince or coerce before entering upon any controversy. Kirsteen stood quite firm.

'No, my lord Duke, I cannot go home,' she said, with a curtsey so respectful that his Grace could only take refuge in the recollection that she was not his clanswoman.

'If ye had been of my name I would not have taken a denial,' he said.

'And she would have been of your name if she had married Glendochart,' cried the Duchess exasperated.

But Kirsteen stood firm. She would hear of no post-chaise. She did not repeat what had been wrung out of her in the first assault that her father would never again receive into his house the fugitive who had escaped from it. Kirsteen had been very well aware of this fact, however, from the beginning, and in her soul it supported her, like a rock to which she had set her back. Her own heart might fail. It did fail often when she thought of her mother. Some-times she would start up in the night with a wailing cry for Kirsteen ringing in her ears; and at these moments it would seem to her that to set out at once with no easements of a post-chaise, but on foot like a pilgrim, guilty of treason to the first love of life, was the only thing for her to do. But these compunctions of affection died away before the recol-lection of her father's lowering face and the fire in his fierce eyes. She had known it when she stole forth in the dark that miserable morning, escaping from all the limitations of her youthful life. Had there been more time to think, had there not been the terror upon her of his summary and unhesitating tyranny, some other way might have been found. But having once taken such a step Kirsteen knew that no way remained of going back. Like Anne she would be already swept out of the record of the family. No one would be permitted to name her name. And even her mother who wanted her most would weep, and acquiesce, and find comfort in an additional plaint. Kirsteen was profoundly acquainted with that prosaic course of common life which closes over all events in such a family as her own. It would be like a stone in the water with ever widening, ever fainter circles; and then the surface would become smooth again. It had been so in the case of Anne. She remembered well enough the awed and desolate sensation of the moment, the story about the candle dying in the socket, and the cold wind blowing through the house from the open door; and then a little blank of vacancy, and terror of the forbidden name which would come to their lips unawares; and then – forgetfulness. Kirsteen knew that the same process would take place in her own case; the father's ban – forbidding that she should be called a child of his or her name mentioned in his house, and the mother's sob, but consent. No romantic superstitions about a father's curse were in Kirsteen's mind. It roused her only to self-assertion, to something of a kindred pride and wrath, and resistance; nor did the thought of her mother's acquiescence in the sentence wound her. Poor mother! The girl was glad to think that there would be no secret struggle in the ailing woman's soul, but only a few tears and all over. Kirsteen had the steadying force of experience to subdue all exaggerated feelings in her own bosom. She knew exactly how it would be. But she knew at the same time that the sentence she had herself called forth was fixed and would not be changed.

And to speak the truth Kirsteen felt the activity and occupations of the new life to be much more congenial to her own energetic and capable spirit than the dull quiet of the old, in which there was no outlet. That she should be seized with a yearning now and then for the sound of the linn, for the silence of the hills, for the wholesome smell of the peats in the clear blue Highland air, was as natural as that she should hear that wail for Kirsteen in the midst of her dreams. These longings gradually built up in her mind an ideal picture of the beauty and perfection of nature as embodied in her own glen, such as is a stay and refreshment to many a heart in the midst of alien life – to many a heart which perhaps in presence of that glen not idealized would be unconscious of any beauty in nature. The glen, and her mother, and little Jeanie – the time would come when she would shower secret gifts and comforts upon all – when they should find out what Kirsteen was by the good things that would come from her – the things soft, and lovely, and comforting, and sweet, which Marg'ret would convey and the father never find out. Go back! Oh, no; she would not if she could go back, and she could not if she would. So what did it matter what Duke or Duchess might say? The post-chaise remained unordered: the girl curtseyed to his Grace and her Grace, and stood firm. And by and by that power came in which is of such force in all human things. Duchess and Duke, and Miss Jean, and even Kirsteen herself, carried on by the tide of daily life with its ever new occurrences – forgot; and the little world about settled down calmly as if the present state of affairs was that which had always been.

Some time, however, after these events a significant incident occurred in the history of Miss Jean Brown's mantua-making establishment. A carriage, unknown as yet with liveries and devices which never had appeared before, appeared in Chapel Street and set down a little party of ladies at Miss Jean's door. She advanced to meet them, as was her wont, to the door of the showroom, with a curtsey which would have done no discredit to a queen's drawing-room. But the ladies made a pause, and whispered together, and then the eldest said – 'Oh, it is Miss Douglas we want. We wish to give our orders to Miss Douglas. We have never been here before. And it is Miss Douglas we want to see.'

Miss Jean, surprised, indicated Kirsteen, who happened to be in the room, with a wave of her hand, and withdrew a little in dignified watchfulness not without a shade of offence.

'Oh, Miss Douglas!' cried the elder lady, while the others fluttered round, enclosing Kirsteen in the circle. 'We wish to have some things made, my daughters and I. And we were so anxious to see you. We know all your romantic story. And though, as the Duchess says, it may not be a

very good example, yet we felt we must come at once
and patronize you. It is so disinterested of you – and so
romantic.'

'So interesting – like a story out of a novel.'

'So dramatic! It might go on the stage.'

Kirsteen stood and listened with a surprised face and an
angry heart while these exclamations fluttered round. Four
ladies all rustling in silks and laces – no doubt likely to be
excellent customers and therefore not to be too much
discouraged, but each more exasperating than the other.
Dramatic! On the stage! Kirsteen had been brought up to
believe that the stage was a sort of vestibule of a region
which the Scotch ministers of her period had no hesitation
in naming. All the blood of the Douglases rushed to her
cheeks.

'I think your ladyships must be deceived,' she said; 'we
have no romantic stories nor stage plays here.'

'Oh, you must not think you can escape, you interesting
creature! For it was your friend Lady Charlotte, the great
beauty, who told us all about it; and we all vowed that henceforward nobody should dress us but you.'

'Lady Chatty is my friend indeed,' said Kirsteen, 'and
she is a bonny creature; but what a friend may know is
nothing to the world. And I am not the mistress here to
undertake your work. Perhaps, Miss Jean, you will tell the
ladies whether you can receive their orders or not. They are
recommended, it would seem,' she added, addressing her
somewhat mortified and indignant principal over the heads
of the newcomers, 'by Lady Chatty, who is just full of
fancies. And the workroom is very full. But you will know
best yourself what you can do.'

With this Kirsteen withdrew into the further part of the
room occupying herself again with the box of flowers which
had already played its part in the beginning of her new life;
and Miss Jean advanced into the middle of the scene. It
had never before occurred to that good woman to treat a
new customer arriving in a coroneted carriage with liveries
which lighted up the street with indifference. But she was
much mortified and affronted, and readily took up the
cue.

'We are very busy, madam, as this young lady says. I
cannot tell whether we can take the advantage of your

ladyship's favours. We have gowns making for the Queen's
Ball more than I remember for years. There is the Duchess
herself, and Lady A., and Lady B., and the Marchioness,
and Miss L., the Maid of Honour, and I cannot tell how
many more – all old patronesses of mine,' said Miss Jean
with a slight curtsey that emphasized her pause.

'But oh, mamma, we can't be sent away! for I vowed to
Lord John I would have a gown,' cried one of the young
ladies, 'from,' she glanced at Kirsteen with a little alarm,
then added in a low voice with a little laugh, '*la belle couturière.*'

'My name is Brown, madam, and not Bell – ye have
perhaps made a mistake,' said Miss Jean, grimly holding her
ground.

This the young ladies received with much laughter and
fluttering among themselves, as an excellent joke; while
their mother, half indignant, half disappointed, eyed Miss
Jean as if she would have liked to annihilate with a glance
the presumptuous seamstress. But the refusal itself was
such a new and startling effect, and the list of fashionable
names was so overwhelming that any humiliation seemed
better than failure. And Miss Jean after a while allowed herself to be mollified. Kirsteen on her part left the room, with
a little offended pride mingled with some mischievous
enjoyment. 'They shall come to me with petitions not with
orders,' she said to herself, 'before all's done.'

Miss Jean kept a grave face for the rest of the day. She
had ended by accepting with apparent reluctance and
doubts as to the possibility of executing it, a large commission, and entering very readily into her new role had
received the enthusiastic thanks of her new customers for
her compliance with their request. Miss Jean had humour
enough to be highly tickled by this turning of the tables, as
well as practical good sense to see the enormous advantage
to herself of assuming such a position should she be strong
enough to do it. But at the same time it opened up grave
questions which completely occupied her mind. Her business had grown into an important one through the best and
simplest agency, by means of good work and punctuality
and the other virtues that specially belong to honest trade,
and rarely fail of success in the long run. She had that
mingling of aristocratic predilections and democratic

impulses which belongs to her race. An old family which
was poor, a gentle lady of what she called real nobility, were
always served with her best, and with a delicacy about pay-
ment for which nobody gave the old Scotswoman credit –
but a haughty speech would fire her blood and change her
aspect even from the most admired and genuine gentility –
and a new peeress, much more a city lady, were subjects for
lofty politeness and veiled disdain and princely bills.
Kirsteen's suggestion had therefore fallen into prepared
soil. The pride of Marg'ret's sister, though she had begun
her life as a lady's maid, was scarcely less than that of
Marg'ret's young mistress who had the blood of all the
Douglases in her veins. And Miss Jean's keen practical
faculty was sharpened by much experience and in her
limited way by great knowledge of the world. She had now
a problem before her of more importance than how best
to make a skirt fall or a bodice fit, which had been till now
the chief problems with which she had troubled herself.

She carried a grave countenance and many thoughts with
her during the remainder of the day. Kirsteen, who noted
this serious aspect with some alarm, made out to herself a
little theory, to the effect that Miss Jean had taken serious
offence and would not suffer the presence of an interloper
who drew away the attention of her customers from herself
– yet she did not fully adopt this either, in consideration
of the great generosity towards her and unfailing kindness
of Miss Jean. But the evening brought a certain suppressed
excitement to both. It was a quiet house when all was over
in the establishment – the workrooms closed and dark, the
workwomen all dispersed to their homes or asleep in their
garrets – in which the mistress of the household and her
young guest were alone. They still occupied this relation to
each other, Miss Jean treating Kirsteen with great ceremony
as an honoured stranger, notwithstanding that her distinguished visitor was so condescending as to take part in the
conduct of her work. When supper was over Miss Jean
drew her chair towards the window which was open, for the
spring by this time was advanced and nearly bursting into
summer. The window admitted nothing more sweet than
the faint and smoky lamplight of the streets into the room,
to mingle with that of the candles; and though Chapel
Street was always quiet, there were vague sounds from

more distant streets, rolling of coaches and cries of the linkboys, which were scarcely musical. Nevertheless Miss Jean
was able to say that the evening air coming in was sweet.

'And that reminds me, Miss Kirsteen,' she said, 'that ye
have been quite a long time in London, three months and
more. And how do you like what you have seen?'

'I like it very well,' said Kirsteen. 'It is not like the
Hielands; there is no comparison to be made. But for a
town it is a very good town – better than Glasgow, which is
the only other town I ever saw.'

'Glasgow!' said Miss Jean with disdain. 'Glasgow has no
more right to be named with London than the big lamp at
Hyde Park Corner, which burns just tons of oil, with the
little cruse in my kitchen. It's one of the points on which
the Scots are just very foolish. They will bring forward
Edinburgh, or that drookit hole of a Glasgow, as if they
were fit to be compared with the real metropolis. In some
ways the Scots, our country-folks, have more sense than all
the rest of the world, but in others they're just ridiculous.
I hope I've sense enough to see both sides, their virtues and
their faults.'

Kirsteen did not see how she was involved in this tirade,
and consequently made no reply.

'But that's not what I was going to say, Miss Kirsteen.
You have seen all about us now, both the house and the
work and the place. And ye seem to have made up your
mind that whatever is said to you, whether by the Duchess
or the Duke or myself, ye will not be persuaded to go
home.'

Kirsteen, still very dubious as to the probable issue of
these remarks, looked in Miss Jean's face with a smile and
shook her head.

'Well, I will not say but what I think you very well able
to manage your own affairs. Miss Kirsteen, that was a very
clever thing ye did today.'

'What was the clever thing?' asked Kirsteen surprised.

'Just to turn those leddies over in that prideful way to
me, as if they were not good enough to trouble our heads
about. My word,' cried Miss Jean with a laugh, 'but ye
made them dight their eyne, if ye will excuse a vulgar
phrase. I'm thinking yon's the way to deal with newcomers,'
she said after a little pause.

'Well,' said Kirsteen, 'there is nobody so good as you, so far as I can hear, in all London. And it's a favour ye do them, to keep on and take all the trouble when ye have no need for it.'

'I would not just say that – that I've no need – though I have put something by. And I would not say either that there was nobody so good. I've been good enough in my day, but I'm getting old – or at least older,' said Miss Jean.

'We're all older today than we were yesterday,' said Kirsteen cheerfully.

'Ay, but in my case it's more than that. I could never have struck out yon invention of yours for Lady Chatty with the silver gauze – though I saw it was just most beautiful when ye did it. And what's more, I could never have gotten the better of those leddies like you – I see it all, nobody clearer. Ye're just a gentlewoman ye see, Miss Kirsteen, and that's above a common person, whatever anybody may say.'

'So far as I can see it makes very little difference,' said Kirsteen, contradicting, however, the assurance in her own heart.

'It makes a great deal of difference; it gives a freedom in treating them that I cannot help feeling are my superiors. Well; this is just what I have to propose. Ye will not go home whatever anybody may say. And ye will not mairry, though I hear he's just a very nice gentleman. And ye will get cleverer and cleverer every day as ye get more knowledge of the world. It's just this, Miss Kirsteen; that you and me, we should enter into partnership and carry on the business together. And I think,' said Miss Jean with modest confidence and a triumphant light in her eyes, 'that between us we could just face the world.'

'Into partnership!' cried Kirsteen in astonishment.

'Say nothing hastily, my dear – just go to your bed upon it. And we will not compromise an honoured name. We'll say Miss Brown and Miss Kirsteen – the English, who are very slow at the uptake, will think it's your family name, and that will compromise nobody,' Miss Jean said.

CHAPTER XXVI

It is difficult to calculate the exact moment at which it shall
be found out by the members of a family that one of them
has disappeared and gone away. It is easy to account for
temporary absence; to think that the missing one has
walked out too far, has been detained by some visit, has
somehow been withdrawn unexpectedly and not by any will
of his, from home. Kirsteen did not appear at breakfast;
there were a few questions, 'Where is Kirsteen?' 'She will
be with my mother.' Her mother on the other hand was
asking Jeanie, who had taken up her breakfast, 'Where is
Kirsteen?' 'She is gone out for a walk – or something,' said
Jeanie. It was not till after the second meal, at which there
was no sign of her, that anything like alarm was excited.
'Where is Kirsteen?' her father cried in what the children
called his Bull of Bashan's voice. 'I am not my sister's
keeper – no doubt she's just away on one of her rovings,'
said Mary, whose mind, however, by this time was full of
curiosity. She had been early struck by the complete disappearance of Kirsteen and every trace of her from about the
place. Neither in the glen, nor by the linn, nor in the
garden, was there any sign of her, no evidence that she had
passed by either in parlour or in kitchen. She had not been
in her mother's room, Mrs Douglas had already asked for
more than a dozen times where was Kirsteen? – requiring
her for a hundred things. It was only, however, when she
found Marg'ret anxiously attempting to do Kirsteen's
special business, to pick up the lost stitches in Mrs
Douglas's knitting, to arrange her pillows and help her to
move, that a real suspicion darted through Mary's mind.
Could Kirsteen have gone away? And could Marg'ret know
of it? On being interrogated the boys and Jeanie declared
that neither on the way to school nor at the merchant's,
which they had passed on their return home, had any trace
of her been seen. And Mary thought that Marg'ret's eyes
were heavy, that she looked like a person who had been up
all night, or who had been crying a great deal, and observed,

which was more extraordinary still, that she alone showed no curiosity about Kirsteen. Had all been natural it was she who would have been most easily alarmed. This acute observation helped Mary to the full truth, or at least to as much of it as it was possible to find out. 'Where's Kirsteen?' she said suddenly in Marg'ret's ear, coming down upon her unawares, after she had left Mrs Douglas's room.

Marg'ret was drying her eyes with her apron, and the sound of a sob which she had not time to restrain, breathed into the air as Mary came upon her. 'Oh, what a start ye gave me!' she answered, as soon as she could recover her voice.

'Where is Kirsteen?' said Mary again. 'You cannot conceal it from me – where is she, and what have ye done with her? I will not tell upon you if you will explain it to me.'

'Kirsteen – what is all this stir about Kirsteen? She will just have gane up the hill or down the linn, or maybe she'll have gone to see her old auntie at the toun.' Here Marg'ret betrayed herself by a heave of her solid shoulders that showed she was weeping, though she attempted with a broken laugh to conceal the fact. 'It's no so many – diversions – the poor thing has.'

'You know where she is, Marg'ret – and ye've helped her to get away.'

'Me!' cried Marg'ret, with convulsive indignation; then she made a great effort to recover herself. 'How should I ken where she is? Yes, I do that! she's on her way home no doubt over the hillside – or down the loch coming back.'

'You'll perhaps tell me then what you're greetin' for?'

'I have plenty of things to make me greet,' Marg'ret said; then after a pause – 'Who said I was greetin'? I just canna be fashed with endless questions, and the haill family rantin' and ravin'. Ye can go and find your sister for yourself.'

'And so I will – or at least I'll satisfy myself,' said Mary with a determination which, though mild and quiet, was not less assured than the bold resolutions of Kirsteen. She went softly upstairs and proceeded to visit her sister's room, where her keen perceptions soon showed her a certain amount of disarray. 'She cannot have two gowns on her back, both the blue and the brown,' said Mary to herself.

'She would never put on her spencer and bonnet to go out on the hillside. She would not have taken that little box with her that she keeps her treasures in and that aye stands by her bedside, had she only gone to see Auntie Eelen. She's just gone away – and there is an end of it.' Mary stood reflecting for some time after she came to this decision. It did not distress her for the moment, but lit a spark of invention, a keener light than usual in her mild brown eyes that never had been full of light like Kirsteen's. After a few minutes of consideration, she went to her own room and dressed herself carefully to go out – carefully but not too well, not with the spencer, the Sunday garment which Kirsteen had taken. Mary put on an old cloth pelisse, and a brown bonnet which was not her best. 'I am not going on a journey, I will only be about the doors,' she said to herself.

Marg'ret was standing outside when she came downstairs, with a look of anxiety on her face, which changed into subdued derision when Mary appeared. 'Ye'll be going after her?' she said. 'Well, I wish ye may find her; but if she's gane, as ye think, she'll have gotten a long start.'

'I'm going – to put some things right,' said Mary enigmatically. The consciousness that Marg'ret stood and watched as she went along the road quickened her senses, and confirmed her in her conviction. It was afternoon, and the wintry sun was shining red through a haze of frost out of the western sky. It dazzled her with its long level lines of light as she walked down the road. There would be a moon that night, so that the visitor who was expected at Drumcarro would have light enough to ride home by, however late he might be; yet he was a little late, and Mary was anxious to meet him at some distance from the house. She walked very quickly for about half a mile towards the hamlet, in which the merchant's shop stood surrounded by three or four cottages. And then she perceived in the distance riding over the little bridge which crossed the stream, the red light catching the metal buttons of his riding-coat and the silver top of his whip, the trim figure of Glendochart coming towards her. At such a distance his grey hair and the lines of his face were of course quite invisible, and he rode like a young man, with all the advantages of good horsemanship and a fine horse to set off his well-formed figure. Mary slackened her pace at once. She looked at him

with a little sigh. What a happy windfall would that be to
one, which to another was a hardship and misfortune! She
herself would not have objected at all to Glendochart's age.
She would have liked him the better for it, as likely to make
a more complaisant husband. However, it was not to her
that he had come wooing, but to Kirsteen, with whom he
had no chance, so troublesome and contrary were the deci-
sions of fate.

Mary gave a sigh to this thought, and turned over in her
mind rapidly the purpose with which she had come out and
what she was to say. She decided that even if Kirsteen came
back, which was not probable, she could do no harm by
warning Glendochart. It would save him a refusal at least, it
would let him know the real state of affairs. She walked
more and more slowly as the horseman advanced. There
was a corner of the road where a projecting rock formed a
sort of angle, shutting out a little the noise of the brawling
burn and making a natural halting-place. She contrived that
she should meet the wayfarer here. Glendochart perceived
her as he came along before they actually met. She appeared
just beyond the corner, recognized him, paused a little,
and then waving her hand to him turned back. Nothing
could be more evident than that she had something to say.
When he had reached the corner he found her standing,
modest and quiet, within the shadow of the rock.

'I hope nothing's wrong, Miss Mary, at the house?' he
said hurriedly.

'Well,' she said, 'that is as maybe. I have perhaps done a
bold thing, but I was wanting a word with ye, Glendochart,
before you go on.'

'What is the matter?' he cried with alarm. He was evidently very unwilling to be detained. 'Your father is expecting me, Miss Mary,' he said, 'and I hope your sister—'

'It is just about Kirsteen, Glendochart, that I wish to
speak to you.'

'What is it?' he said. 'Is she ill – has anything happened?'

'There has just this happened,' said Mary. 'I would not
let ye have a trouble or a shock that I could spare you –
Kirsteen has left her home.'

'Left her home!' His ruddy colour disappeared in a
moment; he threw himself off his horse. 'What do you
mean? I do not understand you!' he cried.

'Glendochart,' said Mary seriously, 'nobody has told me; but I don't think you were meaning to make any secret of it, that it was after Kirsteen you were coming to our house.'

The elderly lover coloured a little. 'I would not hide it from you that that was my intention. It was her,' he said with a little apologetic wave of his hand, 'that I saw first of the family, and upon her I fixed my fancy; not that all the daughters of Drumcarro were not worthy of every admiration.'

'Oh, Glendochart, ye need not apologize. Fancy is free, as is well known. I saw it well from the first, for a sister's eyne are quick to observe; but if ye will believe me, the one that never noticed was just Kirsteen herself.'

'Not possible!' said the wooer, with this time a little flush of offence.

'But it is just very possible – her mind was not set on anything of the kind. And it was her opinion that just friendship and kindness – for all the family—'

'Did she bid ye tell me this?'

'No, no – she said nothing, poor thing. If she had but spoken either to me, that could have explained for her, or to you that would never have forced her—'

'Forced her!' cried the old beau, who had always prided himself upon the fact that his was neither the form nor the eye

> Which youthful maidens wont to fly.

'Well, I know that!' said Mary with fervour; 'and there are few that would have needed any fleeching, if I may say so. But I reckon that she just heard it from my father, very suddenly. My father is a dour man, Glendochart. Whatever ye may have to say he will never hear ye speak. He will listen to the boys – whiles – but to us never. Just you must do this, or you must do that, and not a word more.'

'Drumcarro,' said Glendochart, now full of passion, 'has done me a cruel wrong in putting my suit before any lady in such a way. Your sister was free to have taken it or left it, Miss Mary. Me press a proposition that was not acceptable! – not for all the world!'

'I am well aware of that,' said Mary with feeling; 'but my father is a dour man, and he would say "Not a word!

just take the offer and be thankful." And indeed,' said Mary
diffidently, 'in most cases there would be little difficulty,
but Kirsteen is one that is very much set upon her own
way.'

'She had but to say so,' cried the offended suitor; 'I
promise she would have had no more trouble with me!'

'Oh, Glendochart, do not be angry – I am just sure that
he would not let her say a word. She has not been like herself this week past. It has just been on her mind night and
day. And at last she has taken a despair, seeing no way of
getting out of it – and she has gone away.'

'I am not in the habit,' said Glendochart, 'of finding
myself a bugbear. I would seem to cut a pretty figure in all
this – a sort of old Robin Gray,' he said with a furious
laugh. 'I am sure I am obliged to you all! "With tears in his
e'e, said Jenny, for their sake will ye marry me?" I beg to
say, Miss Mary, that this was not my attitude at all.'

'Do you need to say that to me, Glendochart?' said Mary
reproachfully. 'Oh, no! nor even to poor Kirsteen either,
who would have been fain to hear every word ye had to say
– for she was very fond of ye, Glendochart.'

'It is a strange way of showing it,' he said, but he was
mollified in spite of himself.

'As we all were. It will be a great heartbreak and a great
downfall if ye come no more to the house because of
Kirsteen. But she would have been fain, fain to hear whatever ye had to say, if it had not been—'

'What hindered her, then?' he said.

'It's no for me to betray her secrets,' said Mary, 'and
indeed she never told them to me, for she was not one that
opened her heart. But there is little that can be hidden from
a sister's eye. And it was just this – there was one before
ye, Glendochart. If she had seen you first I am very sure she
would never have thought of him – for to my mind there's
no more comparison – but, poor thing, she had given her
word. Take what you offered her and be mansworn to the
other lad was all that was before her; and no true to you
either, for she would never have dared to tell you.'

Glendochart was still much offended and disturbed. He
had fastened his horse to a tree, and was now pacing about
the road within the corner of the rock with mingled rage
and pain. But he was moved by the soft voice and pleading

accents of the very mild and pleasing intercessor, whose suggestion of her own superior taste was put in with so much gentle insistence. Mary's eyes, which were cast down when he looked at her, but raised with much meaning to his face when he did not seem to be observing, softened his mood in spite of himself.

'If that was the case,' he said, 'there was perhaps an excuse for her, though when she knew it was so she should not have encouraged and drawn on – another man.'

It was Mary's policy to give a very charitable representation of Kirsteen's action, and it was also quite congenial to her feelings, for she was not spiteful nor malicious, notwithstanding that it seemed to be a very sensible thing to turn her sister's failure to her own advantage if that could be done.

'Glendochart,' she said, 'there's some things in which gentlemen never can understand the heart of a girl. She had no thought of encouraging and drawing on. That never came into her head. She liked you well, and she thought no harm in showing it.'

'Because,' cried Glendochart, with mingled offence and emotion, 'she thought I was an old man, and out of the question! That is easy to see—'

'It was not that,' said Mary, softly. 'She saw that you were kind to all of us – every one. Perhaps she may have thought that you had – other intentions. And, oh,' said the gentle girl, raising her eyes to his, 'it made such a difference to us all! It's been so lightsome and so heartsome, Glendochart, to see ye always coming. There is little diversion at Drumcarro. My fafher is a very dour man, wrapped up in the boys, and my mother, she is always ailing, poor body; and we see nobody; and to have you coming just like sunshine, with a smile to one and a kind word to another, and thinking no shame to be pleasant even to me – that ye thought nothing of – or little Jeanie, that is but a bairn.'

Glendochart was very much touched. He took Mary's hand in both his. 'Do not say that I thought nothing of you, for that would be far from the case: and how am I to thank you now for taking so much thought for me? You have just behaved like an angel so far as I can see, both to me and to her.'

'Oh, Glendochart, not that! But just what I could do in the way of kindness,' she said.

CHAPTER XXVII

The result of this interview was that Glendochart turned and rode home, very full of wrath and disappointment, yet soothed in his *amour propre* by the kind expedient of the angelic girl, who returned to Drumcarro very demurely with the consciousness that her time and exertions had not been lost. She had indeed decided perhaps too summarily that Kirsteen's disappearance was a permanent one; but as the day crept on, and there was no appearance of her return, the temporary qualm which had come over Mary's mind dispersed again. She had the satisfaction of seeing that her father was very much disturbed by the non-appearance of Glendochart. He came out of his den from time to time, and took a turn round the house and stood out at the gate straining his eyes along the road. 'Is it Kirsteen ye are looking for, father?' Mary said. Drumcarro asked with a fierce exclamation what he was caring about Kirsteen. Let her go to the devil if she liked. What he was looking for was quite a different person. 'But maybe,' said Mary, 'the other person will not be coming if Kirsteen is not here.' Her father asked fiercely, what she knew about it? But he was evidently impressed by the remark, for he went up and down stairs and out to the side of the linn, shouting for Kirsteen in a way that filled all the echoes. 'Where is Kirsteen all this day, and why cannot she come when her father is crying on her? He will just bring down the house,' Mrs Douglas had said, putting her hands upon her ears. 'She might maybe have a headache, and be lying down upon her bed,' said little Jeanie, to whom a similar experience had once occurred, and who had felt the importance it gave her.

The anxieties of the family were soothed by this and other suggestions until the early wintry night fell and it was discovered that nobody had seen her, or knew anything about her. Marg'ret in her kitchen had been in an intense suppressed state of excitement all day, but it had not been discovered by anyone save the astute Mary that she showed no curiosity about Kirsteen, and asked no questions. When it came to be bedtime the whole household was disturbed. The boys had gone out over the hill, and towards the merchant's along the road to see if any trace could be found of her, while Jeanie stood under the birch trees – now denuded of all their yellow leaves – outside, looking out through the dark with all that sense of desolation and mystery which is in the idea of night to the mind of a child. Jeanie stood very quiet, crying to herself, but thinking she heard footsteps and all kinds of mysterious movements about her, and fully making up her mind to see Kirsteen carried home, murdered or dead of cold and exposure, or something else that was equally terrible and hopeless; and though she would have been overjoyed, yet she would also have been a little disappointed had she seen Kirsteen walk in with no harm or injury, which was also more or less the frame of mind of Jock and Jamie, who fully expected to stumble over their sister among the withered bracken, or to see her lying by the side of the road.

There was, however, a moment of mute despair when they all came back and looked at each other for an explanation of the mystery. Then the children burst out crying one after the other, the boys resisting the impulse till nature was too strong for them, and producing a louder and more abrupt explosion from the fact of the attempted restraint. Their father stood looking round upon them all, his fierce eyes blazing, looking for some way of venting the rage that was in him. The lass disappeared, confound her! And Glendochart drawing back, the devil flee away with him! Drumcarro was indeed in evil case. When Jock, who was the last to give way, burst out without a moment's notice into a violent boo-hoo, his father caught him suddenly a box on the ear which sent him spinning across the room. 'Haud your confounded tongue, can't ye – and no wake your mother.' 'Eh, my poor laddie! Ye need not punish him for me, for here I am, and what is the matter with everybody?' said the weak voice of Mrs Douglas at the door. She had been left alone during all this excitement, and her repeated calls had brought nobody. So that querulous, displeased, and full of complaining, unable to bear the silence and the want of information, the poor soul had wrapped herself in the first garments she could find, and tottered downstairs. She appeared a curious mass of red flannel, chintz, and tartan, one wrapped over the other. 'What is the matter?' she said, looking eagerly round upon the troubled family. 'Oh, mother,' cried little Jeanie weeping, running to her and hiding her face and her tears in one of these confused wrappings. 'Kirsteen has gone away. She's *run* away,' said Jeanie, afraid not to be believed – and then the commotion was increased by a wail from the mother, who sank in a state of collapse into her large chair, and by the rush of Marg'ret from the kitchen, who perceiving what had happened flew to give the necessary help. 'Could you not all hold your tongues, and let her get her night's rest in peace?' Marg'ret cried. The scene was dismal enough, and yet had thus a rude comedy mingled with its real pain. Drumcarro stalked away when this climax of confusion was reached. 'I was a fool ever to mind one of them,' he said. 'Ye little whinging deevil, get out o' my way. You're no better than a lassie yourself.'

Mary had done her best to save the story from becoming public by warning the expectant suitor, who on his side had thought himself safely out of the ridicule of it by his quick withdrawal. But the voices of the servants and the children were not to be silenced. 'Have ye heard the news?' said Duncan the carter at the toll-bar. 'The maister up at the house is neither to haud nor to bind. Our Kirsteen has ta'en her fit in her hand and run away, the Lord kens where, for fear he would mairry her against her will to auld Glendochart.' 'Eh, do ye ken what's happened?' said Marg'ret's help in the kitchen as soon as she could find an excuse to run to the merchant's. 'Miss Kirsteen, she's aff to the ends of the earth, and the mistress near deed with trouble, and Marg'ret raging just like a sauvage beast.' The boys whispered it to their mates at school with a certain sense of distinction, as of people to whom something out of the common had happened, and Jeanie, who had no one else to communicate the wonderful fact to, told the little girl that brought the letters, by whom it was published far and near. Miss Eelen heard it the next morning by means of Jock, who rode the pony over almost before daylight to inquire if his sister had been seen there. 'Indeed she might have been too proud to have had the offer of Glendochart,' the old lady said. 'He should just take Mary instead.' 'He will maybe think that's not the same thing,' said Mr Pyper, the minister, who went over to the town in his gig soon after about some Presbytery business, and to hear what people were saying. 'Well, it will be very near the same thing,' Miss Eelen said.

This was how it had come to the ears of the Duke and Duchess and all the best society in the county, who were immensely entertained, and told a hundred stories about the gallant wooer whose attempt at courtship had been so disastrous. He went away himself the next day, sending a letter to Drumcarro to say that he had heard that his suit was disagreeable to the young lady, and that nothing could induce him to press it after he knew this fact; but that he hoped on his return to pay his respects to Mrs Douglas and the young ladies. Drumcarro was not to be spoken to by any member of his family after this happened for several days. Had he met with the gallant old gentleman who had thus, in his own opinion, retired so gracefully, it is to be feared the trim Glendochart might have found his martial science of but little avail against 'the auld slavedriver's' brutal energy and strength. But after a while Mr Douglas calmed down. He flung Kirsteen's little possessions out of doors, and swore with many oaths that whoever named that hizzy's name again should leave his house on the moment. But when Glendochart, coming back in the spring, came out formally to pay a visit at Drumcarro, bringing boxes of French chocolate and other tokens of his residence abroad, the laird, though he gave him the briefest salutation, did not knock him down, which was what the family feared. And by dint of a diplomacy which would have done credit to any ambassador, Mary continued so to close her mother's mouth that no reference should be made to the past. Mrs Douglas was too much afraid of her husband to introduce Kirsteen's name, but she was ready with a hundred little allusions. 'Ah, Glendochart, when ye were here last! That was before our last misfortune. I will never be so well again as I was in those days, when I had one by me that never forgot her mother.' She would have sympathized with him and claimed his sympathy in this furtive way from the moment of his arrival. But Mary had taken by this time very much the upper hand and brought her mother into great subjection. 'Ye will just drive him away if ye say a word.' 'I am sure,' Mrs Douglas said weeping, 'her name never crosses my lips.' 'But what does that matter when you are just full of allusions and talk of her that's away.' 'Alas! there is another that I might be meaning,' said the poor mother; 'two of them, bonny lasses as ever lived, and one with weans of her own that I will never see.' 'Oh, mother, why should ye make such a work about them that never think of you? They would have bided at home if their hearts had been here. But it's a grand thing for the boys and Jeanie,' said the astute elder sister, 'that Glendochart should come back. It sets us right with the world, and see the things he's always bringing them.' 'Mainy sweeties are not good for children, though thae chocolate ones are maybe wholesome enough,' said Mrs Douglas. 'And what does he ever do for them but bring them sweeties?' 'Mother, it's just education for them to hear such a man speak,' cried Mary, which silenced Mrs Douglas at the end.

Mary apparently felt the full force of what she said. She listened to him devoutly; she persuaded him to talk with little murmurs of pleasure. 'Eh, it's just as good as a book to hear ye, Glendochart' – and other such ascriptions of praise. Few men are quite superior to this kind of flattery, and one who has been slighted in another quarter and has felt the absence of any just appreciation of his deserts, is more than usually open to it. Glendochart fell into his old habit of frequent visits to Drumcarro, and he was pleased by the universal interest in him – the delight of the young ones, and the gentle devotion of Mary. A soft regret, a tender respect was in her tone. The only time in which she ever displayed a consciousness of the past was when she thanked him with almost tears in her eyes for coming; 'Which we could never have expected.' It was not, how-ever, until a day in spring, in the month of April, when the beauty of the country was awakening, that the old gentle-man was completely subjugated. The linn was subdued from the volume of its wintry torrent, but was roaring over the rocks still with the fullness of spring showers one bright afternoon when he met Mary on the road taking a walk, as she said. They returned, without any intention passing the house and continuing their walk unconsciously, drawn on by the tumult of the stream. Glendochart stood at the head of the little glen, and looked down the ravine with many thoughts. Mary had drawn aside from its edge. 'I cannot go down that dreadful way. It makes me giddy,' said Mary. 'I never liked that steep bank; the others run up and down just like goats – but not me! If ye will excuse my weakness, Glendochart, and go a little round by the road, we'll come out at the foot just the same.'

Now it had been with a rush of recollection that Glen-dochart had come to the linn side. He remembered well how Kirsteen had rushed on before him as airy as a feather, trying the stones with her light weight, to find which was most steady, like a bird alighting upon them, putting out her hand to help him – she the young lady who ought to have been indebted to him for help. And he remembered the slip he had made and his fall, and the tremble in her voice which he had feared meant laughter, and the effort he had made to look as if a tumble on the wet sod was nothing, a thing he did not mind. Mary had far more sense to go round by the road. He felt himself in so much better a position agreeing with her that it was too steep for a lady, and gallantly guiding her round the safer way. It was a soft evening with no wind, and a delightful spring sky full of brightness and hope. In the spring a young man's fancy lightly turns to thoughts of love, and the fancy of an old young gentleman who has been led to think of these matters and then has been cruelly disappointed, is if anything more easily awakened. Glendochart gave Mary his arm to help her along the gentler round of the road, and his mouth was opened and he spoke.

'Miss Mary,' he said, 'ye were very kind a few months back in a matter which we need not now enter into. I can never cease to be grateful to you for the warning ye gave me. And ye have been more than kind since I came home. It has been a great pleasure to come to Drumcarro, though I did it at first mostly out of a sense of duty. But to see you gave it a charm.'

'Oh, Glendochart, you are very kind to say so,' said Mary. 'We just all of us have a debt to you that we can never repay.'

'Not a word about debt, or I would soon be on the wrong side of the balance. It has been a great part of the pleasure of my life to come – but now I will have to be thinking whether I should come again.'

'Oh, Glendochart! and wherefore so?' cried Mary with alarm in her eyes.

'My dear young lady,' said the Highland gentleman, 'I am getting an old man – I was mangrown (and perhaps a trifle more) before ye were born.'

She had said 'Oh, no!' softly while he was speaking, with a gentle pressure upon his arm – and now when he paused she lifted her dove's eyes and said, 'What does that matter?' in tones as soft as the wood pigeon's coo.

'You must understand me,' he said, 'which I am afraid was more than your sister, poor thing, ever did – I have been experiencing a great change of feeling. She was a bright young creature, full of pretty ways – and I was just beguiled – the like of that may blind a man for a time, but when his eyes are opened to the knowledge of a more excellent way – that he had not observed before—'

'It is true,' said Mary in a faltering voice; 'my poor Kirsteen had a great deal of the child in her. And it would not be my part to be affronted if ye had seen another that was maybe better adapted to make you happy. Oh, no! it would be ill my part – though I might regret.'

'Ye have no guess,' said Glendochart with a tender touch of the hand that clung to his arm, 'who that other is, who is the only person I will ever think of?'

'No,' said Mary with a sigh. 'I'm not sure that I want to hear – but that's a poor sentiment and it shall not be encouraged by me. On the contrary it will not be my fault if that lady – who will have a happy lot, I am sure – does not find kind friends here.'

'If she does not it will be most unnatural,' said Glendochart, 'for the person I am meaning is just yourself and no other. And if ye think she will have a happy lot – my dear, take it – for it will never be offered to any woman but you.'

'Oh, Glendochart!' said Mary, casting down her eyes.

It was very different from his wooing of Kirsteen and in many ways much more satisfactory – for far from running away in horror of his suit which is a thing to pique the pride of any man, Mary was unfeignedly proud of having won the prize which she had at once felt, failing Kirsteen, it would be a good thing to keep in the family. She saved her old lover every trouble. She would not have him go to

her father, which was what he proposed with great spirit
to do at once. 'No,' she said, 'it is me that must tell him.
My father is a strange man; he is little used to the like of
you; but I know all his ways. And I will tell him; for ye
must mind, Glendochart, if ye mairry me that I will not
have ye taigled with all my family. The boys and little Jeanie
now and then if ye please for a short visit, or my mother
for a change of air, but just at your pleasure, and not like a
thing you're obliged to do. I will take that into my own
hand. Ye can leave it all to me.'

Glendochart rode away that night with great satisfaction
in his mind. He felt that he had wiped out his reproach;
after having failed to marry Kirsteen it was a necessity to
vindicate himself by marrying somebody – and he particularly felt (after the consolation that had been drawn from
Mary's gentle speeches and ways) that to marry out of this
very house where he had been slighted would be the most
complete vindication. And he was delighted with his second
choice; her good taste, her good sense, her clear perception
of all that was necessary filled him with satisfaction and
content. He rode away with something of the ardour of a
young man joined to the more reasonable satisfaction of an
old one, in the consciousness of having secured the most
devoted of housekeepers, a lady who would 'look well at
his table-head', who would take care of his interests and
would not even allow him to be taigled with her family. He
kissed his hand to his bonny Mary, and his soul was filled
with delightful anticipations. There was no doubt she was a
bonny creature, far more correct and satisfactory than that
gilpie Kirsteen with her red hair. Glendochart was thus
guilty of the vulgar unfaithfulness of disparaging his own
ideal – but it is a sin less heinous in an old lover than in a
young one – for how many ideals must not the old gentleman have lived through?

Mary walked in straight to her father's door – who took
as little notice of Glendochart as possible in these days. He
was sitting with a map of the old Douglas property before
him, painfully ruminating whether he could anyhow
squeeze out of the family living enough to buy a corner of
land that was in the market; and wondering, with a sort of
forlorn fury, whether Sandy or even Sandy's son, might be
able to gather all that land back again to the Douglas name.

This was his ideal; all others, such as love, or affection, or the ties of human fellowship having died out of his mind long ago, if they had ever occupied any place there. He looked up angrily as Mary came in. What could she want, the useless woman-creature that was good for nothing, never could bring a penny into the house, but only take out of it as long as she should live?

'Well! what are you wanting now?' he said sharply.

'I am wanting to speak to you,' Mary said.

'A fool would understand that, since ye've come here; which is a place where there's no room for weemen. Speak out what you've got to say, and leave me quiet, which is all I desire from ye.'

'I am afraid,' said Mary sweetly, 'that I will have to give ye a little trouble, father; though it will save you a good deal of fash later.'

'Give me trouble is what you do night and day. Save me fash is what I've never known.'

'It will be so now,' said Mary, 'for to provide for your daughters would be a great fash to you, and one that would go sore against the grain. So you should be glad, father, however little ye think of us, when we can provide for ourselves.'

'How are ye going to do that?' said Drumcarro derisively. 'No man will have ye. I'm sick of the very name of ye,' he said; 'I wish there was not a woman in the house.'

'Well,' said Mary, with imperturbable good temper, 'ye will soon be quit of one. For I'm going to be marriet, and I've come to tell you.'

'To be marriet! I don't believe it; there's no man will look at ye,' said the indignant father.

'It is true we never see any men,' said Mary; 'but one is enough, when ye can make up your mind to him. Father, we would like to name an early day, seeing that he has been disappointed already, and that there is no time to lose. It is Glendochart I am intending to marry,' she said demurely, looking him in the face.

'Glendochart!' He got up from his chair and swore a large round oath. 'That hizzy's leavings!' he said. 'Have ye no pride?'

'I will have a great deal of pride when I'm settled in my own house,' replied Mary. 'He will be here tomorrow to settle everything; but I thought I would just tell you tonight. And I hope, father,' she added with great gravity, 'that seeing I'm here to protect him you will keep a civil tongue in your head.'

CHAPTER XXVIII

These events were communicated by letter to the members of the firm of Misses Brown and Kirsteen, Dressmakers to her Majesty, Chapel Street, Mayfair. The medium of communication was Marg'ret, whose letters to her sister had become, to the vast enlightenment of the only member of the Drumcarro household who was qualified to collect circumstantial evidence, suspiciously frequent. Mary, it may be supposed, had not much time to give to correspondence, while the facts lately recorded were going on; but when all was settled she slipped into Marg'ret's hand a letter containing the important news. 'I am not asking where she is – I am thinking that through your sister, Miss Jean, in London, ye might possibly find a means of getting it to Kirsteen's hand.'

'It's an awfu' expense for postage, and a double letter. I will just be ruined,' said Marg'ret; 'and my sister Jean might not ken anything about the address.'

'You could always try,' said Mary derisively.

'That's true, I might try – for she's a very knowledgeable person, my sister Jean; but that will make a double letter – and how is the like of me to get a frank or any easement?'

'I will ask Glendochart – for he has plenty of friends in the Parliament houses.'

'I will have none from Glendochart! The Lord be praised, I have still a shilling in my pouch to ware upon my friends.'

'Ye are just a jealous woman for your friends,' said Mary with a laugh of triumph.

'Maybe I am that, and maybe I am not. I would neither wile away my sister's joe, nor tak' what anither's left,' cried Marg'ret with unreasonable indignation. But Mary turned away with a demure smile. She had no such ridiculous prejudices. And perhaps it will be best to give in full her letter to Kirsteen explaining how everything came about.

DEAR CHRISTINA, – I am writing you a letter on the risk of perhaps not finding you; but I have the less fear of that that I have always been conscious Marg'ret Brown knew very well at the time where you were to be found. And the letters she gets and sends away have just been ridiculous. I would say one in a fortnight, never less. It stands to reason that it would not be her sister Jean she was writing to so often. So I made sure you were for something in it. And therefore it is with no little confidence that I send this. If ye do not receive it, you will not be able to blame me, for I will have done everything I could.

And I have a great deal to tell you, and in particular about Mr Henry Campbell, of Glendochart, who was abroad for his health in the beginning of the year, and afterwards took up his old practice of visiting at Drumcarro, which was, you know, very well liked by every person: for he was very kind to the children, and brought them beautiful boxes of fine sweeties made of chocolate from Paris, which they consumed from morning till night, my mother being always afraid it would put their stomachs out of order; but no harm followed. Now you know, Christina, that in former times when you were at home it was commonly believed by all the family that Glendochart was coming for you. But it would appear that this had been a mistake. Perhaps it was that his fancy was not fixed then between us two, being sisters and about the same age, which I am told is a thing that sometimes happens. But anyhow the other day him and me being on the road down to the linn – not that awful steep road that you were always trying to break your own neck and other folks' upon, but the road round that goes by the side of the hill – he began to talk to me very seriously, and to say that he had long been thinking upon a Person that would make him a good wife. And I said – that he might see there was no ill-will or disappointment – that I was sure she would be a happy woman, and that she should always find friends at Drumcarro. And on this he took courage and told me he hoped so, for it was just Me that was the Person, and that the offer he made me was one that he would not make to any other woman. I was very much surprised, thinking always that it had been You – but you being gone, and there being no possibility in that quarter, and being always very favourable to Glendochart myself and sure he would make a very good man – besides that it would be real good for my mother to get a change of air from time to time, and that it is better to be a married woman in your own good house, than a lass at home with nothing but what her father will lay out upon her (and you know how little that is), or even an Old Maid like Auntie Eelen, though in many ways she is very comfortable. But taking all things into consideration I just thought I would take Glendochart, who is a very creditable person in every way, and a fine figure of a man; though not so very young. And I hope you will have no feeling upon the subject as if I did wrong to take what they call my sister's leavings, and other coarse things of that kind. For of course if you had wanted him you would have taken him when you had the offer, and it can do you no harm that another should have him, when you would not have him yourself.

So after all, dear Christina, this is just to tell you that on the 1st of June we are to be married by Mr Pyper at Drumcarro. I will wear a habit which it was my desire should be of green cloth, with a little gold lace; but they all rose against me, saying that there was an old rhyme to the effect that –

> The bride that is married in green
> Her sorrow will soon be seen –

so I yielded about that, and it is to be French grey, with a little silver upon the coat-tails and the cuffs and pockets, and a grey hat with a silver band and a grey veil; which will be very pretty and useful too, for grey does not show the dust as red would have done, which was what my mother wanted, being the fashion in her time. We will stay quietly for a week or two at our own house of Glendochart, and then he has promised that he will take me to London. I hope you will let me know by Marg'ret where I can find you, and I will come and see you. Perhaps in the changed

circumstances you would rather not see Henry, though
he has a most kindly feeling, and would never think
of being guided by my father's ban which you might
be sure would be placed upon you. Neither would I
ever give in to it, especially as a married woman, owing
no duty but to her husband, and him a real
enlightened man. So there would be no difference
made either by me or him, but very glad to see you,
either in the place where you are, or at Glendochart,
or wherever we might be. If I don't hear anything more
particular I will come to Miss Jean Brown's when I
get to London in hopes that she will tell me where to
find you, especially as I cannot be in London without
taking the opportunity to get a new gown or perhaps
two, and I hear she is very much patronized by the first
people, and in a very good position as a mantua-
maker.

Now, dear Christina, I hope you will send me a
word by Marg'ret about your address; but anyway I
will come to Miss Brown's and find you out, and in
the meantime I am very glad to have had the
opportunity of letting you know all our news, and I
remain
          Your affectionate sister,
                MARY DOUGLAS.
     P.S. My mother keeps just in her ordinary.

This letter was given to Kirsteen out of the cover which
Miss Jean opened with great precaution on account of the
writing that was always to be found on the very edge of the
paper where the letter was folded, and under the seal. Miss
Jean shook her head while she did so and said aloud that
Marg'ret was very wasteful, and what was the good of so
many letters. 'For, after all,' she said, 'news will keep; and
so long as we know that we are both well what is the object
in writing so often? I got a letter, it's not yet three weeks
ago, and here's another. But one thing is clear, it's not for
me she writes them, and we must just try to get her a few
franks and save her siller.' But she gave what she called a
skreigh as soon as she had read half a page. 'It's your sister
that's going to be married?' that was indeed a piece of news
that warranted the sending of a letter. Kirsteen read hers

with a bright colour and sparkling eyes. She was angry,
which was highly unreasonable, though I have remarked it
in women before. She felt it to be an offence that Glendochart had been able to console himself so soon. And she
was specially exasperated to think that it was upon Mary
his choice had fallen. Mary! to like her as well as me!
Kirsteen breathed to herself, feeling, perhaps, that her inti-
mate knowledge of her sister's character did not increase
her respect for Mary. 'Having known me, to decline on a
range of lower feelings.' These words were not written then,
nor probably had they been written, would they have
reached Kirsteen, but she fully entered into the spirit of
them. Mary! when it was me he wanted! She did not like
the idea at all.

'Yes,' she said sedately, 'so it appears'; but her breathing
was a little quickened, and there was no pleasure in her
tone.

'And is your sister so like you?' said Miss Jean.

'She is not like me at all,' said Kirsteen. 'She is brown-
haired and has little colour, and very smooth and soft in all
her ways.' Kirsteen drew a long breath and the words that
she had spoken reminded her of other words. She thought
to herself but did not say it, 'Now Jacob was a smooth
man.' And then poor Kirsteen flamed with a violent blush
and said to herself, 'What a bad girl I am! Mary has never
been false or unkind to me – and why should not she take
Glendochart when I would not take him? And why should
the poor man never have anybody to care for him because
once he cared for the like of me?'

Miss Jean did not, of course, hear this, but she saw that
something was passing in Kirsteen's mind that was more
than she chose to say. And, like a kind woman, she went on
talking in order that the balance might come right in the
mind of her young companion. 'They will be coming to
London,' she said, 'just when the town is very throng – and
that is real confusing to folk from the country. If it will be
pleasing to you, Miss Kirsteen, I will ask them to their
dinner; that is if they will not think it a great presumption
in the like of me.'

To tell the truth Kirsteen herself felt that Marg'ret's sister
was not exactly the person to entertain Glendochart and
Mary, who were both of the best blood in the country; but

she was too courteous to say this. 'It would be very kind
of you, Miss Jean,' she said, 'but I am not sure that it would
be pleasing to me. Perhaps it would be better to let them
take their own gait and never to mind.'

'I have remarked,' said Miss Jean, 'in my long experience
that a quiet gentleman from the country when he comes
up to London with his new married wife, has often very few
ideas about where he is to take her to. He thinks that he will
be asked to his dinner by the chief of his name, and that
auld friends will just make it a point to be very ceevil. And
so they would perhaps at a quiet time; but when the town
is so throng, and people's minds fixed on what will be the
next news of the war, and everybody taken up with themselves, it is not so easy to mind upon country friends. And
I have seen them that come to London with very high
notions just extremely well pleased to come for an evening
to a countrywoman, even when she was only a mantua-
maker. But it shall be just whatever way you like, and you
know what my company is and who I would ask.'

'Oh, it is not for that!' cried Kirsteen. By this time she
knew very well what Miss Jean's company was. There was
an old Mrs Gordon, who had very high connections and
'called cousins' with a great many fine people, and had a
son with Lord Wellington's army, but who was very poor
and very glad to be received as an honoured guest in Miss
Jean's comfortable house. And there was the minister of the
Scots church in the city, who announced to everybody on
all occasions that there was nobody he had a higher respect
for than Miss Jean, and that her name was well known in
connection with all the Caledonian charities in London.
And there was Miss Jean's silk-mercer, to whom she gave
her large and valuable custom, and who was in consequence
Miss Jean's very humble servant, and always happy to carve
the turkey or help the beef at her table, and act as 'landlord'
to her guests – which how she expressed it. He had a
very quiet little wife who did not count. And there was a
well-known doctor who was one of the community of the
Scots kirk, and often called on Sabbath morning to take
Miss Jean to Swallow Street in his carriage. Besides these
persons, who were her habitual society, there was a floating
element of Scotch ladies who were governesses or housekeepers in great families, and who had occasion to know

Miss Jean through bringing messages to her from their
ladies and being recognized as countrywomen. It was a very
strongly Scots society in the middle of Mayfair, very racy
of Scotch soil, and full of Scotch ideas though living exclu-
sively in London. It had been a little humiliating to Kirsteen
herself to meet them, with the strong conviction she had
in her mind that she herself with her good blood must be
very much above this little assembly. But she had been
obliged to confess that they had all been very agreeable, and
old Mrs Gordon had quoted her fine relations to so much
purpose that Kirsteen had been much ashamed of her
instinctive resistance and foregone conclusion. All the same
she did not think Glendochart would be elated by such an
invitation, or that he would consider it a privilege to introduce his wife to the circle at Chapel Street. His wife! She
thought with a momentary thrill that she might have been
that important personage, ordering new gowns from Miss
Jean instead of sewing under her, driving about in a handsome carriage and doing just what she pleased, with an
adoring slave in attendance. And that he should have taken
Mary in her place! And that Mary should possess all that
had been intended for Kirsteen! She thought she could see
the quiet triumph that would be in her sister's eyes, and the
way in which she would parade her satisfaction. And wherefore not? Kirsteen said to herself. Since she had paid the
price, why should she not have the satisfaction? But it cost
Kirsteen an effort to come to this Christian state of mind –
and she did not reply to Mary's letter. For indeed she was
not at all a perfect young woman, but full of lively and
impatient feelings, and irritability and self-opinion – as
belonged to her race.

CHAPTER XXIX

London was more than *throng* when Glendochart and his young wife arrived. It was mad with joy over the great Battle of Waterloo which had just been fought, and the triumph of the British arms, and the end of the war which nobody had been sure might not be another long war like that of the Peninsula. When the pair from the Highlands reached town travelling in the coach, for Mary thought a post-chaise an unnecessary expense, they met, a short distance from London, the coach which carried the news, all decorated with laurels, the conductor performing triumphant tunes upon his horn, the passengers half crazy with shouting, and feeling themselves somehow a part of the victory if not the first cause, flinging newspapers into passing carriages and meeting every wayfarer with a chorus only half intelligible about the Great and Glorious Victory. The bride was much excited by these announcements. She concluded that now there would be nothing but balls and parties in London, and that Glendochart would receive sheaves of invitations from all quarters; and finally that it was quite essential she should go at once to Miss Jean Brown's, not only to ask after Kirsteen, but to get herself one or two gowns that should be in the height of the fashion and fit to appear at the dinner table of the Duke and Duchess, who she made no doubt would make haste to invite so important a member of the clan. 'That will no doubt be the first place we will go to,' she said to her husband. 'Oh, yes, my dear; if his Grace thinks about it I have no doubt he will mention it to the Duchess, and if they would happen to have a free day—' 'Is that all you say, Glendochart, and me a bride?' cried Mary. But the old bridegroom, who was more or less a man of the world, would not promise more. And he was as much excited by the news as anyone, and from the moment when he could seize one of the papers that were flying about, and read for himself the brief dispatch from the field of battle, there was nothing else to be got from him. There was another old soldier in the coach, and the two began to reckon up the regiments that had been engaged and to discuss the names of the officers, and to speculate on the results of this great and decisive victory, and whether Boney would ever hold up his head again. Mary felt almost deserted as she sat back in her corner and found all the caresses and whispers of the earlier journey stopped by his sudden excitement. She did not herself care very much for the victory nor understand it, though she was glad it was a victory. She was half glad also, and half sorry, that none of the boys were with Lord Wellington – sorry that she was deprived of the consequence of having a brother with the army, yet glad that she was thus free of the sad possibility of being plunged into mourning before her honeymoon was over.

But when these thoughts had passed through her mind, Mary turned to her own concerns, which were more interesting than any public matters. Flags were flying everywhere as they drove through the streets and a grand tumult of rejoicing going on. The very sound of it was exhilarating, the great placards that were up everywhere with the news, the throngs at every corner, the news-vendors who were shouting at the top of their voices imaginary additions to the dispatches and further details of the victory, the improvised illuminations in many windows, a candle stuck in each pane after the fashion of the time, that to a stranger from the country had a fine effect seen through the smoky haze of the London streets, which even in June and at the beginning of the century was sufficiently apparent to rural perceptions. Mary was not carried away by this fervour of popular sentiment as her old husband was, who was ready to shout for Wellington and the army on the smallest provocation, but she was agreeably stimulated in her own thoughts. She already saw herself at the grand dinners which would be given in celebration of the event in the Duke's great mansion in Portman Square – not placed perhaps by his side, as would in other circumstances have been her right as a bride, but yet not far off, in the midst of the lords and ladies; or perhaps his Grace, who was known to be punctilious, would give her her right, whoever was there, were it even a princess of the blood, and she would have the pride and the felicity of looking down upon half the nobility seated below her at the feast. The chief of

Glendochart's name could scarcely do less to one of the Douglases entering his clan at such a moment. Mary lay back in her corner, her mind floating away on a private strain of beatific anticipation, while Glendochart hung half out of the window in his excitement, cheering and asking questions. She imagined the princess of the blood, who no doubt would be present, asking of the Duke who the young lady was in her bridal dress who occupied the place of honour, and hearing that she was one of the Douglases, just entered into his Grace's connection by her marriage with Glendochart, the princess then (she almost saw it!) would request to have the bride presented to her, and would ask that the Duchess should bring her one day to Windsor perhaps to be presented to Queen Charlotte, or to Hampton Court or some other of the royal palaces. Mary's heart beat high with this supposition, which seemed more or less a direct consequence of Waterloo, as much so as Boney's downfall, and much more satisfactory than that probable event.

When they arrived in the city where the coaches from the north stopped, and she had to get out, somewhat dazed by all the tumult round her, and the crowd, and the struggle for baggage, and the absence of any coherent guidance through that chaos of shouting men and stamping horses, and coaches coming and going, and everywhere the shouts of the great and glorious victory, Mary was in the act of receiving a pressing invitation from the princess to pass a week with her, and meet all the first people in London. She was half annoyed to be disturbed in the midst of these delightful visions, but comforted herself with the thought that it was but a pleasure deferred.

And it may be imagined that with all this in her mind it became more than ever important to Mary to make an early call upon Miss Jean and provide herself as rapidly as pos-sible with a dress that was fit to be worn among such fine company. The riding-habit which she had worn at her marriage, though exceedingly fine and becoming, was not a garment in which she could appear at the dinner table in Portman Square. There are some rare geniuses who have an intuitive knowledge of what is finest and best without having learned it, and in respect to society and dress and the details of high life Mary was one of these gifted persons.

Her habit had been very highly thought of in the country.
It was a costume, many rustic persons supposed, in which it
would be possible to approach the presence of Queen Charlotte herself. But Mary knew by intuition just how far this
was possible. And she knew that for the Duke's table a
white gown was indispensable in which to play her part as a
bride; therefore, as there was no saying at what moment
the invitation might arrive, nor how soon the dinner might
take place, she considered it expedient to carry out her
intention at once. Happily Glendochart next morning was
still a little crazy about the victory, and anxious to go down
to the Horse Guards to make inquiries, if she would excuse
him, as he said, apologetically. Mary did so with the best
grace in the world. 'And while you are asking about your
old friends,' she said, 'I will just go and see if I can find out
anything about my poor sister—' 'That is just a most kind
thing to do, and exactly what I would have expected from
you, my dear,' said Glendochart, grateful to his young wife
for allowing him so much liberty. And he hastened to
secure a glass coach for her in which she could drive to
Miss Jean, and 'see all the London ferlies', as he said, on
the way. It was not a very splendid vehicle to drive up to
Miss Jean's door, where the carriages of the nobility
appeared every day; but Mrs Mary felt herself the admired
of all beholders as she drove along the streets, well set up
in the middle of the seat as if she had been the Queen. Her
heart beat a little when she reached the house, with mingled
alarm as to Kirsteen's reception of her, and pride in her
own superior standing, far above any unmarried person, as
Mrs Campbell of Glendochart. The name did not indeed
impress the maid who received her, and who asked twice
what it was, begging pardon for not catching it the first
time, and suggesting 'Lady Campbell of –?' 'Mistress Campbell,' said Mary. She felt even in that moment a little taken
down. It was as if the maid was accustomed to nothing less
than my lady. She was so agitated that she did not perceive
the name of Miss Kirsteen in connection with that of Miss
Brown upon the brass plate of the door.

  She had, however, quite recovered herself before
Kirsteen appeared in the showroom to answer the
summons, and advanced rustling in all her new ribbons to
meet her sister. 'Oh, Kirsteen, is that you? Oh, are you

really here? I thought I could not be deceived about Miss Jean harbouring ye and helping ye, but I did not think I would just find ye in a moment like this.'

'Yes,' said Kirsteen, 'I am here, and I have been here ever since I left home.'

'Ye have turned quite English, Kirsteen, in the time ye've been away.'

'Have I? It's perhaps difficult to avoid it – if ye have anything of an ear for music.' This was perhaps an unkind thing to say, for it was well known in the family that Mary had no ear for music and could not 'turn a tune' to save her life. With a compunction Kirsteen turned to a more natural subject. 'And how is my mother?'

'Oh,' said Mary, 'she is just wonderfully well for her. The marriage was a great divert to her, settling how it was to be and the clothes and everything. She was dressed herself in a new gown that Glendochart presented to her for the occasion, with white ribbons in her cap, and looking just very well. "It's easy to see where ye get your looks from," Henry said to me: which I thought was a very pretty compliment to both of us, for if ever a man was pleased with his wife's looks it should be on his wedding-day.'

'Very likely,' said Kirsteen drily, 'but I have no experience. I got your letter, with an account of what you had on.'

'Yes, it was considered very becoming,' said Mary. 'And Jeanie was just beautiful in a white frock; I will have her with me at Glendochart when she gets a little older, and bring her out, and maybe take her to Edinburgh for a winter that she may have every advantage. I would like her to make a grand marriage, and there is nothing more likely when she's seen as she ought to be in a house like Glendochart.'

'I have yet to learn,' said Kirsteen with dilating nostrils and quivering lips (for she too intended Jeanie to make a great match, and to marry well, but under her own auspices, not her sister's), 'I have yet to learn that a Campbell who is the Duke's clanswoman can give credit to a Douglas that comes of the first family of her own name.'

'Maybe you think too,' said Mary with all the force of ridicule founded on fact, 'that the house of Drumcarro is a good place for letting a young thing see the world.'

Kirsteen was silenced by this potent argument, but it by no means softened the irritation in her mind. She had thought of Jeanie as her own, her creation in many ways, between whom and every evil fate she was determined to stand. To have the child taken out of her hands in this calm way was almost more than she could bear. But she compelled herself to patience with a hasty self-argument: Who was she to stand between Jeanie and any advantage – when nobody could tell whether she would be able to carry out her intentions or not? And at all events at the present moment Jeanie being only fourteen there was not much to be done. Mary's smooth voice going on, forbade any very continued strain of thought.

'And Kirsteen, what is to be done about yourself? We would be real willing to do anything in our power – But oh! it was rash – rash of you to run away – for you see by what's happened that it was all a mistake, and that Glendochart—'

Kirsteen's milk-white brow again grew as red as fire. To have your old lover console himself with your sister is bad enough; but to have her explain to you that your alarm was a mere mistake of vanity, and that the only person who was ridiculous or blameable in the business was yourself – this is too much for mortal flesh and blood!

'I am much obliged to you,' she said with a self-restraint which was painful, 'but I am very happy where I am. It was no mistake so far as I am concerned. It was just impossible to live on down yonder without occupation, when there are so many things to be done in the world.'

'Dear me!' cried Mary astonished with this new view. But at this moment Miss Jean fortunately came in, and was very happy to see the lady of Glendochart and very anxious to show her every attention.

'I consider it a great honour,' said Miss Jean, 'that you should come to see me the first morning; though well I know it's not for me but for one that is far more worthy. Miss Kirsteen is just the prop of this house, Mistress Campbell. Not a thing can be done without her advice – and though I had little reason to complain, and my basket and my store had aye prospered just wonderful, it's a different thing now Miss Kirsteen is here, for she makes all the fine ladies stand about.'

'Dear me,' said Mary again, 'and how can she do that?' But she was more anxious about her own affairs than the gifts and endowments of her sister. 'There is one thing I must say,' she added, 'before we go further, and that is that I am wishing to get a new gown; for we will likely be asked to our dinner at the Duke's, and though I have all my wedding outfit I would like to be in the newest fashion and do my husband credit with the chief of his name. So perhaps you would show me some white silks, just the very newest. And I would like it made in the last fashion; for Glendochart is very liberal and he will wish me to spare no expense. Being Marg'ret's sister as well as having been so kind to Kirsteen, it was just natural that I should choose what little custom I have to give into your hands. But I would want it very quickly done, just as quick as the needles can go – for we cannot tell for what day the invitation might come.'

Miss Jean with a smile upon her face, the smile with which she received an order, and a bow of acquiescence which made the ribbons tremble in her cap, had taken a step towards the drawers in which her silks were kept; but there was something in Kirsteen's eyes which made her hesitate. She looked towards her young associate with a half-question – though indeed she could not tell what was the foundation of her doubt – in her eyes.

'Miss Jean,' said Kirsteen promptly, 'you have then forgotten our new rule! You will maybe think I want you to break it in consideration of my sister? But ye need not depart from your regulations out of thought for me. And I am sure I am very sorry,' she said turning to Mary, who stood expectant with a smile of genial patronage on her face – 'but it's not possible. Miss Jean has made a rule to take no orders from commoners – except them that have been long upon her list. It would just be hopeless if we were to undertake it,' Kirsteen said.

'No orders – from commoners?' cried Mary in consternation and wrath.

'Just that; we would have all London at our tails, no to speak of persons from the country like yourself – just pursuing us night and day – if we were to relax our rule. And there are many of the nobility,' said Kirsteen turning to Miss Jean with a look of serious consultation, 'whom I

would wish to be weeded out – for there are titles and titles,
and some countesses are just nobodies however much they
may think of themselves. You will never get to the first
rank,' continued Kirsteen still addressing Miss Jean, 'unless
ye just settle and never depart from it, who you are to
dress, and who not.'

'Do you mean, Miss Jean,' cried Mrs Campbell of Glendochart, 'that ye will not make me my gown?'

Miss Jean was torn asunder between natural politeness
and proper subjection to her superiors, and a still more
natural partisanship, not to speak of the glance of fiery
laughter in Kirsteen's eyes. 'What can I do,' she cried,
'when you hear with your own ears what Miss Kirsteen has
said? I am wae to put you to any inconvenience, but it's just
true that we cannot get through the half of our work –
and we've plenty with the nobility and old customers to
keep us always very *throng*. But I could recommend ye to
another person that would willingly serve ye though I
cannot take your order myself.'

'Oh, I'll find somebody,' said Mary in great offence. 'It
cannot be that in the great town of London you will not get
whatever you want when you have plenty of money in your
hand.'

'No doubt that's very true,' said Miss Jean, 'and ye may
find that ye are not in such a great hurry as ye think, for the
Duchess has a number of engagements upon her hands,
and will not dine at home for about ten days to my certain
knowledge – and probably she will have her table full then
if ye have not already received your invitations – for town
is just very *throng*, and everything settled for the grand
parties, weeks before.'

CHAPTER XXX

Miss Jean it must be allowed turned to her young companion with some dismay when Mrs Campbell of Glendochart had been ceremoniously seen to her hackney coach, and deeply cast down and discomfited, had driven away to the respectable person who had been recommended to her to make her new gown. 'Were you meaning yon?' Miss Jean asked with solicitude. 'Or what were you meaning?'

'I was meaning what I said,' cried Kirsteen holding her head high and with an unusual colour upon her cheeks. 'You know yourself that we have more work than can be done if we were to sit at it day and night.'

'For the moment,' said Miss Jean prudently; 'but to refuse work just goes to my heart – it might spoil the business.'

'It will do the business good,' said Kirsteen. 'We will let it be known, not just yet perhaps, what I said, that we will take no commoners' orders – that persons who are nobodies need not come here. You did not take me with you into the business just to go on like other folk.'

'No – that's quite true,' said Miss Jean, but with a little hesitation still.

'By the time,' said Kirsteen, 'that you have turned away half a dozen from your door, your name will be up over all the town; and whether in the season or out of it, you will have more to do than you can set your face to, and thanks for doing it. Will you trust me or not, Miss Jean? For I allow that I am inexperienced and perhaps I may not be right.'

'It would be very strange if ye were always right,' said Miss Jean with a smile of affectionate meaning, 'for all so young and so sure as ye are. But ye have a great spirit and there's something in me too that just answers till ye. Yes, I'll trust ye, my dear; and ye'll just go insulting all the poor bodies that are not good enough to please ye, till ye make a spoon or spoil a horn for yourself; for it does not matter so very much for me.'

'Not the poor bodies,' said Kirsteen, 'but the folk with money and nothing else, that come in as if they were doing us a favour – women that Marg'ret would not have in her kitchen; and they will come in here and give their orders as if it was a favour to you and me! I would like to learn them a lesson: that though we're mantua-makers, it's not for the like of them – a person with no name to speak of – and giving her orders to one of the Douglases! We will learn them better before we are done.'

'Oh, pride, pride!' said Miss Jean, 'there's something in me that answers till ye, though well I wot I have little to be proud of; but these half and half gentry they are just insufferable to me too.'

In all this there was nothing said of Mrs Mary, to whom none of these descriptions applied, for she was of course one of the Douglases as well as her sister, and Glendochart was as good a gentleman as any of his name. But while Miss Jean Brown, the daughter of a Scotch ploughman, felt something in her that answered to the pride of the well-born Highland girl, there was much in the other that resembled the 'half and half gentry', of whom the experienced mantua-maker had seen many specimens. Miss Jean's prognostics, however, were carried into effect with stern certainty in the disappointment of the country visitors. They did indeed dine in Portman Square, but chiefly because of Lady Chatty's desire to see the personages of the story which she was so fond of telling, and then only on a Sunday evening when the family were alone. Alone, or all but alone, for there was one guest to meet them in the person of Miss Kirsteen Douglas, who was not a stranger in the house nor awkward, as the bride was in her new gown and much over-dressed for the family party. It was impossible for Kirsteen to meet Glendochart, whose wooing had been of so much importance in her life, without a warmer tinge of colour and a slight shade of consciousness. But the good man was so completely unaware of any cause for feeling, that she came to herself with a little start and shock, which was highly salutary and chastised that pride which was Kirsteen's leading quality at this period of her career. Glendochart was so completely married, so pleased with his young wife, and with himself for having secured her, that all former dreams had departed totally from his mind – a

discovery which Kirsteen made instantaneously so soon as
their eyes met, and which went through and through her
with angry amazement, consternation, wonder, mingled
after a little while with a keen humorous sense of the
absurdity of the situation. He came after dinner and talked
to her a little about her circumstances, and how difficult it
was to know what to do. 'For your father is a very dour
man, as Mary says, and having once passed his word that
you are never to enter his door, it will be hard, hard to
make him change. You know how obdurate he has been
about Anne; but we will always be on the watch, and if the
time ever comes that a word may be of use—'

'I beg you will take no trouble about it, Glendochart. I
knew what I was risking; and but for my mother I have little
to regret. And she has not been any the worse,' Kirsteen
said, almost with bitterness. Nobody seemed to have been
the worse for her departure, not even her mother.

'No, I believe she has been none the worse. She is coming
to pay us a visit so soon as we get back.'

Kirsteen could have laughed, and she could have cried.
She could have seized upon this precise, well-got-up elderly
gentleman and given him a good shake. To think that she
should have been frightened almost out of her wits, and
flung all her life to the winds, because of him; and that he
was here advising her for her good, as well satisfied with
Mary as he ever could have been with herself!

Miss Jean proved, however, a true prophet in respect to
the disappointment of the newly married couple with their
reception in London, and their willingness eventually to
accept the hospitality of the mantua-maker, and meet her
friends, the minister, the doctor, the silk-mercer, and the
old lady of quality, at her comfortable table. Miss Jean gave
them a supper at which all these highly respectable persons
were present, along with another who gave a character of
distinction to the assembly, being no less a person than
young Captain Gordon, promoted on the field of battle and
sent home with dispatches, the son of the old lady above
mentioned, who was not too grand, though all the fine
houses in London were open to him, to come with his
mother, covering her with glory in the eyes of the humbler
friends who had been kind to her poverty. This encounter
was the only one which brought Glendochart and his wife

within the range of the commotion which was filling all
society and occupying all talk. Afterwards, when they
returned home, it was the main feature of their record, what
Captain Gordon had said, and his account of the battle –
'which, you see, we had, so to speak, at first hand; for he
got his promotion upon the field, and was sent home with
dispatches, which is only done when a young man has distinguished himself; and a near connection of the Huntly
family.' I am not sure that Mary did not allow it to be
understood that she had met this young hero at the Duke's
table in Portman Square, but certainly she never disclosed
the fact that it was at the mantua-maker's in Chapel Street,
Mayfair. Captain Gordon proved to be of much after
importance in the family, so that the mode of his first introduction cannot be without interest. The old lady who
patronized Miss Jean by sharing her Sunday dinners, and
many other satisfactory meals, felt herself, and was
acknowledged by all, to have amply repaid her humble
friend by bringing this brilliant young hero fresh from
Waterloo to that entertainment, thus doing Miss Jean an
honour which 'the best in the land' coveted. Alick, so far as
he was concerned, made himself exceedingly agreeable. He
fought the great battle over again, holding his auditors
breathless; he gave the doctor details about the hospitals,
and told the minister how the army chaplain went among
the poor Highlanders from bed to bed. And he accepted an
invitation from Glendochart for the shooting with enthusiasm. 'But they will want you at Castle Gordon,' said the
proud mother, desirous to show that her son had more
gorgeous possibilities. 'Then they must just want me,' cried
the young soldier. 'They were not so keen about me when
I was a poor little ensign.' Everything was at the feet of the
Waterloo hero, who was in a position to snap his fingers
at his grand relations and their tardy hospitality. Kirsteen in
particular was attracted by his cheerful looks and his high
spirit, and his pleasure in his independence and promotion.
It was in accord with her own feeling. She said that he put
her in mind of her brothers in India – all soldiers, but none
of them so fortunate as to have taken part in such a great
decisive battle; and thought with a poignant regret how it
might have been had Ronald Drummond continued with
Lord Wellington's army instead of changing into the

Company's service. It might have been he that would have been sent over with the dispatches, and received with all this honour and renown – and then! – Kirsteen's countenance in the shade where she was sitting was suffused with a soft colour, and the tears came into her eyes.

'They get plenty of fighting out there,' said the young soldier, who was very willing to console the only pretty girl in the room; 'and if it's not so decisive it may be just as important in the long run, for India is a grand possession – the grandest of all. I will probably go there myself, Miss Douglas, for though Waterloo's a fine thing, it will end the war, and what's a poor soldier lad to do?'

'You will just find plenty to do in your own country, Alick,' said his mother eagerly.

'Barrack duty, mother! it's not very exciting – after a taste of the other.'

'A taste!' said the proud old lady. 'He's just been in everything, since the time he put on his first pair of trews. I know those outlandish places, as if they were on Deeside, always following my soldier laddie – Vimiera, and Badajos, and down to Salamanca and Toulouse in France. I could put my finger on them in the map in the dark,' she cried with a glow of enthusiasm; then falling into a little murmur of happy sobbing, 'God be thanked they're all over,' she cried, putting her trembling hand upon her son's arm.

'Amen!' said the minister, 'to the final destruction of the usurper and the restoring of law and order in a distracted land!'

'We'll just see how long it lasts,' said the doctor, who was a little of a free thinker and was believed to have had sympathies with the Revolution.

'We'll have French tastes and French fashions in again, and they're very ingenious with their new patterns it must be allowed,' said the silk-mercer; 'but it will be an ill day for Spitalfields and other places when the French silks are plentiful again.'

'There's ill and good in all things. You must just do your best, Miss Jean, to keep British manufactures in the first place,' the minister said. 'It's astonishing in that way how much the ladies have in their hands.'

'Were you at Salamanca – and Toulouse?' said Kirsteen in her corner, where she kept as far as possible from the light of the candles, lest anyone should see the emotion in her face.

'Indeed I was, and the last was a field of carnage,' said the young soldier. 'Perhaps you had a brother there?'

'Not a brother – but a – friend,' said Kirsteen, unable to restrain a faint little sigh. The young man looked so sympathetic and was so complete a stranger to her that it was a relief to her full bosom to say a word more. 'I could not but think,' she added in a very low tone, 'that but for that weary India – it might have been him that had come with glory – from Waterloo.'

'Instead of me,' said the young soldier with a laugh. 'No, I know you did not mean that. But also,' he added gravely, 'both him and me, we might have been left on the field where many a fine fellow lies.'

'That is true, that is true!' Kirsteen did not say any more; but it flashed across her mind how could she know that he was not lying on some obscure field in India where lives were lost, and little glory or any advantage that she knew of gained? This gave her, however, a very friendly feeling to young Gordon, between whom and herself the tie of something which was almost like a confidence now existed. For the young man had easily divined what a friend meant in the guarded phraseology of his countrywomen.

It was not till long after this that there came to Kirsteen a little note out of that far distance which made amends to her for long waiting and silence. The letter was only from Robbie, whose correspondence with his sisters was of the most rare and fluctuating kind, yet who for once in a way, he scarcely himself knew the reason why, had sent Kirsteen a little enclosure in his letter to his mother, fortunately secured by Marg'ret, who was now everything – nurse, reader, and companion to the invalid. Robbie informed his sister that Jeanie's letter about old Glendochart had 'given him a good laugh', and that he thought she was very right to have nothing to say to an old fellow like that. Before the letter arrived there was already a son and heir born in Glendochart house, but Robbie was no further on in the family history than to be aware of the fact that Kirsteen had gone away rather than have the old lover forced upon her. He told her how on the march he had passed the station where Ronald Drummond was, 'if you mind him, he is the one that left along with me – but you must mind him,' Robbie continued, 'for he was always about the house the last summer before I came away.'

He was keen for news of home, as we all are when we meet a friend in this place. And I read him a bit of Jeanie's letter which was very well written, the little monkey, for a little thing of her age; how old Glendochart followed you about like a puppy dog, and how you would never see it, though all the rest did. We both laughed till we cried at Jeanie's story. She must be growing a clever creature, and writes a very good hand of writing too. But it was more serious when we came to the part where you ran away in your trouble at finding it out. I hope you have come home by this time and have not quarrelled with my father; for after all it never does any good to have quarrels in a family. However, I was saying about Ronald that he was really quite as taken up as I was with Jeanie's letter, and told me I was to give you his respects, and that he would be coming home in a year or two, and would find you out whether you were at Drumcarro or wherever you were, and give you all the news about me, which I consider very kind of him, as I am sure you will do – and he bid me to say that he always kept the little thing he found in the parlour, and carried it wherever he went: though when I asked what it was he would not tell me, but said you would understand: so I suppose it was some joke between you two. And that's about all the news I have to tell you, and I hope you'll think of what I say about not quarrelling with my father. I am in very good health and liking my quarters – and I am,

Your affect. brother,
R. D.

If this had been the most eloquent love-letter that ever was written, and from the hand of her lover himself, it is doubtful whether it would have more touched the heart of Kirsteen than Robbie's schoolboy scrawl, with its complete unconsciousness of every purpose, did. It was the fashion of their time when correspondence was difficult and dear and slow, and when a young man with nothing to offer was too honourable to bind for long years a young woman who in the meantime might change her mind; although both often held by each other with a supreme and silent faithfulness. The bond, so completely understood between themselves with nothing to disclose it to others, was all the dearer for never having been put into words; although it was often no doubt the cause of unspeakable pangs of suspense, of doubt – possibly of profound and unspeakable disappointment if one or the other forgot. Kirsteen read and reread Robbie's letter as if it had been a little gospel. She carried it about with her, for her refreshment at odd moments. There came upon her face a softened sweetness, a mildness to the happy eyes, a mellowing beauty to every line. She grew greatly in beauty as her youth matured, the softening influence of this sweet spring of life keeping in check the pride which was so strong in her character, and the perhaps too great independence and self-reliance which her early elevation to authority and influence developed. And everything prospered with Kirsteen. Miss Jean's business became the most flourishing and important in town. Not only commoners, whom she had so haughtily rejected, but persons of the most exalted pretensions had to cast away their pride and sue for the services of Miss Brown and Miss Kirsteen; and as may be supposed, the more they refused, the more eager were the customers at their door. Before Kirsteen was twenty-seven, the fortune which she had determined to make was already well begun, and Miss Jean in a position to retire if she wished with the income of a statesman. This prosperous condition was in its full height in the midst of the season, the workroom so *throng* that relays of seamstresses sat up all night, there being no inspectors to bring the fashionable mantua-makers under control, when the next great incident happened in the life of our Kirsteen.

CHAPTER XXXI

There were no inspectors to look after the workrooms of the dressmakers in these days, but perhaps also, at least with mistresses like Miss Jean, there was little need for them. If the young women in the workroom had sometimes to work for a part of the night it was only what at that time everybody was supposed to do in their own affairs or in their masters', when business was very urgent, or *throng* as was said in Scotland. The head of the house sat up too, there were little indulgences accorded, and when the vigil was not too much prolonged, there was a certain excitement about it which was not unpleasing to the workwomen in the monotony of their calling. One of these indulgences was that something was now and then read aloud to them as they worked.

Miss Jean herself had ceased to do much in the ordinary conduct of business. She gave her advice (which the workwomen now considered of the old school and wanting in sympathy with advancing taste), and now and then suggested a combination which was approved. But on the whole she took a less and less active share in the work during the morning and evening hours in which she was not wanted in the showroom to receive the ladies who were her patronesses, or whom she patronized (according to Kirsteen's new arrangements) with whom the younger partner had no desire to supplant her. And when Miss Jean resigned the needle and even the scissors, and no longer felt it necessary to superintend a fitting on, or invent a headdress, she developed another faculty which was of the greatest use, especially at moments of great pressure. She read aloud – I will not assert that she had any of the arts of the elocutionist, which were much esteemed in those days – but in a straightforward, plain way, with her Scotch accent, to which of course all the young women were accustomed, her reading was very distinct and satisfactory.

She read in the first instance stories out of the *Ladies' Museum* and kindred works, which were about as absurd as

stories could be, but being continued from week to week,
kept up a certain interest among the girls to know what
happened to Ellen as an example of youthful indiscretion,
or Emily as a victim of parental cruelty. What a jump it was
when Miss Jean brought in with triumphant delight a book
called *Waverley; or, 'Tis Sixty Years Since*, I can scarcely
venture to describe. No doubt the young women accustomed only to Ellen and Emily were a little confused by the
new and great magician with whom they were thus suddenly
brought face to face; but they were greatly stirred by the
Highland scenes and Fergus MacIver's castle, and the beautiful Flora, for and against whom they immediately took
sides, a certain party hoping against hope that she would
finally marry the hero, while the other faction strongly supported the claims of Rose Bradwardine. The humours of
the tale scarcely penetrated perhaps those unaccustomed
bosoms, and nothing in it was so important to the imagination of the workwomen as this. Miss Jean finished the book
one night when all were working very late, the night before
a state ball. It was an unusually heavy night because of Lady
Chatty, now an acknowledged beauty and leader of fashion,
who had invented a new mode a day or two before; that is
to say Kirsteen, who was entirely devoted to her beautiful
friend, had produced an effect by the looping up of a train
or the arrangement of a scarf which had dazzled all
beholders, and had become at once the object of a rage of
imitation such as sometimes occurs in the not uneventful
annals of fashion. So many ladies had argued and implored,
adjuring Miss Jean by all her gods, pointing out to her the
urgent duty of not leaving a client or countrywoman in the
shade; of not crushing the hopes of a young *débutante*,
perhaps spoiling a great marriage or bringing about some
other catastrophe, that the head of the establishment had
been melted, and had indiscreetly consented to execute
more orders than it was possible to do. Miss Jean had been
very shy of meeting Kirsteen after, and had confessed her
indiscretion almost with tears, but her young partner with
no further remonstrance than a shake of her head had
accepted the responsibility. To do something miraculous is
always a pleasure in its way, and Kirsteen laid the circumstances before the young women, and inspired them with
her own energy. She herself was up the whole night never

flagging, while the others managed it by relays, snatching an hour or two of sleep, and returning to work again. They had a tea drinking at midnight, when the fine-flavoured tea which Miss Jean herself affected was served to the work-women all round, with dainty cakes and cates, and, highest solace of all, Miss Jean herself sat up and finished *Waverley*, at the risk of making a few needles rusty by the dropping here and there of furtive tears. The excitement about Flora MacIver and the gentle Rose, and the keen disappointment of Flora's partisans who had all along hoped against hope that she would relent, kept drowsiness at bay. This was not the chief point of interest in the book perhaps, but these young women regarded it from that point of view.

I tell this chiefly as an illustration of the manner in which Miss Brown and Kirsteen managed their affairs. But as a matter of fact Miss Jean often read aloud when there was no such urgent call for it. She read the newspapers to the girls when there were any news of interest. She had read to them everything about Waterloo, and all the dispatches and the descriptions of the field, and anecdotes about the battle, as they came out bit by bit in the small square news-paper of eight pages, which was all that then represented the mighty *Times*. One of the young women lost a brother in that battle. This made the little community feel that all had something special to do with it, and brought tears into every eye, and justified them in shaking all their heads over the cost of blood by which the great victory had been achieved, even in the midst of their enjoyment of the illumi-nations and all the stir and quickened life of town at that great moment.

It was long after Waterloo, however, when the incident I am about to record occurred. Years had passed, and the newspapers were no longer so exciting as in those days of the Peninsula, when a fight or a victory might be always looked for. War died out from among the items of news and the long calm – which ended only after the Great Ex-hibition of '51 had made as people thought an end of all possibility of fighting – had begun; people had ceased to be afraid of the newspaper, and the tidings it might bring. It is true there was always fighting going on in India more or less, little battles now and then, skirmishes, expeditions of which the world did not know very much, but in which without any demonstration, a few brave lives would end from time to time, and hearts break quietly at home, all to the increase and consideration of our great Indian territory, and the greatness of Great Britain in that empire upon which the sun never sets.

Some six years had passed from the time when Kirsteen came friendless to London knowing nobody but Marg'ret's sister. She was now a power in her way, supreme in the house in Chapel Street, Mayfair, feared and courted by many people who had once been sufficiently haughty to Miss Jean. At twenty-six when a young woman has gone through many vicissitudes of actual life, when she has been forced into independence, and stood for herself against the world, she is as mature as if she were twenty years older, though in the still atmosphere of home twenty-six is very often not much more than sixteen. Kirsteen had become in some ways very mature. She had that habit of authority which was so well set forth long ago by the man who described himself as saying to one ' "Go," and he goeth, and to another "Come," and he cometh.' She had but to speak and she was obeyed – partly from love, but partly also from fear: for Kirsteen was not the laird of Drumcarro's daughter for nothing, and she was very prompt in her measures, and quite indisposed to tolerate insubordination. And her young womanhood was so withdrawn from the usual thoughts and projects of her age that Kirsteen had put on something of the dignified manners of a person much older, although her fresh youthful colour, the milk-white brow and throat, the ruddy hair all curly with vigour and life, showed no premature fading, and her person, which was always beautifully clothed, and fitted to perfection, had improved in slenderness and grace. It was not that propositions of a sentimental kind had been wanting. Lord John (but his name always brought a blush of displeasure to Kirsteen's cheek) had done his best to find her at unguarded moments, to beguile her into talk, and to use all the covert arts which were still supposed to be part of the stock-in-trade of a young man of fashion, to attain her interest if not her affection. What he intended perhaps the young man did not himself know, perhaps only to attain the triumph of persuading a young woman whom he admired to admire him. But Kirsteen considered that it was through his means alone that the difficulties of her position were really brought home to her, and the difference between a mantua-maker exercising her craft, and a young lady of family at home, made apparent. This was a mistake, for Lord John would have considered himself quite as free to attempt a flirtation with Drumcarro's daughter in Argyllshire as in London, and with as little intention of any serious result, the daughter of a poor laird however high in descent, being as entirely below the level of the Duke's son as the mantua-maker. But it gave a keen edge to Kirsteen's scorn of him, that she would have believed he was ready to take advantage of her unprotected state.

Also there was Miss Jean's friend the doctor, who would very willingly have made a sensible matrimonial alliance with a young person getting on so very well in the world – while Miss Jean's nephew, he who had already calculated how many years it would take him to reach the elevation of Lord Mayor, worshipped in silence the divinity whom he durst no more approach than he durst propose for one of the princesses, knowing well that Miss Jean would bundle him indignantly out of doors at the merest whisper of such a presumption. But none of these things touched Kirsteen nor would have done had they been much more attractive. 'Will ye wait for me till I come back?' was the whisper which was always in her ears. And since the arrival of Robbie's letter there had come a certain solidity and reality to that visionary bond. A man who was so near on the verge of return that in a year or two, 'in two-three years' he might be back, was almost as close as if he were coming tomorrow – for what is next year but a big tomorrow to the faithful soul? The only feeling that ever marred for a moment the anticipation in Kirsteen's mind was a fear that when he came he might be wounded a little by this mantua-making episode. It vexed her to think that this might be the case, and cast an occasional shadow upon her mind from which she was glad to escape as from the sight of a ghost. He might not like it – his mother, who was a proud woman, would not like it. Kirsteen did not if she could help it, think of this possibility, yet it crossed her mind from time to time.

And in the meantime in those weary years, the fortune that was for little Jeanie, and that which would make

Ronald at ease even in his half-pay when he came back, was quietly growing.

With such a business, the most fashionable in London, and customers praying almost on their knees to be put on the lists of Misses Brown and Kirsteen how could it do otherwise than grow?

Kirsteen was twenty-six, the season was at its climax, the workroom very *throng* when Miss Jean came in one morning with the newspaper in her hand. Her little air of satisfaction when there were news that would be interesting to read was very well known. Miss Smith touched Miss Robinson with her elbow saying, 'Look at 'er,' and Miss Robinson communicated to Miss Jones her conviction that there was something stirring in the paper. Miss Jean came in and took her seat at the lower end of the table with her back to the broad uncurtained window by which all possible light was admitted. She liked to have the light falling well upon her paper. 'Now, my dears,' she said, 'I am going to read something to you – it's very touching, it's an account of a battle.'

'I thought all the battles were done,' said the forewoman who ventured to speak on such occasions.

'Oh, yes, on the Continent, heaven be praised – but this is in India,' said Miss Jean, as if nobody could ever expect battles to be over there. Kirsteen was at the other end of the table arranging some of the work. She was working with the rapidity of an inventor, throwing a piece of stuff into wonderful folds and plaitings of which no one could say what the issue was to be. She knew herself what she intended; but even when one knows what one means to do, the hand of genius itself has sometimes a great deal of trouble before the meaning can be carried out. She glanced up for a moment at the name of India, but only for a moment: for indeed there was always fighting in India, yet nothing had happened to any of those she cared for during all these years.

Miss Jean read out the details of the fight in her steady voice. It had been intended for nothing more than a reconnaissance and it turned into a battle which might have very important and momentous results. She read about the swarms of a warlike tribe who had been engaged by the Sepoys and a few British troops – and how well all had behaved – and how the enemy had been driven back and completely routed and dispersed and the authority of the Company established over a large region. 'Now,' said Miss Jean looking up over her spectacles, 'this is the interesting bit.

' "The victory, however, was a costly one – the casualties among the officers were unusually great. Out of nine actually engaged no less than five brave fellows were left on the field dead or seriously wounded. One young officer of the greatest promise who had led his battalion through a great deal of hot work, and who was down for immediate promotion, is among the number of the former. He was found lying struck through the heart by a native weapon. A curious and affecting incident is recorded of this unfortunate gentleman. After he had received his death stroke he must have found means of extracting a handkerchief from the breast of his uniform, and lay when found holding this to his lips. The handkerchief was extricated from his grasp with some difficulty and was sent home to his mother, who no doubt will cherish it as a most precious relic. It was slightly stained with the brave young fellow's blood." '

Miss Jean's voice faltered as she read that the handkerchief had been sent to the young man's mother. 'Poor leddy, poor leddy!' she said, 'the Lord help her in her trouble.' And little exclamations of pity and emotion rose from various voices – but suddenly they were all stilled. No one was aware how the consciousness first arose. By means of a communication swiftly and silently conveyed from one to another, the eyes of all were suddenly turned towards Kirsteen who, with the light from the large window full upon her, sat surrounded by trails of the beautiful silk which she had been manipulating. She had looked up, her lips had dropped apart, her hands still holding the silk had fallen upon her lap. Her face was without a trace of colour, her bosom still as if she were no longer breathing. She looked like someone suddenly turned into marble, the warm tint of her hair exaggerating, if that were possible, the awful whiteness. They expected her every moment to fall down, like something inanimate in which no life was.

But she did not do this – and nobody dared interfere, partly from fear of this sudden catastrophe whatever it was, partly from fear of her. They all sat not venturing to move, looking at her, ready to spring to her assistance, not daring to take any step. After a moment, she drew a long breath, then with a little start as of awakening raised her hands and looked at them, all enveloped as they were in the silk. 'What – was I – doing?' she said. She moved her hands feebly, twisting the silk round them more and more, then tore it off and flung it from her on the floor. 'I can't remember what I was doing,' she said.

'Oh, my dear,' cried Miss Jean, coming towards her putting down the paper, 'never mind what you were doing – come to your own room.'

'Why should I come – to my own room? What's there?' A gleam of consciousness came over her colourless face. 'It's not there! – it cannot be there!'

'Oh, my darling,' cried Miss Jean, 'come away with me – come away, where you can be quiet.'

Kirsteen looked up in her face with quick anger and impatient sarcasm. 'Why should I be quiet?' she said. 'Have I nothing to do that I should be quiet? That's for idle folk. But read on, read on, Miss Jean. It's a bonny story – and there will be more.'

Miss Jean retired again to her seat, and all the workers bent over their work, but not a needle moved. Kirsteen picked up the silk again. She tried to restore it to its form, plaiting and twisting with swift impatient movements now this way and now that. All the young women watched her furtively, not losing a movement she made. She twisted the silk about, trying apparently to recover her own intention, pulling it here and there with impatient twitches and murmurs of exasperation. Then she piled it all upon the table in a sort of rage, throwing it out of her hands. 'Go on, go on with your paper,' she cried to Miss Jean, and took up a half-made dress from the table at which she began to stitch hurriedly, looking up every moment to cry, 'Go on, go on. Will ye go on?' At length Miss Jean exceedingly tremulous and miserable began to read again in a broken voice. Kirsteen stitched blindly for half an hour, then she rose suddenly and left the room.

CHAPTER XXXII

Kirsteen did not seclude herself for long. While the girls were still whispering to each other, not without some awe, of the sudden shock which she had evidently received, of her deathlike look, her struggle to maintain her composure, her rejection of all inquiries, she had returned among them, had taken up the silk again, and resumed what she was doing. There was scarcely a word said after Kirsteen came back. The young women all bent over their sewing, and their needles flew through their work. The presence among them of this one tragic face, perfectly colourless, self-commanded, silent, wrapped in an abstraction which nobody could penetrate, had the strangest impressive effect upon them. They did not dare to speak even to each other, but signed to each other for things they wanted, and worked like so many machines, fearing even to turn their eyes towards her. Miss Jean, quite unable to control herself after this mysterious blow which she had given without knowing, had retired to the parlour, where she sat alone and cried, she knew not why. Oh, if she had but held her tongue, if she had not been so ready to go and read the news to them! Kirsteen, so busy as she was, might never have seen it, might never have known. Miss Jean read the paragraph over and over again, till she could have repeated it by heart. She found lower down a list of the names of those who had been killed and wounded, but this brought no enlightenment to her, for she did not know Drumcarro, or the names of the neighbours near. She had to lay it away as an insoluble mystery, not able to comprehend how, from so few details as there were, and without even hearing any name, Kirsteen should have at once been killed, as it were, by this mysterious blow. How did she know who he was, the poor gentleman who had died with the white hand-kerchief pressed to his dying lips? It was a very touching incident, Miss Jean had herself thought. No doubt, she had said to herself, there was a story under it. She had shed a sudden, quick-springing tear over the poor young man on the field of battle, and then, in her desire to communicate the touching tale had hurried to the workroom without further thought – how, she asked herself, could she have known that it would hurt anyone? What meaning was there in it that Kirsteen alone could know?

It was late when the workwomen, who lived out of doors, went away. They had gone through a long and tiring day, with no amusement of any sort, or reading or talk to brighten it. But somehow they had not felt it so – they all felt as if they had been acting their parts in a tragedy, as if the poor young officer on the Indian plains had held some relationship to themselves. The silence which nobody enjoined, which nature herself exacted from them, burst into a tumult of low-breathed talk the moment they left the house. They discussed her looks, the awful whiteness of her face, the shock of that sudden, unsoftened communication, without asking, as Miss Jean did, how she could have known. Miss Jean heard their voices, first low and awe-stricken, rising in eagerness and loudness as they got further from the house. But it was not till some time later that Kirsteen came in. She had been at work in a violent, absorbed, passionate way, doing with incredible swiftness and determination everything her hand had found to do. She had an air of great weariness, the exhaustion which means excitement and not repose, when she came in. She threw a glance round the room looking for the paper which Miss Jean had put carefully out of sight. Kirsteen went to the table and turned over everything that was on it, groping in a sort of blind way.

'You are looking for something, my dear?'

'Yes – where is it?'

'What might ye be looking for?' said Miss Jean, trembling very much and with the tears coming to her eyes.

'Where is it?' Kirsteen said. She was perfectly still and quiet, her voice low, her face very white, her eyes cast down. It was evident that she felt no need of explanation, nor power of giving one. There was but one thing for her in the world and that was the paper with the news – which at the first hearing had gone like a stone to the bottom of her heart, like a sword piercing through and through.

Miss Jean had no power to resist or to pretend that she

did not understand. She rose, trembling, and unlocked her escritoire and brought the paper out, fumbling in the depths of a pigeonhole in which she had buried it that it might never be seen more. She was very tremulous, her face drawn, her eyes full of moisture. 'I canna think how you could make anything out of that,' she said almost querulously in the excess of her feeling. 'There's nothing, nothing in that, to say who it was. No person could divine. It might be somebody you never heard of.'

It is possible that after the utter and undoubting convictions of the first moment, such a thought might have come to Kirsteen's mind too. She put out her hand for the paper. Miss Jean kept on talking in a fretful tone.

'You've had no tea, not a thing since two o'clock, and now it's eleven at night – you've had no rest – work, work, as if your bread depended on it; and it's no such thing. I suppose you think you're made of something different from the ordinary, no mere flesh and blood.'

Kirsteen paid no attention. She did not hear, the words were as a vague accompaniment, like the sound of wheels and faint voices and footsteps out of doors. She opened the paper with steady nervous hands that did not tremble, and read over again every word. Then she turned to the list 'Casualties'. Casualties! Accidents! – was that a word to use for the list of the dead? When she had read it her hands dropped on her knee with the paper held in them, and from her colourless lips there came a faint sound, inarticulate, hoarse, the knell of hope. There had not been any hope in her heart: but to say that and to know that hope is over, are two things. In the one there was still a possibility – the other was death itself. Oh, the possibility had been very faint, very feeble! She had worked on all day, struggled on to preserve it, not asking for conviction. Sometimes to know the worst is what we desire. Sometimes we would prefer to put it from us, not to make sure, for a little. But there it was: no further doubt, 'Captain Drummond': his name and no other. 'Will ye wait till I come back?' He was standing by her, saying it – and lying there – with the handkerchief. It was all past, the whole story, as if it had happened a hundred years ago.

'Miss Kirsteen – most likely you are making yourself miserable about nothing. How can ye tell by a story like that who it is? Oh, my bonny dear, I am asking no questions, but to see you like that just breaks my heart.'

Kirsteen smiled in spite of herself at the idea of any heart being broken but her own, of anyone being miserable who had not known him, who had never seen him, who did not even know his name. She said nothing for a few moments and then she spoke with a voice quite tuneless and flat, but steady, 'Miss Jean, I will have to go for a day or two – to the Highlands.'

'Certainly, my dear – whatever ye please,' said Miss Jean, though not without a catching of her breath; for who would look after the work, with herself so much out of the use of it, and the season still so *throng*?

'Not to leave you – with so much in hand – why should I?' said Kirsteen, 'it's not as if it was for anybody but me? But so soon as can be: just the time to go and to come back.'

'Oh, my dear young lady – whenever ye please, and for as long as ye please: but ye will come back?'

Kirsteen smiled again faintly: 'Oh, yes, I will come back – there will be nothing more, no fighting nor battles – nothing to stop me – and nobody – to wait for me' – she added, 'as I would have been content to wait – I was very content – just to think he was coming – some time. But that's over – just an old story. It is time to shut up the house and go to our beds.'

'Oh, my darlin' bairn! Dinna shut it all up like that. Tell me about it – or if you will not tell me, oh, dear Miss Kirsteen, let the tears flow!'

'My eyes are dry and so is my throat, Miss Jean, I cannot speak – I cannot cry – I'm not one for telling – Good night – I will just go away to my bed.'

She lighted her candle which threw a strange new light upon her colourless face, and the rings of hair upon her milk-white forehead out of which nothing could take the colour. Kirsteen's face even now had not the meekness and patience of a saint, but her hair was like an aureole round her wan countenance. She was going out of the room without any more, when she suddenly bethought herself, and coming back went up to Miss Jean, and kissed her – a very unusual ceremony between these two shy Scotswomen. The old lady coloured to the edge of her grey hair with pleasure and surprise. 'Oh, Miss Kirsteen,' she said—

'You are very kind – you are just a mother. You are like my Marg'ret,' Kirsteen said. That name brought a rush of tears to her eyes for the first time. Marg'ret alone in all the world would know – Marg'ret would not need to be told. If she could lay her head on Marg'ret's shoulder then her heart might break in peace. She had to bind it up now with bands of iron – for there was nobody in the world save him, and her, and Marg'ret that knew—

The workroom continued very *throng* for ten days or so longer, and during this time Kirsteen worked like two women. She had never been so inventive, so full of new combinations. With her white face, and without a smile, she stood over Lady Chatty, that grand lay-figure and advertising medium for the mantua-maker, and made her glorious with beautiful garments – beautiful according to the fashion of the time and all that Kirsteen knew: for no genius (in dress) can overstep these limits. Lady Chatty, full of affection and kindness, soon discovered the something which was wrong. She put her hands on either side of Kirsteen's face, and compelled her friend to look at her. 'What ails you, Kirsteen? Oh, what ails you?' 'Nothing,' Kirsteen said. 'Oh, don't tell me it is nothing. You look as if you had died and it was the ghost of Kirsteen that was here.' Kirsteen smiled upon the beautiful face looking so anxiously into hers, and said, 'Maybe that is just true,' but would say no more. And the business in the workroom was done with a sort of passion by everybody there. They had heard that as soon as the press was over Miss Kirsteen was going away. They did not exchange any exhortations, but by one consent they addressed themselves to their work with an unspoken thought that the sooner they were done the sooner she would be released. It was partly that the sight of her became intolerable to these emotional spectators, who had each a private vision of her own of the tragedy. Had Kirsteen wept and raved and got over it, they would have wept with her and consoled her – but the anguish which did not weep, which said nothing – was more than they could bear. They were all silent round the long table, bending over their work, working, as someone of them said, 'as if it were a large mourning order and all for

sum'un of one's own'. And the season was just at its end –
Kirsteen held her place till the last great ball was over, and
then she went away.

No difficulty now about paying for the coach or procuring her seat. She was no longer afraid of any danger on
the road, or of the world unknown. The whirl of progress
through the great country, through the towns and villages,
across the long level plains of England, no longer filled her
with that vague mystery and ecstasy of being which
belonged to her first journey. The movement it was true
gave a certain solace to her pain. The complete silence in
which no one could ask her a question, fenced off as that
was by the surrounding of incessant sound, the tramp of
the horses, the jar of the wheels, the murmurs of the voices,
was a relief to her from the daily intercourse of ordinary
life. After she got to Glasgow she had to think over her
further route. She had no desire to reveal herself, to let
anyone know she had come. Her mission was almost a
secret one; to make it known would have gone against all
the sanctities of memory; therefore, Kirsteen would not
even give herself the pleasure of seeing Marg'ret, of sending
for her at some wayside corner, or in some village as she
had once thought of doing. She drove from Glasgow in
post-chaises where it was possible, in country gigs or carts,
where no better could be had, avoiding all the places where
she might be recognized. She embarked in a smack upon
the Clyde and sat forlorn upon the deck watching the hills
and islands drifting by, as if they were part of a much prolonged and almost endless dream. It was July, the brightest
month of the year, and the weather was one blaze of brightness as if to mock Kirsteen whose heart was sick of the
sunshine. There was nothing but sunshine everywhere, over
the hills, bringing out the glistening of a hundred burns
over their slopes, and making the lochs and the great river
into shimmering paths of gold. It made her heart sick to see
it all so bright, and him lying far away, with that handkerchief to his lips.

And at last Kirsteen came in the gloaming, at the softened
hour, the hour most full of love and longing to his mother's
gate.

CHAPTER XXXIII

'Kirsteen!'

It was Agnes Drummond who made this astonished outcry coming into the old-fashioned drawing-room, where she had been told there was one who wanted a word with her. 'Just say there is one that would fain speak a word,' had been Kirsteen's announcement of herself. Agnes was about Kirsteen's age, but she had never left the shelter of her home, nor ever thought for herself or taken any step in life alone – and she was in reality ten years younger than the matured and serious young woman who was her contemporary. She was tall and slim, a willowy girl gliding into the dim room in her deep mourning, like a shadow. Kirsteen was also in black, but without any of those insignia of crape which mark the legitimate mourner. She was standing in front of one of the dim windows, deep set in the thick wall, with small panes and heavy woodwork, intercepting as much light as possible. Agnes recognized Kirsteen rather from something characteristic in her figure and movement than by her face.

'It is just me,' Kirsteen said, with a quick drawing of her breath.

'Have ye come home?' Then Agnes paused, and with something of the importance of a person to whom a great and mournful distinction has come, added, 'Ye know what great trouble we are in?'

'It is for that that I came here!'

'You are very kind!' said Agnes with some surprise, and then she added, 'We knew that – ye were friends!'

'I am not come,' said Kirsteen, 'to talk – for that I cannot do – I have come to ask you, travelling night and day – come to ask you – for the handkerchief he had in his hand!'

A sob escaped her as she spoke, but her eyes were dry.

'The handkerchief! Oh, Kirsteen, what are ye asking? Anything else; my mother will not part with it while she lives, there is upon it,' the girl stopped, struggling with her tears, 'a stain – of his blood.'

For some minutes there was no sound in the dark room, but of Agnes's voice, weeping, and from Kirsteen now and then a sob which seemed to rend her breast.

'She must give it to me,' said Kirsteen at last, 'for it is mine. He took it out for my sake. Oh, a mother's dear, dear! she has had him all his days, his name and his memory's hers, and no one can take him from her. But that's all I have, for my life. And I will have it, for it is mine!'

'Kirsteen, you need not be violent nor speak like that, for how could my mother give it up – the last thing he ever touched, that he put to his lips? – like a kiss to us – her and me!'

'No,' said Kirsteen, 'for none of you; it was mine, his name is marked in the corner in my coarse red hair, that nobody ever thought anything of. He said it was like a thread of gold. He bade me to wait till he came back. Now he'll never come back – but I'll wait – till I go to him. Give me my handkerchief with his kiss upon it; there's nobody has a right to touch it – for it is mine!'

Agnes in her mild reasoning was no match for this fiery spirit. She could only cry helplessly standing like a ghost among the shadows, but the early moon came in at the window and shone full upon Kirsteen who was neither ghost nor shadow. The aspect of command that was in her daunted the other. 'I will go and ask my mother,' she said.

'Tell her,' said Kirsteen, 'that I have come straight from London travelling night and day. I have scarce tasted bite nor sup, nor slept in my bed since the news came. I knew it was him without any name, for I knew that was what he would do. She has many, many a thing to mind her of him, the house he was born in, and his picture and all, and his dear name. And I have nothing but that. And I will have it, for it belongs to me!'

'I will go and ask my mother,' Agnes said.

The moon shone in through the small window, throwing upon Kirsteen's figure the reflection of the solid wooden framework, so that she looked as if she were in a prison looking out upon the outside world through black iron bars. She stood quite still for some time with her white face turned to it looking through those bars to the light. And she never forgot that moment when she stood gazing up into the white orb in the clear summer sky which had looked down upon him lying silent upon the field. It seemed to Kirsteen in the fever of her weariness and exhaustion that she could see that scene, the awful silence, and the other dead lying about in dark muffled heaps, and the moon shining upon the handkerchief in his hands. There were faint sounds in the house of doors opening and shutting, and of voices. A sudden cry – which perhaps was from his mother. It would be natural that his mother should resist, that she should wish to keep it. But Kirsteen felt that nothing could stand against herself and her right.

In a few minutes Agnes came back, still crying. 'I am sorry,' she said, 'to keep you in this dark room, but I've told them to bring the candles!'

'The candles are not needed, there's nothing needed but one thing.'

'Oh, Kirsteen,' said Agnes, 'be content with something less than that! My mother says she cannot – oh, she cannot! give that up.'

'Did ye tell her it was mine, and I've come to get my own?'

'Oh, Kirsteen! her heart's broken!'

'And what is mine? She will get away to him. She will go where he is. But I'm young, and we are all dour livers, that will not die – I'll live – maybe a hundred years,' cried Kirsteen with a hard sob and a wave of her hand as if in demonstration of the hardness of her fate.

Here a maid entered the room bearing two lighted candles which shone upon a rosy tranquil face, the common unconcerned life coming in upon the exaltation of the other. She closed the other windows one by one as if that had been the only thing to do, but when she approached that at which Kirsteen stood with the bars of shadow upon her, drew back with a frightened look and went away.

This enforced pause made them both a little calmer. 'Ye will stay all night,' said Agnes, faltering, 'now that you are here. Take off your bonnet, Kirsteen. And ye must take something.'

'Do you think,' said Kirsteen, 'that I have come here to eat or to drink – or to bide? – oh, no, oh, no – but get me the thing I have come for and let me go.'

'How can I get it when my mother will not give it up?'

said Agnes overcome, falling into the natural refuge of
tears.

'Let me see her,' said Kirsteen.

'She has seen nobody, not even the minister. She will
scarcely look at the light. She cannot cry like me. She's just
like stone. He was her only son, and she just moans and
says she never believed the Almighty would deal with her
so.' Agnes with the impatience of a patient and gentler
nature of this intolerable grief was relieved to be able to
make her plaint. But it did not seem unnatural to Kirsteen
that the mother should be like stone.

'When she sees me,' she said, 'perhaps the tears will
come.'

'Oh, Kirsteen, but I dare not ask her.'

'I will not bid you ask her, I will just go ben.'

'Oh, Kirsteen!'

She knew the way well, across the outer room which
was not called a hall to the door on the other side within
which Mrs Drummond was sitting with her woe. There was
nothing but the moonlight in the hall making a broad strip
of whiteness as it came in unbroken by the open door. The
two black figures passed across it like shadows, the daughter of the house following, the stranger leading. Mrs Drummond sat by the side of the fire, which was a feeble
redness in the grate, unneeded, supposed to add a little
cheerfulness, but in its unnatural, untended smouldering
making things rather worse than better. Her white widow's
cap was the highest light in the room, which with its dark
wainscot and faint candles looked like a cave of gloom. The
windows were all closed and curtained shutting out the lingering light of day. A large Bible was open on the table,
and in Mrs Drummond's lap lay the knitting with which
her fingers were always occupied. But she was neither reading nor working; her white hair was scarcely distinguishable
under the whiteness of her cap. Her face rigid with sorrow
was grey in comparison. She sat without moving, like
marble. Calamity had made her severe and terrible, she who
had once been kind. She took no notice at first of the fact
that someone had come into the room, believing it to be
her gentle Agnes, who was nobody, the helpless hand-
maiden of this despair.

Kirsteen went round the table to the other side of the fire

and stood before his mother, saying nothing. Mrs Drummond raised her eyelids and perceived her with a faint cry. 'Who is this come to disturb me? I gave no leave to anybody to come, I can see nobody. Kirsteen Douglas, what are ye wanting here?'

Kirsteen put out her hands with a gesture of supplication. 'It is mine,' she said, 'it was for me. It is all I have to keep my heart. You are his mother. And I am nothing to him – but for that—'

'No, you were nothing to him,' said the mother looking at her fixedly.

'Except just this,' cried Kirsteen roused to the full assertion of her claim, 'that it was me he thought upon – yonder – that he had my handkerchief – and took it from his breast – and put it to his mouth.'

'Lassie,' said Mrs Drummond, 'how dare ye tell that like an idle tale and put it into common words? It's written here,' putting her hand on the Bible, 'so that I cannot see the word of God; and it's written here,' she added laying it on her breast, 'on the bosom that nursed him and the heart that's broken. What are you, a young thing, that will love again and mairry another man, and have bairns at your breast that are not his.' She broke off here, and said again after a moment abruptly, ' "He was the only son of his mother, and she was a widow" – but the Lord took no notice of him nor of me!'

Kirsteen sank down upon her knees before this tearless mourner. 'Will I tell ye what I am?' she said. 'I am young, and we're a long-lived race – I will maybe live to be a hundred. No bairn will ever be at my breast – no man will ever take my hand. He said to me, "Will ye wait till I come back?" And I said to him, "That I will," and he took the little napkin from the table that had R. D. on it for Robbie (but yet I thought on him all the time) in my red hair. My mother said her colour was best but he said it was like a thread of gold – and he touched my arm and made me look, and he put it to his mouth. And he said "Will ye wait?" And here we sit forlorn!' said Kirsteen, her voice breaking into a shrill and heart-piercing cry.

There was a long pause. And then the rigid woman in the chair rose up like a marble image, her white cap and pallid countenance awful in the dim room like the face and head coverings of one who had died. She took her keys from a pocket which hung by her side and went across the room to an old-fashioned cabinet, which lent a little glimmer of inlaid mother o' pearl and foreign woods to the dim glimmering wainscot. From this she took a box which she carried back with her to her seat, and unlocking it with a trembling hand, took from it again a little packet wrapped in a piece of faded silk. She held it for a moment as if she would have opened it, then suddenly thrust it into Kirsteen's hands. 'Take it,' she said, 'and not another word. But if ye're ever unfaithful to him send it back to me – or bury it in my grave if I'm not here.'

'In yours or in mine,' was all that Kirsteen could say. She put her lips trembling to the hand that had given this treasure: then being hastily dismissed by a gesture of that hand rose from her knees and went away. In a moment more she was outside in the mild delightful summer night, all made up of pleasures which knew no chill, no fading, no sorrow; the young moon softly shining as if for pure joy, the unseen burns softly tinkling, the graceful birch trees waving their feathery branches in the soft air. Such a night! a visionary daylight lingering in the west, against which rose the fantastic majestic outline of the hills – the glen penetrating far into the soft gloom towards the east, caught by a ray of moonlight here and there, the wind upon the face of the wayfarer like a caress – the air all full of love and longing and sweet dreams. Kirsteen passed through it holding her treasure against her breast, a kind of happiness possessing her, her bosom lightened for the moment by reason of the very climax of emotion through which she had passed, the exhaustion of sorrow which at times feels like ease to the worn-out soul. She had a long walk to the village where her post-chaise waited for her. The road came out upon the sides of the loch which shone like a sheet of burnished silver in the moonlight. As she approached the village one or two people met her and turned to look back at the unknown figure which it was evident did not 'belong'. There was a little commotion in the small village public-house where her carriage was waiting, the horses harnessed and the lamps lighted as she had ordered. A post-chaise with an unknown lady in it was a strange occurrence in such a place. The people at the little alehouse were very anxious

to see her veil lifted, to know if she would have anything.
Just outside the village was the road that led to Drumcarro.
Kirsteen did not even remark it as she drove past in the soft
darkness. There was no room in her mind for any thought
but one.

Posting all through the summer night which so soon
expanded into a glorious summer morning, revealing her to
herself as a veiled and pallid shadow fit rather for the darkness than the light, Kirsteen reached Glasgow in time to
take the coach again for London. Then followed two days
more of monotonous, continual motion, with villages and
fields whirling past in one long continuous line. She arrived
the second night dazed with fatigue and exhaustion in the
great gleaming city, throwing all its lights abroad to the
evening sky, which was now her only home. It had been but
a temporary dwelling-place before, to be replaced by a true
home, perhaps in her own Highlands, perhaps – what did
it matter? – in the incomprehensible Indian world, when he
came back. Now he would never come back: and Kirsteen
recognized that this was her established place, and that her
life had taken the form and colour which it must now bear
to the end. She had accepted it for his sake that she might
be faithful to him, and now it was to be for ever, with no
break or change. There had sometimes crossed her mind a
dread that he would not like it – that the mantua-maker in
Mayfair would wound the pride of all the proud Drum-
monds if not of himself. Now that fear was buried like the
rest. There was no one to object any more than to praise.
She was independent of all the world, and bound to that
work for ever.

It was not till Kirsteen had reached the house, which she
recognized as now her permanent resting-place, that she
undid out of its case the precious thing she had gone to
seek. She bought a little silver casket, a gem of workmanship and grace, though she knew nothing of this but only
that it seemed to suit the sacred deposit, and unfolded the
little 'napkin' to take from it once, like a sacrament, the
touch of his dying lips. There was the mark, with her thread
of gold shining undimmed, and there, touching the little
letters, the stain – and even the traces of his dead fingers
where he had grasped it. She folded it up again in his
mother's cover and put with it the little blue Testament

with the intertwined initials. The silver casket stood in Kirsteen's room during her whole life within reach of her hand. But I do not think she opened it often. Why should she? She could not see them more clearly than she did with the eyes of her mind had they been in her hands night and day. And she did not profane her sacred things by touch; they were there – that was enough.

And thus life was over for Kirsteen; and life began. No longer a preparatory chapter, a thing to be given up when the happy moment came – but the only life that was to be vouchsafed to her in this earth so full of the happy and of the unhappy. She was to be neither. The worst had happened to her that could happen. No postscriptal life or new love was possible to her. Her career was determined, with many objects and many affections, but of that first enchantment no more. She took up her work with fresh vigour, and immediately began to make many alterations in the house, and to change the workroom according to her own ideas and to reorganize everything. Miss Jean looked on well pleased. She was the nominal head, but Kirsteen was her head, her strength, and soul. She was as well satisfied with all the plannings and alterings as a mother is with things that please and occupy her child. 'It takes off her thoughts,' Miss Jean said. She herself was a happy woman. She was like the woman in Scripture whose reproach is taken away, and who becomes a joyful mother of children when all hope is over. She had no need to do anything but to be happy in her child.

CHAPTER XXXIV

Some time after this when everything connected with this incident was over, Kirsteen received one morning a visitor, very different from the usual frequenters of the house. The subsequent mails had brought no further details of Ronald's fate, at least to her. His mother had done everything of which a woman's magnanimity was capable in giving her that sacred relic; but to make further communication of the further news that came in fragments from one correspondent and another was not in either of their thoughts. Information was not what these women thought of. They had no habit of learning every detail as we have now. The event came like a bombshell upon them, shattering their hearts and hopes – and that was all, they looked for no more. It was accordingly with no expectations of any kind that Kirsteen received the visitor, who was Major Gordon, the young Waterloo man whom his mother had brought to honour the little gathering at Miss Jean's house. He had been in India since all the fighting had ceased in Europe, for his living and fortune depended upon active service, and India meant increased pay and increased opportunities under the liberal sway of the Company, without any derogation from the pretensions of the King's officers who thought more of themselves than the leaders of the Company's troops. Major Gordon was a brave officer, and had been in as much fighting as any man of his years could boast. But he was somewhat shy when he called on Kirsteen, and stood with his hat in his hand moving from one foot to another, as if he had not been a perfect master of his drill. He said that his mother had thought he had better call to see Miss Douglas after his return – that he had been so fortunate as to meet Colonel Douglas in India, who was hoping soon to have a furlough home – and that he hoped he saw Miss Douglas well, and Miss Brown too, who had always been so kind to his mother. Kirsteen in her black gown was a somewhat imposing figure, and the thought that this visitor had come straight from India took the colour, which had begun to come back, from her cheek. A black dress was not then, as in our days, the commonest of feminine garments – and his eyes seemed to take an expression of anxiety as they returned again and again to her, which Kirsteen did not understand. He told her that he had come home with his regiment sooner than he had expected, for that India was now the only place in which a soldier could push his fortune.

'Or lose his life,' she said.

'One may lose one's life anywhere – but to vegetate without the means of doing anything, without being able to take a step of any kind – to settle – to marry,' said the young soldier with a slight blush and laugh – 'to take a place of one's own.'

'Oh,' said Kirsteen, 'to live and do well will be enough to make your mother happy – and others that belong to you – if you think of them that have been left lying on many a field—'

'I acknowledge that,' he said – 'many and many a better man than I – but to die a soldier's death is always what one looks forward to – better than living an idle life and cumbering the ground.'

'You will not do that,' said Kirsteen with a smile. She might have been his mother's contemporary instead of his own – so far remote did she feel from all such agitation as was expressed in the young man's awkwardness and earnestness. It did not occur to Kirsteen as it might have done to an ordinary young woman of her age that these agitations could have any reference to herself. She smiled upon him as over a long blank of years – 'You are not one that will ever stay still long enough to cumber the ground.'

'Miss Douglas,' he said, 'I have seen several of your family – I feel a great interest. Will you forgive me if I take a liberty? You are in mourning?'

The light faded altogether out of Kirsteen's face. She made a little pause for a moment clasping her hands. 'Not for any of my family,' she said.

He begged her a thousand pardons, brightening up in a moment. She fell back into the pale shadows; he roused up to pleasant brightness of life. These two different moods do not understand each other. They are almost antagonistic without some special bond of sympathy. He went on after a moment,

'I saw much of your family – in Argyllshire – before I went to India. You will perhaps remember that Glendochart invited me for the shooting – which was very kind.'

Kirsteen's attention flagged. She assented merely with a bow.

'I have been three years in India,' said the young man. 'She was nearly seventeen when I saw her last.'

'Who was nearly seventeen?'

'Oh, Miss Douglas, forgive me! – your lovely little sister – a flower that seemed born to blush unseen.'

The light came back to Kirsteen's face. 'Jeanie!' she said with a little flush of pleasure, 'is she so bonny? I always thought she would be so – but it's long, long since I have seen her.'

'Bonny is not the word,' said the young soldier, 'though bonny is a very bonny word. She is – she is – I wish,' he cried, breaking off abruptly with a nervous laugh, 'that I could show you her picture – in my heart.'

'Is that so?' Kirsteen raised her head and looked at him with a searching glance from head to foot: the young man instinctively squared himself, drawing up his head as under inspection. 'Ye are well to look at, Major Gordon – but I cannot see into your heart.'

'No,' he said, 'and how can I tell you what I think of her? It's not her beauty – she's just as sweet as the flowers. I wish I had the tongue of Robbie Burns – or some of those new poets that would wile a bird from the trees –' and he began to murmur some words that were not so familiar to the ear as they have come to be since then.

> 'She shall be sportive as the fawn
> That wild with glee across the lawn
> Or up the mountain springs;
> And hers shall be the breathing balm,
> And hers the silence and the calm
> Of mute insensate things.

> 'The floating clouds their state shall lend
> To her; for her the willow bend.
> Nor shall she fail to see
> E'en in the motions of the storm
> Grace that shall mould the maiden's form
> By silent sympathy.

'The stars of midnight shall be dear
To her; and she shall lean her ear
In many a secret place
Where rivulets dance their wayward round,
And beauty born of murmuring sound
Shall pass into her face.'

The major paused a moment, and then he added, with a rising colour, another verse –

'Three years she grew in sun and shower,
Then Nature said, "A lovelier flower
On earth was never sown:
This child I to myself will take;
She shall be mine, and I will make
A lady of my own."'

Kirsteen, though she was in London where everything that is new should be best known, had little acquaintance with the new poets. She had heard part of the *Ancient Mariner*, which was to her like a great piece of music, thrilling her being, but imperfectly understood of her intelligence. She had heard much of Byron who was raved of by every apprentice, and whom consequently this high aristocrat in verse as in all other things, held in a certain scorn. She listened surprised to the lines which Gordon stammered forth somewhat shamefacedly, finding himself embarked in a kind of recitation which he had not intended.

'Who said it? – they are very bonny words. I am much beholden to him, whoever he is, for such a bonny picture of my little sister – if it is not yourself?'

'I,' cried the major. 'Oh, be not profane! It is one Words-worth that lives on the Borders – but she is like that.'

'I can well believe it,' said Kirsteen; 'nevertheless, if it was Jeanie he was meaning, though it may be all true, it did not need that to make a lady of my sister,' she said with an ineffable visionary pride.

The major did not argue, or make any stand for his part, though he had all the enthusiasm of an early member of the sect. He would have indeed sacrificed Wordsworth and all the poets without a thought at the shrine he was approaching. 'That is, alas! what daunts me,' he said. 'How am I, a poor man, to make your father hear me? He will want, and well I know how justly, what I have not to give.'

'I am no authority as to what my father will do, Major Gordon. You may have heard why I, a Douglas, and not the least proud of the family, am here.'

'But she adores you, Miss Kirsteen!'

'Does she that? My bonny Jeanie! And well I wot she is the dearest thing to me.' Kirsteen paused with a flood of pleasure and anguish inundating her heart. The visions of the past rose up before her. Ah, why had the image of the little sister come so persistently into all her dreams of a future that was never to be? Because, she said to herself, putting down that climbing sorrow, it was a life that was never to be – and Jeanie was the consolation that remained.

'Major Gordon,' she said, 'if it may so be that Jeanie's happiness is bound up in yours, all that I can do will be too little. But what is there that I can do? She is in the hands of her parents; and I that have broken my bonds, and am a rebel, having nothing to say.'

'It will not last like that between them and you.'

'It has lasted for six years. My father is a dour man and does not change. If Alexander were to come back, that is the next in the family to my father—'

'He is coming, he is coming – when men in India speak of two or three years they think it is nothing – but it's an eternity to me.'

'And sometimes it is an eternity,' Kirsteen said solemnly. She asked then suddenly without intending it, if he had ever been at Ahmednugger where the battle was.

'I was in the battle,' he said simply. 'I had my orders home, but I was there. It was a kind of chance, no one expected it.'

Major Gordon was much surprised when Miss Douglas, who was so reserved and dignified, caught him by the arm and made him sit down by her side. She was as white as the cambric kerchief on her neck. She said with a little moan, 'Oh, not a chance, not a chance, but God's grace, I must think that. And tell me all ye know. Oh, tell me all ye know!' He began to say (with astonishment, and so startled that it was difficult to put his recollections in order) that it had all been caused by a mistake, that no one knew how strong the native powers were, and that on the British side all might have been lost, but Kirsteen stopped him with an imperative movement of her hand. 'Begin,' she said, 'where it began, and tell me who was there and all. Oh, tell me everything – for I have heard nothing – except that so it was.' Her intent face, her trembling clasped hands, the tragic eagerness with which she sat herself down to listen, overwhelmed the young soldier who knew nothing of her connection with that fatal field. With a rapid review and calculation he made out to himself that no Douglas had been there. It was then someone else in whom she was interested: he looked at her again and her black dress, her composed gravity as of one whose life was set apart, and an indefinable change that he had remarked without comprehending it, showed him, as by a sudden revelation, that whoever it was in whom Kirsteen was interested he was dead. But who was it? And how was he to give her dead hero the place her heart would crave for, if he did not know who that was?

He began, however, as best he could his story of the fight. As was made very apparent afterwards, Major Gordon had a soldier's skill in the arrangement of his tale. He made the listener see the movements of the troops, the gradually growing alarm, the scouts coming in with news, the officers, anxious and harassed, gathering to their rapid council, the bold advice that was first received with a sort of horror then adopted. 'We should all have been cut to pieces but for that – not one would have escaped to tell the tale; but he did not live to get the benefit himself, poor fellow. His name was Drummond, a Peninsula man who had seen a great deal of fighting. He and I were old friends. We had gone through many a hot moment together. His plan was adopted after a great deal of discussion. And by the blessing of God it saved many a man's life – but not his own!'

He gave a start as he looked up at her, for Kirsteen's countenance was transfigured. Her paleness glowed as if with a light behind, though there was not a particle of colour in her face. He had found the way to her heart without knowing, without meaning it, his testimony all the more prized and valuable for that. He went on with details which I cannot repeat, setting all the field before her. And then with his voice trembling he told her the end. How he had seen his friend fall, and then the little story of the handkerchief. 'None of us knew what it meant,' he said, 'for Drummond never was one to talk much of himself, but we were all sure there was some story. He lay there on the field with that white thing on his lips. It was hard – to take it out of his hand.'

The major's voice was a little strained. A man cannot cry like a girl, but he had to stop and swallow something that was in his throat. Then to his great surprise Miss Douglas rose and without a word went out of the room. He asked himself in his astonishment had he been wrong after all? Had he been talking of someone for whom she did not care, leaving out the name she wanted to hear? He sat wondering, listening while her steps went upstairs to a room above. Then he heard her coming down again. She came back into the room with a silver box in her hand, and opening it without a word took out something wrapped in a piece of faded silk. The young soldier felt his heart in his throat, an intolerable overwhelming pang of sympathy taking all voice and utterance from him. He knew the little handkerchief which he had taken from Ronald's dead hand. She did not say a word, but looked at him with a faint mournful smile and that transfiguration on her face. Then putting back her treasure locked it away again in its shrine, and gave him her hand.

'Now,' she said after some time, speaking with difficulty, 'you know, and there will be no need of words between you and me. I will never forget what you have told me. It's been like a bit of God's word, all new. And ye will never doubt that if I can serve ye, it's in my heart to do – whatever a woman can do. Oh,' cried Kirsteen, 'take the blessing of God from a heartbroken woman and go away, Major Gordon! He was but Captain – never more, and he's lying yonder, and you standing here. Oh, go! and let me see ye no more.'

When the rapture of sorrow that was in her had softened again, Kirsteen sent many messages to the young officer by his mother; but she could not endure the sight of him at that time. Everything she could do – with Jeanie or anyone – but not to see him, not to see him, he who had come home living and loving and promoted and with everything that had not come to the other. She could not bear that.

CHAPTER XXXV

During the six years which had passed since she left Drumcarro, Kirsteen had heard but little of the home which she
had sacrificed perhaps too passionately, too hastily.
Marg'ret's letters indeed were very regular, if few and
scanty in detail, but these were conditions natural to the
time, and Kirsteen had never expected more. 'Your mother
is just in her ordinary.' This seemed satisfaction enough to
a mind unaccustomed to correspondence, brought up in
the philosophy of long silences, of little intercourse, of
blank years which went over on all sides in an understood
routine, and in which the nearest relations when they met
each other, remarked upon the external 'ageing' of so many
additional years with a placid sense that it must be so. Mary
also, dutiful to all the necessities of the family, communicated periodically to Kirsteen the course of events in her
own particular family, as well as a more or less vague report
of the paternal house. She had by this time three little children in whom, naturally, all her chief interests centred.
Old Glendochart had become 'papa' to his wife, and was
reported as being very hale and hearty for his time of life,
and very much taken up with his young family. While 'my
mother is just in her ordinary', remained the habitual
report, differing only from Marg'ret's in the pronoun
employed. Now and then indeed Mary would open out into
an account of the company that had been at Glendochart
for the shooting, and there was one subject on which she
was even eloquent, and that was the beauty of Jeanie, the
younger sister in whom her family pride was gratified, as
well as perhaps the only bit of romantic and generous feeling which was in Lady Glendochart's well-regulated bosom.
'Our Jeanie!' From her babyhood the sisters had all been
proud of her. And Mary was pleased with the distinction
she herself had over Kirsteen in having a house to which
she could invite Jeanie, and where the praises of the young
beauty could delight her ears, ever reflecting back again, as
she felt, an honour upon herself. There was nobody far and

near who had not heard of Drumcarro's lovely daughter. She was the Lily of Loch Fyne. The visitors at the Castle took long rides all about Drumcarro, and the linn had been elevated into one of the sights of the district, all with a view of procuring a glimpse, if possible, of the beautiful Highland girl. And Lord John, Mary had reported, was particularly civil, and a very great admirer, words which were deeply underlined, and which filled Kirsteen with indignation. To think that after all the rebuffs she had herself given him he should endeavour to beguile the guileless Jeanie! Kirsteen had at once written a warning letter to Mary, informing her very decisively that Lord John was not a man to be allowed the enjoyment of Jeanie's company. 'For he can have no right meaning, and is only a useless idle person,' Kirsteen said. This had produced a warm reply from Mary under a frank received from the Duke, by means of the same Lord John.

'You are very ready with your letters, and a heavy postage to pay,' Mrs Campbell wrote, aggrieved, 'when you have really no news to give us. And as for the warning about Lord John, I hope me and Glendochart have sense enough to take care of Jeanie; and what can you, a mantuamaker in London, know about a young gentleman of such high family, the best of our name? I would advise you, my dear Kirsteen, not to encourage a spirit of envy. For if you never received such attention yourself it is partly the fault of Providence that gave you red hair and no beauty, and partly your own that cast away all the advantages of your family. But you cannot think that me and Glendochart are likely to go to you for counsel upon affairs of which you can have no experience.'

This letter did not please Kirsteen, as may well be supposed. We are all made up of great feelings and of petty ones, and are not always at our best. Kirsteen had a heart of the noblest constancy, and held the contents of her little silver casket above all that the world could give. But at more vulgar moments it sometimes gave her a sting to know that, notwithstanding all her passion of love and faithfulness, prosaic Mary, who had never known a throb of profound feeling in her life, would assume airs of superior importance, and pity the sister who had no man, and would be an old maid all her life. A woman may be capable of taking

her part in a tragedy such as Kirsteen's, yet resent the
comedy, generally more or less contemptuous, that winds
itself about an unmarried woman's life, and more at that
period than now. She was very angry at the neglect of her
warning, but this was only an incident and soon dropped
into oblivion.

One day, however, late in the year in which she had performed her rapid and melancholy journey, Kirsteen
received, by private hand, and in the shape of a small brown
paper parcel, concealing a letter in many wrappings, news
of a very distressing kind. It was supposed in those days of
dear postage to be illegal to send a letter by the private
hand, which most simple country people infinitely preferred as at once surer and cheaper than the post. This, as
Marg'ret informed her in the hurried scrawl enclosed, was
to be taken by a lad from the village who was going straight
to London, and had promised to deliver it at once. It was
to tell Kirsteen that her mother was very ill, so ill that
Marg'ret had given up all hope. 'I have never done so
before,' Marg'ret wrote, 'so you may trust me that this is
not a fright on my part. And she just yammers for Kirsteen
night and day – little, little has she ever said till now – she's
full of complaints, poor body, but yet she's more patient
than words can say. Ye must just come without a moment's
delay; and if he will not let you in, I will let you in, for
she shall not be crossed in her last wish by any man, if he
was three times her husband – so, my dear bairn, just come,
and let there be no delay.' Kirsteen obeyed this summons,
as she was commanded, at once. To go so soon again over
the same ground, and undertake once more such a weari-
some and protracted journey was very unusual, and was
thought something dreadful by all who heard of it. 'You
will feel as if you were always on the road,' Miss Jean said;
and she felt an inclination to blame her sister who thought
that the pleasure of her dying mistress was worth the great
disturbance of Kirsteen's life which must result. 'What
good will it do her, a dying woman? It will just disturb her
when her mind should be taken up with other things,' said
Miss Jean.

But it was perhaps natural that Kirsteen should not take
it in the same way. She set off that evening, by the night
coach, arriving in Glasgow on the morning of the second

day. But this time Kirsteen remembered her kindred, and finding with difficulty the new house of Dr Dewar, now a fine tall 'self-contained' house with a main door and a brass plate upon it, suddenly appeared at the breakfast table where Anne and her doctor presided over a party consisting of two tall children of nine and ten, and two more set up in high chairs to reach the board. Anne was so much absorbed in the feeding of those small creatures that she scarcely observed the stranger, whom Dr Dewar rose with an apology and a little embarrassment to meet, thinking her a patient improperly introduced into the domestic scene. An exclamation, 'It's your sister Kirsteen, Anne!' roused the absorbed mother, at that moment holding a spoonful of porridge to the mouth of one of the babies. Anne had developed much since her sister had seen her last. She had become stout, yet not unpleasantly so, but in a manner which suggested the motherly hen whose wings can extend over many chickens. She wore a cap with plaited lace borders tied under her chin, encircling a rosy face, which, though still young, was losing its higher aspect a little in the roundness of comfort and ease. Her soul was absorbed in the little ones, and in domestic cares. She thrust the spoon into the baby's mouth before she rose with a wondering cry of 'Kirsteen!' And all the children stared, knowing nothing of aunts, except some on the side of the doctor who were not of the same kind as the fashionably dressed London lady in her black fur-trimmed pelisse. Kirsteen was still in something of the solemnity of her first mourning. Her natural colour was subdued, she was slighter than ever she had been, graver, more pale. Her hair once so rebellious was smoothed away. She looked many years older, and very grave, serious and imposing. The two elder children looked at each other with mingled pride and alarm. This grand lady! The doctor was the only one who fully retained his wits. He put a chair to the table for the newcomer. 'You will have arrived this morning by the coach? And the first thing wanting will be a good cup of tea?'

'Yes, I will take the tea thankfully, for it is very cold, but what I have come for is Anne. There will be a post-chaise at the door in an hour.'

'Are you going to run away with my wife?' said the doctor with a smile.

'A post-chaise!' cried Anne in dismay.

'Anne! – my mother is dying.'

'God save us, Kirsteen!'

'I want you to come with me; take your warmest cloak; there will be no change of clothes necessary that I know of, for we will most likely be back tomorrow.'

'To go with ye?' faltered Anne – 'to – to Drumcarro, Kirsteen?' All the blood forsook her face.

'Where else? My mother is there, and she's dying, and crying for us.'

'Oh, I dare not – I dare not! Oh, I cannot go with ye, Kirsteen! You don't know, you've got great courage – but me I'm just a coward. Oh, I canna go.'

'My mother is dying,' said Kirsteen, 'and crying for you and me. Can we let her go down to her grave without a word? We've both left her in her life, and maybe we were to blame; but to leave her to die is more than I can do. Anne, you must come.'

Anne fell back in her chair, her rosy face the colour of ashes, her plump person limp with terror and dismay. 'Oh, I canna go. Oh, I canna leave the bairns! Oh, David!' She turned to him with a gasp, terrified by the blazing of Kirsteen's eyes.

'Well, my dear,' said the doctor, 'your sister's right, and ye ought to go. But when ye get there,' he added, turning to Kirsteen, 'have you any surety that they will let you in? To go all that way for nothing would be little good to your mother; and I will not have my wife insulted with a door steekit in her face – even if it is her father's door.'

'I have this surety,' said Kirsteen, feeling herself to tower over them though she was not very tall, 'that I will see my mother, whoever steeks the door in my face, nor think twice if it was the King himself.'

'The King's the first gentleman in the country,' said the doctor shrugging his shoulders, 'but your father?'

'He is just my father, Dr Dewar, and Anne's father, and we will say no more; the question is my mother, that never harmed living creature nor said an unkind word. How can ye stop to consider, Anne? Your mother! The more ye cherish your bairns the more ye should mind upon her.'

'I think, my dear,' said the doctor, 'that it's your duty to go. It might pave the way to a reconciliation,' he added, 'which would be good for us all and good for the bairns. I think you should go.'

'Oh, David!' was all that Anne said.

Kirsteen stood and looked upon them all with a flash of scorn. Was this the effect of marrying and being happy as people say? The little plump mother with her rosy face no longer capable of responding to any call outside of her own little circle of existence, the babies delving with their spoons into the porridge, covering their faces and pinafores, or holding up little gaping mouths to be fed. It had been a delightful picture which she had come in upon before at an earlier stage, when Anne had wept at her mother's name, and cried wistfully for a message from home, and longed to show her children. That had all been sweet – but now it was sweet no longer. The prosaic interior, the bondage of all these little necessities, the loosening of all other bonds of older date or wider reach, was this what happiness meant? Sometimes a sudden *aperçu* of this kind will flash through the mind of one for whom those ties are forbidden, and give a consolation, a compensation, to the fancy. But the thought only passed as swiftly as a breath through the mind of Kirsteen.

However when the post-chaise came to the door, Anne, who had been hurried into her black silk gown and cloak more by pressure of the doctor than by any will of her own, was ready to step into it with her sister. Kirsteen did not quite know how it was done. She would have retired from the conflict and left her sister with the children and their porridge, but Dr Dewar was of a different mind. He had never given up the hope of having it fully recognized that his wife was one of the old Douglases; and here there seemed to him an opportunity of bringing about that hope. He half led, half followed her, into her room, having himself summoned one of the maids to look after the children. 'Ye must just put the best face upon it, Anne; your sister is right. It would be unnatural, and a thing that would be generally blamed if you did not try to see your mother. And as for your father he won't bite you whatever he does.'

'Oh, David! he'll just say things that would make you tremble; he'll take me and put me to the door,' said Anne, crying with fright and reluctance.

'Nonsense, woman; and if he does you must just put up with it; you have a good home to come back to, and you will be none the worse, and ye'll have done your duty; but he'll maybe be much softened by the circumstances,' said the doctor, 'and there is no saying what might happen. It would have a very good effect if it were known you had gone to Drumcarro, and think what a fine thing it would be for the bairns. Take your warmest cloak as your sister said, and my plaid to put over your knees. It will be a very cold journey.'

'Oh,' cried Anne, 'I will just be perished, I know. And very likely turned to the door in the cold, and never see my mother at all.'

'Well, ye must just try,' said Dr Dewar, bringing her out of her room triumphantly, and fully equipped. Anne cried for an hour, sobbing by Kirsteen's side over her deserted children and home, and with a certainty that everything would go wrong while she was away. 'David will get no right dinners, and the two eldest will be late for the school in the morning, and the little bairns neglected all the day. There's no confidence to be put in servants when the mistress is not there. And most likely I will never get a glimpse of my mother, and my father will put me to the door.'

'Oh, Anne, is that all you think of her that never was hard upon any of us – that always was kind – and suffering so long, weary in body and in soul?'

'You need not instruct me about my mother, Kirsteen. I am the eldest, and I am a mother myself, and who should know if I don't?' said Anne roused at last. Kirsteen was glad to accept the position of inferiority thus allotted to her on all sides. She was neither mother nor wife, nor ever would be so. The others took a higher position than hers. She acquiesced without a word, with a faint smile, and was thankful to be allowed to sit silent listening to Anne's querulous murmurs, and still more thankful when in the unusual movement and silence Mrs Dewar dropped to sleep. The journey was doubly sad to her who had so lately travelled along the same road in the first force of her passionate misery. That seemed to be long, long ago; as if a dull subduing lifetime had passed between. The dreadful thing was to think of the long life to come, which might go on and on for so many years.

CHAPTER XXXVI

'What will ye do now?' said Anne.

Once more Kirsteen had left her carriage in the village where so short a time before she had paused on a different mission. Every detail of that journey had been brought back to her by this. The six months had softened a little the burning of that first bitter wound. The calm of acknowledged loss had settled down, deep and still upon her life – but all the breathless excitements of the previous quest, when she knew not whether the only satisfaction possible to her now might be given or not, and saw in anticipation the relic that was to make assurance sure, and felt in her breast the burning of the murderous steel – all these returned to her soul with double and almost intolerable force, as she retraced the same road. An ailing and feeble mother not seen for years – who would not hasten to her bedside, weep over her failing days, and grieve – but not with the grief that crushes the heart? That anguish is soft, even after a time sweet. It is the course of nature, as we say. The life from which ours came must fade before ours. The light of day is not obliterated by that natural fading. Kirsteen had set out at an hour's notice, and was prepared to risk any encounter, any hardness or even insult in order to answer her mother's call. She was not reluctant like Anne, nor did she grudge the trouble and pain. But as she returned in thought to her previous lonely flight into these glens the acuter pang swallowed up the lesser. She had not spoken to her sister for a long time. Her recollections grew more and more keen, as in another twilight, yet so different, she again approached the glimmering loch, the dimly visible hills. Anne's unsteady grasp upon her arm brought her to herself.

'What must we do? We must just leave the chaise here, it can go no further. To drive to the door would frighten them all, and perhaps betray us. It is not a very long walk.'

'Are ye going to walk? I am not a good walker, Kirsteen.

And in the dark by that wild road? I never could get so far
– Oh, I'm so used to town ways now – I couldn't take such
a long, dreadful walk.'

'Anne!'

'It would be far better to leave me here. You could send
for me if I was really wanted; I'm very tired already, and
not fit – oh, not fit for more. You're younger – and ye
always was so strong – not like me.'

'Would you like your bairns to leave ye to die alone –
for the sake of a two miles walk? Would ye like them to lie
down and sleep and rest, and you dying two miles away?'

'Oh, Kirsteen, you are very cruel to me! What can I do
for her?' cried Anne. 'She will have plenty without me.'

It was no time for controversy, and as Anne trembled
so that she could scarcely stand, Kirsteen had to consent to
take the post-chaise on as far as was practicable without
rousing the household at Drumcarro. For herself the chill
of the wintry night, the cold freshness in the air, the wild
sweep of sound all round her, in the swelling burn, and the
rustle of the naked trees and all those inarticulate murmurs
of silence which come down from the heights of unseen
hills, were salutary and sweet. When they paused at last
upon the lonely road and stepped out into the blackness of
the night with the lantern that was to guide them on their
further way, the descent into the indecipherable dark, with
all the roaring of wind and stream about them, had indeed
something in it that was appalling. Anne, not able even to
complain more, clung to Kirsteen's arm with a terrified
grasp and listened among all the other storms of sound to
the rolling of the wheels going back as if her last hope was
thus departing from her. She that ought to have been warm
and safe at home, putting the children to bed, sitting
between the bright fire and the pleasant lamp waiting for
David, to think that she should be here in a darkness that
might be felt, with the burn on one side rushing like some
wild beast in the dark, and the wind lashing the bare
branches on the other, and only Kirsteen, a woman like herself, to protect her! A weak woman with a strong husband
loses all faith in other women. How could Kirsteen protect
her? She shivered with cold and terror clinging to her sister's arm but without any faith in it, and thinking of
nothing but her own terrors and discomfort. Kirsteen on

her side felt the stimulus of the cold, the tumult of natural
sounds, the need of wary walking, and the responsibility of
the burden upon her arm as something that subdued and
softened the storm of recollections in her heart.

When they came suddenly upon the house of Drumcarro, almost unexpectedly, although the added roar of the
linn coming nearer made them aware that the house could
not be far off, Anne broke down altogether. The house was
faintly lighted, one or two windows upstairs giving out a
faint gleam through the darkness in honour of the
approaching event. The house door stood half open, the
shutters were not closed in the dining-room. That air of
domestic disarray, of the absorption of all thoughts in the
tragedy going on upstairs which is habitual to such
moments, had stolen into the house. The two wayfarers
standing outside, both of them trembling with the strangeness of it, and fear and emotion, could see someone sitting
by the fire in the dining-room, with a bowed head. They
grasped each other's hands when they saw it was their
father. He was sitting by the side of the fire, bending for-
wards, his profile brought out against the dark mantelpiece
by the ruddy glow. Even Kirsteen's stronger frame trembled
a little at sight of him, and Anne, no better than a helpless
lay figure, hung upon her sister's arm without power of
movement, stifling by force a terrified cry. It would not
have reached him in the tumult of natural noises outside,
but she became more frightened and helpless still when this
cry had burst from her lips. 'Oh! come away, come away, I
dare not face him,' she said in Kirsteen's ear. And Kirsteen
too was daunted. She abandoned the intention of entering
by the open door, which had been her first thought, and
softly took the path which led to Marg'ret's quarters
behind. Drumcarro heard the faint click of the latch as she
opened the gate. He rose up and listened while they shrank
into the shelter of the bushes. Then he came out of the
door, and stood there looking out into the darkness with a
faint candle showing his own lowering countenance to the
watchers outside, but to him nothing. 'I thought it might
be the doctor,' he said to himself, then went again to his
seat by the dull fire. Anne was no more than a bundle
upon Kirsteen's arm. She dragged her as softly as might be
to the lighted kitchen behind, and looking in at the un-

curtained window had the good fortune to catch Marg'ret's eye.

'Ye have brought her with ye,' said Marg'ret half reproachfully when Anne had been placed in a chair before the fire.

'She had the same right as I. We have both deserted the old house.'

'Oh, my bonny dear, but not the same. Kirsteen, my lamb – ye're all well, all well?'

Marg'ret searched with longing eyes the face that had so long been lost to her. Some things she knew, many she divined. She asked no question, but looked and saw, and sighed and shook her head. The face was not the girl's face she knew; but she was not aware that the change in it had come within the last six months, the setting of the mobile lines with a certain fixedness, the mysterious depths that had come into the laughing, flashing, soft, fierce eyes she knew, the eyes that were made of light. Behind the light there was now a deep sea, of which the meanings were hidden and manifold.

'There's no question of me,' said Kirsteen, meeting her look steadfastly, 'but of my mother—'

'She is just herself,' said Marg'ret, 'just herself, poor body. The end is coming fast, and she has little fear of it. Oh, I think very little fear; but taken up with small things as she always was.'

'I will just go up—'

'Will ye go up? – the laird is about the house: and I am feared he will make some stramash when he sees ye. If ye were to wait till he is in bed? She has not said a word about ye all day, but I've seen her as if she was listening. She'll maybe have had some inkling from the Lord that her bairn was coming. She's real peaceable and contented,' said Marg'ret, putting her apron to her eyes. 'The Almichty is just dealing with her like a petted bairn. She's no feared – her that aye thought the grasshopper a burden – I ken fine that she has been looking for ye the livelang day.'

'I will just go up,' said Kirsteen again.

'And what am I to do with her?'

'Marg'ret, it's Anne.'

'I ken weel who it is, Dr Dewar's wife; you might just have let her bide with her bairns. What am I to do with her? It's no her mother she's thinking o'. The laird will never thole her in the house. He'll just take her with his foot like a bundle of claes, which is what she is, and put her to the door.'

'You will take care of her, Marg'ret,' said Kirsteen. There was some justice in Marg'ret's description. Anne sat huddled up in a chair by the fire holding out her hands to it now and then, moaning a little. She had asked no question as they came in; perhaps she had heard the reply to Kirsteen's anxious inquiry. She was cold no doubt and miserable, and beyond all afraid. When there was any sound in the house she drew herself together with a shudder. 'You will just take care of her, Marg'ret; let her lie down upon your bed, and keep her warm, and when my father has gone to his bed—'

'You will not wait for that yoursel'?'

Kirsteen's answer was to walk away. She went through the passage with her heart beating, and mounted the dark stair; there were few lights about the house, a solitary miserable candle at the top of the stair waving about in the wind that blew in from the open door, and another placed on a small table near the head of Mrs Douglas's bed. The invalid herself was quite in the dark shade with a curtain between her and this light. The whiteness of her worn face on the pillow betrayed where she was, but little more. But by the bedside with the gleam of the candle upon her soft, beautiful hair, and her face, which Kirsteen thought was like the face of an angel, stood Jeanie, Jeanie woman-grown, the beauty that all her sisters had expected her to be, radiant in colour and expression. For the first moment the light that seemed to ray from Jeanie was the only thing that Kirsteen saw. It was what she had expected. It gave her almost a pang of sudden exquisite pleasure by her mother's deathbed.

'Did ye hear somebody, Jeanie, coming up the stair?'

'It will be Merran, mother, with the things for the night.'

'It canna be Merran: I know one foot from another though I'm a little dull, just a little dull in my hearing. Look out and see if your sister's come.'

'Do you mean Mary, mother?'

'No, I'm not meaning Mary. She's the one of all my bairns most like me, folk say – the same coloured hair – not like your red heads – and Alexander he was aye a brown-haired laddie. Eh, to think that I will never see one of them again! – and I'm just quite content, not frettin' at all. They'll be taken care of – they'll get wives of their own. When they get wives – or men either – there's but little room for their mother. But I'm not heeding – I'm just not heeding. I'm quite content. Look out, Jeanie, and see if that was your sister at the door.'

Jeanie turned to do her mother's bidding, and found herself almost face to face with a lady whom she thought at first she had never seen before. She gave a little cry of instinctive alarm.

'Is she there?' said the mother faintly from the bed. 'I knew she would be there. Come to the other side, Kirsteen, that I may get the light upon ye and see it's you. Ay, it's just you – my bonny woman! – but you've changed, you've changed.'

'No, mother – just the same Kirsteen.'

'In one way, I dinna doubt ye, my dear; but ye've come through trouble and sorrow. I'm thinking there was something I had to say, but it's clean gone away out of my mind.' She had put out her hand to Kirsteen, and was smiling faintly upon her from amidst the pillows. 'I knew ye were coming – I just heard the coach rattling all the day.'

'But, mother, tell me how you are? That's the most important thing – you're easy, at least in no pain?'

'Oh, I'm just very easy. I'm easy about everything. I'm no tormenting myself any more. I aye told ye I would never live to see my boys come back. Ye would not believe me, but ye see it's true. One thing's just a great blessing – I'll be away myself before the next laddie goes.'

'Oh, mother, never mind that; tell me about yourself.'

Mrs Douglas lay silent for a little while, and then she asked in her soft, small voice, no longer querulous, 'Kirsteen, have ye got a man?'

'No, mother.'

'It's maybe just as well – it's maybe better. You'll give an eye to the rest. Ye were always more like a mother than Mary. Give an eye to them. This puir lassie here; she'll be a wee forlorn when I'm away.'

'Oh, mother!' cried Jeanie, with an outburst of vehement tears.

'There's something I wanted to tell ye – but it's gone out of my mind. Eh, when I think how many of ye have lain at my breast, and only the two of ye here; but it's no maitter, it's no maitter. I've aye been a complaining creature. Fourteen bairns is a heavy handful, and three of them dead. My first little girlie of all I lost, and then one between you and Robbie, and then – all of you weel in health, and like to live, but just thae three. But that's plenty to keep a woman's heart. I have a notion I'll find them still little things when I win up yonder,' said the dying woman, with a flicker of her feeble hand towards the dim roof. A faint, ineffable smile was upon her face. 'She was Alison, after my mother,' she said.

The two daughters, one on each side of the bed, stood and watched while this little monologue went on, Jeanie shaken now and then by convulsive fits of weeping, Kirsteen too much absorbed in her mother for any other sensation.

'So ye have no man?' said Mrs Douglas again. 'It's maybe just as well; you will be a stand-by for them all, Kirsteen, my bonny woman. I'm thankful there's one that is not marriet. You will just tell them all when they come hame that I knew I would never see them more, but just wore away at the last very easy, very easy and content. I'm waik, but just bye ordinar' comfortable, awfu' light like, as if I could just mount up on angels' wings, ye mind, and flee—'

'It's wings like eagles, mother,' said Jeanie, anxious for accuracy.

'Well, well, there's little difference. Kirsteen, she's very young, younger than you were at her age. Ye'll aye give an eye to Jeanie. She may have need of it when her auld mother's away. I've not been much protection, ye'll think, but still it's a loss to a woman bairn. Jeanie's my youngest and Alison my firstborn, and yet Jeanie's a woman and Alison a little playing bairn at heaven's gate. Isna that strange?' A little sound of laughter came from the bed. Never was dying so easy, so pleasant and gentle. The sand was ebbing out a grain at a time. Suddenly she roused herself a little, and put out again her hand to Kirsteen. A little change came over her face. 'I hear your father's step coming up the stair. But ye'll no forsake me, Kirsteen – ye'll not go away?'

'Never while you want me, mother.'

'It will not be for long,' said the dying woman. Her gratitude was disturbed by a little alarm; she grasped Kirsteen
with her shadowy hand, and held her fast.

CHAPTER XXXVII

'Weel – how are ye now?' said Drumcarro, coming to his wife's bedside. His shaggy eyebrows were drawn together, so that his eyes gleamed small from among the manifold puckers round them. He was not altogether without feeling. He was sorry now that she was dying. He had never taken much notice of her constant illness before. His voice was still gruff and abrupt, and he had no kind things to say, but in his way he was a little affected by the fact that she was lying, this weak creature to whose presence and complaints he had been accustomed for so many years, on the brink of the grave.

'I'm just very comfortable. Never you mind me, Neil, my man. Just go to your bed, and if anything should happen Jeanie will give ye a cry. Your father was never a man that could do without his night's rest. And there's no need; I'm just as easy as I can be, and well taken care of.' Mrs Douglas was past the little wiles which women fall into when there is a domestic despot to deal with. She forgot that it was a sin against her husband that Kirsteen should be there. She turned her head from one side to the other with a smile. 'Real weel taken care of – between them,' she said.

Drumcarro lifted his head and gazed fiercely at the figure on the other side; the folds of his eyelids widened and opened up, a fierce glance of recognition shot out of them. 'How dared ye come here?' he said.

'To see my mother,' said Kirsteen.

'How dared ye come into my house?'

'I would have gone – to the gates of death when my mother wanted me. Let me be, as long as she wants me, father; she's so quiet and peaceable, you would not disturb her. Let her be.'

He looked at her again, with a threatening look, as if he might have seized her, but made no other movement. 'Ye've done less harm than you meant,' he said; 'ye've brought no canailye into my house; ye'll just pass and drop with no importance, and have no mention in the family. Be it so. It's

no worth my while to interfere; a lass here or a lass there
maitters nothing, so long as there's no canailye brought into
my house.'

'Neil,' said the mother from the bed, 'we must just pray
the Lord to bless them a' before we pairt. Fourteen of them
between you and me – I've just been naming them a' before
the Lord. Alison, she was the first; you were terrible disappointed thinking there might maybe be no more.' Mrs
Douglas once more laughed feebly at this mistake. 'And
then there was Alexander, and ye were a proud man. And
then Donald and William, and then Anne, my bonny Anne,
my first lass that lived—'

'Hold your peace, woman. Put out that name, damn her!
confound her. She's none o' mine.'

'And Neil that ye called Nigel, but I like it Neil best,' said
the low voice rippling on without interruption. 'And syne
Mary, and syne— But eh, it wearies me to name them a'.
Their Maker just knows them a' well, puir things, some in
heaven, and some in India – and some— Just say with me,
God bless them a', fourteen bonny bairns that are men and
women now – and some of them with bairns of their ain.
To think all these lads and lassies should come from me,
always a waik creature – and no a blemish among them all –
not a thrawn limb, or a twisted finger, straight and strong
and fair to see. Neil, my man, take my hand that's a poor
thin thing now, and say God bless them all!'

'What good will that do them? I'm for none of your
forms and ceremonies,' said Drumcarro, putting his hands
deep in his pockets, 'ye had better try and get some sleep.'

'I'll get plenty sleep by and by. Kirsteen, I would like to
turn upon my side, to see your father's face. Neil, ye've
been a good man to me.'

He started a little, evidently not expecting this praise.

'On the whole,' said the dying woman. 'I was a silly thing
when I was young, but the bairns were always a great
pleasure. But you're a dour man, Neil – ye canna forgive
nor forget. Kirsteen, that ye put your curse upon, she'll be
the stand-by for the whole house. Mind you what I say.
She'll have no man, and she'll be the stand-by—'

'No man will ever have her, ye mean. She'll just live and
die an auld maid,' said Drumcarro, with a hoarse laugh.

'She'll be the stand-by,' said Mrs Douglas. 'And maybe

my poor Anne—' She paid no attention to the interruption
he made. 'I would not wonder,' she said with a faint smile,
'if my poor Anne— Eh, I would like to see her little bairns,
Kirsteen. Why are they not here?'

'If one of the confounded set comes to my door—'

'Oh, father,' cried Kirsteen, 'hold your peace, and let
her be.'

'That minds me,' said the dying woman, 'give me your
hand, Neil – or rather take a hold of mine, for I'm very
waik – like the time we were marriet. Ay, that's the way.'
Though she was so weak her faint fingers closed over the
hard hand that unwillingly humoured her whim, and took
hers. 'Now,' she said, 'ye know it's the man that's the priest
and king in his own house. I'll just say the Amen. Neil,
God bless them a' every one, and all belonging to them, for
Jesus Christ's sake, Amen – Amen! that's for His Son's
sake, ye know, in whom He is ever well pleased. Amen!
And many thanks to ye, my man, for doing my last bidding.
The Lord bless them a', and all belonging to them, in
heaven and in earth, and the far places of the earth, for
Jesus Christ's sake. Amen!'

Drumcarro said no more, his rugged countenance low-
ered like a thunder cloud, yet there were workings in the
muscles of the weatherbeaten cheeks and throat half
covered with grizzled hair. He drew his hand out of hers,
and looked for a moment at the marks of the weak fingers
which had so closed upon it, leaving an impress which died
out as he gazed, like the fingers themselves disappearing
out of sight.

'Now we'll all go to our beds,' said the faint voice cheerfully. 'I'm real glad we've just had that moment: for the
man's the priest – the man's the priest. I just said Amen –
ye all heard me, just Amen. Neil, my man, go away to your
bed.'

He hesitated a moment, then turned away. 'Ye can give
me a cry if there's any change,' he said to Jeanie as he
passed; and then they could hear his heavy steps going
slowly along the passage, stopping for a moment to blow
out the flickering candle, and then the closing of his door.

'I'm going to my bed, too. I'm real happy and easy, and
just ready for a sleep; was it no a grand thing to get your
father in such a good key, and hear him bless them all?' said

the patient with a little proud flutter of joy, and then her eyes closed like the eyes of a child. Kirsteen sent her younger sister also to bed, and made what arrangements she could for the comfort and quiet of the dying woman. Many of the appliances of nursing did not exist in those days, but affection and good sense are perhaps after all the best appliances.

She sat down by the bedside, with a strange sensation as if she were in a dream. The peacefulness about her was wonderful, so different from anything she had expected. She had feared to find her mother as querulous and wailing as ever, and to have probably a struggle over her bed; possibly to be expelled from the house. Instead of this all was quiet; everything given over into her hands. She sat going over the wonderful things that had happened since she had left the place, her terror of the step she had felt herself bound to take, her trembling helplessness, the sustenance of her sweet and tender hope. And now that hope was gone for ever, and all dreams, and every inspiring expectation. Her life was blank, though so full – no hidden heart in it any longer. She would be the stand-by of her family. 'That I will!' Kirsteen said to herself; the same words she had said to him when he had whispered, 'Will ye wait?' She remembered this too with a forlorn sense of her own life as of a thing apart, which went on shaping itself different from all anticipations. She to be the stand-by of the family who had fled from it so helpless and unfriended! And she to have that dim blank before her, with no light ever to come out of it, whose heart had been fixed so early upon such a hope! Perhaps the second pledge might end too in unfulfilment like the first. At least she would have soothed the conclusion of her mother's fading life.

It was in the middle of the night that Anne was introduced to her mother's bedside. She had fallen asleep in Marg'ret's bed, and had not awakened for hours, sleeping the heavy sleep of fatigue and unaccustomed excessive emotion. To travel in a post-chaise all day, to take a terrible walk in the dark with the light of a lantern, she who was accustomed to Glasgow streets, to lie down to sleep fully dressed on a strange bed, she who was used to retire punctually to rest at ten o'clock, with the baby in its cradle beside her, and her husband to see that all was right! When

Anne woke and realized all the horrors of her position, come here to attend a deathbed (of which, as of other painful things, she had a great terror), and with the risk of being seen and seized by her father, perhaps exposed to personal violence, perhaps turned out into the dark night – and everything she was used to out of her reach – her sensations were almost those of despair. If it had not been for the superadded horrors of the dark road, she would have stolen out of the house, and escaped. But she dared not alone face the darkness and solitude, and the raging burn and roaring wind, which were like two wild beasts on either side of the way. She thought of David sleeping quietly at home, and all the children in their beds, with a wild pang of mingled longing and injury. They could sleep while she was surrounded by these terrors; and David had made her come in spite of herself, in spite of her certainty that it would kill her. She got up in the wildest feverish nervousness and misery, and looked at herself in Marg'ret's little looking-glass – a wild, pale, red-eyed, dishevelled creature, so entirely unlike Mrs Doctor Dewar. Oh, what should she do? The terrors of the cowardly and ignoble are perhaps more dreadful than anything that can be experienced by minds more highly endowed. No barrier of reason or possibility appeared to Anne to limit the horrors that might happen to her. She might be murdered there for anything she knew.

And it was with the greatest difficulty that she was got upstairs. She was afraid of everything, afraid of the creak of the stairs, of her father's door, lest it should open upon her suddenly, and of her mother's deathbed. Anne was terribly afraid of death – always with a personal terror lest she should see or hear something ghastly and dreadful. 'Oh, Kirsteen, it will just kill me,' she said. 'What will kill ye?' cried Kirsteen in indignation. 'It is just a sight for the angels.' But Anne was beyond the verge of such consolation. She dropped down a helpless heap of clothes and tears by her mother's bedside, scarcely venturing a glance at the blanched and shrunken white image that lay in her mother's bed. And by this time the dying woman had wandered beyond the consciousness of what was about her. She smiled and opened her eyes for a moment when she was appealed to, but what she said had no connection with the circumstances about her. 'Mother, it is Anne – Mother, Anne's here, Anne's come to see ye – Mother, have ye not a word for Anne?' 'Anne, is that her name? No, my bonny dear, but Alison after my mother. She's the biggest of the three, and look at her gold hair like Jeanie's.' The white face was illuminated with the most beautiful smile – the half-opened eyes had a dazzled look of happiness. She opened them faintly with the one recognition that remained in them. 'Eh, Kirsteen, but it's bonny, bonny!' 'Mother,' cried Kirsteen, with her arm under the pillow gently moving and changing the position of the sufferer, as she turned from one side to another. 'Mother! one word for poor Anne!' Her mother only turned once more those dazzled faint eyes with the last spark of mortal consciousness in them to Kirsteen and smiled. She had gone out into the green pastures and by the quiet waters, and recognized earthly calls no more.

'Oh, Kirsteen, never mind, oh, never mind. Now that I've seen her I'll just creep away.'

'Come here,' said Kirsteen, full of pity, 'and ye can give her a kiss before ye go.'

Anne dragged herself up, trembling and tottering. She would rather have dared the dark road than touch that white face. But what her sister ordained she had to do. She bent over the bedside with terror to give the required kiss.

Something had roused Drumcarro at that moment from his disturbed slumbers. He had thrown himself on his bed half dressed, being after all human and not without some feeling in respect to the poor companion of so many long years. Perhaps he had heard something of the progress of Anne and her supporters up the stairs. He came out now with a swing of his door, pushing open that of the sick room. The first thing he saw was the distracted face of Anne put forward reluctantly towards her mother, against the dark moreen curtains of the bed. She saw him at the same moment, and with the shriek of a wild creature at the touch of the slayer sank out of sight, prone upon the floor, keeping a despairing hold upon the folds of Kirsteen's dress. Scorn of the coward no doubt was in Drumcarro's mind as well as rage at the intruder. He made a stride across the room, and caught her by the shoulder forcing her to her feet. The unusual sounds roused the dying mother. She struggled up, looking wildly round. 'What was that, what was that? Oh, dinna make a noise, bairns, and anger your father.' Then her dim faculties returned to their previous impression. 'Neil, Neil – you're the priest – Say it once more – The Lord bless them a' and all belonging to them, for Jesus Christ's sake, Amen – for ever and ever, Amen!'

She put her wasted hands upon her breast and fell back on her pillows. The end had come – and everything had now to give way to the presence of death. Drumcarro thrust his trembling daughter violently from him with a muttered oath, and all except Anne gathered round the bed. The solitary candle flickered with a faint light upon the group, Kirsteen on one side with her arm under the pillow to ease the faint movements of the dying, the father's dark and weatherbeaten countenance lowering over the bed, Marg'ret behind, and Jeanie more like an angel than ever in her white nightdress, startled by the sensation that had gone through the house, appearing in the doorway. A last gleam of light in the mother's fading eyes rested upon this white angelic figure. No doubt the departing soul took it for the guide that was to lead her to the skies.

Mr Douglas put his hand, not without reverence, over the closing eyes. He took out his watch to note the time. To kiss the dead face, or make any demonstration of love or sorrow would have been impossible, and a contradiction of all his habits and tenets; but the man was subdued, and there was something in this presence which obliterated for the moment all violent impulses. He said aloud but softly, 'Twenty minutes past three in the morning,' and closing his big watch with a sharp sound which jarred upon the silence turned away. He even laid his hand almost tenderly for an instant upon the golden head of Jeanie as he passed her, and closed his own door with little noise. It was his only tribute to the dead, and yet it was a real tribute. No harsh sound nor violence could intrude there. Perhaps he was ashamed to have startled her, and thankful even in his arbitrary soul that she had not known what it was.

Some moments of absolute silence passed during which Anne did not know what to do. She had time to steal away, but was afraid to do so – not sure that her father might not be lurking, lying in wait for her outside of the door. The grip of his fingers on her shoulder seemed still to burn her, and yet she had not received any harm. And this was not all – for awe and superstitious fear and some natural feeling also kept her still. She might see some white image of her mother, more terrible still than the wrath of the other parent, if she ventured out of the shelter of human society even in the death chamber. Tears were hot behind her eyes, waiting to burst. She did not dare to approach, to look again at the face out of which life had just departed. The only movement of which she was capable was to put forth a hand to grasp Kirsteen's dress, as at last, after that moment of silence and homage to the departed life, the watchers began to move again.

How soon that had to be! A few inevitable tears, a sense of utter quiet and relief after the struggle, instinctive little cares which Marg'ret could not postpone, to close the eyes, to straighten the dead arms, to smooth the sheets in the decorum of death. Marg'ret's eyes were full of tears, but she knew well all that had to be done. 'You must go and lie down, my dear, and leave the rest to me,' she whispered. 'All's done that you can do.' And it was only then that Anne recurred to their minds, an anxiety the more, and that Kirsteen felt as she moved her sister's hold upon her dress.

Four o'clock in the morning, the darkest moment of the winter night! The little troubled feminine party withdrew to the warm kitchen, the only place in the house where there was warmth and light, to consult what they should do. It had been Kirsteen's intention to leave her father's house at once as she had come, her duty being over. But Jeanie's anxious entreaty bursting forth among the tears in which her simple sorrow found relief, and a sense of the charge she had seemed to take from her mother's hand like some office and trust conferred, changed the mood of Kirsteen. Her father had endured her presence, her young sister needed her; Anne was her chief hindrance in these circumstances. But even for Anne the bitterness of death was past. It was all over, and she had sustained little harm; all that anyone could ask of her now was to get away as quietly as possible; the worst was over; Anne was capable of enjoying the cup of tea which Marg'ret made haste to prepare. She even was persuaded to 'try an egg' with it, as she had 'a journey before her'. It is true that for a moment she was thrown into fresh despair by the suggestion that Kirsteen was not to accompany her home.

'Oh, what will I do?' cried Anne, 'walk that awful way in the dark, and take up the chaise at the end, and all alone, with nobody with me? Oh, Kirsteen, if I had known, you would never have got me to leave my family, me that never goes a step without my man!'

'It's a great pity,' said Marg'ret, 'that you put Mrs Doctor Dewar to all that trouble, Kirsteen.'

'And so it is,' said Anne. 'I told her so; I said I was not fit for it, to be trailed away to the Highlands at a moment's notice. And my poor mother that was too far gone to mind, or to ask about my family. And what good could I do? But you might as well speak to the rocks as to Kirsteen when she has taken a thing into her head. And now what is to become of me?'

CHAPTER XXXVIII

The question how to dispose of Anne was finally settled by the evident necessity of sending Duncan, the man from the farm, into the town for various necessary things, and to call at the merchant's and other indispensable errands. Marg'ret decided that he should take the cart, and convey Mrs Doctor Dewar to the place where the post-chaise had been left, an arrangement to which Anne did not object, for Anne was one of the women who have not much confidence in other women, and she was very willing to exchange Kirsteen's protection and care for that of a man, even though he was only Duncan. She made her preparations for departure more cheerfully than could have been supposed, and even set out in the dark with Kirsteen and the lantern to walk a part of the way so that the sound of the cart might not be heard by Drumcarro, with resignation. They were interrupted, however, as they stole out of the house, by a sudden rush upon them of Jeanie who had been sent back to bed, but lying weeping there had heard the little stir of the departure, carefully as they had subdued every sound. Jeanie thought it was Kirsteen who was abandoning her, and rose and rushed to the door still in her nightdress to implore her sister to stay. 'Oh! if ye will not stay, take me with you, oh, take me with you, Kirsteen!' she cried, flinging herself upon her sister's shoulder.

'Oh, Jeanie, whisht, whisht! you will make a noise and wake my father. I am not going away.'

'Oh, take me with you, Kirsteen!' cried the girl, too much excited to understand what was said. 'Oh! dinna leave me here.' She clung to Kirsteen's arm, embracing it in both her own. 'You would not leave me if you knew! Oh! you would take me with you if you knew. Kirsteen! Kirsteen!'

It was Anne who interfered with words of wisdom. 'Are you out of your senses, Jeanie?' she said. 'Take ye away from your home, and your father's house? Kirsteen may be foolish enough, but she is not so mad as that.'

'Oh! Kirsteen,' continued Jeanie imploring, putting her

wet cheek against her sister's, rubbing herself against her like a child, 'hear nobody but me! Bide with me, Kirsteen, or take me with you. I will just die – or worse – if I am left here.'

It was not until Marg'ret had come alarmed from her kitchen to bid them, 'Oh, whisht, bairns, or ye'll waken your father!' that Jeanie could be persuaded to silence, and to believe in her sister's promise to return. The sounds though so subdued still made a whispering through the hall, and an alarming movement that shook the house sounded overhead as if Drumcarro himself had been roused to see what was going on. This precipitated the departure of Anne, who, frightened as she was for the dark road and the chill of the morning, was still more alarmed at the idea of her father's appearance, and hastened out from the one danger to dare the other, almost with alertness pulling Kirsteen with her, with a clutch of her other arm. Anne's spirit was roused by the episode which had just passed. She was aware that she was not herself strong or able to move about unprotected, or take any separate step on her responsibility, but she had a great confidence in her own judgment respecting others. She almost forgot to think of the terrors of the dark in her desire to make Kirsteen see her duty in respect to Jeanie, and to set everything right. She panted a little as she spoke walking on in the darkness, with the lantern throwing a faint light upon the ground at her feet, but though it affected her breath, it did not affect her certainty of being able to give good advice.

'Kirsteen – ye will be very wrong – if ye yield to that bairn. She is little more – than a bairn. She is maybe nervish with a person dead in the house. You will say it is weak – but I'm nervish myself.

'Kirsteen!' Anne had made a longer pause to take breath – 'ye had aye a great confidence in yourself. But you see you make a mistake whiles. Like bringing me here. David – was just silly as well as you. He thought, if I came, it might mend – maitters – and be good for the bairns. But I – was right ye see. When a person's dying – they've no time to think – about other folk.'

'All that my mother thought was about other folk – if you call her children other folk.'

'Ay, in a kind of a general way. But she never said,

"Where's Anne? how many bairns has she? – and is the
doctor doing well?" – which is what I would have expected.
No that I did – expect it,' said Anne, panting. 'Oh, Kirsteen,
we'll be in – the burn – if ye do not take care! She never –
asked for me, at all,' Mrs Dewar continued; 'I might have
been safe – in my bed – at home. A long day in a post-chaise
– and now another long day – and I'll get back perished
with hunger and cold – and if I havena an illness, as
Marg'ret says – and just for nothing,' said Anne – 'nothing!
for all you said – David and you.'

Kirsteen said nothing in reply, but instinctively quickened her pace a little. She heard the rumble of the cart in
the darkness round a corner which was to deliver her from
Anne's wisdom and helplessness, the first of which was
worse than the last. And after a while the gleam of another
lantern, the horse's hoofs and jog of the cart guided them
to the spot where Duncan stood, his ruddy face grave with
sympathy. He made a little remark about the waeful occasion, and the need of supporting God's will, raising his
bonnet reverently; and then Mrs Dewar was helped into the
cart, and went rumbling away into the darkness, still
relieved for a time by the gleams growing fainter and fainter
thrown by Duncan's lantern from side to side.

The wind had fallen and the burn ran more softly, as
Kirsteen walked home. She was very tired, in that state of
exaltation which extreme exhaustion and sorrow sometimes
bring, as if lifted out of herself altogether into a clear, still
atmosphere of utter sadness, yet relief. The active suffering
was over, she was incapable of further pain, but unutterably
sad and sorrowful, hushed out of all complaining. The
darkness enveloped her and soothed her, hiding her from
all the world so that she could go on, weeping all to herself
with no one to ask why or how.

> True loves I may get many an ane,
> But minnie ne'er anither.

These words kept wandering through her mind involuntarily while the tears fell down, and her mouth quivered
with something like a smile. The futile contrast now; to her
who could have no true love but one, and no second
mother. She went on very softly in the dark, as in a dream,
feeling in her face the freshness of the mountain air and

the turn of the night towards morning – silently weeping
as she walked. The greater of her losses was altogether
secret, a thing to be known of none. Neither of her sorrows
was for the public eye. Her life, which was so far from this
and so different, awaited her with labours and cares
unknown to this solitude, and she had much to do with
which no loss or sorrow could interfere. She was to be the
stand-by of the family, she who had fled from it to find a
shelter among strangers. She must not even sit down to
weep for her mother. Only thus could she allow herself the
indulgence of tears. The darkness was sweet to her, wrap-
ping her round, keeping all her secrets. The heavens did not
open to show her any beatitude; the landscape which she
loved was all hidden away as if it did not exist. Nor were
there any ecstatic thoughts in her heart of reunion or
heavenly rapture. There was a long, long weary road
stretching before her, years that seemed endless going on
and on, through which she must walk, weeping only in the
dark, smiling and busy through the day. Kirsteen made up
her mind to all that was before her in that solitary walk,
going towards her desolate home. In a day or two she would
have left it, probably for ever, and gone back to a manifold
and many-coloured life. The stand-by of the family! She
had always intended this, and now there was consecration
on her head.

The lights in Drumcarro shone blurred through the dark,
a window here and there, with rays of reflection round it
hanging suspended in the night, no walls visible, a faint
illumination for the dead. Duncan's wife had come in to
help, and a silent, solemn bustle was going on, sad, yet not
without an enjoyment in it. Merran went and came up and
down stairs with an occasional sniff and sob, and the importance of a great event was in the hushed house. Save for a
birth or a marriage there had never been so much suppressed excitement in Drumcarro – even Marg'ret was
swept by it, and moved about, observing many punctilios,
with a tremor of emotion which was not altogether painful.
She had put the best sheets upon the bed, and covered the
looking-glass with white, and put away everything that
belonged to the usages of life. Kirsteen paused for a
moment to look at the white, serene face upon the pillow,
with all the white, cold surroundings of the death chamber

– and then went noiselessly into the room which had been
her own, where Jeanie lay fast asleep, exhausted with
sorrow and trouble, upon one of the beds. She undressed
for the first time since she had left London, and lay down
on the other. But she was too tired and overworn to sleep.
She lay with wide-open eyes in the dark, thinking over and
over all the circumstances through which she found herself
again an inmate of her father's house. It seemed an endless
time before the first greyness of dawn crept into the room,
carrying with it a whole world of the past, beginning, as it
seemed to Kirsteen, a new life of which she but dimly
realized the burdens and anxieties. There was her father to
think of, how he would receive her now that the protection
of her mother's dying presence was withdrawn. Whether
he would allow her to stay – and what she could answer to
Jeanie's cry of distress, 'Oh, take me with you!' Anne was
a fool and yet she had spoken wisely. The daughter who
had herself escaped from home was the last who could take
another away. Perhaps the bonds of nature seemed all the
stronger now to Kirsteen because she had herself broken
them, because even now she shuddered at the thought of
being again bound by them. Even when it is but an interval
of a few years which has made the change, a woman who
has gone out into the world and encountered life is slow to
believe that a girl's troubles can be so heavy as to warrant
such a step. They were in her own case she may allow – but
how to believe that there is anything in a father's power
tragic enough to make life unbearable for another, or how
in Jeanie's childlike existence such a necessity should arise,
made Kirsteen smile with half shame of herself who had set
the example, half amazement at her little sister's exaggerated
feelings. It could be nothing surely but fear of her father's
jibes and frowns. Neither of these things alarmed Kirsteen
now. And who could be harsh to Jeanie? – not even her
father, though she was but a girl.

While the elder sister thought thus, the younger stirred
a little and turned towards her. The daylight was still grey
but clear enough to make the sweet little countenance
visible. Jeanie's yellow hair was all decently smoothed away
under her nightcap according to the decorous fashion of
the time. And the little frilled cap surrounding her face
made her look something between an infant and a nun,

unspeakably childlike, innocent and pure to her sister's admiring eyes. But Jeanie's face grew agitated and unquiet as the faint light stole over it and the moment of waking approached. She put out her hands and seemed to clutch at something in the air – 'I will not go – I will not go – I will go with none but Kirsteen,' she cried in her sleep. Then, her voice growing thick and hurried, 'No – no – I'll not do it – I'll never go – no, no, no.' Jeanie struggled in her dream as if she were being dragged away struggling with something stronger than herself. Suddenly she woke, and sat up in her bed with a dazed look round her, and trouble in every line of her puckered eyelids. 'What is it, Jeanie?' She turned round and saw Kirsteen, with a sudden lightening of her countenance, as if the sun had risen. 'Oh, Kirsteen! if you're there! nobody will meddle with me if you're there!' 'What is it – what is it, Jeanie?' Jeanie looked round again as if still unassured. 'I was only dreaming,' she said.

And there was little time for further inquiries since Marg'ret just then came into the room. She was very tender to Jeanie but anxious to get her roused and dressed and sent downstairs, 'to give the laddies, poor things, their breakfast'. Marg'ret had restrained herself with a great effort that neither might be disturbed before the time after such a broken night. She herself had not been in bed at all, and felt it quite natural that it should be so, her fatigue going off with the coming of the morning, and a still excitement filling all her veins. The loss of the mistress was perhaps more to Marg'ret than to anyone in the house; but Kirsteen too was more to her than any other. She would have a long time to indulge her grief, but not long to hear the story and enter into all the feelings of her child. She had restrained with what was a true self-sacrifice her eagerness and loving curiosity. When she sat down now by Kirsteen's bedside it was with a sigh of satisfaction and relief. 'And now, my own bairn, the pride of my heart!' Marg'ret said.

The conversation lasted a long time. Their letters had been frequent for the habit of the time, once every quarter of a year at the least they had exchanged their good wishes and such information to each other about the other as could be conveyed by 'hand o' write'; but neither of them had any habit of letter writing, and there was much to be added, to fill in the framework of fact which Kirsteen had communicated from time to time. Everything indeed had to be told from the time of her arrival in London until the present moment. Marg'ret sat crying softly holding her hands, keeping up a low murmur of commentary. 'Eh, but I'm glad my sister Jean had it in her power.' 'Eh, but she's a fortunate woman to have ye!' 'Eh, if I had but been there!' she exclaimed at intervals, pride and satisfaction mingled with an envy of her sister which Marg'ret's better feeling could scarcely overcome. 'I am just an ill woman, full of envy and all uncharitableness. I would fain, fain have been the one. I would have held ye up in my arms, and let no harm come near ye! I couldna have seen your bonny fingers spoilt with sewing,' she cried with outbursts of tears. But when Kirsteen came to the story of the last year, Marg'ret listened upon her knees, her head bent down upon the hands which she held clasped in her own, a few sobs bursting from her breast, her lips pressed in a passion of sympathy which had no words upon Kirsteen's hands. The story was told very briefly in a few words. And then that chapter was closed, and no more was said.

'What is it that ails Jeanie?' asked Kirsteen, after she had come to the end of her tale, and Marg'ret had resumed her seat by the bed, 'tell me what has happened to her; there is something on her mind.'

'Hoots,' said Marg'ret, drying her eyes, 'there is little on it, but what is on most lassies' minds – most likely a braw marriage so far as I can see. There is a gentleman that is up in yon lodge on the hill above Glendyer. It's said to be for the fishing – but first it was said to be for the shooting – and my opinion is it's neither for the one nor the other but for our bit bonny Jeanie. It is just what I always said, even to the laird himself. She is the bonniest creature in all this country from Clyde to the sea.'

'But she would not start in her sleep like that, nor cry and pray to me to take her with me, if that was all. And who is the man?'

'Not like Glendochart, though he's a clever gentleman and a real good man to her that has the wit to guide him. A young lad, long and straight and with a bonny black e'e – and a clever tongue, but leein', for he says very ceevil things to me. He's ceevil to everyone about the place, and great friends with the laird – and I canna tell what ails her at him, if there's anything ails her at him. She was just real pleased to see him till twa-three weeks ago; and then she took an ill turn – but wherefore I canna say. Wha can say what whimsies come into a lassie's mind? – and I've been muckle taken up,' said Marg'ret. She paused a moment, and if she had been a Roman Catholic would have crossed herself; the impulse was the same, though nothing would have more horrified a Scotch Protestant than to be told so. She paused, and in a low voice said, 'Muckle taken up – with her that needs nae mortal's service mair—'

And there was silence between them for a moment, and thought, that travels so fast, stopped remorseful with a sense of compunction, feeling how recent was the event, and how swift was the current of life which had already begun to flow—

'You have not told me who he is?' said Kirsteen presently in a subdued tone.

'Well,' said Marg'ret rousing herself with a smile of pride and pleasure, 'his is a kind of what they ca' incognity at the Lodge; but I'm thinking, though I'm not quite sure, that it's just one of the Duke's sons.'

'One of the Duke's sons,' cried Kirsteen aghast.

'Well, my bonny dear! And wherefore no? – the Douglases are as good blood as any in Scotland, if it were the Queen herself—'

'Oh, Marg'ret,' cried Kirsteen, 'my poor little Jeanie! Do ye think she cares for this man?'

'I make nae doubt ye are used to grander persons than that; but it's no just ceevil to call the young lord "this man".'

'Ye don't understand – Oh! ye don't understand,' cried Kirsteen, wringing her hands. 'The blood of the Douglases may be a very fine thing, but it will not make her a match for the Duke's son – Marg'ret, you that have so much sense! And what does my father say?'

'I mind the time,' said Marg'ret, 'when ye wouldna have said I didna understand. Maybe my sister Jean – Oh, my bonny dear, forgive me, I'm just a jealous fool, and I didna mean it. But there's naething in it that's hard to understand; a bonny lad that's young, and ganging his ain gait – and he sees a bonny lass, that is just like a flower, the pride of the place. Is he to wait and reckon, will my father be pleased?

and will my leddy mother be pleased? Set them up! not to
be overproud of a Douglas in their house, and a beauty like
Jeanie. The pride used to be on our side once,' said
Marg'ret, tossing her head, 'if a' tales be true.'

'It must have been a long time ago,' said Kirsteen; 'and
my father, what does he say?'

'I never saw the laird so fatherlike – no since the day
when I put your brother Alexander into his arms, that's
now the Cornel and a great man among the blacks in India.
I mind the gleam in his face when he got his son, and
thought upon all the grand things that would come with the
lad bairn. Ye ken yoursel' he never heeded a lass he had.
But when he sees my lord coming like a little colley doggie
after our Jeanie, following her wherever she goes, there's
the same look upon his face. I was the first to tell him,' said
Marg'ret with pride, 'that it wasna just a bonny lass that
bairn would be, but a beauty to be kent about the world.
And now he sees it himsel'. What your father says? – He
just says naething for pleasure and pride.'

'Oh, Marg'ret – I fear, I fear, that this will be the worst
of all.'

'And what is there that's ill among ye, that ye speak of
the worst of a'? There's Mrs Doctor Dewar just a very comfortable like person, that's done weel enough for hersel'.
She's a poor creature with little heart, wrapt up in her
common man and her little vulgar bairns. But that is just a'
she would have been fit for whether or no. And there's
Leddy Glendochart that is a real credit to the family, and
has travelled, and can knap English with the best – far
better than you. And there's yourself, Kirsteen, that makes
all the grand London leddies stand about. And where is
the ill among ye, that our bonny little Jeanie should be the
worst of a'?'

Marg'ret raised her voice unconsciously as she gave forth
this flourish, with her head in the air and all her banners
waving. But the sound of her own utterance brought her
back with a shock to the reality of things. She gave a low
cry. 'Eh, to think I should forget myself and brag and boast
– with her, just an angel of God, lying ben the house.'

And once more Marg'ret paid a little hasty hot tribute
of tears to the presence, now so solemn, but which till now
had counted for so little amid the agitations of the family.

During those days of mourning at least the mistress could not be altogether forgotten.

Mary and her husband arrived from Glendochart in the afternoon of that day. She was very full of explanations as to how it was impossible to come sooner, and how the illness had gone on so long, she had no belief in its speedy ending. She went up dutifully to the death chamber, and shed a natural tear or two and came down again with her handkerchief to her eyes. 'I thought my mother would have seen us all out. I never mind of her anything but ill,' she remarked, her ideas still being Scottish though her voice since her visit to London had taken on what she considered an English accent. 'We had got to think, Glendochart and me, that she would go on as long as any of us. It was a great shock. If I had thought there was danger, I would have been here.'

Then there was a little natural family conversation and a few more natural tears. And Kirsteen gave her sister an account of the last hours which she had witnessed, which Mary listened to with due gravity and a little feeling, saying at intervals, 'My poor mother!' 'She had always a very feeling heart!' 'She was always so proud of her family!' as occasion required. 'And what did my father say when he saw you, Kirsteen? I did not think you would dare to come, but Glendochart thought ye would dare anything, and it appears he knew better than me.'

Kirsteen repressed the spark of resentment which this speech called forth. 'My father said little to me. He made no objection, but he was not kind to Anne.'

'To Anne!' Mary cried with horror, looking round lest anyone should hear.

'I brought her, that she might see her mother before she died. But I am not unwilling to allow,' said Kirsteen, 'that it was a mistake. My mother took no notice of her, and my father – I did it for the best, but she came against her will – and it was a mistake.'

'Little doubt of that,' said Mary; 'but I'm very glad ye see it, Kirsteen, for it's not often ye'll yield to say ye have made a mistake. And it will be a lesson to you another time.'

'Let us hope so,' said Kirsteen. 'There is one thing I would fain have ye do, and that will save me maybe from

making another. Mary, our little Jeanie is not happy, I
cannot tell why.'

'It would be very unnatural if she were happy, when her
mother died this morning.'

'It is not that. Grief is one thing and trouble is another.
She has something on her mind. Will ye take her back with
ye to Glendochart, and take care of her, when I go away?'

'Take her back? And who would be left with my father,
to keep him company? And the two callants, that have
nobody to look after them?'

'Marg'ret would look after them. And my father wants
no company. Jeanie will miss my mother more than any of
us.'

'You will not miss her,' said Mary; 'I well believe that.
But me that came to see her every six months.'

'Still that is different from Jeanie that has been always
here. The little thing will be very solitary. There may be
people about that are not company for the like of her. I
could not take her, it would not be allowed.'

'I hope, Kirsteen, you will put nothing like that into
Jeanie's head. You to take her! There are many things ye
must have forgotten to propose that.'

'I do not propose it. On the contrary, I ask you to take
her. I am not easy about her. I would not like to have her
left here.'

'Do you think because you could not put up with your
home that nobody can put up with it?' said Mary. 'Ye are
just far mistaken, Kirsteen. Jeanie is a contented creature,
of a quiet mind, and she'll do very well and keep very
happy doing her duty to her father. None of us want to be
hard upon you, but perhaps if my mother had not had all
the charge left upon her, poor body, she might have had a
longer and a more peaceful life; when the daughters of the
house just take their own way.'

'You did not stay long after me,' said Kirsteen, out of
patience.

'I was very different,' said Mary holding up her head. 'I
had my duty to my husband to think of; a married woman
cannot please herself. You it was just your own fancy, but
I had to think of Glendochart, for the Scripture says ye are
to leave your parents and your father's house.'

Kirsteen was silent and said no more.

CHAPTER XXXIX

The funeral, according to the dreary custom of the time, did not take place for nearly a week, and in the meantime there was a great subdued bustle in the house of mourning. It was rather the house of what they all called 'mournings', or *murninse*, in the plural, than of grief. The mistress lay still and white in her coffin, locked up and shut away, more drearily separated from all living thoughts and ways than had she been in the grave; but the black gowns and bonnets that were intended to 'show respect' to her were being manufactured everywhere, in almost every room but hers. Miss Macnab was throned in the parlour as at the time when she came to make the ball-dresses, and not less absorbed in the perfection of her art and the fit of every garment, while Kirsteen looked on with something of the suppressed amusement with which a great scholar contemplates the village pedagogue who taught him his first Latin, or an artist the house-painter who first showed him the uses of the brush. How far already had all their thoughts drifted from the dead mother who was the cause of this subdued commotion, and of so much more stir and life than for a long time had been in the house! But yet there were many things that were intimately connected with that poor lady. All her little secrets were disclosed. Mary began almost immediately to clear out the drawers and wardrobes in which her mother's old dresses and old stores of every kind had accumulated. She turned out the old pockets, of which Mrs Douglas had many, some made in silk to wear outside her gown, some of strong linen to wear below, and which were emptied out with all their countless stores, pathetically insignificant, not without many a critical remark. 'There was never anybody like my mother for rubbish in her pockets. It's just like a clatter of old iron to hear the keys jingling. And what did she ever do with keys? – with everything in Marg'ret's hand. I cannot tell what to do with these old gowns, unless we give them to the old bodies in the clachan, for they're past fashion and past wearing, and just rubbitch like all the rest.'

'Could you not let them be? Such as they are, they are part of my mother – at least to me,' said Kirsteen.

'Why would I let them be? Just to gather dust and cumber the earth, and fill presses that there may be need of for living folk. I am not a wasteful person, as maybe in London and among all your heaps of claes you may be tempted to be. They are little more than old rags, and what my mother could mean by keeping them I cannot divine, but still they might be of use to the old bodies in the clachan. Just bring them all down into the parlour in your arms, Merran, and I'll sort them there. And ye can clear out the big hanging press; it might be wanted for Miss Jeanie, or when I come over myself on a visit, for there's very little room for hanging up a good gown in this house.'

Kirsteen left her sister to this congenial occupation, feeling the sight of the old, well-remembered gowns, upon which she had hung in her childhood, a sight too pitiful to be endured. But Mary divided them into bundles, and tied them up in napkins, apportioning to the 'poor bodies' about, each her share. 'If they will not do for themselves, they'll make frocks out of them for their grandchildren,' Mary said. She was very thoughtful and considerate of the poor bodies; and she gave Jeanie many lectures upon her duties, now that she was the only one left at home. 'I hope you'll not allow yourself to be led away by anything Kirsteen can say to you. Of course we will be aye glad to see you at Glendochart, but in the meantime your duty is at home. What would my father do without a woman in the house? And what would come of the callants? It may be a little dull for you at first, but you must just never mind that. But don't let yourself be led away by Kirsteen, who is just wilfulness itself,' said Mary. Jeanie sat very still, and listened, looking wistfully at her mother's old gowns, but she had nothing to say in reply.

Miss Eelen came over to Drumcarro for the funeral, but not with the intention of following the mournful procession to the grave. This was a thing which was contrary to all Scotch customs – a thing unheard of. The men attired in their 'blacks', with deep white 'weepers' on their cuffs, and great hatbands with flowing ends of crape, formed a long line marching two and two, with pauses now and then to change the bearers along the mournful wintry road. The women sat within, keeping together in one room, and firing off little minute guns in the way of mournful remarks, as they sat solemnly doing nothing, not even looking out to see the object of this lugubrious ceremony carried away to her last rest. Miss Eelen bore the part of a kind of mistress of the ceremonies on this sad occasion. She sat in her weepers and her crape, which was not new like the others', but kept for such occasions, in the high chair which had been Mrs Douglas's, with a white handkerchief in her hand, and said at intervals, 'Poor Christina – she was a fine creature. Your mother, my dears, was a real, right-thinking woman. She was from the south, and ignorant of some of our ways, but her meaning was always good. She was very fond of her family, poor body. All those laddies – and not one of them to help to lay her head in the grave, except the two little ones, poor things.'

Kirsteen stood leaning against the window watching through the shutters the mournful black line as it moved away, while Jeanie at her feet, holding by her dress, followed vicariously through her sister's eyes the progress of the procession. They heard the tramp, recognizable among the others, of the bearers, as they straightened themselves under their burden, and then the sound of the slow, irregular march. 'Can ye see it, Kirsteen? Is it away? Is that it passing? Oh, my mother, my mother!' cried Jeanie. She held fast by Kirsteen's dress, as if there was strength and support in it; and Kirsteen stooped and raised her up when the sound of the measured tramp had died away. 'Now,' she said, 'all is gone – the very last. And the time is come when we must begin our common lives again.'

'She was indeed a fine creature,' said Miss Eelen with a little flourish of her handkerchief. 'I mind when she came first here, a delicate bit thing, that never looked as if she would live.'

'She was always delicate,' said Mary, taking up the response.

'And to think of all the bairns she had – a fine stirring family.'

'Fourteen of us,' said Mary.

'Eleven living, and all a credit – that is to say – but I name no names,' said Miss Eelen.

'It is perhaps better not,' said Mary.

Kirsteen whispered in her little sister's ear that she could bear this no longer, and taking Jeanie's hand rose to leave the room. She was stopped by Mary's reproving voice – 'Where are ye taking Jeanie, Kirsteen? Ye are not going out on the day of my mother's funeral?'

'At least leave the innocent bairn,' said Miss Eelen in a voice of solemn command. 'A day like this should be like a Lord's day in a house.'

'Or worse,' Mary added with tremendous seriousness – 'for the Sabbath comes once in a week, but your mother's funeral but once in a lifetime.'

The words came surging back into Kirsteen's mind again,

> True loves I may get many an ane
> But minnie ne'er anither.

Her heart felt as if it must burst, and yet it was something like a laugh that broke from her, as she was thus reproached for levity. 'I am not likely to forget that,' she said. Jeanie clung to her as she left the others to their Antiphone. The sound of the familiar linn seemed to have come back to dominate all sounds as before, when she stole out at the back of the house, Jeanie always following. It was a grey mild wintry day, a day such as is consolatory to the overwrought spirit. The two sisters seated themselves on the fallen trunk of a tree on the bank near the head of the linn. The softened rush of the water with no storm and but little wind in the air filled the atmosphere with a soothing hush of sound. Jeanie laid her head upon her sister's knee, hiding her face, and sobbing softly like a child in its mother's lap when the storm of woe is overpast. Kirsteen, who had no tears at her command save those that welled quietly into her eyes from time to time without observation, smoothed tenderly with one hand the girl's soft and beautiful hair.

'Just sob out all your heart,' she said, 'my little Jeanie – it will do you good.'

'Oh, Kirsteen, it is not all for her, but for me too that am so forlorn.'

'Jeanie, my dear, it's a hard thing to say, but soon ye will not be so forlorn. We will all go back to our common work, and your heart will maybe not be light again for many a long day; but the sun will begin to shine again.'

'Kirsteen,' said Jeanie raising her head, 'you are my sister next to me, and I am a woman grown. There is not such a long, long way between us; but you speak as if it was a hundred years.'

'It is more I think,' said Kirsteen; 'for you will have all that life can give, and I will have nothing, except maybe you, and being a stand-by for the family as my mother said.'

'Why should you not too have all that life can give?'

Kirsteen smiled and shook her head. 'It is too long a story; and I would rather speak about you, Jeanie. Tomorrow I am going away.'

Jeanie seized Kirsteen's hands and held them fast. 'I will be no trouble,' she said, 'I will do whatever you please, but take me with you, Kirsteen.'

'I cannot, Jeanie. It would be to steal you away; I dare not do it. If I have been right or wrong in what I did for myself I cannot always tell; but for you, I dare not take it upon me. You heard what Anne said – and it was true.'

'Kirsteen,' said Jeanie raising her face to her sister. 'I have more cause than you. Oh, listen to me, Kirsteen; would you like to see shame at Drumcarro? Would you like to see the name you all think so much of rolled in the dust? Oh, hear what I'm saying, Kirsteen! I have more cause than you.'

'Jeanie, my dear! my dear!'

'Kirsteen, there is one that is here, and they all think much of him, and he follows me wherever I go. Kirsteen, are ye listening?' The girl grasped her hands fiercely as if her own had been made of steel. 'Kirsteen! It's not to marry me he is seeking me. Do ye hear what I am saying? It is not – for anything that's good.'

And Jeanie who had been very pale, hid her face which was blazing with sudden red in Kirsteen's lap, and sobbed as if her heart would burst.

Kirsteen caught her in her arms, held her to her breast, murmured over her every tender word; but profoundly as Jeanie was in earnest, gave no faith to what she said. 'What has put that dreadful thought in your mind? Oh, my darling, if there was such a villain in the world it's not here he would dare to come – with everybody round you to defend you – to our father's house.'

'Who have I to defend me?' cried Jeanie raising her head. 'Jock is away and Jamie is so young; how should he understand? and my father that notices nothing, that thinks it will be a grand marriage and a credit to the family. Even Marg'ret!' – cried the girl with sudden exasperation, 'they will none of them understand!'

Kirsteen took her young sister's face between her hands – 'An ill man could have no power but what he got from you. Jeanie, Jeanie, has he got your heart?'

'Oh, how can you tell, you that have never been tried?' cried the girl drawing herself out of her sister's hold. Little Jeanie had her experience too. 'No, he has not got my heart; but he gives me no rest night nor day, he sends me letters – I might put them in the fire. But there's little to keep you living at Drumcarro – and I read them, I canna help it. And then he's waiting for me about the door whenever I stir. And his tongue would wile the bird off the tree. And he's not like the rough men you see, young Glenbowie or the like of that, he's a fine grand gentleman. And oh, Kirsteen, take me with you! take me away! For my father's one that will not understand, and Jamie is but a laddie, and even Marg'ret! – And how am I to fight and stand all alone by myself?'

The girl's eyes were full of tears and her face of trouble. She held fast by Kirsteen's hand as if by an anchor of salvation. 'He has not got my heart,' she said, 'but oh, I canna trust my head. He wiles me away. And there's nobody in the world, nobody else, that is heeding what becomes of me, or where I go, unless it's maybe you, Kirsteen. Oh, take me with you, Kirsteen! for I cannot trust myself and live here.'

'Jeanie, Jeanie, ye love this man.'

'No,' cried the girl rising to her feet. 'No! no! If it was my last word, No! but I'm lone, lone in the house, and nobody to speak a word, and him with his flattering tongue. And oh, Kirsteen, if you will do anything for Jeanie, take her away.'

'There is nothing I would not do for Jeanie,' said the elder sister, drawing her again to her arms. 'My dear, there was one I saw in London before I came away.'

'One you saw in London?'

'That had his heart set upon my little sister, one I could serve with my life.'

Jeanie's agitated face was again covered with a burning blush. She withdrew herself from Kirsteen's arm. 'How can I tell who ye might see in London? It's far, far from here.'

'And maybe you never thought upon him, though his heart is set on you.'

Jeanie turned from red to pale. She trembled, drawing herself from within her sister's arm. 'How can I tell who it is!' she said with an indignation which made her breathless, 'when you never tell me? And there has never been any person – oh, never any person!' Her eyes were unquiet, seeking Kirsteen's face, then withdrawn hurriedly not to meet her look; her hands were nervously clasping and unclasping in her lap. 'Men,' she cried, 'never care! I've read it in books and I know it's true. They look at you and they speak and speak, and follow you about, and when their time is come they go away, and you hear of them no more!'

'Where have you learned all this, my poor little Jeanie,' said Kirsteen tenderly, 'for ye seem to have knowledge of things that are beyond me?'

'We learn the things that come our way,' said the girl. Her lips quivered, she was too much agitated to keep still. 'Who would that be that you saw in London?' she asked with a forced, almost mocking smile.

'He has been in India since then, and wherever there was fighting. His name is Major Gordon.'

Kirsteen was conscious once more of the grudge in her heart at Gordon's life and promotion, and the title she had given him; but she had no time for thought. For Jeanie rose up from her side in a passion of mingled feeling, anger and indignation and wistfulness and pain.

'How dared he speak?' she cried. 'How dared he name my name? Him! that came when I was but a bairn, and then rode away!'

'Jeanie!'

'Oh! I thought you understood,' cried Jeanie in a kind of frenzy. 'I thought you would know, but you've aye had peace in your heart though ye think you're so wise. There has nobody ever come and gone and made ye feel ye were a fool and unwomanly, and all that Marg'ret says. You have never known what it was to have your heart burnt like hot irons on it, and to scorn yourself, and feel that ye were the poorest thing on earth! To let a man think that, and then to see him ride away!'

Scorching tears poured from Jeanie's eyes. Tears like a fiery torrent, very different from those which had been wept for her mother. She sat down again on the log but turned her back to Kirsteen, covering her face with her hands. 'It is just for that,' she said to herself, 'just for that that I'm tempted most – just for that!'

'I would have thought,' said Kirsteen, with intense and sorrowful indignation to think that where there was life and love there should be this perversity, 'I would have thought that a touch of true love in the heart would save ye for ever and ever from all temptations of the kind.'

'You would have thought!' cried Jeanie scornful in her passion, turning her soft angelic countenance, in which there were so many things unintelligible to her elder sister, all flushed and wild to Kirsteen. 'And me that thought you would understand!' she cried.

There was a pause, and Kirsteen's heart ached with feelings inexpressible. She had never been accused of not understanding before, and it is a reproach which is hard to bear. She sat silent, painfully wondering into what strange places these young feet had wandered where she could not follow. She had expressed the only conviction that was possible to her one-ideaed soul. The touch of true love had been to herself the one and only touch, never to be obliterated by baser contact. She sat gazing wistfully into the dim air, perplexed and troubled, her eyes filling with tears, her heart with heaviness. To be tempted was the one thing which in her austere and spotless womanhood, a widowed maiden, Kirsteen could not understand.

Jeanie had been sobbing passionately by her side for a minute or more, when suddenly she turned and flung herself again upon her sister, once more hiding her face in Kirsteen's lap. 'Oh!' she cried, 'take me with you, Kirsteen! Do you not see now that I cannot be left! You're holy like a saint, but me, I want more, I want something more. Is it not natural to be happy when you're young – to get what you like, and see what's bonny and bright, and get out into the world? I'm not one that can be patient and bide at home. Oh, Kirsteen! I cannot just sew my seam, and read my book like good girls. Even with my mother here – and now that she's gone – Kirsteen, Kirsteen! he will wile me away to my shame if you will not save me, you that are the only one.'

She said all this half intelligibly, clasping her arms round her sister, now raising her head with an imploring look, now burying it again on Kirsteen's shoulder or in her lap. Such an impassioned creature was unlike anything that Kirsteen had ever known before. She soothed her with soft words saying, 'My dear, my darlin', my bonny Jeanie!' the tears falling from her eyes as she caressed and stilled the excitement of the other. What could she do? How could she take her? How leave her? She who was herself on sufferance allowed to be here by reason of her mother's death, but bound to go away tomorrow, and with so little likelihood that anyone would pay attention to what she said. She dared not steal her little sister away. She dared scarcely plead for her, for more care, for closer guardianship! Alas, was this all that was to come of the post she had undertaken, she who was to be the stand-by of the family? She who from the beginning had thought of Jeanie as the one for whom everything was to be made bright?

CHAPTER XL

Kirsteen, up to this time, had kept as much as possible out
of her father's way, and he had taken no notice of her presence in the house. When she came within his range of
vision he turned his back upon her but said nothing. It
appeared to her now, however, that it was necessary to
change her procedure. If she were to do anything for Jeanie
she must take a more decided part. Accordingly, on the
evening of her mother's funeral, Kirsteen appeared at the
family table among the others. Her father perceived her as
he took his place, and gave her a somewhat fixed look from
under his eyebrows, along with a muttered exclamation;
but he said nothing, and suffered her presence without any
demonstration of displeasure. The evening was like and yet
unlike one of the former ceremonials of the house, on the
eve of the departure of sons. It was a celebration like that,
but the hero of the occasion was not there, and the party at
table after a week of composed quiet, subdued voices, and
melancholy subjects, showed a certain relief in the fact that
all was over, and nothing further required to show their
respect. The black ribbons in Miss Eelen's cap nodded as
she moved her head, and Mary was very careful of the crisp
new crape which ornamented her dress, while Mr Pyper,
the minister, would make an occasional remark in con-
formity with what were supposed to be the feelings of the
bereaved family. But these were almost the only signs of
mourning. Jeanie, after all the agitation of the morning, presented a changeful aspect, and her eyes were heavy and a little red with tears; and Jamie, the last of the boys, had an
open-eyed, wistful, almost startled look, feeling very solitary, poor boy, and wishing to be away like the rest. There
was no one who had felt the mother's death, or perhaps it
would be almost more just to say the presence of death in
the house, as this boy, more imaginative than the rest, to
whom the week's interval had been a terrible one. He was
pale under his freckles, with a dismal look in his wide eyes,
the impression of the funeral still too strong upon him for

any other feeling. But the others were relieved; it is impossible to use another word.

'The country will be very quiet this year with nobody at the Castle,' said Mary in subdued tones.

'It will make little difference to ainy of you,' replied Miss Eelen, her black bows nodding in her cap, 'for if there had been fifty balls, ye could not in decency have gone to ainy one o' them.'

'There are more folk in the country than us,' said Mary, with a little sharpness. 'But I hear Lady Chatty's far from happy, poor thing. For my part I never had any confidence in the man.'

'The man was well enough; there's nothing to be said against the man; they're just both spenders, and no siller to spend.'

'That is what I am saying,' said Mary. 'The Duke's daughter, and her beauty, and her fashion, and all that – and at the last to take up with a poor man.'

'What do you think, Drumcarro, of this Catholic Emancipation that is making such a noise?' said Glendochart, as the ladies continued to argue over the subject of Lady Chatty.

'I just think that we'll have all the wild Irish and the wild North on our hands before we know where we are – and Jesuits going to and fro over the face of the earth like Sawtan in the Scriptures – if the Government doesn't stand firm.'

'I cannot but think, however,' said Glendochart, 'that there's something to be said on the other side. A large number of our country folk just put out of the question altogether.'

'There's nothing to be said on the other side of the question,' cried Drumcarro, with his fierce look. 'Fellow subjects! just thae deevils of Irish and a whean idle Crofters that will neither fish the seas nor delve the land – and a horde of priests at the head of them. Them that think the Pope of Rome should have a hand in governing this country will get little backing from me.'

'I allow,' said Mr Pyper, 'that it's a difficult question with modern notions of toleration, and all that – but violent evils must have violent remedies – and when ye think, Glendochart, what this country has suffered from Papal rule—'

'I would just have no dealings with the pooers of darkness,' said Mr Douglas, bringing down his hand upon the table with a force which made everything tremble.

'Bless me,' cried Miss Eelen, 'what's wrong with ye, Drumcarro? Ye'll break all the glasses. Eh, but the pooers o' darkness are no so easy to make or meddle with. The minister will tell ye that they are just in our hearts and at our doors.'

'Ye may say that, Miss Eelen,' said Mr Pyper, shaking his head professionally; 'but it was in the sphere of politics our friend was meaning. It would be a fine thing if, with all our progress, we were to find ourselves back again in the hands of the Inquiseetion and yon wild Irishman O'Connell.'

'I would learn them a lesson,' cried Drumcarro, 'there's none o' them to be trusted. I would let them know there would be no trafficking with treason. We've had enough in Scotland of the thumbscrew and the boot – no but what judeeciously employed,' he added a moment after, 'with the ignorant, when ye cannot get at them in any other way—'

'I hope ye don't advocate torture, Drumcarro; that would be a curious way of opposing Catholic Emancipation,' said Glendochart.

'I'm not saying, sir, that I advocate torture; but I've seen cases – when deevilish obstinacy had to be dealt with,' said the old slave-driver, with a gleam of fire from under his shaggy eyebrows.

'Well, well,' said the minister softly, raising a large hand in deprecation of the argument, 'that's perhaps departing from the immediate question. I hear there's like to be trouble in your parish, Glendochart, about the new presentee. The Duke has been maybe a little hasty – an old tutor that had to be provided for.'

'If he manages the parish as ill as he managed some of the young lords,' said Glendochart, with a shrug of his shoulders.

'I will not have a word said against the young lords,' cried Mary. 'They're just very pleasant – and as ceevil young men as ye could meet anywhere – there's Lord John that we know best.'

Miss Eelen shook her head till the black bows fluttered as if in a strong wind. 'You're all just infatuate about Lord

John. I would not trust him, not a step out o' my sight. I have no faith in your Lord Johns. Begging your pardon, Glendochart, they're not a true race, and Lord John he is the worst of a'.'

'I think you might know better, Aunt Eelen, than to bring up accusations against the head of my husband's name.'

'Your husband quotha!' cried Miss Eelen. 'It was said of them for hundreds of years before your husband was born or thought of.'

The minister again intervened to smooth matters down with instances of the power and value of the race thus called in question. Jeanie was seated at the other end of the table out of reach of the principal personages who kept up the conversation, but she started at the name of Lord John, and her pale face with the faint redness round the eyes, which appealed so powerfully to Kirsteen's sympathies, grew suddenly crimson. She cast a terrified look at her sister who sat silently by her, and caught Kirsteen's hand under the table with a clutch as of despair. Lord John! Kirsteen had made no attempt to identify Jeanie's wooer whom the girl held in such strange terror. Her own heart gave a bound of alarm yet disdain. She asked with her eyes, 'Is that the man?' and received from Jeanie an answering look of confusion and trouble. There were no words exchanged between them. Kirsteen shook her head with a gesture which to Jeanie's eyes expressed not only disapproval but surprise and scorn; and Jeanie let go her hold of her sister's hand with an impulse of impatience much like that with which she had cried, 'I thought you would understand!' This little conversation by pantomime made the heart of the elder sister ache. 'Lord John,' she said to herself, 'Lord John!' with mingled fear and astonishment. That Jeanie should be in danger from him – that he should dare! that her little sister with that angelic face, who had once been touched as Kirsteen said by true love, should feel a temptation in the flattering words of the man from whom she yet desired to escape, conscious that he was not a true man! Kirsteen's experiences had been of a simple kind hitherto. She was acquainted with no such problems. It cost her a painful effort to bring herself even to the threshold of Jeanie's confused mind. She could not comprehend the conflict that was going on there. And yet she could not forsake her little sister even though the circumstances were such as she did not understand.

'Glendochart,' said Mary when the ladies had retired to the parlour leaving the gentlemen to consume their toddy, 'has had a letter from Major Gordon that we first met in London, Kirsteen. I cannot call to mind where my husband met him, if it was at the Duke's or where. But we had him down for the shooting, and two or three times he just went and came – and admired Jeanie – but that's no wonder, for there's nobody but what admires Jeanie. He's wanting to come again if we'll ask him. But I doubt if I'll do it – for Jeanie – where is she? I hope she cannot hear me – is on the way to something far grander or I'm much mistaken – and I'm not one that makes mistakes in that way.'

'If ye paid any attention to me,' said Miss Eelen, 'I would say ye were making the greatest mistake ye ever made in your life.'

'That's because it's not one of your Douglas allies – and you're full of auld world freats and proverbs about names, but I would like to hear in our family who had anything to say against my husband's name.'

'If you mean Lord John – do you know he has not a good reputation? Very ill things are said of him.'

'In London,' said the lady of Glendochart with a superior smile. 'My experience is that there's just nothing but scandal in London. But in his own country he's the Duke's son and one of the first of his name.'

'There are some things that one learns in London,' said Kirsteen with a little of that quick growing identification of one's self with one's habitation which changes the point of view; 'and Mary, if you will let me say it, this is one. The Duke's son does not match with a country laird's daughter however bonny she may be, unless he may be one of the romanticks that will make a sacrifice – but Lord John, he is not one.'

'I would hope not,' cried Mary. 'The romanticks you are meaning are just fools and fantastic persons like—' She was about to have said like yourself, but forbore.

'He would need to be fantastic that went to the Duke his father, and said I am going to be married to Jeanie Douglas, of Drumcarro.'

'Ye go a little too far, Kirsteen,' said Miss Eelen. 'The

Douglases might match with princes so far as blood goes.
But I'm not saying (for I know their ways) that there is not
reason in it. He will just get up a talk about the lassie and
then he will go away.'

'Ye are two ravens,' said Mary; 'he will do nothing of
the kind.'

'I wish you would take her to Glendochart, Mary. She is
not happy. If it is Lord John or something else I cannot tell.
She says she would like to come with me – but what would
my father say?'

'Say! just what we all would say – that we would not
permit it. A mantua-maker's house in London for Jeanie
Douglas. Oh, you need not blaze up, Kirsteen; ye have
made your bed and ye must lie on it – but Jeanie!'

Kirsteen did not blaze up. Her eyes flashed, her colour
rose; but she restrained herself with a great effort – for what
would be the use? 'The more reason,' she said, 'that you
should step in – you that are no mantua-maker but a lady in
your own house. Take Jeanie with you, and keep her safe
– and if you will take my advice ask Major Gordon. He is
not rich but he has a very good name.'

'I mind now,' said Mary, 'that these Gordons were
friends of yours – and you want to keep Jeanie down, just
in a mean position when she might take her place among
the highest. I would not have thought ye were so little,
Kirsteen. But I have nothing of that. I've always been proud
of Jeanie and I'm not minding if she's put over my head. I'll
bring no man here to distract her mind – and I'll put no
spoke in her wheel, my bonny little sister. She shall be the
first and grandest of us all, if I can do it. And then her ladyship,' cried Mary, 'will know who was her best friend.'

'Perhaps I think less of ladyships being more used to
them,' cried Kirsteen irritated beyond her self-control. 'If
ye bring her to shame instead of grandeur who will she
thank then?'

'To shame!' cried Mary. 'Let them say that word that
dare.'

'But I dare! And I know them all, and what they think
of him in his own family. And that he's not safe for a girl
like Jeanie to know. Aunt Eelen, you know them as well,
and you know if what I say is true.'

'Young weemen,' said Miss Eelen, 'if ye think that words

of strife are seemly in a house where the mother's buried that day, it's not my opinion. Kirsteen goes too far, though I would not say but there was reason in it,' she added after a moment. 'Whisht both of you – here is the poor bairn herself.'

The next morning Kirsteen, in her despair, took a still bolder step. She went to the door of the room in which Drumcarro was, and knocked for admittance. He stared at her as she came in with a lowering brow, and *humph!* of ungracious surprise, and stopped in his reading of the paper, but said nothing.

'Father,' said Kirsteen, 'I am going away today.'

He gave her another lowering and stormy glance. 'It is the best thing you can do,' he said. 'You were never wanted here.'

Kirsteen, wounded, could not refrain from saying, 'My mother wanted me,' which was met solely by that impatient indifference which we render badly by the word *humph!*

'But I did not come to speak of myself. I know,' she said, 'father, that you like where you can to add on a little of the old Douglas lands to what you have already.'

He gave her a more direct look, astonished, not knowing what she meant; then, 'What o' that?' he said.

'No more than this – that money's sometimes wanting, and I thought if the opportunity arose – I have done very well – I have some siller – at your command.'

Drumcarro was very much startled; he dropped the newspaper which he had been holding before him, as an intimation that her visit was an interruption, and turning round stared at her for a moment with genuine surprise. Then he said, 'Your mantua-making must have thriven. I would like to know one thing about ye, have you put my name intill your miserable trade?'

'No,' she said; 'so far as any name is in it, it is Miss Kirsteen.'

He gave a sigh of relief. 'I'm glad at least that ye have not brought disgrace upon the name of Douglas.'

'The name of Douglas will never get disgrace from me,' cried Kirsteen proudly, with an answering glance of fire. 'There is no one that bears it that has more care of it than me. If you keep it in as great honour at home—'

He laughed grimly. 'My lass, you may trust me for that.'

'I hope so, father; I hope there will be no speaking got up about the bonniest of us all – the youngest and the sweetest.'

His fiery eyes gave forth a gleam of mingled exultation and anger. 'I see,' he said, 'you're jealous, like all your kind. A woman can never stand another being mounted o'er her head. Trust you me, my woman, to take care of Jeanie; it's my place.'

'Yes,' she said, 'it's your place.' Then hesitating, Kirsteen continued: 'She would have liked – to go to London with me.'

'To London with you!'

'It is excusable,' said Kirsteen; 'it is natural that a young thing should desire to see a little of the world.'

Mr Douglas expressed his feelings in a harsh and angry laugh. 'Out of a mantua-maker's windows,' he cried; then added with solemnity, 'and her mother dead just a week today.'

'It's not for want of heart,' said Kirsteen. She paused again, and then speaking quickly with all the courage she could summon up: 'Oh, father, yon Lord John – there's no truth in him; there's no trust to be put in him! She's frightened for him, father.'

'Hold your peace!' he cried. 'I'll have none of your slandering here.'

'Father, mind – you'll have to be both father and mother to Jeanie. If it should come to pass that every old wife in the clachan had a hold of her bonny name!'

Perhaps it was not unnatural that Drumcarro should resent this speech. 'If ye will mind your own concerns,' he said grimly, 'I will take care of mine. The sooner you go your own gait the better; there will be more peace left behind.'

'I have delivered my soul,' said Kirsteen; 'the wyte will be upon your own head if you close your eyes. Farewell, father, if we should never meet again.'

She stood for a moment waiting his reply; then made him a curtsey as she had done when she was a little girl. Something perhaps in this salutation touched Drumcarro. He broke out into a laugh, not so harsh as before. 'Fare ye well,' he said, 'you were always upsetting, and wiser than other folk. But I'll mind what you said about the siller, which was not without reason. And I've little doubt but I'll see ye again. You're too fond o' meddling not to come back now ye've got your hand in.'

This was all the leave-taking between father and daughter, but Kirsteen's heart was touched as she went away. It was at once a sign of amity and a permission – a condoning of her past sins and almost an invitation to return.

CHAPTER XLI

'Then you are going, Kirsteen?'

'I must go, Jeanie. There is no place, and no wish for me here.'

'And I am to bide – alone. Oh, there are plenty of folk in the house. My father to gloom at me, and Marg'ret to make me scones, and take care that I do not wet my feet – as if that was all the danger in the world! – and Jamie to sit at his books and never say a word. And on the other side – oh, the deevil, just the deevil himself aye whispering in my ear.'

'Jeanie, Jeanie! ye must not say such words.'

'It's like swearing,' said the girl with a scornful laugh, 'but it's true.'

'Jeanie,' said Kirsteen anxiously, 'you will say again that I do not understand. But, my dear, I cannot think but you're terrifying yourself in vain; when true love has once come in, how can the false move ye? It will be no temptation. Oh, no, no. There can be but one, there cannot be two.'

'Where is your one?' said Jeanie. 'I know nothing about your one.' She shook her head with a sudden flush of burning and indignant colour, too painful to be called a blush, as if to shake all recollection away. 'I have none to take my part,' she said, 'but him that says "Come." And I know that it's the ill way, and not the good, he's leading to. But if you leave me here, and leave me alone, that's the way I'll go.'

'Oh, Jeanie, my darling, what can I do? I cannot bide – and I cannot steal you away.'

'I will ask no more,' said Jeanie. 'You will maybe be sorry after – but then it will be too late.'

Kirsteen put her arms round her young sister, who turned her shoulder towards her, holding off as far away as was possible, with a reluctance and resistance that were almost sullen. 'Jeanie,' she said, 'if I send you Lewis Gordon instead?'

Jeanie wrenched herself indignantly out of her sister's arms. 'I will never speak nor look at ye again! A man that never said a word to me. What would Lewis Gordon do here? The shooting's near over, and the fishing's bad this year. Men that come to the Highlands for sport had better stay at home.'

'Jeanie! if he never spoke it was for poverty and not for want of love; and you were so young.'

'Oh, yes, I was very young – too young to be shamed and made a fool of by him or any man. And if you send him here, Kirsteen, out of pity to save Jeanie – Oh!' the girl cried dashing her clenched hands in the air, 'I will – I will – just go headlong and be lost in the darkness, and never be seen more!'

It was true that Kirsteen did not understand. She could only look wistfully at her little sister, in whose young bosom there were tumults unknown to herself. What could she do but soothe and try to subdue her endeavouring all the time to represent to herself that it was but the impatience of Jeanie's nature, the hasty temper of a spoilt child, sharpened by offence and misunderstanding of the man whom she really loved. After a time Jeanie yielded to Kirsteen's caresses and consolations with a sudden recovery of her self-control which was almost more wonderful and alarming than the previous abandon. 'It's no matter,' she said, and recovered her calm with almost an indignant effort. What did it mean? Both the despair and the recovery were mysteries to the more steadfast spirit which knew no such impulses and was ignorant both of the strength and weakness of a passionate superficial nature eager to live and to enjoy, unable to support the tedium and languor of life.

Kirsteen had little more success with Marg'ret to whom she appealed next. 'You will look after my poor little Jeanie. Oh, Marg'ret, don't let her out of your sight, keep her like the apple of your eye.'

'And do you think, Kirsteen, you that are full of sense, that I could keep any grip of her if I did that? Never let her out of my sight! I canna keep her in my sight for an hour.'

'Marg'ret, my heart's just sick with fear and trouble.'

'Hoot,' said Marg'ret, 'there is nae occasion. What should possess the bairn to terrify ye as she seems to do, I canna tell. There's nae reason for it. A man is none the worse that I can see for bein' a young lord – maybe he's none the better; I'm putting forward nae opinion – but to come to Drumcarro with an ill meaning if he were the greatest of his name – no, no, I'll never believe that.'

'It is hard to believe; but it's harder still to think of the Duke's son coming here for his wife.'

'If it was a king's son, and the bride was our Jeanie,' Marg'ret cast her head high, 'they're no blate that think themselves above the Douglases, whatever their titles or their honours may be!'

Kirsteen shook her head, but in her heart too that superstition was strong. Insult the Douglases in their own house! She thought again that perhaps all her sophisticated thoughts might be wrong. In London there was a difference unspeakable between the great Duke and the little Highland laird whom nobody had ever heard of – but at home Drumcarro was as good blood as the Duke, and of an older race – and to intend insult to the house of as good a gentleman as himself was surely more than the wildest profligate would dare. She tried to persuade herself of this as she made her preparations for going away, which were very small. While she was doing this Jamie, the only boy now left at home, the one of the family who was studious, and for whom not the usual commission but a writership in India had been obtained, came to her shyly; for to him his sister Kirsteen was little more than a name.

'There was a book,' he said, and then hung his head unable to get out any more.

'There was a book? It is something you want, Jamie?'

Jamie explained with many contortions that it was – a book which he wanted much, and which there was no chance of getting nearer than Glasgow, but which Mr Pyper thought might be found in London if anyone would take the trouble. Kirsteen promised eagerly to take that trouble. She laid her hand upon the big boy's shoulder. He was only eighteen, but already much taller than herself, a large, loosely made, immature man.

'And will ye do something for me?' she said. Jamie very awkward and shamefaced pledged himself at once – whatever she wanted.

'I want you to take care of Jeanie,' said Kirsteen; 'will ye go with her when she takes a walk, and stand by her what-ever happens, and not let her out of your sight.'

'Not let her out of my sight!' cried Jamie, astonished as Margaret had been. 'But she would soon send me out of the way. She would never be bothered with me.'

'I meant not long out of your sight, Jamie. Oh! just keep a watch. She will be lonely and want kind company. Ye must keep your eye upon her for kindness, and not let her be alone.'

'If you mean I'm to spy upon her, I couldn't do that, Kirsteen, not for all the books in the world.'

'That is not what I mean,' Kirsteen cried. 'Can you not understand, Jamie? I want you to stand by her, to be with her when you can, not to leave her by herself. She's very lonely – She's – not happy – She's—'

Jamie gave an abashed laugh. 'She's sometimes happy enough,' he said, then recollected himself and became grave all at once. 'I was meaning, before—' Presently he recovered again from this momentary cloud and added, 'She's no wanting me; there are other folk she likes better.'

'Jamie – it is just the other folk, that frighten me.'

Jamie made a great effort to consider the matter with the seriousness which he saw to be expected from him. But the effort was vain. He burst into a great laugh, and with heav-ing shoulders and a face crimson with the struggle swung himself away.

In the meantime, Mary, not without a great deal of satis-faction in the removal of the restraint which Kirsteen's presence enforced, was preparing officiously for her sister's journey. The gig which Kirsteen could herself drive, and in which Miss Macnab could be conveyed back to her home, was ordered in time for the further journey to Glasgow which Kirsteen was to make by post-chaise. The ease with which she made these arrangements, her indifference to the cost of her journey, her practical contempt of the diffi-culties which to the country people who had to scheme and plan for a long time before they decided upon any extra expense, had a half-sinful appearance, and was very trying to Mary's sense of innate superiority. 'She does not heed what money she spends. It's come light, gang light,' said the lady of Glendochart. 'I have heard that was the way with persons in business, but I never thought to see it in a sister of mine. I do not doubt,' she added, 'that Kirsteen would just order an expensive dinner at an inn if it took her fancy; but I'm saving her the need of that at least, for I'm putting her a chicken in her basket, and some of Marg'ret's scones and cakes (oat-cakes were meant) to keep her going.' 'I am sure, mem, you are very considerate,' said Miss Macnab, to whom this explanation was given. 'But I get very little credit for it from Kirsteen,' Mary answered with a sigh.

These preparations to get rid of her, and the disappearance of Jeanie who had shut herself up in her room and would see nobody, had a great effect upon Kirsteen. She had taken up, with a heroic sense of having something henceforward to live for, her mother's half-charge, half-statement that she would be the stand-by of the family. All brighter hopes being gone that was enough to keep her heart from sinking, and it was not always she knew that the stand-by of a family received much acknowledgment, thanks or praise. But to find herself forsaken and avoided by her young sister, hurried away by the elder, with a scarcely veiled pleasure in her departure, were painful things to meet with in the beginning of that mission. She went out of the house in the weary hours of waiting before the gig was ready, to lighten if possible the aching of her heart by the soothing influence of the fresh air and natural sounds. The linn was making less than its usual tumult in the benumbing of the frost, the wind was hushed in the trees, the clouds hung low and grey with that look of oppressed and lowering heaviness which precedes snow. The house too – the home which now indeed she felt herself to be leaving for ever, seemed bound in bands of frost and silence. The poor mother so complaining in her lifetime, so peaceful in her death, who had wanted for so little while she was there, seemed to have left a blank behind her quite out of correspondence with the insignificance of her life. There was no one now to call Kirsteen, to have the right of weakness to her service and succour. With a sharp pang Kirsteen recollected that Jeanie had called and she had refused. What could she do but refuse? Yet to have done so troubled her beyond anything else that could have happened. It came upon her now with a sense of failure which was very bitter. Not her mother but her mother's child, the little beautiful sister who from her birth had been Kirsteen's joy. She had called, and Kirsteen had refused. She went up the hill behind the house and sat down upon a rock, and gazed at the familiar scene. And then this remorse came upon her and seized her. She had failed to Jeanie's call. She had allowed other notions to come in, thoughts of other people, hesitations, pride, reluctance to be thought to interfere. Was she right to have done so? Was she wrong? Should she have yielded to Jeanie's instinct instead of what seemed like duty? It was rare to Kirsteen to be in this dilemma. It added to the pang with which she felt herself entirely deserted, with nobody to regret her or to say a kind word. If misfortune should come to Jeanie, if anything should happen as people say, how deeply, how bitterly would she blame herself who might have helped but refused. And yet again what but this could she do?

The sound of someone coming down the hill, wading among the great bushes of the ling, and over the withered bracken scarcely roused her; for what did it matter to Kirsteen who came that way? She was still sitting on the rock when a man appeared round the turning of the path; she paid no attention to him till he was quite near. Then her heart suddenly leapt up to her throat; she started, rising from her seat. He on his side recognized her too. He stopped with a low whistle of dismay, then took off his Highland bonnet, less with an air of courtesy than with that of not daring to omit the forms of respect.

'So it is you, Miss Kirsteen,' he said.

'It is me – at my father's door. It's more wonderful to see that it's you, my Lord John.'

'Not so very wonderful either,' he said, 'for I may say I am at my father's door too.'

'You are on the lands of Drumcarro – the Douglas lands, that never belonged to one of your name.'

'You don't expect me to enter into old feuds,' he said with a laugh; 'would you like to have me seized by your men-at-arms, Miss Kirsteen, and plunged into the dungeon below the castle moat?' He paused and looked down at the grey, penurious house standing bare in the wilds. 'Unhappily there is neither moat nor castle,' he said again with a laugh.

'There's more,' said Kirsteen proudly, 'for there's honour

and peace, and he that disturbs either will not pass without his reward. Lord John, I would like to know what you are wanting here?'

'You have always treated me in a very lordly way, Miss Kirsteen,' he said. 'What if I were to doubt your right to make any such inquiry? I am wanting, as you say, to pay my respects to my kinswoman of Glendochart, and ask for the family, who I hear have been in trouble.'

Kirsteen paused with a look at him to which he answered with a smile and bow. What could she say? To let him know that he was a danger to Jeanie was but to stimulate him in his pursuit: and she could not herself believe it even now.

'Lord John,' she said. 'I met you once upon another hill-side; you had done me a great service but you did not know who I was – a gentlewoman as good as yourself. But when I bid you as a gentleman to stand by and let me pass, ye did so. You could not stand against me when I said that. I ask you now again, but I ask more. As ye are a gentleman, Lord John, go away from here.'

He shook his head. 'The argument served its turn once,' he said, 'you must not scorn my intellect so much as to try it again.'

'Go,' she said, putting herself in his way, 'those that are dwelling down there are too high for one thing and not high enough for another. Go away, Lord John, if you're what a gentleman should be. If ye do not, I'll promise you this, that you will repent it all your days.'

He stepped past her amid the heather bushes and short brushwood. 'Not even an angel with a flaming sword could bar the road,' he said waving his hand, 'on a hillside like this. Farewell, Miss Kirsteen, I'm going about my own affairs and doing no harm to you.'

In a moment he had passed, finding another path for himself among the windings of the heather and bracken. He took off his bonnet again with a mocking salutation as he disappeared down the hill. And Kirsteen felt herself left behind with a sense of mortification and helplessness intolerable to her high and proud spirit. How could she have hoped to stop him? What power had she? But this did not make her feel her failure less. 'You will repent it all your days,' she called after him, raising her voice in the vexation of her soul. He turned and lifted his bonnet again with a

mocking salutation. That was all. She might have known,
she said to herself with angry tears of humiliation in her
eyes.

But when Kirsteen came down the hill there was no trace
of Lord John. Mary and Jeanie were in the parlour waiting
for her to say goodbye. And there was an air of agitation
about her younger sister, which Kirsteen in her troubled
mind set down to the visit for which no doubt Jeanie had
been called from her room. But nothing was said. They
accompanied her to the door where the gig was now standing with Miss Macnab already mounted into her seat. There
was no time or opportunity for further leave-taking; Jeanie
gave her cheek to be kissed with averted eyes; and not
even with Marg'ret could Kirsteen speak another word in
private. In a few minutes more she had turned her back
upon Drumcarro; was it for ever? To her wounded and
impatient heart, impatient above all the sense of utter futility and failure, this seemed the thing most probable. Why
should she ever come again, the stand-by of the family?
Perhaps if they should want money, and she should have it
– but in no other way.

She was roused by the mild voice of the country artist
at her elbow. 'You will find a great change in everything,
Miss Kirsteen, coming back from London?' she said.

Kirsteen did not immediately reply. 'I find more change
in myself than in anything else,' she said at last, bringing
herself back with difficulty from more urgent thoughts.

'That was partly what I was meaning. Ye'll find a great
interest in life in yon muckle London, where there must
always be the bonniest new things to see.'

'When your heart's away,' said Kirsteen, yielding in spite
of herself to the natural desire of unburdening her mind a
little, 'it does not matter much what bonny things there
may be to see.'

'That's true too,' said the dressmaker; 'but my experience
has aye been, that where we canna have what we want, and
eh, how few of us have that advantage, it's just a great thing
to please your e'e, and fill your mind with what e'e can
see, and the best ye can see. There's even pleasure in a new
fashion book when ye have little else. And with all the
bonny leddies and their court dresses, and just to dress
them like a picture.'

Kirsteen looked at this humble artist with a sigh. 'Perhaps you were not always so resigned,' she said.

'I'm not saying that I'm resigned. I would just like to see the Queen's court, and the princesses in their plumes and trains, before everything in the world, but it's a comfort,' said the mild philosopher, 'when ye can make it up to yourself with a bonny person like Miss Jeanie, just to make the line of her gown perfitt, if ainything can ever be called perfitt,' she added piously, 'in this imperfitt world.'

CHAPTER XLII

There came a great sense of desolation and misery into the heart of Jeanie after she had witnessed, with eyes averted and without a sign of affection, wrapped up in offence and estrangement, the departure of her sister. She was angry with Kirsteen and deeply disappointed, and incapable of comprehending that it must be so, and that she, Jeanie, was to be crossed at last and after all, her plaint disregarded, her prayer refused. It had been her lot hitherto to get all her little requirements in the end, however her mother or Marg'ret might at first stand out. And the boys had been much ruled by Jeanie's will, and had yielded to her as big brothers often fail to do. She had never been crossed, in the end. Opposition had been made to her, difficulties insisted upon, but in the end they had always given way. Only once before had Jeanie come face to face with a disappointment, which could not by anything she could do be changed into happiness and content. It was the central incident in her life, but it had been up to this moment the exception, the one adverse event she had ever known. And it had been so great, so startling and astonishing that the girl's pride and all her strength had been roused to conceal and surmount it, so that no one should ever suspect that to her, Jeanie, any slight had ever come. To nobody but to Kirsteen, and to her only when taken utterly by surprise, had this secret ever been betrayed. Young Gordon had visited Glendochart from time to time during the last years. He had come in the intervals of his service while Jeanie grew and blossomed into womanhood. While she was still half child, half woman, he had awakened in her heart that first delicious and strange sense of power which is so great a revelation to a girl. His eyes had said a thousand indistinct sweetnesses to her, which his lips had not ventured to confess. He had been reverent of her extreme youth. He had been kept back by his own uncertain prospects, by his want of money and unsettled life, a soldier seeking advancement wherever it was to be found. But none of these honourable reasons had been taken into account by the girl, who, convinced as she had been of his love, had seen him go away with an amazement and shock of feeling scarcely comprehensible out of the first absolutism and certainty of youth. He had gone away, saying never a word. That he was overwhelmed with agitation and distress when the summons to join his regiment (for which he professed to be looking eagerly) came; that he had spoken of returning, of hopes that were involved in his return, with allusions and suggestions that the poor fellow thought plain enough, had all been invisible to Jeanie, or disdained by her, as so many evidences of falsehood. Her little imperious soul had been shaken as by a tempest. She to be forsaken, wooed and abandoned, she before whom everyone bowed, the flower of the Highlands, as they called her!

And now Kirsteen had done the same. Once again, till the last moment Jeanie had believed that her sister would yield, and she would have her way. Just as she had expected that word which never came from Lewis Gordon, she had expected from Kirsteen if it were but a word, a whisper of consent at the last. Even while she held her cheek to be kissed, turning away her eyes which were sullen with anger yet expectation, the girl expected that Kirsteen might still whisper – 'Come.' She had contrived all in her own mind ready for that last moment – Kirsteen would say, 'Come, I'll wait for you at the clachan' – and all unsuspected, the stranger having visibly departed, Jeanie would steal out, nobody taking any notice, and fly along the road, and spring up light as a feather beside Miss Macnab. What would it matter to her that there was no room? She had planned it all. At the very last, as her mother used to do, as Marg'ret did, compunction at the sight of Jeanie's averted face would seize upon Kirsteen. None of them could bear to see her vexed – and at the last that feeling would be stronger than prudence or any wise sentiment. Jeanie within herself had been sure of this; but she had been deceived. And after she had watched with incredulous angry eyes full of a mist of bitterness – for tears she would not shed to acknowledge herself defeated – the actual going away without a word of her sister, she had fled to her room and flung herself upon her bed, even now not without an ear intent on any sound that might indicate Kirsteen's return, to say yet the tardy 'Come,' to her little sister. But the wintry afternoon closed down, the light faded away, and stillness fell upon the house. There was nothing to be heard but the echo of the linn which always mingled with everything, and Merran's heavy footstep and Marg'ret's distant voice in the kitchen. Kirsteen was gone. It was impossible to believe it, but it was true. She was gone like *him* – him for whom she had spoken, who was her friend, for like draws to like, Jeanie cried furiously to herself, in the silence. They had gone away – both of them – the man who loved her, and the sister who was evidently born for no such important end as to save and succour Jeanie – both! They had gone away, and she was left alone – to meet her fate.

Jeanie was not of the simple fibre of her family. Perhaps her condition of spoiled child had done something towards the development of a different character, but that character was there in the first place to be developed. Her impatient determination to have what she wanted, to be happy, to get such amusements, privileges, and advantages as were comprehensible to her, without consideration as to whether they were possible or not, or what the result of her satisfaction would be – was very different both from the steadfastness of Kirsteen, and the calm self-seeking of Mary. Jeanie had a passion in her which would not be gainsaid. She did not understand obstacles except as things to be eluded, pushed aside, thrust out of the way, arbitrarily, imperiously, whether they were just or even necessary or not. She could not understand that she had been born for anything but to be paramount, to be loved and admired, and happy. Her lover and heaven itself had wronged her by holding back that happiness that was her due. And when there seemed a prospect that it was to come back to her, Jeanie's heart rushed at the hope with a fervour which was largely made up of fury and indignation. The thought of a future more brilliant than any she could have had with Gordon filled her with fierce delight, principally from the hope that he would hear of it, perhaps see it and recognize her superior bliss and his loss. This, more than a girl's natural vanity in being followed by one so much above her in rank, and far more than any feeling for Lord John, had made his attentions delightful to her. Jeanie had been taken like her sisters before her to the ball at the Castle; but hers were not merely the good looks of Kirsteen or the comeliness of Mary. It had not been possible to keep the little beauty in the background. Even the noble party of visitors and relations who were usually so little interested by the lairds and their belongings were moved by Jeanie. She was introduced among them, danced with, talked to, while the others of her class looked on grim or smiling as their case might be. That Jeanie had been excited and delighted by her triumph it is needless to say; what was much more extraordinary was that her father, though he said nothing, felt for the first time the true sensation of that superiority which he had believed in and asserted all his life. The beauty and brightness which dazzled everybody were but the natural emanation of her blood, to Drumcarro. 'Oh, ay, she's of the real auld Douglas kind,' he said with proud carelessness when compliments were paid him. That the Douglases should gain a triumph through a lassie was a thing that he had scarcely been able to bring himself to believe; but when this triumph was accomplished for him, his pride accepted it as a thing to be looked for. Was not she a Douglas? That explained all.

And when Lord John appeared 'incognity' as Marg'ret said, in the little shooting lodge on the hill, both father and daughter had responded after their kind. Drumcarro had felt the suggestion of an alliance with the other noble house which had outstripped his in honours, but never to his consciousness excelled or even equalled it in antiquity and nobility, to be a gratifying circumstance and high testimonial to his superiority to everything around, but he had not contemplated it with any surprise. To get a Douglas as his wife was honour enough for any duke's son; but the thought of being so closely allied to the Duke gave him on his side a proud satisfaction. It was a great thing for a daughter to do who was only a daughter, and of no account whatever. Jeanie too felt a subtle elation in her veins, a sense of high promotion, but not in so simple a way. When *he* heard of it what would he think? was the burden of her thoughts. He would see that Jeanie Douglas was not one to be deserted, left or taken up again at his pleasure. She pictured to herself meeting him in some vague grandeur of a party in London, and a hundred times in her heart rehearsed the bow she would give him, the sweeping

curtsey, the fine progress past him which she would make
on her husband's arm. The husband himself had a very
secondary place – but that did not occur to Jeanie. He was
understood as the occasion of all that grandeur, the sharer
of it no doubt; but the exquisite revenge of such an encounter was what in her first vague sense of triumph, Jeanie
chiefly pictured to herself.

The girl was not, however, herself enlightened by this
curious evidence of the state of her mind. She had not
begun to think about her thoughts; all was straightforward
and simple with her, as with a young savage. On the other
side Lord John did not leave her in any doubt as to his feelings. His declaration of love was not delayed by any
scruples – but neither was it followed by any of those practical steps which even in Jeanie's limited experience were
usual in the circumstances. It is true that Jeanie herself was
coy, and held off from the warm love-making of her suitor,
keeping him at arm's length; but no reference to her father,
none of the suggestions and arrangements into which happy
lovers rush ever came from Lord John's lips. He spoke
indeed of the time when they should be always together,
but said not a word as to when or how that should be. It
was less difficult to Jeanie to keep such a secret than it
would have been for most girls. Her mother was ill, her
father, as she supposed, utterly indifferent, no sister near to
whom her heart could be opened. And to be secret in love
was one of the traditions of the time and country. But still
after a time she began to feel that there was something, she
could not tell what, unexpected, undesirable, in her lover.
When he spoke of marriage it was with a scoff and jeer.
Even, however, when the moment came in which he told
her that marriage in the ordinary way, with all the publicity
usually surrounding that event, was impossible to him,
Jeanie was not suspicious enough to be defiant. 'You'll have
to steal out some night, and trust yourself to me and let
me carry you away,' he said, 'that's what we'll have to do.
My bonny Jeanie will trust herself to me.'

'That is what Anne did,' cried Jeanie startled. 'My father
would not give his consent; and he has never seen her again.
We dare not say her name. But maybe,' she added after a
pause, 'it would be different with you.'

'I think it would be different with me,' he said, with a

laugh that somehow offended Jeanie, she could not tell how. But then he began to lavish sweet words and praises upon her, so that the girl's vanity was soothed and her imagination excited. He told her where he would take her – to London, and then abroad, which was a word of no tangible import to her ignorance, but meant only everything that was brilliant and splendid – and of all the beautiful places she should see, and the beautiful things she should have.

'I suppose,' said Jeanie, 'we would go to see the King.'

'There is no king, in that way,' he said, with a laugh.

'But there is a court, for we see it in the paper,' said Jeanie. 'If it is the Prince, it would just be the same.'

'We'll not go to the court this time,' he said, with another of those laughs which wounded Jeanie, she could not tell how.

'I thought it was the right way,' said Jeanie, thoughtfully. What she was thinking was, that in that case she would not meet *him*, and that the heart of her triumph would be lost.

'In some cases,' he said, still laughing, 'but not in ours, my lovely dear. We will never think of the world, we'll think only of love. Whatever's pleasantest my Jeanie shall see, but nothing so bonny as herself.'

'There will be many things in London besides the court – there is my sister Kirsteen,' said Jeanie, still musing. 'Oh, I will be glad to see Kirsteen.'

'It's clear I am not enough for my Jeanie, though my Jeanie is enough for me!'

'Oh, it is not that,' said Jeanie, vaguely. In her heart, however, there was no doubt a sensation that to dazzle *him* with her grandeur, and to make her sister a spectator of her new and exalted life, were the things to which she looked forward most.

'I'll not promise to take you to Kirsteen, any more than to take you to court,' he said. 'I'll promise nothing that takes your mind off me. To think of having you all to myself is enough for me. I mean to carry you off to some Italian bower, where there will be nothing to do but love, and love, and—'

'Till you are tired of love, as you call it, and me too,' said Jeanie, with a little disdain.

He gave her a curious look, wondering if at last the little simplicity had fathomed what he really meant. But Jeanie's eyes were all untroubled, and her brow serene. She was disappointed and dissatisfied with his way; but only because it was not her way, and contrary to her expectations, not that she had divined the shame that was in his heart.

But one day a gleam of strange light burst upon the girl. He had been telling her of one of his friends, who had gone to those Italian bowers, and of the life he led; the lake, the moonlight, the myrtles and roses in the middle of winter, till Jeanie's eyes grew bright. 'We will get him to look for a place for us, on the water's edge,' Lord John said. No thought of suspicion, or of finding her lover out, was in Jeanie's mind. She asked, as a girl does, eager to hear of others in the same circumstances as herself, 'And is he married, too?'

For the moment she could not comprehend the hurried demonstration, the embarrassment of Lord John among his caresses, the laugh, always so distasteful to her. 'They don't think of that out there,' he said, 'they don't put you in chains out there, they trust everything to love – as my Jeanie is going to do.'

What did it mean? She was always shy of these vehement caresses – she freed herself, with a strange chill upon her, and said that she must go. They had been wandering by the side of linn, under the bare, overarching trees; and Jeanie would not listen to the explanations which he was anxious to make, and which she understood no more than the offence. She was sure of nothing but that she must get away.

CHAPTER XLIII

Jeanie fled to her own room, and all that had been said went vaguely rolling and sweeping through her mind like clouds blowing up for a storm. A hundred things he had said came drifting up – singly they had no meaning, and without something in her own soul to interpret them they would have conveyed no enlightenment to the uninstructed Highland girl. Even now, though aroused and frightened, it was very hard for Jeanie to put in shape or to explain to herself, what were the suspicions and the uneasiness she felt – 'They don't think of that out there, they don't put you in chains out there' – what did it mean? Jeanie knew that there was a kind of *persiflage* – though she did not know the word nor yet what it meant – in which marriage was spoken of as bondage, and it was said of a man that he was going up for execution on his marriage-day. That was said 'in fun' she knew. Was Lord John in fun? Was it a jest, and no more? But there was something uncertain, something dissatisfied in Jeanie's heart which would not be calmed down by any such explanation. What, oh, what did he mean? She was not to be taken to court, nor even to see Kirsteen. She was to go to that Italian bower where all was trusted to love. An Italian bower sounded like Paradise to Jeanie. She had not the most remote idea what it was. She was prepared to believe anything, to allow of any difference between the conditions of life there and those she knew. That might be quite right in an Italian bower which was not right in a Highland glen. She was bewildered in her innocence and simplicity; and yet that very simplicity gave her the sensation that all was not well.

After this there was a long interval in her intercourse with Lord John. He wandered about the glen and the hillside, but she took care never to fall in his way, the excitement of eluding him making a kind of counterpoise for the absence of the excitement there used to be in meeting him. And then he began to make frequent calls, to endure interviews with Drumcarro and inquire into Mrs Douglas's

ailments in order to see Jeanie to whom he directed the
most appealing looks. And the impression and suspicion
gradually died away from her mind. When she met him by
accident after this interval out of doors, and he was free to
demand explanations, Jeanie hung her head and said
nothing. How could she explain? She had nothing to
explain. And once more, though with self-reproach, the
daily walks and talks were resumed. In her dull life it was
the only relief. Her mother was growing more and more
helpless and wanted more and more attention. And when
Jeanie stole out from her long nursing for a breath of air no
doubt it pleased and exhilarated her to see him waiting, to
receive his welcome and all the tender words he could think
of. Drumcarro himself saw them together, and made no
remark. Marg'ret saw them together and was glad and
proud to see the favourite of the house courted by the
Duke's son. Thus no one helped Jeanie, but everything
persuaded her against her own perception that all was not
well.

That perception, however, grew stronger and stronger,
but with it a longing, of Jeanie's forlorn youth for the only
pleasure that remained in her life. He flattered her so, he
conveyed to her in every word and look such evidence of
her own delightfulness, of her power over him, and his
devotion to her! And all the rest of life was so overcast to
Jeanie, so dull and grey, so destitute of pleasure. It was like
a momentary escape into that Italian bower of which he
spoke, to go out to him, to see his eyes glowing with
admiration, to hear of all the delightsome things which were
waiting for her. Day by day it became more clear to Jeanie
that Lord John's love was not like that of those downright
wooers at whom she had once scoffed, who would have her
answer yes or no, and left nothing vague in respect to their
wishes. It occurred to her too, though she would not permit
it to put itself into words, even in her mind, that his love
was not like that which she had been so sure of in Lewis
Gordon's eyes, but which had never been spoken. Lord
John was bold, there was no timidity nor reverence in his
look, he was confident, excited, sure that he had her in his
toils. All these the girl saw with the perspicacity of despair
– yet could not free herself or break away. With him she
divined there might be shame lying in wait for her, but with

him, too, was all that was brilliant and fair in life. A time
of splendour, of pleasure, of joy, if after that despair –
while within her own possibilities there was nothing but the
given routine, the dull existence in which nothing ever
stirred, in which no pleasure was. Oh, if only something
would come, she cared not what. Death or a saviour – what
did it matter? – to carry Jeanie away.

And now Kirsteen had come and gone. Kirsteen who
was her natural saviour, the only one who could have done
it. Kirsteen who knew *him*, and said that he was true. The
wail, 'Take me with you!' had come from Jeanie's very
heart. But Kirsteen had gone away, and every hope had
failed. And as for the party at home they were all elated by
the visits of Lord John, all expectant of a grand marriage,
which would bring back something of the old prestige to
Drumcarro. 'When ye are so near the head, Jeanie, I hope
you'll be mindful of the branches,' said Mary. 'It's not just
an invitation to the ball which everybody is asked to, that
will satisfy me then.' No thought of possible wrong was in
the innocent fancies of all these people. They ought to have
known, but they did not. They ought to have taken fright,
but no alarm came to them. The man who would try to
wrong a Douglas, Mary thought, could never be born.

There had been again a pause during the time when the
atmosphere of death had surrounded the house. Jeanie had
seen him pass from a window. She had heard his voice at
the door inquiring for the family. He had sent some flowers,
an unusual and unexpected compliment, to decorate the
death chamber, for to put flowers on a coffin or a grave was
not then the habit in England and still less in Scotland. All
these attentions had added to the elation and pleasure of
the others, but had not silenced the terror in Jeanie's heart.
And now all was over, the pause for her mother's death,
the visit of Kirsteen, the hope she had of something or of
someone, who would interfere to save her. Even to hear of
Lewis Gordon had added to the fire in Jeanie's veins. She
would not have him come to find her at his disposal, to
know how she had suffered in the thought of his desertion.
No! he should find that there was someone else who did
not hold back, someone who would not let her go, someone
– oh, hapless Jeanie! – whom she could no longer escape,
towards whom she was drifting without any power to stop

herself though it should be towards tears and shame. Better even that, Jeanie said to herself, than to wait upon the leisure of a man who thought he could let her drop and take her up again at his pleasure. Her mind was disturbed beyond description, confused and miserable. She was afloat upon a dreadful current which carried her away, from which some-one outside could save her, but not herself, against which she seemed now to have no force to struggle more.

Jeanie made still another stand, lashing herself, as it were, against the violence of that tide to the companions whom for the moment she had in the house with her, even to Mary by whom she could hold, a little in want of other help. Mary was not a very enlivening companion for the girl – all she could talk about was her children, and the vicissi-tudes of her household, and the wit and wisdom of little Colin. But Mary was not exigent as to her listeners. So long as she was allowed to go on in her monologue her com-panion was called upon for no reply. And thus Jeanie's thoughts had full scope, and increased instead of softened the tension of being in which she was; she seemed unable to escape that current which drew her unwilling feet.

She met him again on the last day of the Glendocharts' stay. Though Mary gave her so little help, Jeanie regarded with terror the time of her sister's departure. She felt as if then her last hope would fail her. There would be no longer anything to which to cling, any counterpoise to the in-fluence which was hurrying her to her destruction. She had gone out in the afternoon with a bad headache, and a still worse tremor and throbbing in her heart, feeling that need for the fresh air and the stillness outside, and a moment's exemption from the voices and the questions within, which people in agitation and trouble so often feel. She had not thought of Lord John at all, or of meeting him. She felt only that she must breathe the outer air and be alone for a moment, or else die.

She sat down upon the same fallen tree on which she had sat with Kirsteen. The voice of the linn was softer than ever, stilled by the frost into a soothing murmur. The bare trees stirred their many branches over her head, as if to shield her from any penetrating look, whether from earth or sky. 'Oh, what am I to do?' she said to herself. How often these words are said by people in mortal perplexity, in difficulty and trouble. What to do, when you have no alternative but one, no temptation but one? But everything was against Jeanie, and all, who ought to have protected her, fought against her, and made it more and more difficult to resist. She bent down her face into her hands, and repeated to herself that question, 'What am I to do? – What am I to do?' Jeanie did not know how long she had been there, or how much time had elapsed before, with a start, and a sense of horror, her heart struggling to her throat, she felt a pair of arms encircle her, and a voice in her ear: 'Crying, Jeanie! Why should you cry – you who should never have a care? You would never have a care if you would trust yourself, as I am imploring you to do, to me.'

Poor Jeanie's heart was sick with conflicting emotions, with the temptation and the strong recoil from it. She could make no reply, could not lift her head, or escape from his arms, or control the sudden access of sobbing that had come upon her. Her sobbing became audible in the stillness of the wintry scene, through the sound of the linn and the faint rustling of the trees. 'Oh, go away and leave me! Oh, let me be!' Jeanie said among her sobs. Perhaps she did not altogether mean it, neither the one thing nor the other – neither that he should go nor stay.

He stayed, however, and talked more earnestly than he had ever done before. Not of the Italian bower, but of the two living together, sharing everything, never apart. He had the house all ready to which he would take her, he said; a house fit for her, waiting for its mistress – everything was ready but Jeanie. And why should she hold back? Did she not know he loved her? Had she any doubt? She could not have any doubt; all his study would be to make her happy. She knew that he had no other thought. 'Jeanie, Jeanie, only say yes; only yield that pride of yours; you know you have yielded in your heart.'

'No,' cried Jeanie, sitting upright, drawing herself from him. 'No, I have not yielded. There is but one way. Go and ask my father, and then I will go with you. I will go with you,' she repeated, one belated sob coming in breaking her voice, 'wherever you want me to go.'

'Speak to your father? But you know that is what I cannot do. I have told you already I would have to speak to my father, too. And he – would put me into a madhouse or a prison. You know, my sweet love, for I have told you – but must we be parted by two old fathers with no feeling left in them? Jeanie, if you will be ready by ten o'clock, or any hour you please, I will have a post-chaise waiting. Oh, Jeanie, come! Just a little boldness, just one bold step, and then nothing can harm us more; for we'll be together – for ever!' said the young man in his fervour. She had risen up, putting him away from her, but he pressed to her side again. 'You have gone too far to go back now,' he said. 'Jeanie, I'll take no denial. Tonight, tonight, my lovely dear.'

'No,' she said, her heart throbbing as if it would break, putting one hand against his shoulder to push him away from her. 'Oh, no, no!' but her eyes met the glowing gaze of his, and the current was seizing her feet.

'That means yes, yes – for two no's make a consent,' cried Lord John, seizing her again in his arms.

Drumcarro had scoffed at Kirsteen and her warning, but like many another suspicious man, he had remembered the warning he scorned. He had kept an eye upon all Jeanie's movements since that day. On this afternoon he had seen her steal out, and had cautiously followed her. It was not difficult on the soft grass, doubly soft with the penetrating moisture like a bank of green mossy sponge, to steal along without making any noise; and the trees were thick enough to permit a wayfarer to steal from trunk to trunk un-discovered, especially when those who were watched were so altogether unafraid. Thus Drumcarro, his tall shadow mingled with the trees, had come close to the log on which they sat, and had heard everything. No scruple about listen-ing moved his mind. With his hand grasping a young birch, as if it were a staff, he stood grim and fierce, and heard the lovers talk. His eyes gave forth a gleam that might have set the wood on fire when he heard of the post-chaise, and the young tree shivered in his hand. Jeanie was at the end of her powers. She put up her hand to her face to cover it from the storm of her lover's kisses. His passion carried her away. She murmured, *No, no!* still, but it was in gasps, with her failing breath.

'You'll come, you're coming – tonight – and hurrah for love and freedom,' cried Lord John.

At this moment he was seized from behind by the collar of his coat – a furious hand full of force and passion caught him with sudden, wild, overpowering strength – Lord John was young but not strong, his slim form writhed in the sudden grasp. There was a moment's struggle yet scarcely a struggle as Drumcarro assumed his choking hold. And then something dashed through the air with the speed and the force of a thunderbolt – flung by sheer force of passion. A gasping cry, and an answering roar of the linn as if to swallow down in its caves the object tossed and spinning down – a flash far below. And in another moment all was still.

What was it that had been done? Jeanie looking up to see her father's transformed and impassioned face, and finding herself free, had fled in the first impulse of terror. And on the log where the lovers had been seated, the old man sat down quivering with the strain he had made, wiping the drops of moisture from his forehead. He was old, but not beyond the strength of his prime; the unaccustomed effort had brought out the muscles on his hands, the veins upon his forehead. The blood was purple in his face. His capacious chest and shoulders heaved; he put his hand, the hand that had done it, to his mouth, to blow upon it, to relieve the strain. He sat down to recover his breath.

How still everything was! – as it is after a rock has fallen, after a tree has been torn up, the silence arching over the void before any whispering voice gets up to say where is it. The waters and the sighing branches both seemed still – with horror. And Drumcarro blew upon his hand which he had strained, and wiped the perspiration from his face.

After a while he rose, still panting a little, his feet sinking into the spongy grass, and went homeward. He met nobody on the way, but seeing Duncan in the yard where he was attending to the cattle, beckoned to him with his hand. Duncan came at the master's call, but not too quickly. 'Ye were wanting me, sir,' he said. 'No – I was not wanting you.' 'Ye cried upon me, maister.' 'No, I did not cry upon you – is it me that knows best or you? Go back to your beasts.' Drumcarro stood for a moment and watched the man turn back reluctantly, then he raised his voice: 'Hey, Duncan – go down yonder,' pointing his thumb over his shoulder – 'and see if anything's happened. I'm thinking there's a man – tummult over the linn.' Having said this the master went quietly to his own room and shut himself up there.

CHAPTER XLIV

Duncan gave a great start at this strange intimation – 'Tummult over the linn!' That was not an accident to be spoken of in such an easy way. He put down the noisy pail he had been carrying in his hand. 'Lord!' he said to himself; but he was a man slow to move. Nevertheless after two or three goings back upon himself, and thoughts that 'the maister must have gone gyte', Duncan set himself slowly in motion. 'A man tummult o'er the linn – that's a very sarious thing,' he said to himself. It was a great ease to his mind to see Glendochart coming down the path from the hill, and he stopped until they met. 'Sir,' said Duncan, 'have ye noticed anything strange about the maister?' 'Strange about Drumcarro? I have noticed nothing beyond the ordinary,' was the reply. 'What has he been doing, Duncan?' 'He has been doing naething, Glendochart. But he just came upon me when I was doing my wark in the yaird. And I says, "Are ye wanting me, maister?" And he says, "Me wanting ye? No, I'm no wanting ye." But afore I can get back to my wark I hear him again, "Duncan!" "What is it, maister?" says I. And says he, "I think there's a man tummult over the linn. Ye can go and see." '

'Tumbled over the linn!' cried Glendochart. 'Good Lord! and did ye go and see?'

'I'm on the road now,' said Duncan, 'a man cannot do everything at once.'

'The man may be drowned,' cried Glendochart turning round quickly. 'Run on, Duncan, for the Lord's sake. I'm not so surefooted as the like of you, but I'll follow ye by the road, as fast as I can. A man over the linn! Dear me, but that may be a very serious matter.'

'I was just saying that,' said Duncan plunging down upon the spongy grass. He slid and stumbled, tearing long strips of moss off the roots of the trees with which he came in heavy contact, striding over the fallen trunk which had played so great a part in the drama of that afternoon. There were signs of footsteps there, and Duncan slid on the slippery and trampled soil, and came down on his back, but got up again at once and took no notice. This accident perhaps delayed him for a moment, and the need of pre-caution as he descended after such a warning. At all events Glendochart coming quickly by the roundabout of the road arrived only a moment after, and found Duncan dragging out upon the bank an inanimate figure which had appar-ently been lying half in half out of the stream. Duncan's ruddy face had grown suddenly pale. 'Lord keep us! Do ye think he's dead, sir?'

'I hope not, Duncan,' said Glendochart kneeling down by the body; but after a few minutes, both men scared and horror-stricken bending over the figure on the grass, 'God preserve us,' he said, 'I fear it is so. Do you know who it is?' – then a hoarse exclamation burst from them both: 'It's the young lord from the lodge on the hill – it's Lord John! God preserve us!' cried Glendochart again. 'What can this mean? But a man that's drowned may be brought to life again,' he added. 'How are we to get him home?'

Duncan, roused by the wonderful event which had thus come in a moment into the tranquil ordinary of his life, rushed along the road calling with a roar for help, which it was not easy to find in that lonely place. However, there proved to be one or two people within call – the game-keeper who lived at the lodge inhabited by Lord John, and the blacksmith from the clachan, who had been carrying some implement home to a distant mountain farm. They managed to tie some branches roughly together to make a sort of litter and thus carried the dead man to Drumcarro, which was the nearest house. The sound of the men's feet and Glendochart's call at the door, brought out every member of the household except the laird who remained in his room with the door closed and took no notice. Glendo-chart and the gamekeeper had both some rude notion of what to do, and they acted upon their knowledge, roughly it is true but with all the care they were capable of. Duncan on horseback, and less apt to spare his horse's legs than his own, thundered off for a doctor. But the doctor was not easily found, and long before his arrival the rough methods of restoring animation had all been given up. Lord John lay on the mistress's unoccupied bed to which he had been carried, like a marble image, with all the lines that a careless

life had made showing still upon the whiteness of death,
the darkness under the eyes, the curves about the mouth.
His wet clothes which had been cut from the limbs to which
they clung, lay in a muddy heap smoking before the now
blazing fire. They had piled blankets over him and done
everything they knew to restore the vital heat – but without
avail.

'How did it happen?' the doctor said – but this no man
could tell. They gathered together in an excited yet awe-
stricken group to consult together, to put their different
guesses together, to collect what indications might be
found. Duncan thought that the collar of the coat was torn
as if someone had grasped the poor young man 'by the
scruff of the neck'. There was a bruise on his throat which
might have come from the hand thus inserted – but his face
had several bruises upon it from contact with the rocks,
and his clothes had been so torn and cut up that they
afforded little assistance in solving the problem. To send
for some member of his family, and to make the sheriff
aware of all the circumstances was evidently the only thing
to do.

Jeanie had fled without a word, without a look behind
her, when her lover's arm loosened from her waist, and her
father's hoarse and angry voice broke in upon the scene.
No thought of any tragedy to follow was in Jeanie's mind.
She had never seen her father take any violent action; his
voice, his frowns had always been enough, there had been
no need for more. She thought of an angry altercation, a
command to come near the house no more, so far as she
thought at all. But she scarcely did think at all. She fled,
afraid of her lover, afraid of her father, not sure, to tell the
truth, which she feared most – glad that the situation was
over, that she could escape by any means. She sped up the
wooded bank, out of the shadow of the bare trees about the
linn, like a frightened bird – flying, never looking behind.
Pausing a moment to take breath before she ran round to
the house door, she was thankful to hear no voices in anger,
but all fallen into quiet again, nothing but the sound of
the linn, louder she thought for the cessation of other
sounds; and concluding rapidly in her mind that her father
had reserved his anger for her, and let Lord John go – not
a just, but according even to Jeanie's small experience, a

sufficiently usual turn of affairs – she went on more quietly to the house, that no hasty rush on her part, or self-disclosure of agitation, might call forth Mary's remarks or the questions of Marg'ret. But the agitation of the moment was not over for Jeanie. She saw someone approaching the door from the road as she came within sight. It was too late to escape, and she instinctively put up her hand to smooth her hair, and drew a few long breaths to overcome altogether the panting of her heart, that the stranger, whoever he might be, might not perceive how disturbed she was. But when Jeanie had taken a step or two further, her heart suddenly made a leap again, which swept all her precautions away. 'Oh!' she cried, with almost a shriek of agitated recognition, 'now of all moments in the world! That he should come now—'

'I am afraid,' he said, 'I cannot think that cry means any pleasure to see me, though I am so glad to be here.'

Oh, to think he should be able to speak, to use common words, as if they had parted yesterday – as if nothing had happened since then!

'Oh, Captain Gordon,' she said, breathless; then added, not knowing what she said, 'You've been long away.'

'Not with my will. I've nothing but my profession, and I was forced to do all I could in that. If it had been my will—'

'Oh,' said Jeanie, 'I cannot talk; my sister is here, you will want to see her – but for me, I cannot talk. I am – not well. I am in – grief and trouble. Don't stop me now, but let me go.'

He stood aside, without a word, his hat in his hand, looking at her wistfully. His look dwelt in her mind as she hurried upstairs. It was not like the look of Lord John – the look that terrified, yet excited her. He had come for her, for her and no one else; but he would not stop her, nor trouble her. It was of her he thought, not of himself. Jeanie's heart came back like an unbent bow. This was the man that she loved. She fled from him, not daring to meet his eyes – but she felt as if some chain had been broken, some bond cut. Lord John! What was Lord John? She was afraid of him no more.

Major Gordon did not know what to do. He lingered a little, unable with the excitement in his veins of having seen

his love again, to knock presently at the door and ask for
the lady of Glendochart. After a time the sound of a heavy
step caught his ear, and the loud interchange of words
between Duncan and his master. Then the heavy steps came
on towards the door. It must be Drumcarro himself who
was coming. Major Gordon drew aside to await the coming
of Jeanie's father. Mr Douglas came round the side of the
house, with his hands thrust deep into his pockets and his
shoulders up to his ears. He was staring before him with a
fierce intensity, the kind of look which sees nothing.
Gordon made a step forward, and said some common
words of greeting, at which Drumcarro lifted his puckered
eyelids for a moment, said 'Eh?' with a sort of hasty interro-
gation, and then turning his back, went in and closed the
door behind him, leaving the stranger astonished. What did
it mean? Gordon thought at first a studied slight to him,
but farther thought showed him that this was absurd, and
with some surprise he set it down to its true cause – some
secret trouble in Drumcarro's mind, some thought which
absorbed him. After a moment's astonished pause he
turned back upon the road, concluding that whatever his
excitement was, by and by it would die away. He walked,
perhaps a mile, occupied by his own thoughts, by Jeanie,
who was more lovely, he thought, than ever, and by eager
speculations what she would say to him; whether perhaps
after all she might not be glad to see him when she had got
over the first surprise; whether it was merely haste and that
great surprise that made her turn away. Gordon had occupation enough for his thoughts had he walked on the whole
afternoon; but presently he turned back, remembering what
Jeanie had said, that her sister was at Drumcarro, and glad
to think of so reasonable a way of getting admittance. He
had just come up to the house again, and was approaching
the door, when he was met by the group of men coming
down from their hopeless attempts to resuscitate the dead.
He was much surprised to see this party come to the door,
and stepped out of the way with vexation and annoyance,
feeling himself and his urgent affairs thrust as it were into a
secondary place by this evidence of something going on at
Drumcarro. The men, of whom at first he recognized none,
were exchanging grave observations, shaking their heads,
with puzzled and troubled looks. At the sight of him there

was a visible stir among them. One of them stepped forward hastily, and caught him by the arm. 'Who are you?
And what are you doing here!'

'Glendochart, you seem to have forgotten me. I am Lewis
Gordon, whom you were once very kind to.'

'Captain Gordon!'

'Major, at your service; I got my step in India.'

'Gordon!' repeated Glendochart. It was natural enough
that every new idea should chime in with the terrible one
that now possessed his mind. He remembered in a moment
who the young man was, and all that had been said and
thought of him. He had been Jeanie's lover. It seemed to
throw a sudden gleam of illumination on the mystery. 'Step
in, step in here, and come you with me,' he said, laying his
hand on the doctor's arm. With a slight summons at the
door, but without waiting for any reply he led them into his
father-in-law's room. Drumcarro was sitting at his usual
table with his head leant upon his hands. He turned half
round but did not otherwise change his attitude, as these
newcomers entered, darkening the little room.

'I beg your pardon, Drumcarro,' said Glendochart, 'but
it's urgent. I must ask this gentleman a few questions in the
presence of some responsible person – Captain Gordon,
or Major if ye are Major, answer me for the love of God.
Ye may do a hasty act, but you're not one that will shrink
from the consequence, or I'm far mistaken in you. When
did you come here?'

'This is a strange way of receiving a friend,' said Gordon
with surprise. 'I came here about half an hour ago.'

'But you did not come in?'

'No – I saw – one of the family.'

'And then? Still you did not come in?'

'No, I walked back a mile or so to wait – and then hearing
that you were here, and Mrs Campbell – I returned.'

'Why did you not come in?'

'I really cannot tell you the reason,' said Gordon, a little
irritated. 'There was no particular reason.'

Said the doctor, perceiving where Glendochart's questions were tending: 'It will be far better for you to tell the
truth. It might be an accident, but denial will do no good.'

'Am I accused of anything?' said the stranger in great
surprise.

'A stranger about the place at such a time is very sus-picious,' said the doctor shaking his head. 'The best thing you could do, Glendochart, would be to detain him till the sheriff comes.'

Drumcarro raised his head from his supporting hands. His habitual redness had changed to grey. He spoke with some difficulty moistening his lips. He said, 'Whatever ye may be thinking of, this lad's tale's true. I saw him come, and I saw him go. If there's any man to blame it's not him.'

They all turned round to where Mr Douglas sat; the after-noon light was by this time waning, and they had difficulty in seeing each others' faces. Drumcarro after a moment resumed again. The want of light and the deep sound of his voice, and the scene from which they had just come, made a strange horror of impression upon the men. He asked, 'Is he dead?'

'Yes, he is dead. And that minds me it was you that gave the alarm. What did you see, Drumcarro?'

'I heard a rumbling as if the linn rose up to meet him, like hell in the Scriptures to meet that king – and a thud here and there upon the rocks – that's all I heard.'

Nobody made any reply. No suspicion of the truth had occurred to any mind, but something in the voice, and the language not familiar to the man gave a vague sensation of solemnity and horror. The darkness seemed to deepen round them, while this pause lasted. And Drumcarro said no more, but leant his head upon his hands again. The silence was broken by the doctor who said in a subdued tone: 'We'll better leave Mr Douglas quiet. It is a time of trouble – and the shock of this accident on the top of all the rest—'

Drumcarro did not move, but he said between the two hands that supported his head, 'That man has nothing to do with it. I saw him come. And now ye can let him go his way.'

They filed out of the room in silence with a vague dread upon them all. Something strange was in the air. The dark figure by the table never moved, his head on his hands, his big frame looking colossal in the quivering twilight. The fire in the grate behind burned up suddenly and threw a little flickering flame into the gloom revealing still more that motionless shadow. 'It has been too much for the old gentleman,' the doctor said in a whisper, as he closed the door.

'He's none so old,' said Glendochart with a little irritation, mindful of the fact that he was not himself much younger, and feeling the thrill of nervous discomfort and alarm.

'I doubt if he'll live to be much older. I do not like the looks of him,' the doctor said.

It seemed to have become almost night when they came out into the hall. The blacksmith and the gamekeeper and Duncan were standing in a group about the door, the sky full of a twilight clearness behind them, and one star in it, like a messenger sent out to see what dreadful thing had happened. The air blew cold through the house from the open door, and Mary crying and nervous stood at the door of the parlour behind. The mother's death which she had taken with such calm propriety was in the course of nature, but the dreadful suddenness of this, the mystery about it affected even her calm nerves. A second death in the house, and the Duke's son! It comforted Mary when Gordon left the group of men whose meaning he did not even yet comprehend and joined her, to hear the whole story, and yet not all.

The other men still stood consulting when the Glendochart carriage arrived at the door; everybody had forgotten that the departure of the visitors had been settled for that afternoon. Glendochart seized the opportunity at once. 'I will send the ladies away, this is no place for them with all these new troubles,' he said, 'and the express to the Duke can travel so far with them.' It had occurred to Glendochart that the less that could be made of Lord John's intercourse with the family at Drumcarro the better. He had not discouraged it himself; had it come to a marriage which would have allied himself and his children so much more nearly with the ducal family, it would have been no bad thing; but now that there could be no marriage it was clear that it was neither for Jeanie's advantage, nor indeed for his own, to give any more publicity than was necessary to the cause of Lord John's presence here. And thus it was that Jeanie without knowing why, yet willing enough to be carried off at such a crisis even to Glendochart, found herself within half an hour seated by her sister's side driving off, with the darkness of night behind her, and the clearness in the west reflected in her startled eyes. Jeanie neither knew nor suspected that anything dreadful had happened; but to escape her father's eye and his questions after the discovery he had made was relief enough to make her forget the bustle and haste with which she was carried away. They were to give Major Gordon 'a lift as far as the town', but Jeanie did not know this until he followed her into the carriage, and then her heart so jumped up and choked her with its beating that she thought no more of Drumcarro's wrath, nor of the deliverance from Lord John which she knew her father's interposition would make final.

And so Drumcarro House was once more, but with a deepened mystery and terror, left with its dead. Mr Douglas did not leave his room all the evening. The call to supper made first by Marg'ret, then by Glendochart knocking cautiously at his door, produced only the response of a growl from within. No light was visible from under the door. No sound was heard in the room. To all appearance he remained without moving or even lighting his candle, until late at night his heavy step was heard going upstairs to bed.

Without a light, that was the strangest thing of all to the keen but silent observers. There could be nothing on the master's mind or he could never have sat all the evening through, knowing what it was that lay in his wife's room upstairs, without a light. They could not imagine indeed how in any circumstances Drumcarro, an old man, could have had anything to do with the death of Lord John, a young one, nor what reason there could be for seeking his death, yet an uneasy fear was in the air, and there was no one else who could be thought of. But that circumstance cleared him. Without a light no man could sit who had been instrumental in causing a man's death, while that man lay dead in the same house. Glendochart, whose mind was disturbed by many miserable surmises, was comforted by this thought, though almost unconsciously to himself.

And nobody knew what thoughts were going on in the dark in that closed room. They were not thoughts specially about Lord John. They were the bewildering circling of a mind suddenly driven into tragic self-consciousness, about the entire chapter of his life now perhaps about to be brought to an end. The sudden pang of the moment, his clutch upon his victim (his hand hurt him still from the strain, and still now and then he raised it to his mouth, to blow his hot breath upon it), the whirl of that figure through the air, came back at intervals like a picture placed before his eyes. But between those intervals there surged up all manner of things. Old scenes far off and gone, incidents that had taken place in the jungle and swamp, cries and sounds of the lash, and pistol shots all long over and forgotten. One face, not white like Lord John's, but grey in its blackness, like ashes, came and wavered in the darkness before him more distinct than the others. No ghost, he had no faith in ghosts, nothing outside of him. Something within from which even if they should hang him he knew he would not get free. Lord John – he thought very little of Lord John! And yet his hand hurt him, the picture would come back, and the scene re-enact itself before his eyes. Sometimes he dozed with his head in his hands. The chief thing was that he should not be disturbed, that no one should come in to question him, to interfere with his liberty, that night at least. That he should be quiet that night if nevermore.

CHAPTER XLV

The Duke arrived with his eldest son as soon as post-horses could bring him. He had been in the north, not very far away, so that the interval, though it represented much more difficult travelling than the journey from one end to the other of Great Britain nowadays, was not very long. Lord John had been a trouble to his family all his life. He had followed none of the traditions of prudence and good sense which had made his race what they were. The scrapes in which he had been were innumerable, and all his family were aware that nothing but embarrassment and trouble was likely to come to them from his hand. Sometimes this state of affairs may exist without any breach of the bonds of natural affection; but perhaps when a man is a duke and accustomed to have many things bow to his will, the things and persons that cannot be made to do so become more obnoxious to him than to a common man. No doubt a shock of natural distress convulsed the father's mind at the first news of what had happened, but after a while there came, horrible as it seems to say it, a certain relief into the august mind of the Duke. At least here was an end of it; there could be no more to follow, no new disgraces or inconveniences to be encountered. Scarcely a year had come or gone for many years past without some fresh development of John's powers of mischief, now, poor fellow! all was over; he could do no more harm, make no more demands on a revenue which was not able to bear such claims, endanger no more a name which indeed had borne a great deal in its day without much permanent disadvantage. On the whole there was thus something to set against the terrible shock of a son's sudden death by accident. A few questions thrown into the air as it were, a general demand upon somebody for information burst from the Duke during that long drive. 'Where is this linn, do you know? What could he have wanted there? On the land of that old ruffian, Drumcarro? And what did he want there?' But to the last question at least no one could make any reply. Even to speak of Drumcarro's lovely daughter as an inducement would have been a jarring note when the poor fellow was so recently dead. And the Duke could answer his own question well enough; any petty intrigue would be reason enough for John, the worse the better. His only fear was that some dark story of seduction and revenge might unfold itself when he got there.

It was Glendochart who received his chief when he reached his journey's end, and told him the little there was to tell. It was supposed that Lord John had somehow missed his footing when at the head of the linn. Someone had heard the sound of a fall, and the body had been found below at the foot of the waterfall. This was all that could be discovered at the end of two or three days which had elapsed. The Duke saw, with a natural pang, his dead son laid out upon the mistress's bed, and then he visited the scene of the tragedy. He inspected everything with a clouded countenance, asking brief, sharp questions from time to time. To Glendochart he seemed suspicious of violence and foul play, a suspicion which was lurking in Glendochart's own mind, with strange surmises which he could not put into words, but which his mind was on the alert to find some clue to. This, however, was scarcely the Duke's frame of mind. After he had visited the spot where the body had been found, and looked up the foaming fall of the linn, and heard everything that could be told him, he put a sudden question which dismayed Glendochart. 'Have you any suspicions?' he said. 'Has there been any suggestion – of violence?'

'The idea has no doubt been suggested,' Mr Campbell replied, 'but I can find nothing to give it any countenance. There were signs as of stamping of feet at one place near the fallen tree, but the man who found the body accounted for that as having slipped and fallen there.'

'It has been suggested then?' said the Duke, with another cloud coming over his face. 'Glendochart, I may speak freely to you that would bring no discredit on the name. Was there any story, any reason for his staying here?'

Glendochart felt his countenance redden, though it was of that well-worn colour which shows little. He suddenly realized, with a sense of relief unspeakable, what it would have been had Lord John lived and thriven, to have intimated to the chief that his son had married Drumcarro's daughter. Glendochart had himself been flattered by the idea. He saw the reverse of the medal now.

'I know of none,' he said, 'my Lord Duke. He was more at this house than at any other house round about.'

'And there was no story – no lass, disappointed perhaps – or angry father? You know what I mean, Glendochart. One of my own name, and not so far from me in blood, I know that I can trust you. You know, too – what my poor boy was.'

'I understand what your Grace means,' said Glendochart. 'I have heard of nothing of the kind.'

'And who was it that heard the fall?'

'It was my father-in-law, Drumcarro himself. He was taking his usual walk. I don't imagine he ever thought it was so serious. He called to the man in the byre to see to it, that he thought he had heard a fall.'

'I will see Drumcarro, I suppose.'

'If it will satisfy your Grace better – but he is an old man, and much shaken with his wife's death which took place only a fortnight ago.'

The Duke gave his clansman what looked like a suspicious glance. But he only said, 'It will be better not to disturb him. I would have thought,' he added, 'that old Drumcarro was tough enough to stand the loss of his wife or anything else.'

'We sometimes do men injustice,' said Glendochart, a little stiffly; 'and the shock of having another death, so to speak, in the house, has had a great effect upon his mind – or I should perhaps say his nerves.'

'Well, well, I will not disturb him,' said the Duke. He said no more until they reached again the head of the linn. Then he stood for a few minutes amid the spray, looking down as he had looked up the boiling foam of waters. The cloud had gone off his face. He turned to his son, by his side, who had said little all this time. 'I think we may satisfy ourselves that it was pure accident,' he said.

'I think so,' said the taintless heir, with a solemn nod of his head.

The Duke stood there for a moment more, and then he took off his hat and said, 'Thank God.' With all his heart, Glendochart echoed the surprising words. He thought that he indeed had cause for thankfulness – that he should never have had the occasion to approach his chief with news of an alliance that would have been so little to his mind. That Jeanie's name should have been kept out of the matter altogether, and no questions put to the old man whose nerves had been so strangely shaken. He had indeed cause for thankfulness; but the Duke, why? Glendochart came to understand later why the Duke should have been glad that no new scandal was to be associated with the end of his son's life.

And so Lord John was carried in great state to the burial place of his fathers, and was rehabilitated with his family, and mourned, by his mother and sisters, like other men. And whatever the tragedy was that attended his last hours it was buried with him, and never told to man. There is no coroner in Scotland; and in those remote regions, and at that period, the Duke's satisfaction that his son's death was caused by accident was enough for all.

Drumcarro scarcely left his room while that solemn visitor was in the house. He appeared after, a singularly changed and broken man, and fell into something like the habits of his old life. There had been no secret in his strange retirement, but there was no doubt left in the mind of any who surrounded him, that something had happened which was not in the peaceful routine of existence. They formed their own impressions at their leisure; it was nothing to the laird what they thought. He had deceived no man, neither had he confided in any man. When Glendochart left the house, taking charge of the mournful conveyance which carried Lord John home, life at Drumcarro would, in any circumstances, have been a wonderfully changed and shrunken life. It was the first time that the diminished family had been left alone since the death of the mistress. At the family table, once so well surrounded, Drumcarro sat down with his one remaining son, and the vast expanse of the wide tablecloth vacant save in that corner. It did not occur to anyone to substitute a smaller table for the long-stretching board where there had been room for all. Jamie, who was never seen without a book, compensated himself for the silence and anxiety of this tête-à-tête by reading furtively, while his father sat with his shoulders up to his ears, and his eyes, almost lost in his shaggy eyebrows, glaring out now and then with a glance of gloomy fire. It was rarely that he addressed the boy; and the boy escaped from him into his book. The mother was gone, Jeanie was gone, everyone who could make that empty board a little brighter. The father and son swallowed their meal side by side, but did not prolong it any more than was possible. The sight of them affected Merran's nerves when she served them, though that ruddy lass might well have been supposed to have no such things in her possession. 'There's the laird just glowering frae him as if he saw something no canny, and Jamie with his book. And me that minds all that fine family!' cried Merran. 'Ye must just go ben yourself, Marg'ret, for I canna do it.' And there is no doubt that it was a piteous sight.

Jeanie, on the other hand, recovered her spirit and her ease of mind with singular rapidity under the sheltering roof of Glendochart. She was not told of Lord John's death for some time, and never of the rapidity with which it followed her interrupted interview. She was very much moved and excited when she heard of his death, wondering with natural self-importance whether her resistance of his suit had anything to do with the breaking down of his health. It half relieved, half disappointed Jeanie to discover after that his death was caused by an accident and not by love. But indeed she had then only a limited space to give in her thoughts to that lover of the past. He of the present had the command of the situation. Determined as she had been not to understand Gordon, the effect of a few days in the same house with him had been marvellous, and when the fairy regions of youthful experience began once more to open before Jeanie, she forgot that she had cause of griev-ance against the companion who opened to her that magic gate. All tragic possibilities disappeared from the path of the girl who had no longer any distracting struggle, but whose desires and inclinations all went with her fate. Her father made no objection to her marriage. 'Let him take her if he wants her. I have no need of her here,' Drumcarro said. Jeanie indeed, instead of brightening the house and soothing the fever in him, excited and disturbed her father: 'I want no lass about the house, now her mother that kept her a little in order is gone.' She was married eventually at Glendochart, the laird making no appearance even. He was said to be ill, and his illness had taken the curious form, a form not unprecedented but much against nature, of strong dislike to certain persons. He could not abide the sight of Jeanie. 'Let her do what she will, but let her no more come near me. Let him take her if he likes, I'm well pleased to be quit of her.' When Jeanie came attended by her lover to bid her father goodbye, the laird almost drove her away. He got up from his chair supporting himself upon its arms, his eyes burning like coals of fire, his now gaunt and worn figure trembling with passion. 'Go away to the parlour,' he said, 'and get your tea, or whatever you've come for. I want none of you here.'

'Father, I just came to bid you goodbye,' said Jeanie.

'Go 'way to the parlour. I suffer nobody to disturb me here. Go 'way to Marg'ret. Ye'll get what ye want from her, and plenty of petting, no doubt. Go 'way to the parlour. Marg'ret! Get them what they want and let them go.'

'Oh, father,' cried Jeanie weeping, 'it's not for anything we've come, but just for kindness – to say goodbye.'

He was a strange figure standing up between his chair and table supporting himself by his hands, stooping forward, grown old all at once, his hair and beard long and ragged in aspect, a nervous tremor in his limbs. Could that be the hale and vigorous man who scarcely seemed beyond middle age? Jeanie assayed to say something more, but the words were checked on her lips by his threatening looks.

'Goodbye,' he said. 'Consider it's done and all your duty paid, and begone from my sight, for I cannot bide to see you.' He added a moment after with a painful effort over himself, 'I'm an old man, and not well in my health. Marg'ret! Ye mind me of many a thing I woud fain forget. Goodbye, and for the love of God go away, and let me see you no more.'

'Is he always like that?' Jeanie asked, clinging to Marg'ret in the parlour, where that faithful adherent prepared tea for the visitors.

'Like what?' asked Marg'ret with a determination to keep up appearances in the presence of the strange gentleman with whom she had no associations. 'The maister's not very well. He has never been in his richt health since your mother died. That made an awfu' change in the house, as might have been expected. Such a quiet woman as she was, never making any steer; it's just bye ordinar' how she's missed.'

'Is it that? Is that all?' cried Jeanie.

'And what else would it be?' asked Marg'ret with a look that could not be gainsaid.

Marg'ret did not know any more than the rest what had happened. Lord John had died of an accident, he had fallen over the linn, and from the Duke himself to the last of the name all were satisfied that it was so. And in Drumcarro House there was not a word said to alter this view. But many heavy thoughts had arisen there of which nothing was said.

Drumcarro did what is also not uncommon in such circumstances, he justified those who explained his strange conduct by illness, and fell ill. The doctor said it was a malady of long standing which had thus developed itself as it was certain to have done sooner or later. He recommended that a doctor should be sent for from Glasgow, who had become very famous for his practice in this particular malady. It is doubtful whether Glendochart, who had the conduct of the business, knew anything about Dr Dewar. At all events, if he did, it did not prevent him from sending for that special practitioner. The result was a curious scene in the chamber of the patient, who raised himself from his bed to stare at the newcomer, and after contemplating him for some time in doubtful silence between wrath and astonishment, suddenly burst out into a great guffaw of laughter. 'This was all that was wanted,' he said. But he allowed Anne's husband to come in, to examine him, to prescribe, and with a grim humour saw him wave away the offered fee. 'Na, it's all in the family,' said the grim patient with a sudden sense of the grotesque illumining the darkness of his sick room. He was not insensible to this irony of circumstance, and he made no resistance. It was the only thing that produced a gleam of amusement in these latter days.

CHAPTER XLVI

In his newly developed condition as an invalid Mr Douglas had gone on for more than a year. During this time he had taken no active steps of any kind. Jamie had been left to read as he pleased, every book he could lay his hands upon, from Mr Pyper's old-fashioned theology to D'Urfey's *Pills to Purge Melancholy*, a curious if not very extensive range. Only these two, the dreary boy with his books, and his possible writership hung suspended so to speak, no one taking any steps to put him forth like his brothers into active life, and the grim invalid, who rarely left his room, or indeed his bed, remained in Drumcarro. Such an emptiness occurs not unfrequently in the story of a house once full and echoing with the superabundant energies of a large family, but the father and son afforded a deeper emblem of dullness and desolation than almost any mother and daughter could have done. They were more separated from life. The laird cared nothing for his neighbours, rich or poor, whether they prospered or were in want. Marg'ret, who had the control of everything, kept indeed a liberal hand, and preserved the reputation of Drumcarro as a house from which no poor body was ever sent away without a handful of meal at least, if not more substantial charity. But her master took no interest in the vicissitudes of the clachan or to hear of either prosperity or need. She still attempted to carry him the news of the district for the relief of her own mind if not for the advantage of his, for to arrange his room in silence or bring his meals without a word was an effort quite beyond Marg'ret's powers.

'The Rosscraig Carmichaels have come to the end of their tether,' she told him one morning. 'There's a muckle roup proclaimed for next month of a' the farm things. I might maybe send Duncan to see what's going, if there's anything very cheap, and folks say the farm itself.'

'What's that you're saying, woman?'

'I'm just telling you, laird. The Rosscraig family is clean ruined – no much wonder if ye think of a' the ongoings

they've had. There's to be a roup, and the estate itsel' by
private contract, or if nae offer comes—'

'Get out of my room, woman,' cried Drumcarro. 'Bring
me my clothes. You steek everything away as if a gentleman
was to be bound for ever in his bed. I'm going to get up.'

'Sir!' cried Marg'ret in dismay. 'It's as much as your life
is worth!'

'My life!' he said with a snarl of angry impatience, but
as he struggled up in his bed Drumcarro caught sight of
himself, a weird figure, lean as an old eagle, with long hair
and ragged beard, and no doubt the spring of sudden
energy with which he raised himself was felt through all his
rusty joints so long unaccustomed to movement. He kept
up, sitting erect, but he uttered a groan of impatience as he
did so. 'I'm not my own master,' he said – 'a woman's
enough to daunton me that once never knew what difficulty
was. Stop your infernal dusting and cleaning, and listen to
me. Where's that lass in London living now? Or is she aye
there? Or has she taken up with some man to waste her
siller like the rest of her kind?'

'Sir, are ye meaning your daughter Kirsteen?' said
Marg'ret, with dignity.

'Who should I be meaning? Ye can write her a letter and
send it by the post. Tell her there's need of her. Her father's
wanting her, and at once. Do ye hear? There's no time to
trouble about a frank. Just send it by the post.'

'If ye were not in such an awfu' hurry,' said Marg'ret,
'there might maybe be an occasion.'

'I can wait for none of your occasions – there's little feeling in her if she cannot pay for one letter – from her father.
Tell her I'm wanting her, and just as fast as horses' legs
can carry her she's to come.'

'Maister,' cried Marg'ret with great seriousness drawing
close to the bed, 'if ye're feeling the end sa near and wanting
your bairns about ye, will I no send for the minister? It's
right he should be here.'

Drumcarro sat taller and taller in his bed, and let forth a
string of epithets enough to make a woman's blood run
cold. 'Ye old bletherin' doited witch!' he said, 'ye old ——'

His eloquence had not failed him, and Marg'ret, though a
brave woman, who had taken these objurgations composedly enough on previous occasions, was altogether over-

whelmed by the torrent of fiery words, and the red fero-
cious light in the eyes of the skeleton form in the bed. She
put up her hands to her ears and fled. 'I'll do your will – I'll
do your will,' she cried. A letter was not a very easy piece
of work to Marg'ret, but so great was the impression made
upon her mind that she fulfilled the laird's commission at
once. She wrote as follows in the perturbation of her
mind—

> Your fader has either taken leave of his senses,
> or he's fey, or thinks his later end is nigh. But any way
> I'm bid to summons you, Kirsteen, just this moment
> without delay. I'm to tell ye there's need of you – that
> your fader's wanting ye. Ye will just exerceese your
> own judgment, for he's in his ordinar', neither better
> nor warse. But he's took a passion of wanting ye and
> will not bide for an occasion nor a private hand as may
> be whiles heard of – nor yet a frank that could be got
> with a little trouble. So ye will have this letter to pay
> for, and ye'll come no doubt if ye think it's reasonable
> – but I cannot say that I do for my part.
> P.S. – The Carmichaels of Rosscraig are just
> ruined with feasting and wasting, and their place is to
> be sold and everything roupit – a sair downcome for
> their name.

Kirsteen obeyed this letter with a speed beyond anything
which was thought possible in the north. She drove to the
door, no longer finding it necessary to conceal her coming.
Marg'ret's postscript, written from the mere instinct of telling what news there was to tell, had already thrown some
light to her upon this hasty summons. Drumcarro lay
propped up by pillows waiting for her, with something of
the old deep red upon his worn face. He was wonderfully
changed, but the red light in his eyes and the passion which
had always blazed or smouldered in the man, ready to burst
out at any touch, even when covered with the inevitable
repressions of modern life, was more apparent than ever.
His greetings were few. 'Eh, so that's you?' he said. 'Ye've
come fast.'
'I was told that you wanted me, father.'
'And maybe thought I was dying and there was no time
to lose.' He noticed that Kirsteen held in her hand a news-

paper, at which he glanced with something like contempt. A London newspaper was no small prize to people so far off from all sources of information. But such things were at present contemptible to Drumcarro in presence of the overwhelming preoccupation in his own mind.

'I see,' he said, 'ye've brought a paper to the old man; but I have other things in my head. When ye were here before ye made an offer. It was none of my seeking. It was little likely I should think of a lass like you having siller at her command – which is just another sign that everything in this country is turned upside down.'

Kirsteen made no reply, but waited for the further revelation of his news.

'Well,' he said with a slight appearance of embarrassment and a wave of his hand. 'Here's just an opportunity. I have not the means of my own self. I would just have to sit and girn in this corner, where a severe Providence has thrown me and see it go – to another of those damned Campbells, little doubt of that.'

'What is it?' she said. Kirsteen had lifted her head too, like a horse scenting the battle from afar. She had not her father's hatred of his hereditary foes, but there was a fine strain of tradition in Kirsteen's veins.

'It's just Rosscraig – our own land, that's been in the Douglas name for hundreds of years, and out of it since the attainder. I would be ready to depart in peace if I had it back.'

Kirsteen's eyes flashed in response. 'If it's possible – but they will want a great sum for Rosscraig.'

'Possible!' he cried with furious impatience. 'How dare ye beguile me with your offer, if it's only to think of what's possible? I can do that mysel'. Does one of your name condescend to a dirty trade, and serve women that are not fit to tie a Douglas's shoe, and then come to me and talk of what's possible? If that's all, give up your mantua-making and your trading that's a disgrace to your family, and come back and look after the house, which will set you better. Possible!' he cried, the fire flying from his eyes and the foam from his mouth. 'For what do you demean yourself – and me to permit it – if it's no possible?' He came to the end on a high note, with the sharpness of indignant passion in his voice.

Kirsteen had followed every word with a kindling countenance, with responsive flame in her eyes. 'Ye speak
justly,' she said, with a little heaving of her breast. 'For
them to whom it's natural a little may suffice. But I that do
it against nature am bound to a different end.' She paused
a little, thinking; then raised her head. 'It shall be possible,'
she said.

He held out his thin and trembling fingers, which were
like eagle's claws.

'Your hand upon it,' he cried. The hot clutch made
Kirsteen start and shiver. He dropped her hand with an
excited laugh. 'That's the first bargain,' he said, 'was ever
made between father and child to the father's advantage – at
least, in this house. And a lass – and all my fine lads that I
sent out for honour and for gain!' He leant back on his
pillows with feeble sobs of sound, the penalty of his excitement. 'Not for me,' he said, 'not for me, though I would
be the first – but for the auld name, that was once so
great.'

Kirsteen unfolded the paper tremulously, with tears
lingering on her eyelashes. 'Father, if ye will look here—'

'Go away with your news and your follies,' he said
roughly. 'You think much of your London town and your
great world, as ye call it, but I think more of my forbears'
name and the lands they had, and to bring to confusion a
false race. Kirsteen,' he put out his hand again, and drew
her close to the bedside, clutching her arm. 'I'll tell you a
thing I've told nobody. It was me that did it. I just took and
threw him down the linn. Me an old man, him a young
one, and as false as hell. He was like the serpent at that
bairn's lug; and I just took him by the scruff of the neck.
My hand's never got the better of it,' he added, thrusting
her away suddenly, and looking at his right hand, blowing
upon it as if to remove the stiffness of the strain.

'Father!' Kirsteen cried, with subdued horror. 'What
was it you did?'

He chuckled with sounds of laughter that seemed to dis-
locate his throat. 'I took him by the scruff of the neck – I
never thought I could have had the strength. It was just
pawsion. The Douglases have that in them; they're wild
when they're roused. I took him – by the scruff of the neck.
He never made a struggle. I know nothing more about it,

if he was living or dead.'

'Ye killed him!' cried Kirsteen with horror. 'Oh, it's no possible!'

'There ye are with your possibles again. It's just very possible when a man's blood's up. He's not the first,' he said, in a low tone, turning his face to the wall. He lay muttering there for some time words of which Kirsteen could only hear 'the scruff of the neck', 'no struggle', 'it's hurt my hand, though', till in the recoil from his excitement Drumcarro fell fast asleep and remembered no more.

He had, however, it appeared, to pay for this excitement and the tremendous tension in which he had been held from the time he summoned Kirsteen to the moment of her arrival. His frame, already so weakened, had not been able to bear it. He was seized during the night by a paralytic attack, from which he never rallied, though he lived for a week or more as in a living tomb. All that had been so important to Drumcarro died off from him, and left him struggling in that dumb insensibility, living yet dead. Kirsteen was never able to let him know that, herself as eager for the elevation of the family as he could be, she had at once opened negotiations for the purchase of Rosscraig, though on terms that would cripple her for years. Sometimes his eyes would glare upon her wildly out of the half-dead face asking questions to which his deadened senses could understand no answer. She at last withdrew from the room altogether, finding that he was more calm in her absence. And all the time there lay on the table beside his bed, rejected first in his excitement, all-impotent to reach him now, the copy of the *Gazette* brought by Kirsteen from London, in which appeared the announcement that Colonel Alexander Douglas, of the 100th Native Regiment, for distinguished valour and long services, had received the honours of a K.C.B. Had it come but a day sooner, the exultation of Drumcarro might have killed him (which would have been so good a thing), but at least would have given him such sensations of glory and gratified pride as would have crowned his life. But he never had this supreme delight.

When Sir Alexander Douglas, K.C.B., came home, he found his patrimony largely increased, but both father and mother and all his belongings swept away. The one whom he found it hardest to approve was Kirsteen. Anne with her well-to-do doctor had nothing now to forgive that her brother could see; Mary had fulfilled every duty of woman. Young Jeanie with her young soldier had all the prestige of beauty and youth, and the fact that her husband was a rising man and sure of promotion to make her acceptable to her family. But a London mantua-maker, 'sewing', so he put it to himself, 'for her bread!' It startled him a little to find that he owed Rosscraig to that mantua-maker, but he never got over the shock of hearing what and where she was. 'Any sort of a man, if he had been a chimney-sweep, would have been better,' Sir Alexander said. And Kirsteen was a rare and not very welcome visitor in the house she had redeemed. They all deplored the miserable way of life she had chosen, and that she had no man. For the credit of human nature, it must be said that the young Gordons, succoured and established by Kirsteen's bounty, were on her side, and stood by her loyally; but even Jeanie wavered in her convictions in respect to the mantua-making. She too would have been thankful to drown the recollection of the establishment in Chapel Street in the name of a man. 'If she had but a good man of her own!' But Major Gordon, soon Colonel and eventually General, as fortunate a man as in piping times of peace a soldier could hope to be, put down this suggestion with a vehemence which nobody could understand. He was the only one to whom Kirsteen's secret had ever been revealed.

In the times which are not ancient history, which some of us still remember, which were our high days of youth, as far down as in the fifties of this present century, there lived in one of the most imposing houses, in one of the prince-liest squares of Edinburgh, a lady, who was an old lady, yet still as may be said in the prime of life. Her eye was not dim nor her natural force abated; her beautiful head of hair was still red, her eyes still full of fire. She drove the finest horses in the town, and gave dinners in which judges delighted and where the best talkers were glad to come. Her hospitality was almost boundless, her large house running over with hordes of nephews and nieces, her advice, which meant her help, continually demanded from one side or other of a large and widely extended family. No one could be more cheerful, more full of interest in all that went on.

Her figure had expanded a little like her fortune, but she was the best dressed woman in Edinburgh, always clothed in rich dark-coloured silks and satins, with lace which a queen might have envied. Upon the table by her bedhead there stood a silver casket, without which she never moved; but the story, of which the records were there enshrined, sometimes appeared to this lady like a beautiful dream of the past, of which she was not always sure that it had ever been.

She was of the Drumcarro family in Argyllshire, who it is well known are the elder branch of all; and she was well known not only as the stand-by of her family, but as the friend of the poor and struggling everywhere. It was a common question in many circles where she was known as to how it was that she had never gotten a man – a question more than usually mysterious, seeing how well off she was, and that she must have been very good looking in her time. She was Miss Douglas of Moray Place, sister to a number of distinguished Indian officers, and to one bookworm and antiquary well known to a certain class of learned readers, but whom Edinburgh lightly jeered at as blind Jimmy Douglas or the Moudiewart – not that he was blind indeed but only abstracted in much learning. Miss Douglas was the elder sister also of the beautiful Lady Gordon whose husband was in command at Edinburgh Castle. There was no one better thought of. And so far as anybody ever knew, most people had entirely forgotten that in past times, not to disgrace her family, her name had appeared on a neat plate in conjunction with the name of Miss Jean Brown, Court Dressmaker and Mantua-Maker, as

MISS KIRSTEEN.

Endnotes

Abbreviations:

Coghill *The Autobiography and Letters of Mrs M.O.W. Oliphant*, edited by Mrs Harry Coghill, with an introduction by Q.D. Leavis. A reprint of the 1899 edition, Blackwood, Edinburgh (Leicester: Leicester University Press, 1974)

Jay *The Autobiography of Margaret Oliphant*, edited by Elizabeth Jay (Ontario: Broadview, 2002)

ODNB Oxford Dictionary of National Biography

OED Oxford English Dictionary

All biblical quotations are taken from the Authorised King James Version.

Ch. I.

Kirsteen: Scots form of 'Christine' or 'Christina' or 'Christian'. Oliphant's *Kirsteen* is based both on a true story told to Oliphant by her friend Christina ('Chrissie') Rogerson and on the character of Rogerson herself. The 1891 one-volume edition of her novel on which this edition is based is 'inscribed with love and respect' to Rogerson who had been compromised during a public divorce case involving Sir Charles Dilke when it was alleged that Rogerson had been Dilke's mistress. In her autobiography Oliphant says of her friend that 'She has had all manner of adventures and gone through all sorts of phases. She is the most varied, complex, bewildering character—', (Jay, p.188).

Douglas: The Gaelic origin – *Dubhglas* means 'dark water/river' – the name derives from the family seat in Lanarkshire which has land around Douglas Water. Oliphant gives the name of Douglas to an Argyllshire family although this name or clan is not common to the area. Parish records of the period 1750-1850 for the whole of Argyll show that there were only 204 births and baptisms registered under the name of Douglas and only 7 of these were in the parish of Inveraray. By contrast there were 10,640 births and baptisms registered under the name of Campbell (see: www.scotlandspeople.gov.uk/search/oprbirth/index.aspx). Presumably, as Oliphant did not wish her heroine to be a Campbell, she simply used the name of another famous Scottish family, but there are various other explanations:

- The Duke of Douglas was a political associate of John Campbell, 5th Duke of Argyll (1723-1806). Their close link was further demonstrated when Douglas Castle in Lanarkshire, begun in 1757, was modelled on Inverarary Castle, the seat of the Campbell clan. The landmarks of Glen Douglas situated between Loch Lomond and Loch Long, and Douglas Bridge and Douglas Water are also indications of a long-standing close relationship between the two families. Early maps of the area such as *Pont's Maps of Scotland* 1580-1590 and *Roy's Military Survey of Scotland* 1747-1755 show that Glen Douglas was already known as such from around mid 16th century. (See Pont. 17). Inter-marrying between the aristocracy of the Campbell and Douglas families also occurred – e.g: Archibald, 1st Marquis of Argyll, married a Margaret Douglas [c.1648] See: Sir Herbert Maxwell, *A History of the House of Douglas: From earliest times to the legislative union of England and Scotland*. (London: Freemantle &. Co, 1902), vol 2. Oliphant may have been aware of this inter-family relationship as she reviewed a number of pieces of writing connected to Argyll – e.g. she reviewed Lord Archibald Campbell, *Records of Argyll: Legends, Traditions, and Recollection of Argyllshire Highlanders* (Edinburgh and London: Blackwood and Sons, 1884), in 'Scotch Local History', *Blackwood's Edinburgh Magazine*, 139 (March 1886), pp.375-97.

• There was a William Douglas, an Edinburgh man settled in Inveraray since 1731, who was a mason to the 3rd Duke of Argyll (1682-1761). This Douglas was reputed in a letter of 1745 from Archibald Campbell of Stonefield, Sheriff Depute and Chamberlain of Argyll Castle, to Lord Milton to be 'soe peevish and unsettled a Creature that I am very unwilling to have any thing to do with him.' Ian G. Lindsay and Mary Cosh, *Inveraray and the Dukes of Argyll*. (Edinburgh: Edinburgh University Press, 1973), pp.72-3. There is an obvious parallel here with Oliphant's character Drumcarro.

• In her *Royal Edinburgh: Her Saints, Kings, Prophets and Poets*, published by Macmillan in 1893, Oliphant documents 'that preponderating influence of the Douglas family in Scotland which vexed the entire reign of the second James, and prompted two of the most violent and tragic deeds which stain the character of the historical figure of the 'Black Douglas'. (Oliphant, 1893, p.91) Oliphant's character indeed echoes the temper and character of the historical figure of the 'Black Douglas' (1286- 1330), who was also fictionalised by Walter Scott in *Castle Dangerous* (1831).

porter's chair: a chair with an arched hood, originally placed in a hallway for a porter or doorkeeper to sit in. OED

Drumcarro: There is no Drumcarro in Argyllshire. Oliphant probably appropriated the name from the settlement of Drumcarro near Cupar, Fife. It was common practice in Scotland to call a farmer or laird by the name of their farm or estate.

de jure: by right according to law.

de facto: in fact, whether by right or not.

she was the only one in the house that was not afraid of 'the maister':

Oliphant's Marg'ret Brown is her own version of the faithful Scots servant who is very often 'caustically critical' of the affairs of the family they serve. See: Oliphant, 'Scottish National Character', *Blackwood's Edinburgh Magazine*, 87 (June 1860), pp.715-31. Marg'ret Brown is recognisably a precursor to Stevenson's Kirsty Elliot in *Weir of Hermiston* (1896) who also rises beyond her class status as a house servant and becomes the mainstay of the family she serves: 'Such an unequal intimacy has never been uncommon in Scotland, where the clan spirit survives; where the servant tends to spend her life in the same service, a helpmeet at first, then a tyrant, and at last a pensioner—' (*Weir of Hermiston*, ch. 5. III). A discussion of the unique position of the Scottish domestic servant can also be found in Dean Ramsay, *Reminiscences of Scottish Life and Character* (T.N. Foulis: Edinburgh and London, 1858).

He turned him right: from an anonymous ballad sung by the character 'Elspeth o' the Craigburnfoot' in Scott's *The Antiquary* (1816), ch.40. Scott's version of this verse is:

He turned him right and round again
Said, scorn na at my mither
Light loves I may get many a ane
But minnie ne'er ane ither

plaiden: twilled woollen cloth woven in distinctive patterns to denote Scottish clan association.

wires: fine knitting needles often used for socks.

clew: a ball of yarn or thread.

cambric: lightweight cotton or cloth originally made in Cambrai, France, in the late sixteenth-century.

Quentin Durward: In Walter Scott's *Quentin Durward* (1823) the hero leaves his poor family home in Scotland to become an archer with the Scottish Guard of Louis XI of France. Hence young men who go out to make their fortunes in foreign military adventures.

the brief peace that lasted only so long as Napoleon was at Elba: Britain resumed war on France in 1803 and its leader Napoleon Bonaparte, who was crowned Emperor of the French in 1804. In March 1814 Paris fell to Britain and its allies and Napoleon was exiled on the Mediterranean island of Elba.

France had been at war almost incessantly for over twenty years. She had lost millions of men and her colonies, her overseas trade was strangled, and she was virtually bankrupt. Although she was treated far more leniently by the Allies than she had a right to expect, the restored Bourbons could scarcely cope with the problems they inherited. Popular disenchantment soon set in. Napoleon, seizing his chance, escaped from exile [in March 1815] and overthrew the monarchy. His reckless gamble lasted but a hundred days, culminating in Waterloo and his second abdication. (David Gates, *The Oxford Companion to Military History*. ed. by Richard Holmes (Oxford: Oxford University Press, 2001), p.626.)

the last campaign in the Peninsula: The 'Peninsular War' (1808-1814), which formed part of the Napoleonic wars, was fought between France and the allied forces of Spain, Portugal and Britain for the control of the Iberian peninsula.

Ch. II.

when the existence of the window-tax curtailed the light: this tax introduced in England in 1696, was first levied in Scotland on 'Houses, Windows or Lights' in 1746 and was repealed in 1851.

cellaret: a cabinet for holding wine bottles usually made from mahogany or rosewood.

Eelen: Scots form of 'Helen'.

a made dish: a special culinary creation conceived and executed by the cook of the household.

the King himself: George III (1760-1820).

he took from it one bottle of champagne: When her brother was made bankrupt, Oliphant offered a home and paid for the education of her nephew, Frank. After attending the Royal Indian Engineering College in Windsor, Frank, like Robbie in *Kirsteen*, set sail for service in India. Oliphant records her desire to make Frank's departure a special and happy occasion saying:

> I was trying to make Frank's last summer at home pleasant, and wanted him within the limits of our small ways to see and do everything possible. There is an incident in one of my own books, in "Kirsteen," which is a sort of illustration of my feeling about him. It was not my own invention, but told me by C.R. [Christina Rogerson] as the family custom in the large, poor, proud family which formed the model through her stories of the family in that book,— the bottle of champagne solemnly produced and drunk by the whole party on the night before the boy went away. I wanted Frank to have his bottle of champagne—(Jay, p.194).

portmanteaux: 'cases' – from the French *porter* ('to carry') and *manteau* ('cloak'). Usually denoted a large leather case hinged in the middle, opening into two compartments.

poorhouse: a house of refuge for poor and destitute people. Oliphant was perhaps unaware that it was not until 1845 that the poorhouse system was firmly established in Scotland following the Poor Law (Scotland) Act. Up until this time it was the responsibility of each individual parish to give alms to destitute people and, to prevent idle beggars, only certain categories of paupers were eligible for relief. See: R. Cage, *The Scottish Poor Law* 1745-1845 *(Edinburgh: Scottish Academic Press, 1981)*.

toddy-ladle: a ladle used to serve toddies – i.e. hot drinks often made from mixing whisky, water, lemon and honey.

it's all sounding brass and a tinkling cymbal to me: 'Though I speak with the tongues of men and of angels, and have not charity, I am become as sounding brass, or a tinkling cymbal—' (I Corinthians 13:1).

There's a time to feast and a time to refrain from feasting: sentiments deriving from Ecclesiastes 3:1-8 which elaborates on the sentiment 'To everything there is a season, and a time to every purpose under heaven—'.

It's like the strange woman that you're warned against in Scripture: possible allusion to Jezebel in Revelations 2: 20-24.

Ch. III.

was as the laws of the Medes and the Persians to these two: An unalterable law. 'Now, O King, establish the decree, and sign the writing, so that it be not changed, according to the law of the Medes and Persians, which does not alter—' (Daniel 6:8).

In those days people were not afraid of strong tea mixed with a great deal of green to modify the strong black Congou: Chinese black tea – Congou – was the preferred tea in Scotland.

> Whereas the East India Tea Company imported from China mostly the basic kind of black tea, called Bohea, Continental companies imported more of the better-quality Congou. They were encouraged in this policy by the attempt in the 1760s of the London wholesalers to defeat the smugglers by bidding down the price of legitimate Bohea at the East India Company auctions. Since the Continental companies were now unable to make a profit by selling Bohea, they dedicated themselves to the importation of Congou, of which the East India Company imported relatively little and which it sold at a relatively high price. The smugglers bought Congou in Europe, and by their efforts turned it into one of the most popular teas in Britain. In Scotland, where there were fewer restrictions on smuggling than in England, virtually all the tea that was drunk was Congou. (A. Barr, *Drink: A Social History* (London: Bantam Press, 1996), p.207).

It was not until the 1850s that tea production in India was established and, as Barr notes, 'the Government did its best to persuade consumers to convert from the China tea that they had been drinking for over a century to the new type of tea that was now being produced in its Indian colony.' (Barr, 1996, p.221) Green tea remains green because it is unfermented.

> But this made it possible for doubts about the healthfulness of green tea to be fostered. [...] In fact, green tea was generally not taken strong in Britain; but for many people, the expectation that

green tea would affect their nerves was sufficient for it to do so.'
(Barr, pp.221-2)

where are they to see men in their own position?: Kirsteen and her
sisters are grand-daughters of a 'fallen' Highland laird who, having supported the failed Jacobite rising of 1745, lost his lands and ancestral
family home. The Douglas sisters, therefore, live a poor and frugal existence but are nonetheless very aware of their lineage. Their lack of a
substantial dowry or landed status makes them a poor attraction for
suitors from their own class.

Ch. IV.

the gig: a light two-wheeled one horse carriage. OED

Inveralton: An invented placename on the model of Inveraray or Inverness. The Gaelic 'Inbhir' refers to the mouth of a river. In the novel it
stands in for Inveraray.

P. and O.: abbreviation for the 'Peninsula and Oriental Steam Naviga-
tion Company', a British shipping line founded early in the nineteenth
century.

the Peninsula: see note, p.390.

an iron to the fire: Before the invention of the electric iron in 1882,
irons were heated in direct heat from the fire or stove.

worsted: here, knitting wool.

pays du tendre: Fr. the domain of love, from the _pays du Tendre_, 'the
name of an imaginary country whose topography symbolized aspects of
love, probably devised by Madeleine de Scudéry (1607-1701) within
her literary circle and described by her in her novel _Clélie_ (1654-1660)'.
OED

fingering: wool or yarn used chiefly in knitting stockings. OED

beef-tea: a hot beverage made by boiling lean strips of beef thought to
benefit the constitution.

morocco: soft leather made from goatskin originating in Morocco,
north-west Africa.

runic: the Runic alphabet was used in north Europe before the adoption of the Latin alphabet. Symbols from the alphabet acquired a semi-
magical significance.

Ch. V.

the disastrous conclusion of the Forty-Five: The failed Jacobite Rising
of 1745 attempted to restore a multi-kingdom monarchy to the exiled
Prince Charles Edward Stuart (grandson of the deposed James II and
VII) which in turn would restore Episcopacy. The effort was supported
by Highland and Lowland Scots as well as Irish Jacobites, but following
the triumphant 'taking' of Edinburgh and a march down through

England as far as Derby, the army turned back as the promised support from English Jacobites never materialised. The army was pursued by King George II's son, the Duke of Cumberland, who savagely destroyed the Jacobite army at Battle of Culloden, fought on Drummossie moor near Inverness, in April 1746. The brutal and unnecessary government repression after Culloden had an apocalyptic effect on Highland culture, as its clan system, its music and language were all but dismantled. The Douglas clan were not Jacobite sympathisers (see Introduction, p.7) and thus Oliphant's positioning of them as supporters is not historically accurate. Oliphant was not particularly interested in the politics of the Jacobite cause but was moved by poignant stories connected to its history – as seen, for example, in a letter of 1865 to John Blackwood where she speaks of her visit to St Germain:

> I was so impressed by it that perhaps I will send you a little paper about it one day or another. I am not in the least disposed to be a Jacobite, and Dundee and Culloden and Professor Aytoun sort of thing have very little effect on me. But there was something wonderfully touching in that long silent terrace and the thought of all the weary days and miserable hopes and disappointments that must have passed without any record – that and the other terrace at Frascati where poor Prince Charlie lies. I was sad enough myself at both places, and no one, being Scotch, could be unmoved by their associations. (Coghill, p.197)

one of the great houses of the district which had passed into alien hands: In reprisals after the '45 Scottish lairds who were known to have supported the Jacobite cause forfeited their estates.

> The Vesting Act of June 1747 authorised the Scottish Court of Exchequer, as guardian of Crown revenues in Scotland, to survey and value these estates, appoint factors, determine claims and pay creditors. In all, fifty-three estates were surveyed, and forty-one of these – the forfeited estates – were taken over by the Barons of Exchequer. Most forfeited estates were sold by public auction to pay creditors, but thirteen estates were inalienably annexed to the Crown by the Annexing Act of March 1752.' (A.J. Youngson, *After the Forty-Five: The Economic Impact on the Scottish Highlands* (Edinburgh: Edinburgh University Press, 1973), p.27)

many accessories of which people in the next generation spoke darkly: a reference to the part played by Scots in the subjugation of the native people in British colonies to enhance both the financial economy of Scotland and their own private fortunes. Opportunities for Scots opened up after the 1707 Union created new trading initiatives. As Douglas Hamilton explains:

> The first acquisition of new land in the Caribbean after the Act of Union, in St Kitts in 1713, offered the chance for Scots to obtain land in the new British empire. The second decade of the eighteenth century saw two Scotsmen as governors of St Kitts, Walter Douglas and Walter Hamilton. During this period, Scots

were prominent among the grantees receiving estates of over 100 acres. The beleaguered refugees from Darien swelled Scottish numbers in Jamaica, and formed the basis of a considerable Argyll community of the western part of the island.' (Douglas J Hamilton, *Scotland, the Caribbean and the Atlantic world 1750-1820* (Manchester: Manchester University Press, 2005), p.4)

Oliphant's Drumcarro however does not appear to have greatly profited financially during his time in Jamaica and only manages to accrue enough money to buy back a very small portion of the family's former estate.

It was more easy in those days to set young men out in the world than it is now: a possible ironic reflection by Oliphant on her own situation. Widowed after only seven years of marriage, she was left to bring up her sons, Cyril ('Tiddy') and Francis Romano ('Cecco'), on her own. Neither of her sons excelled in any sphere of study and, after causing her much anxiety, both died at a young age. In her Autobiography Oliphant alludes to the 'passion and agony of motherhood' while dealing with her sons who were full of 'the folly of youth' which achieved them little. She also complains of the apparent lack of help to further her sons' careers: 'No one indeed, however good they may have been in professions towards me ever did anything to help me in that chief care of my life' (Jay, pp.199- 202).

seven sons is not a quiverful: An ironic allusion to Psalm 127, 3-5: 'Lo, children are an heritage of the LORD: and the fruit of the womb is his reward. As arrows are in the hand of a mighty man; so are children of the youth. Happy is the man that hath his quiver full of them—'. But that number of children is no blessing to a poor man.

tares among the wheat: 'Tares' or weeds found among good grain. 'But while men slept, his enemy came and sowed tares among the wheat, and went his way—' (Matthew 13:25).

without even the meagre education then considered necessary for women: The supposedly egalitarian nature of Scottish education is a myth in regard to the educational opportunities for young women of the early nineteenth century. The domestic sphere and its associated arts was held as the proper place for women and aspirations towards formal learning were viewed as highly unsuitable and suspect. Around the 1860s campaigns for the admission of women to universities began and in 1892 women were finally legally admitted to university courses. See: Lindy Moore, 'Education and Learning', in *Gender in Scottish History since 1770*. ed. by Lynn Abrams et al. (Edinburgh: Edinburgh University Press, 2006), pp.111-39.

The Gentle Shepherd: a pastoral drama by Allan Ramsay published in 1725 – a favourite of Oliphant's judging by her references to it in various places in her writing.

Barbour's *Bruce*: An epic poem by John Barbour (c.1320-1395) which focuses on the period of the Wars of Independence (1286-1332).

Ch. VI.

the Castle: Oliphant does not actually call this castle Inveraray – the seat of the chief of Clan Campbell – but she is obviously suggesting it as Inveralton suggests the town.

the white frocks ought to be obtained somehow: the white frock, or dress, high-waisted, plain and made from muslin, was the usual mode of dress for a young single woman of this period denoting, as it did, her virginal state. This style was influenced by the Classical Revival of the French Revolution. See: S. S Maxwell and R. Hutchison, *Scottish Costume 1550-1850* (London: Black, 1958).

Lord John: The Duke and his family are fictions and Oliphant is careful not to refer to the Duke as the Duke of Argyll nor to duplicate the actual members of the Campbell family who supplied the clan chiefs and Dukes of Argyll. Yet some similarities are teasing. The actual John Douglas Edward Henry Campbell (1777-1847), was brother to the 6th Duke of Argyll (1806-1841). Whereas Oliphant has her Lord John killed as a young man, John Campbell later became the 7th Duke of Argyll at the age of 62 when the 6th Duke died without legitimate issue. Lord John's character, however, is in some ways similar to that of the 6th Duke. See note below.

Lord Thomas: Lady Charlotte Campbell had a son, Thomas, from her first marriage to her kinsman John Campbell of Shawfield in 1796, but here again no specific reference is intended.

the auld slave-driver: As outlined in ch.V n. 3, Drumcarro was part of the infamous part played by Scots in the history of the Caribbean. William Wilberforce spearheaded the abolition of the slave trade within the British Empire which was achieved in 1807. Slavery in British colonies was finally abolished in 1833 and the indentured slavery (or 'apprenticeship system') in the West Indies in 1839.

It was a Glasgow paper: The leading Glasgow newspaper of the day was *The Glasgow Herald* (founded in 1789 as *The Glasgow Advertiser)*, but the reference could be to *The Glasgow Chronicle* (founded 1810) or *The Glasgow Courier* (founded 1791). Drumcarro is reading in late 1814; a few months later after Waterloo, newspapers in Scotland gained great momentum. See: R.M.W. Cowan, *The Newspaper in Scotland: A Study of Its First Expansion* (Glasgow: Outram and Co, 1946).

for marrying and giving in marriage: Matthew 24:38.

the Duke: Oliphant's Duke, the presiding chief of Clan Campbell is fictional. George William Campbell, was the actual 6th Duke of Argyll from 1806-1839. In 1810 the Duke married Lady Caroline Paget (née Villiers) but had no legitimate offspring. The character of this Duke was apparently highly questionable – he is recorded as being 'a dissolute playboy who left a string of debts and illegitimate children'. See: www.inveraray-castle.com

saucy jade: a term of reprobation applied to a woman. *OED*

Ch. VII.

It was not like the grand gowns: This is one of the many instances in
the novel where Oliphant reveals her own interest in fashion. In 1878
Macmillan & Co published her study *Dress* which gives a simple history
of dress from the ancient Greeks to her own Victorian era. In her autobiography Oliphant states how this interest was inherited from her
mother who made all her clothes which were 'finer and more beautifully
worked than ever child's clothes were'. (Jay, p.20)

sitting with our seams: sitting doing simple plain sewing.

The Duke: See note, p.396.

my cairngorms: precious stones of smoky quartz, usually yellow or
wine-coloured originally mined from the Cairngorm mountains of
Scotland, commonly set in jewellery in the nineteenth century.

Ch. VIII.

Vedi Napoli e poi morire: 'see Naples and die'. Sometimes attributed to
Goethe who visited Italy in 1786-1788. It is used here in its commonly
understood sense that Naples is so beautiful that it must be seen before
one dies.

earth could not have etc: 'Earth has not anything to show more fair'
is the opening line of Wordsworth's sonnet 'Upon Westminster Bridge'
(1802).

nécessaire: *Fr.* '— a small case, sometimes ornamental, for personal
articles such as pencils, scissors, tweezers, cosmetics, etc.' *OED.* Here,
for the dressmaker's necessities.

gore: a triangular piece of cloth used in dressmaking to vary the width
of a skirt or bodice.

the fashions of 1814: see above note for: 'it was not like the grand
gowns'

**The Duke in his own country was scarcely second to the far off and
unknown king:** Oliphant refers here to the influence of the clan system
whereby the members of a clan owed their allegiance to their own chief-
tain before any member of the ruling monarchy. When the Scottish
court moved south under the rule of James VI and I the influence of the
crown also moved further away from the Scottish people who viewed
subsequent monarchs as indeed 'far off and unknown' as Oliphant
describes. The ruling monarch at this time was George III who reigned
from 1760 and who was afflicted with what was suggested as porphyria
– a maddening and debilitating metabolic disorder – which may have
disrupted his reign as early as 1765. Personal rule was given to his son,
George, the Prince Regent in 1811. George III died blind, deaf and
insane at Windsor Castle in 1820.

the old and peevish majesty: Charlotte of Mecklenburg-Strelitz (1744-
1818), married George III in 1761 with whom she had fifteen children.

Despite his mental illness Queen Charlotte remained loyal to her husband and he appeared to be devoted to her. Oliphant's version of her as peevish is perhaps a little unjust but her grand-daughter Charlotte did find Windsor dull and restrictive when she was an adolescent.

window tax: see note, p.390.

before the attainder: refers to the outlawing of the clans who had supported the Jacobite Risings as noted in end-note for ch. V, on p.393.

new-fangled Dukes: a reference to the titles given out as a reward for those who had supported the government's repression of Jacobite loyalists.

gig: see note, p.392.

Ch. IX.

the play: the theatre. The reference here is to the Scottish Calvinist view of the theatre as being from the devil, hence depraved. See: Sorensen, 'Varieties of Public Performance: Folk Songs, Ballads, Popular Drama and Sermons', in *The Edinburgh History of Scottish Literature*. ed. by Brown et al. (Edinburgh: Edinburgh University Press, 2007), vol 2, pp.133-42; *A History of Scottish Theatre*, ed. by Bill Findlay. (Edinburgh: Polygon, 1998); Donald Campbell, *Playing for Scotland: A History of the Scottish Stage, 1715-1965* (Edinburgh: Mercat Press, 1996).

Lady Chatty: Lady Charlotte Campbell (1775-1861), was the youngest daughter of the 5th Duke of Argyll. Oliphant has recast this historical figure and fictionalised her as the daughter of the 6th Duke. Lady Chatty possesses some of the characteristics of the real woman. The actual Lady Charlotte married her kinsman Col. John Campbell of Shawfield in 1796 with whom she had a large family. Some nine years after his death she made a second marriage to the Rev. Edward Bury in 1818. She became a Lady-in-Waiting to the Princess of Wales, and achieved some fame as a novelist. She was reputed a great beauty. See: George Douglas, Eighth Duke of Argyll, *Autobiography and Memoirs*, ed. by the Dowager Duchess of Argyll (London: John Murray, 1906).

Pericles: The Athenian general and statesman (c.495-429 BC).

Charlemagne: (c.747-814) 'Charles the Great', King of the Franks and Christian Emperor of the West, he did much to define the shape and character of medieval Europe.

vees-a-vis: this takes its meaning in this context from the literal translation of the French phrase *vis-à-vis* meaning 'face to face', i.e. a couple of dancers facing each other.

quadrille: a dance performed by four couples in a square formation.

St. James's: St. James's Palace, Pall Mall, London: the official and, until Victoria's accession in 1837, the actual residence of the Sovereign.

Ch. X.

Loch Fyne: the longest and deepest of Scotland's sea lochs and famed for its fine fish.

a muslin mutch: a close fitting cap worn by married Scotswomen or elderly women.

Parthian arrow: an arrow discharged at an enemy while retreating or pretending to retreat, as was the custom of the Parthians. Hence a parting shot.

pelisse: a woman's long coat, with armhole slits and a shoulder cape or hood, often made of a rich fabric; (later also) a long fitted coat of a similar style. *OED*. Here a functional rather than a decorative item.

King's Ellwand: The Scottish name for the three bright stars which make up the constellation of Orion, or 'the belt of Orion' as Oliphant footnotes it.

Ch. XI.

when to speak and when to refrain from speaking: possibly a version of Ecclesiastes 3:7 'a time to keep silence, and a time to speak—'.

Ch. XII.

fairings: gifts, traditionally bought at a fair.

escape of Boney: Reference to the escape in 1815 of Napoleon Bonaparte, from his exile on the island of Elba. See note, p.389.

the law of Laban: Allusion to Genesis 29:15-26. Laban had two daughters, Leah (the elder) and Rachel. Their kinsman, Jacob, falls in love with Rachel but is tricked by Laban into sleeping with Leah. As justification for this Jacob states that it is not the custom in his country to give the younger before the elder.

Ch. XIII.

auld Robin Gray: Ballad by Lady Anne Barnard née Lindsay (1750-1825), which tells of a young Scottish girl, Jenny, who, believing her lover lost at sea, and facing the illnesses of her parents and the theft of their cow, marries an elderly man, Robin Gray. When her lover returns shortly after the wedding she sorrowfully remains loyal to her husband.

Ch. XIV.

[No endnotes required]

Ch. XV.

dans son droit: *Fr.* Here: within her rights.

The only art ... is to die—: from Oliver Goldsmith's novel *The Vicar of Wakefield*, 1766, ch.24. Unlike Kirsteen, Olivia in the novel has been seduced and abandoned by her lover.

Ch. XVI.

clachan: *Gaelic* small village, hamlet.

Hell's Glen: Gaelic name is *Gleann Beag* ('small glen'). The English name possibly derives either from the steep gradient of the narrow road which runs through the glen or from the practice of burning charcoal in the area. The glen, which is four miles long, runs from Loch Fyne to the head of Loch Goil.

camlet: fabric made from wool or goat's hair.

the only art her guilt to cover: see note above.

Glen Croe: *Gaelic* 'Glen of the Cattle'.

gillie: *Gaelic* a male attendant on a Highland chief.

for there were as yet no tourists (nay, no magician to send them thither) in those days: a reference to the 'Wizard of the North' i.e. Walter Scott, whose writing is held to have initiated Scotland's tourism culture. 'For Scotland, although Ossian, Burns [...] and later Barrie (Angus) are not without significance, Scott's influence stood head and shoulders above any other writer's, an influence that was to work both in general terms for the country as a whole and for particular locations.' (Alistair Durie, '"Scotland is Scott-Land": Scott and the Development of Tourism' in Muray Pittock, *The Reception of Sir Walter Scott in Europe* (London: Continuum, 2006), p.321).

the Lord, their God the Duke as Robbie Burns calls him: Burns visited Inveraray in 1787 as part of his West Highland tour. His visit coincided with a large house party hosted by the 5th Duke of Argyll. The inn-keeper was apparently too busy with the Duke's guests to have time for other travellers and in disgust Burns wrote the lines of 'On Incivility shown him at Inverarary' on one of the inn windows:

Whoe'er he be that sojourns here
I pity much his case—
Unless he come to wait upon
The Lord *their* God, "His Grace ..."

Ye'll be a Campbell: Campbell is the clan of the Duke of Argyll. As old parish registers record, there were 10,640 births and baptisms under this name in Argyll over the period 1750-1850. See: www.scotlandspeople.gov.uk

Loch Long: *Gaelic* loch of the ship. Contary to popular belief the word 'Long' here is not an English one.

Mrs MacFarlane: Parish records for the district of Argyll indicate that there were 464 births and baptisms registered under this name for the period 1750-1850.

Ch. XVII.

who could speak little English: Oliphant's use of language varieties in *Kirsteen* is eclectic. As a native of the area around Loch Fyne Kirsteen would have been a Gaelic speaker and understood the Highland maid but here there is no suggestion of this. It is true that Kirsteen does not speak as much Scots as other characters do but, for the most part, she speaks in Standard English – thus following the usual practice of total shift from Gaelic to English when the occasion requires. The first half of the maid's sentence: 'Your hair will be like the red gold and your skin like the white milk' reflects Gaelic speech patterning but this is the nearest Oliphant comes to any recognition of the language. The maid also uses the expression 'chappit acht' – a Scots expression which a Highland girl would not have used. As Oliphant's own linguistic heritage lay in Fife she herself was not a Gaelic speaker and there is little suggestion elsewhere in her writing that she was actively interested in Gaelic. Drumcarro speaks Scots – again as a native of Argyll he would be more likely to speak either Gaelic or English. Oliphant's representation of Marg'ret Brown and Mrs Douglas as Scots speakers is however accurate since they are from the lowlands of Scotland. But strict accuracy was probably not Oliphant's aim and she has Kirsteen speak English both for the marketing purpose of widening the novel's readership and also to move away from the type of Scots of utilised by kailyard writers which Oliphant disliked. (Introduction, p.4)

Glasco: this pronunciation is probably influenced by the Gaelic 'Glaschu'.

mantua-makers: Originally a person who made mantuas – a loose gown fashionable especially in late 17th and early 18th centuries. Later, more generally: a dressmaker. The name originates from the city of Mantua in northern Italy. *OED*

Eelensburgh: Scots pronunciation of 'Helensburgh'. Founded in 1776 by Sir James Colquhoun of Luss who named it after his wife Lady Helen Sutherland.

St John's wort: One of the common names of the plant *Hypericum perforatum* which reputedly flowers around St. John's Day, 24th June. St. John's wort, sometimes called 'devil's flight' or 'grace of God', was believed to have magical properties to ward off evil spirits.

Grass of Parnassus: *Parnassia palustris*, a plant with a single white green-veined flower.

dark undress tartan: a version of a clan tartan used for informal occasions.

Whistlefield: Gaelic: *tigh-na-fead*: the house of the whistle. The name is derived from the practice of a whistle being blown at a tavern to announce the arrival of mail coach or to summon a ferry.

Rosneath: this small peninsula in Argyllshire was very familiar territory to Oliphant. She spent some happy summer holidays there in the hamlet of Clynder in the rented villa 'Willowburn'. The first of these came shortly after her return home from Rome following her husband's death and Rosneath was to live up to its name as a place of sanctuary particularly as it was here that Oliphant first met the Rev. Robert Story while researching her biography on Irving. Story was enchanted with the young widow and proposed to her. Oliphant refused him but they remained good friends throughout her life. Oliphant also gifted a stained glass window, in memory of her daughter Maggie, to the Rosneath Parish church (now St Modan's Rosneath Parish Church), as well as a reredos which remains a valued artefact of the church. Her novel *The Minister's Wife* (1869) is set in this area.

Ch. XVIII.

the crackling of thorns under a pot: 'For as the crackling of thorns under a pot, so is the laughter of the fool: this also is vanity—' (Ecclesiastes 7:6).

the dreadful town in which every evil thing flourished: This negative portrayal of Glasgow in the early nineteenth-century is possibly influenced by Oliphant's own childhood memories of her family's move to Glasgow from Lasswade when she was six years old so that her father could take up a post at the Royal Bank. Dorothy Wordsworth offers this description of Glasgow as she experienced it in 1803:

> The suburbs of Glasgow extend very far, houses on each side of the highway, – all ugly; and the inhabitants dirty. The roads are very wide; and everything seems to tell of a neighbourhood of a large town. We were annoyed by carts and dirt, and the road was full of people, who all noticed our car in one way or other; the children often sent a hooting after us. [...] One thing must strike every stranger in his first walk through Glasgow – an appearance of business and bustle, but no coaches or gentlemen's carriages. [...] I also could not but observe a want of cleanliness in the appearance of the lower orders of the people, and a dullness in the dress and outside of the whole mass, as they moved along.' (Dorothy Wordsworth, *'Recollections of a Tour made in Scotland'* in *Journals of Dorothy Wordsworth.* ed. by E. De Selincourt, 2 vols. (London: Macmillan, 1941), vol 1, pp.235-6)

For further description of Glasgow in the early nineteenth-century see: Irene Mavor, *Glasgow* (Edinburgh: Edinburgh University Press, 2000).

and sat looking out from the height of her present elevation upon the green below: the history of Glasgow Green can be traced back to 1450 when James II granted the green to Bishop Turnbull of Glasgow for common grazing. This was its main use until the nineteenth century. When the city expanded and the area beside the Green became more populated it was used by the women of the area to wash and bleach linen.

Ch. XIX.

flichterin' noise and glee: From Robert Burns, 'The Cotter's Saturday Night' (1785):

At length his lonely *Cot* appears in view,
   Beneath the shelter of an aged tree;
Th' expectant wee-things, toddlan, stacher thro'
   To meet their *Dad*, wi'flichertin noise and glee.

Ch. XX.

true loves ye may get many an ane: misquoted from 'Elspeth's ballad' in Scott's *The Antiquary* (1816), vol 2, ch.19:

He turn'd him right and round again,
Said, Scorn na at my mither;
Light loves I may get mony a ane,
But Minnie neer anither.

On land and sea ... more: Possibly an allusion to Robert Burns, 'The Slave's Lament' (1792):

It was in sweet Senegal that my foes did me enthral
For the lands of Virginia -ginia, O:
Torn from that lovely shore, and must never see it more;
And alas! I am weary, weary O:
Torn from etc.

Ch.XI.

ostler: a stableman or groom at an inn. *OED*

Ch. XII.

stuff: light woollen material.

a brown front: a band of false hair, or a set of false curls, worn by women over the forehead. *OED*

nabobs: wealthy, influential people used in the period of British people who had acquired a large fortune in India. *OED*

We're just as the auld Queen said, dry trees: possibly an allusion to the response given by Elizabeth I of England when told of Mary Queen of Scots' delivery of a son in 1566: 'Alack, the Queen of Scots is lighter of a bony son and I am but barren stock.'

Boney's escape: See p.389, note on **'peace only lasted while Napoleon was at Elba'**

but partly to a Scotch shyness: Oliphant wrote on the Scots character a number of times, in particular in 'Scottish National Character', *Blackwood's Edinburgh Magazine*, 87 (June 1860), pp.715-31.

the Prince Regent: See p. 396, note on 'the Duke in his own country'

White Horse Cellar: famous coach inn, Piccadilly, London.

Ladies Museum: The full title was, until 1829 when the word 'Monthly' was dropped, *The Ladies Monthly Museum or Polite Repository of Amusement and Instruction; Being an Assemblage of whatever can tend to please the fancy, interest the mind, or exalt the character of The British Fair.* This was a magazine for women which styled itself as:

> —of a character the most unexceptionable; the purest morals being inculcated in the most fascinating guise of Essays, Tales, and Narratives, and in fused into and impressed on the mind in the most lasting manner, while it is merely searching for amusement; interspersed with Anecdotes, passing Events, and Poetry; co[n]temporary Biography and Portraits; a Print of fashionable Costume, and an occasional piece of Original Music—'. (*The Ladies Monthly Museum* (June 1st, 1817), vol 5, pp.iii-iv)

cumberer of the ground: someone who gets in the way. OED

Ch. XXIII.

The standing feud between the Scotch and English: Reference to the historical tensions between Scotland and England which Oliphant, while not a nationalist, nevertheless noted in essays such as 'Scotland and her Accusers', Sept 1861, *Blackwood's Edinburgh Magazine* and in her *A History of Scotland for the Young* (1895) where she points out that:

> The terms of [the 1707 Union] were more like those dictated to a conquered nation than offered to an equal and independent power. [...] In every stipulation indeed the treaty was favourable to England and unfavourable to Scotland. (Oliphant, *A History of Scotland for the Young* (London: Fisher Unwin, 1895), p.302)

Mr Charles Reade has endowed: Charles Reade (1814-1884), English dramatist, novelist and journalist. The reference here is to the heroine Miss Lucy Dodd (née Fountain), a young single woman in Reade's novel *Love Me Little, Love Me Long* (1859) whom we later meet as a married woman in *Hard Cash* (1863). In October 1869 Oliphant wrote a review 'Charles Reade's Novels' where she applauds Reade's writing and his construction of women. See: *Blackwood's Edinburgh Magazine* 106 (October 1869), pp.488-514.

pelisse: See note, p.398.

Ch. XXIV.

cheval glass: a mirror swung on a frame, and of sufficient length to reflect the whole figure. OED

Ch. XXV.

that the stage was a sort of vestibule ...: See p.397, note on **'the play'.**

la belle couturière: Fr. beautiful dressmaker.

linkboys: boys employed to carry a link [a torch] to light passengers along the streets. OED

Ch. XXVI.

Bull of Bashan: 'Many bulls have compassed me: strong bulls of Bashan have beset me round. They gaped upon me with their mouths, as a ravening and a roaring lion—' (Psalm 22:12 -13).

which youthful maidens wont to fly: from Canto 1, Stanza XX, of Walter Scott's *The Lady of the Lake* (1810).

old Robin Gray: see note, p.398.

Ch. XXVII.

armour propre: Fr. self-esteem. Oliphant was fond of this phrase and often used it when referring to her own literary standing – e.g. In a letter to Mr John Blackwood in 1861 she expresses her disappointment on the return of a manuscript:

> It would be affectation to say that I was not much disappointed and mortified by receiving your packet last night. I should be glad to console my *armour propre* by thinking that the stronger fare to which you are accustomed has given you a distaste for my womanish style. One finds it odd somehow to account for being stupid in one's own person.' (Coghill, p.171)

hizzy: wild young woman.

Ch. XXVIII.

a double letter: a letter written on two sheets and charged double postage. OED. See: A.R.B. Haldane, *Three Centuries of Scottish Posts* (Edinburgh: Edinburgh University, 1971).

a frank or any easement: the superscribed signature of a person e.g. member of Parliament, entitled to send letters post free.

writing that was always to be found on the very edge of the paper: the expense of the postage meant that every inch of the writing paper was used. Letters were also sometimes crossed and even recrossed.

Having known me, to decline on a range of lower feelings: Tennyson's 'Locksley Hall' (1842) where a youthful lover muses on his rejection by a former lover:

Is it well to wish thee happy? —having known me —to decline
On a range of lower feelings and a narrower heart than mine!

Now Jacob was a smooth man: Genesis 27. Jacob who was 'a smooth man', with the assistance of his mother Rebekah, tricked his brother, Esau, who 'was a hairy man', out of his birthright by covering himself with the skin of the kids of goats and presenting himself to his blind father.

silk-mercer: a dealer in silk. Silk-mercers had high social status and economic importance, had invariably served an apprenticeship and sold a range of goods not produced in the locality. *OED*

the Scots kirk: As a result of James VI's arrival in London in 1707 there were many Scots particularly in the area of Westminster who sought a place of worship where they could continue their usual religious practice and meet with their fellow countrymen. Swallow Street Scottish National Church was one of the various responses to this need. Originally sited in Glasshouse Street it removed to Swallow Street in 1709 and continued there until the end of the nineteenth century. See: George G. Cameron, *The Scots Kirk in London* (Oxford: Becket Publications, 1979).

Ch. XXIX.

Battle of Waterloo: Fought in June 1815, the allied forces of the British, German, Belgian, Prussian and Dutch armies fought against the French Grande Armée just south of the village of Waterloo, eight miles from Brussels. The victory of the allied forces saw the end of twenty-six years of fighting between European powers and France.

the Peninsula: see note, p.390.

postchaise: a horse drawn, usually four-wheeled carriage (in Britain usually having a closed body, the driver or postilion riding on one of the horses) used for carrying mail and passengers. *OED*

decorated with laurels: the laurel leaf has been held as a symbol of victory and peace since the Greeks awarded a wreath of laurels to the victor in the Pythian Games.

Lord Wellington: (1769-1852). Arthur Wellesley (formerly 'Wesley'), third son of the Earl of Mornington, Wellington, army officer and prime minister. He was knighted in 1805 for his distinguished military service and is best remembered for his skilful command of the British army at Waterloo in 1815.

Wellington's funeral marked, for all its florid pomposity, the general sense among his countrymen that they had lost a great man. [...] 'The last great Englishman is low', lamented Tennyson in his fine funerary 'Ode on the Death of the Duke of Wellington' (1852). In the years that followed Wellington's name was commemorated in almost every imaginable way, from articles of clothing, streets (fifty-seven in London), barracks, towers, waterfalls, and warships to a public school near Sandhurst, the capital of New Zealand, and the great Californian redwood tree *Sequoia gigantica*. Already in his lifetime anecdotes had begun to cluster around him – some true, some (like 'publish and be damned'), highly doubtful, others (like 'try sparrow-hawks, ma'am'), demonstrably fictitious. That he remains one of the best known characters in English history is not solely due to his military achievements, though these were greater than those of his only two rivals, Cromwell and Marlborough, nor to his unwavering sense of public duty, though it was the general recognition of this that enabled him to ride out his crisis of personal unpopularity in 1829-1832 with undiminished reputation. Besides these outward virtues were the more human and endearing aspects: his ability to reflect with humorous detachment on his astonishing life, and a fundamental simplicity which charmed his friends and disarmed his enemies. *ODNB*

a glass coach: Here: a private coach let out for hire as distinguished from those on public stands. *OED*

and bring her out: Until the practice was abolished by Queen Elizabeth II in 1958, young women of good families were presented to the Monarch at court at the beginning of a season of dinners and balls in London.

Ch. XXX.

make a spoon or spoil a horn: to attempt something at the risk of failure. The phrase refers to the practice of making spoons out of the horns of cattle or sheep.

half and half gentry: as pronounced in the drama 'Virginius' by James Sheridan Knowles (1820), 'I never liked your half and half gentry, they generally combine the bad of both kinds without the good of either'. This Irish playwright was cousin to Richard Brinsley Butler Sheridan whose biography Oliphant published in 1883 in Macmillan's *English Men of Letters* series.

ensign: a commissioned officer of junior rank in the infantry or navy.

Vimiera ... Toulouse: landmark conflicts of the Peninsular War, fought respectively in 1808, 1812, 1812, 1814. 'Badajos' is usually spelled 'Badajoz'.

Spitalfields: In 1682 a royal charter gave permission for a market to be held in this area of East London. In 1685 the refugee Huguenots settled here and brought with them their skills of silk-weaving which helped establish the famous reputation of the market.

Ch. XXXI.

there being no inspectors: Despite 'anti-sweating' initiatives from the 1840s onwards it was not until the early twentieth century that the wages and conditions of women employed in the sewing trade in Britain were regulated by law. See: Sheila Blackburn, "To be Poor to be Honest ... Is this the Hardest Struggle of All": Sweated Needlewomen and

Campaigns for Protective Legislation, 1840-1914', in *Famine and Fashion: Needlewomen in the Nineteenth Century*, ed. Beth Harris (Aldershot: Ashgate 2005), pp.243-57.

Waverley; or, 'Tis Sixty Years Since: Published anonymously in 1814, this landmark historical novel by Walter Scott tells the tale of a young Englishman, Edward Waverley, who has been brought up by an uncle who has Tory and Jacobite sympathies. Through a sequence of events while on unauthorised extended leave from his commission with the government army billeted in Dundee, Waverley falls in love with the Highlands, the beautiful but highly politicised Flora MacIvor and the romance of the Jacobite cause. Encouraged by Flora's brother, the chieftan Fergus MacIvor, Edward marches with the Jacobite army, meets Prince Charles Edward Stuart and takes part in the Battle of Prestonpans where he saves the life of an English colonel who is a close friend of his uncle. This act saves him from severe censure by the British government and allows him to pursue his newly resolved path of marrying the moderate and gentle Lowland woman Rose Bradwardine – a conclusion which symbolises the positive argument for the Union between Scotland and England.

the great Exhibition of '51: Also known as the 'Crystal Palace Exhibition' of 1851, this was a celebration of international industry of manufactured products and was highly influential on the development of many aspects of society including art and design, international trade relations and tourism. Over 13,000 exhibits were displayed and viewed by over 6,200,000 visitors to the exhibition. The exhibition was housed in a giant glass and iron structure in Hyde Park, London which was later relocated to Sydenham Hill where it was destroyed by fire in 1936. Opened by Queen Victoria the exhibition was organised by her husband Prince Albert and members of The Royal Society for the Encouragement of the Arts, Manufactures and Commerce. The exhibition was a resounding triumph and the profits assisted the subsequent building of the Albert Hall, the Science Museum, the Natural History Museum and the Victoria and Albert Museum in London.

cates: delicate food.

"Go" and he goeth, and to another "Come", and he cometh: 'For I am also a man set under authority, having under me soldiers, and I say unto one, Go, and he goeth; and to another, Come, and he cometh; and to my servant Do this, and he doeth it—' (Luke 7:8).

Sepoys: natives of India employed as soldiers under European, esp. British, discipline. OED

Ch. XXXII.

escritoire: a writing desk constructed to contain paper and stationery. OED

Ch. XXXIII.

wainscot: fine wooden panelling on the lower part of the walls of a room.

He was the only son of his mother: In Luke 7: 12-15 Jesus raised the dead son of a widow.

She was like the woman in scripture ...: possible allusion to the story of Sarah, Genesis 17-21.

Ch. XXXIV.

a flower that seemed born to blush unseen: 'Full many a flower is born to blush unseen,/And waste its sweetness on the desert air': from Thomas Gray's 'Elegy Written in a Country Churchyard' (1751).

wile: persuade.

She shall be sportive as the fawn ...: William Wordsworth, 'Three years she grew in sun and shower' first published in *Lyrical Ballads*, 1798. Major Gordon is quoting the version published in Wordsworth's *Collected Poems* in 1815.

the new poets: refers to the poets we now call the Romantics and would in Kirsteen's time include Wordsworth, Coleridge, Byron, Keats and Shelley.

Ancient Mariner: 'The Rime of the Ancient Mariner' by Samuel Taylor Coleridge, written 1797-1798, and published in the first edition of *Lyrical Ballads* in 1798, was revised and republished in 1817.

Byron: Byron had left Britain in 1816 amidst the scandal which attended his separation from his wife.

Ahmednugger: Ahmednagar in India where a serious battle arose between troops of the British East India Company and native people. This incident formed part of the Third Maratha War 1817-1818 and the conclusive British victory secured the supremacy of the British in India. Oliphant appears to date this battle slightly later as news of it is not reported in the novel until c.1820.

Ch. XXXV.

[no endnotes required]

Ch. XXXVI.

still little things when I win up yonder: Oliphant herself was no stranger to the loss of children as all of her children predeceased her. Her first-born daughter Margaret ('Maggie') died age 11, in 1864; her second daughter, Marjorie, died age 1 year, in 1855; her third child, a son, died after only one day also in 1855; her fourth child, Cyril ('Tiddy') died age 34, in 1890; her fifth child, Stephen Thomas, died age

9 weeks in 1858; her sixth and last child Francis Romano ('Cecco') died age 35, in 1894.

Ch. XXXVII.

moreen: strong, ribbed, worsted fabric with a watered finish. *OED*

Ch. XXXVIII.

covered the looking glass with white: It was a funeral custom to cover mirrors with veiling because of the superstition that the deceased's spirit might become trapped in the looking glass.

ye are to leave your parents and your father's house: Genesis 2:24.

Ch. XXXIX.

this was a thing contrary to all Scotch customs: at this time only men accompanied the coffin to the graveside, the women would wait behind to look after children and prepare the refreshment for after the funeral.

weepers: pieces of crape or linen sewn to the sleeves or hat as a sign of mourning.

Antiphone: the response one side of a choir makes to the other in a chant.

Ch. XL.

Catholic Emancipation: Following the Reformation in England and the establishment of the Church of England, only Protestants were allowed to vote or sit in Parliament. With large scale emigration of Irish people to Scotland in the early nineteenth century the impact particularly on Scottish society was significant as the majority of the immigrants were Catholic. A movement for Catholic emancipation began in the early 1800s and culminated in the Catholic Emancipation Act of 1829.

We will have all the wild Irish [...] like Sawtan in the Scriptures: T.M. Devine notes: '[The immigrant Catholic Irish] could not relate to a Scotland which, as a stateless nation, derived its collective identity from Presbyterianism, a creed whose adherents regarded Catholicism as at best superstitious error and at worst as a satanic force led by the Man of Sin himself, the Pope of Rome.' (T.M. Devine, *The Scottish Nation 1700-2000* (London: Penguin, 1999), p.488)

A large number of our country folk just put out of the question altogether: a reference to the parts of the Scottish Highlands which remained Catholic despite the impact of the Reformation in Scotland. See: Ray Burnett, ' "The Long Nineteenth Century": Scotland's Catholic Gaidhealtachd', in *Out of the Ghetto?: The Catholic Community in Modern Scotland,*. ed. by Boyle and Lynch (Edinburgh: John Donald, 1998).

Inquiseetion: Scots pronunciation of the Inquisition – a Roman Catholic tribunal for the discovery and punishment of heresy. Established by Pope Gregory IX in 1233 it was by the fifteenth century associated with Spain and later Portugal. It was never instituted in the United Kingdom.

yon wild Irishman O'Connell: Daniel O'Connell (1775-1847) was a radical democratic Dublin lawyer whose ultimate aim was the repeal of the 1801 Act of Union and the restoration of the Irish Parliament.

the thumbscrew and the boot: instruments of torture.

the new presentee: under the Patronage Act of 1712 landowners could appoint their choice of minister to the parishes within their boundaries. This outraged the Presbyterian community as the revolution of 1690 had abolished patronage as it was viewed as conflicting with the rights of the community itself to choose a candidate.

they are not a true race: the Campbell clan have traditionally had suspicion cast over them since their part in the Massacre of Glen Coe in 1692.

Ch. XLI.

ling: common heather, *Calluna Vulgaris.*

Ch. XLII.

[No endnotes required]

Ch. XLIII.

persiflage: frivolous banter.

Ch. XLIV.

like hell in the Scriptures to meet that king: Isaiah 14:9.

Ch. XLV.

[No endnotes required]

Ch. XLVI.

Dufrey's *Pills to Purge Melancholy*: possibly a printer's error for Thomas D'Urfey's collection of ballads *Wit and Mirth: or, Pills to Purge Melancholy* (1698-1720).

the attainder: see note, p.397.

a K.C.B.: a Knight Commander of the Bath – in the period a military distinction.

where the best talkers were glad to come: Edinburgh in the 1850s still reverberated with the effects of the intellectual stimulus of the Enlightenment which had caused the Scottish capital to become known as the 'Athens of the North'. By the 1820s Edinburgh was the most important financial city outside London as well as being recognised as a major European publishing centre. As an astute business woman, Kirsteen Douglas would have been aware of the status of Scotland's capital – a status remarked by Oliphant elsewhere: 'Even now, when everything tends towards London, Edinburgh preserves a very distinct stamp of her own; but in those days [of the Scottish Enlightenment] she was as individual and distinct as Paris or Vienna' (Oliphant, *Annals of a Publishing House: William Blackwood and his Sons, Their Magazine and Friends*, 3 vols (Edinburgh and London: Blackwood, 1897), vol 1, p.4). See also: James Buchan, *Capital of the Mind: How Edinburgh Changed the World* (London: John Murray, 2003); John Gibson Lockhart, *Peter's Letters to his Kinsfolk* (Edinburgh: William Blackwood, 1819); Krystyn Lach-Szyrma, *From Charlotte Square to Fingal's Cave: Reminiscences of a Journey through Scotland 1820-1824*, ed. by Mona Kedslie McLeod (Tuckwell: East Linton, 2004).

Moray Place: part of the fashionable New Town development of Edinburgh designed by James Craig in 1766 and constructed in the later eighteenth century.

Glossary

The following lists Scots words, phrases or forms that may be unfamiliar. The primary sources consulted are: *Dictionary of the Scots Language/Dictionar o the Scots Leid.* http://www.dsl.ac.uk/dsl; *Dictionary of the Older Scottish Tongue* http://www.celtscot.ed.ac.uk/dost/; *Oxford English Dictionary*

aff: off
ails: troubles
ainy: any
ain: own
airt: art
ance: once
anither: another
auld world freats: superstitious beliefs
bairn: child
bairn-time: child-bearing years
ben: inside
bide: to remain, stay, dwell, live
bit nor sup: food nor drink
blate: shy, timid, modest
blethering: chatting, gossiping
bodies: folk, people
bonnie: beautiful, pretty
braw: good, fine
bring ben: bring inside
burn: brook or stream
callants: young lads
canailye: from the French 'canaille'; rabble, unruly mob
cauld: cold
ceevil: civil
cha'amer: private room/bedroom
chappit acht: struck eight o'clock
chuckie: chicken
colleaguing: conspiring together for the purpose of crime or mischief
colley dogue: sheepdog
collops: minced meat
claes/clo'es: clothes
clachan: small village/hamlet

clanjamfry: rabble of people
daidling: idling/wasting time
dauntoned/daunted: subdued/intimidated
daured: dared
deed: indeed
deevil: devil
dight their eyne: 'to wipe their eyes'; fig., to be taken aback by having been got the better of
ding: drive, force, beat
dishclouts: dishcloths
doited: stupid
donnered: senseless
doo: dove
dour: miserable, sullen
downsitting/doonsitting: a settlement, especially that obtained from a marriage or inheritance
drookit: wet, sodden
eerie: ghostly, strange
faddom: fathom
fain: glad, well pleased
farden: farthing
fash: trouble oneself, worry
fecht: fight, struggle
fend for: to provide for
ferly: curiosity, marvel, object of gossip
fey: behaving as if in touch with something supernatural
fleech: coax, cajole
fyke: laborious work
gaed: went
gait: way
gale: bog myrtle (worn by Clan Campbell in their bonnets)
gane: gone
ganging his ain gait: following his own path or will
gathering straes: dozing: cf.wool-gathering
gilpie: lively young girl, tomboy
girdle: heavy flat iron plate for baking cf. griddle
girn: to snarl, moan
glaikit: empty-headed, foolish
gyte: mad, insane
gowk: fool
greetin': crying
hail/haill: whole

haud: hold
havering: speaking nonsense
heartsome: heart warming
heedin': caring
hirple: limp
hissel': himself
hoot awa' with ye: get away with you!
howkit: dug
jaud: a servant of the lowest order who goes from house to house doing the dirtiest of jobs, a term of abuse for a worthless woman
joe/jo: sweetheart
keepit: kept
ken: know
kirk: church
knap English: to speak English in an affected manner
lane: alone, on one's own
lassies: young women, girls
leddy: lady
leein': lying
lightsome: carefree, joyful
linking in: stepping lightly in, dancing in
linn: waterfall
loup: to jump
lums: chimneys
mair: more
mairry: marry
maist: most
maitters: matters
mansworn: false, perjured
marriet: married
masket: brewed
maun: must
meal pack: a small bag used by beggars for holding food given as alms
mind: remember
minnie: affectionate form of 'mother'
moudiewart: mole
muckle: big, large
muckle taken up: greatly occupied
nae mair: no more
no canny: strange, out of the ordinary

ower: over

paidling lairdie: an insignificant landowner; a 'paidler' is a child learning to walk, a toddler

pairty: party

parritch: porridge

peeny: apron

perfitt: perfect

piece: some food, snack

pingling: demanding

pooers: powers

preen: metal pin

presses: cupboards

quean: young unmarried girl

redd up: to tidy, sort

red-weed: furious, enraged, wild with passion. Cf. OE 'wood': mad

roup: public auction

rubbitch: rubbish

sauvage: wild, ungoverned

Sawtan: Satan

scart of the pen: scribbled note

schule: school

shadit: shaded

shoogly: unsteady

siller: silver, money

skimpit: skimpy, scant

skreigh/skreich: a piercing shriek/scream

steek: to lock or shut

steekit: locked or shut

steer: trouble

stramash: commotion

stravaiging: wandering aimlessly

taigled: hindered, impeded

thole: endure

throng: very busy

tocher: marriage portion, dowry

toun: town

tumult: tumbled

waddlin': waddling

wae/waeful: sad

waik: weak

ware upon: make use of for, lay out upon

weans: children
weariet: weary
weel: well
weel put on: respectably dressed
weemen: women
what ails ye?: what's wrong with you?/what objection have
 you?
wheeling: a coarse thick type of worsted yarn originally
 from uncombed wool spun on the big wheel
wheen: a (good) few, several
whiles: sometimes
whist: be quiet!
win: to find one's way
wyte: blame
yammer: make a din, talk volubly
ye: you
ye've: you have

THE ASSOCIATION FOR SCOTTISH LITERARY STUDIES

ANNUAL VOLUMES

Volumes marked * are, at the time of publication, still available.

1971	James Hogg, *The Three Perils of Man*, ed. Douglas Gifford
1972	*The Poems of John Davidson*, vol. I, ed. Andrew Turnbull
1973	*The Poems of John Davidson*, vol. II, ed. Andrew Turnbull
1974	Allan Ramsay and Robert Fergusson, *Poems*, ed. Alexander M. Kinghorn and Alexander Law
1975	John Galt, *The Member*, ed. Ian A. Gordon
1976	William Drummond of Hawthornden, *Poems and Prose*, ed. Robert H. MacDonald
1977	John G. Lockhart, *Peter's Letters to his Kinsfolk*, ed. William Ruddick
1978	John Galt, *Selected Short Stories*, ed. Ian A. Gordon
1979	Andrew Fletcher of Saltoun, *Selected Political Writings and Speeches*, ed. David Daiches
1980	*Scott on Himself*, ed. David Hewitt
1981	*The Party-Coloured Mind*, ed. David Reid
1982	James Hogg, *Selected Stories and Sketches*, ed. Douglas S. Mack
1983	Sir Thomas Urquhart of Cromarty, *The Jewel*, ed. R.D.S. Jack and R.J. Lyall
1984	John Galt, *Ringan Gilhaize*, ed. Patricia J. Wilson
1985	Margaret Oliphant, *Selected Short Stories of the Supernatural*, ed. Margaret K. Gray
1986	James Hogg, *Selected Poems and Songs*, ed. David Groves
1987	Hugh MacDiarmid, *A Drunk Man Looks at the Thistle*, ed. Kenneth Buthlay
1988	*The Book of Sandy Stewart*, ed. Roger Leitch
1989*	*The Comic Poems of William Tennant*, ed. Maurice Lindsay and Alexander Scott
1990*	Thomas Hamilton, *The Youth and Manhood of Cyril Thornton*, ed. Maurice Lindsay
1991	*The Complete Poems of Edwin Muir*, ed. Peter Butter
1992*	*The Tavern Sages: Selections from the 'Noctes Ambrosianae'*, ed. J.H. Alexander

1993   *Gaelic Poetry in the Eighteenth Century*, ed. Derick S. Thomson

1994*   Violet Jacob, *Flemington*, ed. Carol Anderson

1995*   *'Scotland's Ruine': Lockhart of Carnwath's Memoirs of the Union*, ed. Daniel Szechi, with a foreword by Paul Scott

1996*   *The Christis Kirk Tradition: Scots Poems of Folk Festivity*, ed. Allan H. MacLaine

1997–8*   *The Poems of William Dunbar* (two vols.), ed. Priscilla Bawcutt

1999*   *The Scotswoman at Home and Abroad*, ed. Dorothy McMillan

2000*   Sir David Lyndsay, *Selected Poems*, ed. Janet Hadley Williams

2001   Sorley MacLean, *Dàin do Eimhir*, ed. Christopher Whyte

2002   Christian Isobel Johnstone, *Clan-Albin*, ed. Andrew Monnickendam

2003*   *Modernism and Nationalism: Literature and Society in Scotland 1918–1939*, ed. Margery Palmer McCulloch

2004*   *Serving Twa Maisters: five classic plays in Scots translation*, ed. John Corbett and Bill Findlay

2005*   *The Devil to Stage: five plays by James Bridie*, ed. Gerard Carruthers

2006*   *Voices From Their Ain Countrie: the poems of Marion Angus and Violet Jacob*, ed. Katherine Gordon

2007*   *Scottish People's Theatre: Plays by Glasgow Unity Writers*, ed. Bill Findlay

2008*   Elizabeth Hamilton, *The Cottagers of Glenburnie*, ed. Pam Perkins

2009*   Dot Allan, *Makeshift & Hunger March*, ed. Moira Burgess